THE
PUPPET
SHOW

THE PUPPET SHOW

M.W. CRAVEN

Constable • London

CONSTABLE

First published in Great Britain in 2018 by Constable

Copyright © M. W. Craven, 2018

1 3 5 7 9 10 8 6 4 2

The moral right of the author has been asserted.

A CIP catalogue record for this book is available from the British Library.

ISBN: 978-1-47212-743-3 (hardback)
ISBN: 978-1-47212-744-0 (trade paperback)

Typeset in Caslon Pro by TW Type
Printed and bound in Great Britain by CPI Group (UK) Ltd, Croydon CR0 4YY

Papers used by Constable are from well-managed forests and other responsible sources.

MIX
Paper from
responsible sources
FSC® C104740
www.fsc.org

Constable
An imprint of
Little, Brown Book Group
Carmelite House
50 Victoria Embankment
London EC4Y 0DZ

An Hachette UK Company
www.hachette.co.uk

www.littlebrown.co.uk

This book is dedicated to my wife, Joanne,
and my late mum, Susan Avison Craven.
Without either of them this book wouldn't exist.

Immolation
[im-*uh*-**ley**-sh*uh*-n]
1. To kill as a religious sacrifice.
2. To kill, especially by fire.

The stone circle is an ancient, tranquil place. Its stones are silent sentinels. Unmoving watchers. Their granite glistens with the morning dew. They have withstood a thousand and more winters, and although they are weathered and worn, they have never yielded to time, the seasons, or man.

Alone in the circle, surrounded by soft shadows, stands an old man. His face is heavily lined, and lank grey hair frames his bald and mottled scalp. He is cadaverously thin, and his gaunt frame is racked by tremors. His head is bowed and his shoulders are stooped.

He is naked and he is about to die.

Strong wire secures him to an iron girder. It bites into his skin. He doesn't care: his tormentor has already tortured him.

He is in shock and thinks he has no more capacity for pain.

He is wrong.

'Look at me.' His tormentor's voice is flat.

The old man has been smeared with a jelly-like substance that reeks of petrol. He raises his head and looks to the hooded figure in front of him.

His tormentor holds an American Zippo lighter.

And now the fear kicks in. The primal fear of fire. He knows what's going to happen and he knows he can't stop it. His breathing becomes shallow and erratic.

The Zippo is raised to his eyes. The old man sees the simple beauty of it. The perfect lines, the exact engineering. A design that hasn't changed in a century. With a flick, the top flips open. A turn of the thumb and the wheel strikes the flint. A shower of sparks and the flame appears.

His tormentor lowers the Zippo, drags the flame down. The

accelerant catches. The hungry flames flare, then crawl down his arm.

The pain is immediate, like his blood has turned to acid. His eyes widen in horror and every muscle goes rigid. His hands clench into a fist. He tries to scream but it dies when it reaches the obstacle in his throat. Becomes pitiful and muted as he gargles his own blood.

His flesh spits and sizzles like meat in a hot oven. Blood, fat and water roll down his arms and drip from his fingers.

Black fills his vision. The pain fades. His breathing is no longer rushed and urgent.

The old man dies. He doesn't know that his own fat will fuel the fire long after the accelerant has burnt away. He doesn't see how the flames burn and distort what has been carved into his chest.

But it happens anyway.

CHAPTER ONE

One week later.

Tilly Bradshaw had a problem. She didn't like problems. Her low tolerance for uncertainty meant they made her anxious.

She looked around to see if there was anyone to share her findings with, but the Serious Crime Analysis Section office was empty. She checked her watch and saw it was coming up to midnight. She'd worked for sixteen hours straight again. She thumbed her mother a text, apologising for not calling her.

She turned back to her screen. Although she knew it wasn't a glitch, with results like these there would be an expectation that she had triple checked. She ran her program again.

After making herself a fruit tea, she glanced at the progress bar to see how long she had to wait. Fifteen minutes. Bradshaw opened her personal laptop, plugged in her headphones and typed, 'Back at keyboard'. Within seconds she was fully immersed in *Dragonlore*, a multiplayer, online role-playing game.

In the background her program processed the data she'd entered. Bradshaw didn't check the SCAS computer once.

She didn't make mistakes.

Fifteen minutes later, the National Crime Agency logo dissolved, and the same results appeared. She typed, 'Away from Keyboard', and logged out of her game.

There were two possibilities. Either the results were

accurate, or a mathematically implausible coincidence had occurred. When she'd first seen the results, she'd calculated the odds of it happening by chance, and had come up with a number in the high millions. In case she was asked, she entered the maths problem into a program of her own design and ran it. The result popped up and showed it was within the margin of error she'd allowed. She didn't smile when she realised that she'd worked it out faster than her own computer, using a program *she'd* written.

Bradshaw wasn't sure what to do next. Her boss, Detective Inspector Stephanie Flynn, was usually nice to her, but it *had* only been the week before when they'd had their little chat about when it was appropriate to call her at home. She was only allowed to ring when it *was* important. But . . . as it was DI Flynn who decided if something was important, how was she supposed to know without asking her? It was all very confusing.

Bradshaw wished it were a maths problem. She *understood* maths. She didn't understand Detective Inspector Flynn. She bit her lip, then came to a decision.

She reviewed her findings and practised what to say.

Her discovery related to SCAS's latest target – a man the press were calling the 'Immolation Man'. Whoever he was – and they'd made an early assumption he was male – he didn't seem to like men in their sixties and seventies. In fact, he disliked them so much, he was setting them on fire.

It was the third and latest victim's data that Bradshaw had been studying. SCAS had been brought in after the second. As well as identifying the emergence of serial killers and serial rapists, their role was also to provide analytical support to any police force undertaking complex or apparently motiveless murder investigations. The Immolation Man certainly ticked all the SCAS boxes.

Because the fire had destroyed the bodies to the point they didn't even *look* like bodies, a post-mortem wasn't the only approach the SIO, the senior investigating officer, up in Cumbria had taken. He'd sought advice from SCAS. After the post-mortem, SCAS had arranged for the body to go through a multi-slice computed tomography machine. The MSCT was a sophisticated medical investigative technique. It used X-ray beams and a liquid dye to form a 3D image of the body. It was meant for the living but was just as effective on the dead.

SCAS didn't have the resources to have their own MSCT – no law enforcement agency did – but they had an agreement to purchase time on one when the situation merited it. As the Immolation Man left no trace evidence at the murder scenes or abduction sites, the SIO had been willing to try anything.

Bradshaw took a deep breath and dialled DI Flynn.

The phone answered on the fifth ring. A groggy voice answered. 'Hello?'

She checked her watch to confirm it was after midnight, before saying, 'Good morning, Detective Inspector Flynn. How are you?' As well as talking to her about when it was appropriate to ring her after hours, DI Flynn had also urged her to be politer to her colleagues.

'Tilly,' Flynn grumbled, 'what do you want?'

'I want to talk to you about the case, Detective Inspector Flynn.'

Flynn sighed. 'Can you just call me Stephanie, Tilly? Or Steph? Or boss? In fact, we're not that far away from London, I'll even accept guv.'

'Of course, Detective Inspector Stephanie Flynn.'

'No . . . I mean can you not just . . . Oh, it doesn't matter.'

Bradshaw waited for Flynn to finish before saying, 'May I please tell you what I've found?'

Flynn groaned. 'What time is it?'

'The time is thirteen minutes past midnight.'

'Go on then. What's so important it couldn't wait until the morning?'

Flynn listened to her before asking a few questions and hanging up. Bradshaw sat back in her chair and smiled. She'd been right to call her. DI Flynn had said so.

Flynn was there within half an hour. Her blonde hair was tangled. She wore no makeup. Bradshaw wore no makeup either, although that was by choice. She thought it was silly.

Bradshaw pressed some keys and brought up a series of cross sections. 'They're all of the torso,' she said.

She then went on to explain what the MSCT did. 'It can identify wounds and fractures that the post-mortem might miss. It is particularly useful when the victim has been badly burned.'

Flynn knew all this but let her finish anyway. Bradshaw gave up information in her own time and wouldn't be rushed.

'The cross sections don't really give us that much, DI Stephanie Flynn, but watch this.' Bradshaw brought up a composite image, this time from above.

'What on earth . . . ?' Flynn asked, staring at the screen.

'Wounds,' Bradshaw replied. 'Lots of them.'

'So the post-mortem missed a load of random slashes?'

Bradshaw shook her head. 'That is what I thought.' She pressed a button and they studied the 3D image of the wounds on the victim's chest. The program sorted through the seemingly random slashes. Eventually they all came together.

They stared at the final image. There was nothing random about it.

'What do we do now, Detective Inspector Flynn?'

Flynn paused before answering. 'Have you called your mum to explain why you aren't home yet?'

'I sent her a text.'

'Well, send her another one. Tell her you won't be back tonight.'

Bradshaw began tapping the screen of her mobile. 'What reason shall I give?'

'Tell her we're getting the director out of bed.'

CHAPTER TWO

Washington Poe had enjoyed his day repairing the dry stone wall. It was one of several new skills he'd learned since moving back to Cumbria. It was backbreaking work but the reward of a pie and pint at the end of the day was all the sweeter for it. He loaded his tools and a few spare rocks into his quad's trailer, whistled for Edgar, his springer spaniel, and then began the drive back to his croft. He'd been working on the outer boundary wall today so was over a mile from his home, a rough-stone building called Herdwick Croft. It would take him fifteen minutes or so to get back.

The spring sun was low and the evening dew made the grass and heather shine. Birds chirped territorial and mating songs and the air was fragrant with early flowers. Poe breathed in deeply as he drove.

He could get used to this.

He *had* been planning on a quick shower then a walk over to the hotel, but the closer to home he got, the thought of a long soak in the bath with a good book was far more appealing.

He crested the last peak and stopped. Someone was sitting at his outdoor table.

He opened the canvas bag he always carried with him and removed a pair of binoculars. He trained them on the lone figure. He couldn't be sure, but the person looked female. He increased the magnification and smiled grimly when he recognised the figure with the long blonde hair.

So . . . they'd finally caught up with him.

8

He put the binoculars back in his bag and drove down to see his old sergeant.

'Long time no see, Steph,' Poe said. 'What brings you this far north?' Edgar, the furry traitor, was fussing round her like a long-lost friend.

'Poe,' she acknowledged. 'Nice beard.'

He reached up and scratched his chin. He'd got out of the habit of daily shaves. 'You know I've never been good at small talk, Steph.'

Flynn nodded. 'This is a hard place to find.' She was wearing a trouser suit; navy blue with pinstripes, and judging by how lean and supple she looked, she'd obviously kept up to date with her martial arts training. She exuded the confidence of someone in control. A pair of reading glasses lay folded beside a file on the table. It looked like she'd been working before he'd arrived.

'Not hard enough apparently,' he replied. He didn't smile. 'What can I do for you, Sergeant Flynn?'

'It's Detective Inspector now, although it couldn't possibly make the slightest bit of difference.'

Poe raised his eyebrows. 'My old job?'

She nodded.

'I'm surprised Talbot allowed you to take it,' Poe said. Talbot had been the director when Poe had been SCAS's detective inspector. He was a petty man, and he'd have blamed Flynn for what happened just as much as he blamed Poe. More so perhaps – Poe hadn't hung around; she had.

'It's Edward van Zyl now. Talbot didn't survive the fallout.'

'Good man, I like him,' Poe grunted. When van Zyl was in North West Special Branch they'd worked closely together on a counter-terrorism case. The July 21st bombers had trained in the Lake District, and Cumbrian cops were vital in building up the

9

intelligence profile. It had been van Zyl who asked Poe to apply for the SCAS position. 'And Hanson?'

'Still the deputy director.'

'Pity,' said Poe. Hanson was a politically savvy man and Poe wasn't surprised to learn he'd somehow managed to wriggle out of it. Ordinarily, when a senior manager is forced out due to catastrophic errors in judgement, the next manager in line takes their job. That Hanson hadn't been promoted meant he'd not got away with it completely.

Poe could still remember the smirk on Hanson's face when he suspended him. He hadn't had contact with anyone from the NCA since. He'd left no forwarding address, had cancelled his mobile-phone contract, and as far as he knew, he wasn't on any database in Cumbria.

If Flynn had taken the trouble to track him down, it meant a decision on his employment had finally been made. As Hanson was still in post, Poe doubted it was good news. It didn't matter; he'd moved on months ago. If Flynn was there to tell him he no longer worked for the NCA then that was fine. And if she were there to tell him that Hanson had finally found a way to charge him with a criminal offence, he would just have to deal with it.

There was no point shooting the messenger. He doubted Flynn wanted to be there. 'You want a brew? I'm having one.' He didn't wait for a response and disappeared into the croft. He shut the door behind him.

Five minutes later he was back with a metal espresso maker and a separate pot of boiled water. He filled two mugs. 'Still taking it black?'

She nodded and took a sip. She smiled and raised the mug in appreciation.

'How'd you find me?' His face was serious. His privacy had become increasingly important to him.

'Van Zyl knew you'd come back to Cumbria and he knew

roughly where you lived. Some quarry workers told me there was someone living in an old shepherd's croft in the middle of nowhere. They'd been watching you do the place up.' She looked round as if evidence of this was negligible.

Herdwick Croft looked as though it had grown out of the ground. The walls were made of unrendered stone – too big for any one man to lift and manoeuvre into place – and it merged seamlessly with the ancient moorland it inhabited. It was squat and ugly and looked like it had been frozen in time for two hundred years. Poe loved it.

Flynn said, 'I've been here a couple of hours waiting—'

'What do you want?'

Flynn reached into her briefcase and pulled out a thick file. She didn't open it. 'I assume you've heard of the Immolation Man?'

Poe jerked his head up. He hadn't expected her to say *that*.

And of course he'd heard of the Immolation Man. Even in the middle of the Shap Fells, the Immolation Man was news. He'd been burning men to death in some of Cumbria's many stone circles. Three victims so far, unless there was another he hadn't heard about. Although the press had been speculating, the facts were there if you knew how to separate them from the sensationalism.

The county had its first-ever serial killer.

Even if SCAS had been called in to help Cumbria police, he was on suspension: subject to an internal investigation *and* an IPCC inquiry. Although Poe knew he was an asset to any investigation, he wasn't irreplaceable. SCAS had moved on without him.

So what was Flynn really doing there?

'Van Zyl's lifted your suspension. He wants you working the case. You'll be my DS.'

Although Poe's face was a mask, his mind worked faster than a computer. It didn't make sense. Flynn was a new DI, and the last thing she'd want would be the *old* DI working under her, undermining her authority just by being there. And she'd known him a long time and knew how he responded to authority. Why would she want to be a part of that?

She'd been ordered to.

Poe noticed she'd made no mention of the IPCC inquiry so presumably *that* was still ongoing. He stood and cleared away the mugs. 'Not interested,' he said.

She seemed surprised by his answer. He didn't know why. The NCA had washed their hands of him.

'Don't you want to see what's in my file?' she asked.

'I don't care,' he replied. He no longer missed SCAS. While it had taken him a long time to get used to the slower pace of life on the Cumbrian fells, he didn't want to give it up. If Flynn wasn't there to sack or arrest him, then he wasn't interested in anything else she had to say. Catching serial killers was no longer a part of his life.

'OK,' she said. She stood up. She was tall and their eyes were on the same level. 'I need you to sign two bits of paper for me then.' She removed a thinner file from her briefcase and passed it over.

'What's this?'

'You heard me say van Zyl's lifted your suspension, right?'

Nodding, he read the document.

Ah.

'And you realise that as you're now officially a serving police officer again, if you refuse to come back to work it's a sackable offence? But rather than go through all that, I've been told I can accept your resignation now. I've taken the liberty of getting HR to draw up this document.'

Poe studied the one-page sheet. If he signed at the bottom, he was no longer a police officer. Although he'd been expecting it for a while, he found it wasn't as easy to say goodbye as he thought. If he *did* sign, it would draw a line under the last eighteen months. He could start living.

But he'd never carry a warrant card again.

He glanced at Edgar. The spaniel was soaking up the last of the sun. Most of the surrounding land was his. Was he ready to give all this up?

Poe took her pen and scrawled his name across the bottom. He handed it back so she could check he hadn't simply written 'piss off' on the bottom. Now that her bluff had been called she seemed less sure of what to do next. It wasn't going to plan. Poe took the mugs and coffee pot inside. A minute later he was back outside. Flynn hadn't moved.

'What's up, Steph?'

'What are you doing, Poe? You loved being a cop. What's changed?'

He ignored her. With the decision made, he just wanted her to go. 'Where's the other document?'

'Excuse me?'

'You said you had two things for me to sign. I've signed your resignation letter, so unless you've got two of them, there's still something else.'

She was all business again. Opening the file, she removed the second document. It was a bit thicker than the first and had the official seal of the NCA across the top.

She launched into a rehearsed speech. It was one Poe had used himself. 'Washington Poe, please read this document and then sign at the bottom to confirm you've been served.' She handed over the thick sheaf of paper.

Poe glanced at the top sheet.

It was an Osman Warning.

Oh shit . . .

CHAPTER THREE

When the police have intelligence that someone is in significant and immediate danger, they have a duty of care to warn the victim. The Osman Warning is the official process for discharging that duty. Potential victims can consider the protective measures being proposed by the police, or, if they aren't happy, they can make their own arrangements.

Poe scanned the first page but it was full of officious bullshit. It didn't say who he was at risk from. 'What's this about, Steph?'

'I can only tell you if you're still a serving police officer, Poe.' She handed him the resignation letter he'd just signed. He didn't take it.

'Poe, look at me.'

She held his gaze and he saw nothing but honesty in her eyes.

'Trust me. You need to see what's in this file. If you don't like it, you can always email Hanson your notice later.' She handed him back his resignation letter.

Poe nodded and tore up the letter.

'Good,' she said.

She passed across some glossy photographs. They were of a crime scene.

'Do you recognise these?'

Poe studied them. They were of a dead body. Blackened, charred, almost unrecognisable as a human being. Shrunken, as anything primarily made of liquid is after exposure to extreme heat. The corpse looked as though it had the same texture and weight as the charcoal Poe removed from his wood-burning stove every morning. He could almost feel the residual heat through the image.

'Do you know which one this was?' Flynn asked.

Poe didn't answer. He flicked through the sheaf of photos searching for a point of reference. The last one was a shot of the whole crime scene. He recognised the stone circle. 'This is Long Meg and Her Daughters. This . . .' he pointed at the first photograph, '. . . must be Michael James, the Tory councillor. He was the third victim.'

'It is. Staked in the middle of the stone circle, covered in accelerant, then set on fire. His burns were over ninety per cent. What else do you know?'

'Only what I've read. I expect the police were surprised at the location; it's not as rural as the other two.'

'Not half as surprised as they were at how he'd successfully managed to evade every bit of surveillance they'd put in place.'

Poe nodded. The Immolation Man had chosen a different stone circle each time he killed. It was how the press had come up with the name. Immolation meant sacrificing by burning and, with no other motive, the press jumped on it. Poe would have expected the police to be watching all the circles. Then again maybe not . . . there were a lot of stone circles in Cumbria. Add the barrows, henges and standing stones and you'd have nearly five hundred to watch. Even if they used minimal surveillance details, they'd need a team numbering close to two thousand cops. Cumbria barely had a thousand badged officers as it was. They'd have no choice but to pick and choose where they put their limited resources.

He passed the photographs back. As gruesome as it all was, it didn't explain why Flynn had made the long journey north. 'I still don't understand what this has to do with me?'

She ignored the question. 'SCAS were called in after the Immolation Man's second victim. The SIO wanted a profile.'

It was to be expected. It was the unit's speciality.

15

'Which we did,' she continued. 'Came up with nothing useable, the usual stuff about age ranges and ethnicity, that type of thing.'

Poe knew that profiles could add value, but only when they were part of a multi-strand investigation. He doubted they were talking because of a profile.

'Have you heard of multi-slice computed tomography?'

'Yes,' he lied.

'It's where a machine photographs the body in very thin slices rather than as a whole. It's an expensive process but sometimes it identifies ante- and post-mortem injuries that the conventional forensic post-mortem has missed.'

Poe had been very much a 'need to know what it can do' rather than a 'need to know how it works' kind of guy. If Flynn said it was possible, then it was possible.

'The post-mortem found nothing, but the MSCT found this.' Retrieving another set of photographs, she placed them on the table in front of him. They were computerised images of what appeared to be random slashes.

'These were on the third victim?' he asked.

She nodded. 'On the torso. Everything he does is designed for maximum impact.'

The Immolation Man was a sadist. Poe didn't need a fancy profile to tell him that. He studied each page as Flynn turned them over. There were nearly twenty but it was the last one that caused him to gasp.

It was the sum of all the parts. The computer image where all the random slashes came together to form the picture you were meant to see. Poe's mouth turned to glue. 'How?' he croaked.

Flynn shrugged. 'We were hoping you could tell us.'

They stared at the last photograph.

The Immolation Man had carved two words into the victim's chest.

'Washington Poe'.

CHAPTER FOUR

Poe sat down heavily. Blood leached from his face. A vein in his temple began pounding.

He stared at the computerised mock-up of his name. And it wasn't *just* his name – above it had been carved the number five.

That wasn't good . . . That wasn't good at all.

'We're interested in why he felt the need to carve your name into the victim's chest.'

'And it's not something he's done before? It's not something that's been held back from the press?'

'Nope. We've retrospectively put victims one and two through the MSCT and they're clear.'

'And the number five?' There was only one plausible explanation and he knew Flynn agreed. It was why she'd issued the Osman Warning.

'We assume you're earmarked as the fifth victim.'

He picked up the last photograph. After the crude attempt at the number five, the Immolation Man had given up on curves. All the letter strokes were straight.

Although they were only looking at a computer image, Poe could see the wounds were too crude for a scalpel. His money was on a Stanley knife or similar. The fact that the letters had been picked up by the MSCT meant two things: they were ante-mortem – if they hadn't been, the post-mortem examination would have found them – and they were deep; the burning would have destroyed shallower wounds. The victim's last few minutes must have been hell on earth.

'Why me?' Poe said. He'd spent a career making enemies but he hadn't worked a case involving someone this nutty before.

Flynn shrugged. 'As you can imagine, you're not the first person to ask that question.'

'I wasn't lying when I said I only know what's been reported in the papers.'

'We know that when you were a Cumbria police officer, you had no official contact with any of the victims. I'm assuming you hadn't had any *unofficial* contact with them?'

'Not that I know of.' He gestured to the croft and surrounding land. 'This place takes up most of my time these days.'

'That's what we assumed. We don't think the link is the victims; we think the link is with the killer.'

'You think I know the Immolation Man?'

'We think he knows you, or knows *of* you. We doubt you know him.'

Poe knew that this was the first of many discussions and meetings, and that whether he wanted to or not, he was involved. In what capacity was still up for debate.

'First impressions?' Flynn asked.

He studied the slash marks again. Not including the messy number five, he counted forty-two. Forty-two wounds to spell out 'Washington Poe'. Forty-two individual expressions of agony. 'Other than the victim wishing I'd been called Bob, nothing.'

'I need you to come back to work,' she said. She looked around at the desolate fells he now called home. 'I need you to re-join the human race.'

He stood up, all previous thoughts of resigning dismissed. There was only one thing that mattered: the Immolation Man was out there somewhere, selecting victim number four. If he ever wanted to feel at ease again he had to find him before he reached number five.

'Whose car are we taking?' he asked.

CHAPTER FIVE

As soon as they were out of Cumbria the land flattened and the M6 stretched ahead like a runway. Spring was having delusions of summer grandeur, and Poe found himself having to turn up Flynn's air-conditioning. Sweat pooled in the small of his back. It had little to do with the heat.

An uneasy silence had stifled them. When Poe had dropped off Edgar with his nearest neighbour, Flynn had changed out of her crisp power suit into a more casual outfit of jeans and a jumper, but despite her relaxed attire, she twirled her fingers through her long hair as she stared at the road.

'Congratulations on your promotion,' Poe said.

She turned her head. 'I didn't want your job. You must know that?'

'I do. And for what it's worth, I think you'll make an excellent DI.'

He wasn't being spiteful. She relaxed and said, 'Thank you. You being suspended wasn't exactly how I envisaged getting a DI position, though.'

'They had no choice.'

'They might not have had a choice when they suspended you,' Flynn said, 'but anyone could have made that mistake.'

'Doesn't matter,' he replied. 'We both know there's a clear evolutionary line from that mistake to what happened, Steph.'

Flynn was referring to their last case. *His* last case. A mad man in the Thames Valley area had abducted and killed two women, and

Muriel Bristow, a fourteen-year-old girl, was missing. SCAS had been involved from the beginning. Offender profiles and crime mapping had been completed but it was the geographic profile that led them to their main suspect: Peyton Williams, an MP's aide. Everything fit. He had a previous conviction for stalking, was in the area every time a girl had been abducted, and had a string of failed relationships.

Poe wanted to arrest and question him, but his boss, Director of Intelligence Talbot, had refused. A general election had been called and they were in the pre-election period known as purdah – without evidence, arresting an MP's aide in a marginal seat could be viewed as election tampering. At least it could in Talbot's eyes. 'Go and find something solid,' he'd been told. In the meantime, Talbot told Poe he would inform the MP in question. Tell him they were investigating a member of his staff. Poe begged him not to.

Talbot ignored him. The MP fired his aide.

And told him why.

Poe was furious. Peyton Williams wasn't going to go anywhere near Muriel Bristow now. Not with that kind of attention. If she were still alive, she wouldn't be for much longer. She'd die of dehydration.

He wasn't the type of cop who'd palm off the unpleasant tasks to others. He'd made the trip to the family's home himself. Before he left, he printed off a Family Liaison Case Summary, a heavily sanitised account of what was happening in the investigation. After telling the Bristows what he could, he handed over the file for them to review in their own time.

And later that day, all hell broke loose.

Poe had made a mistake. A terrible mistake. As well as printing off the Family Liaison Case Summary, he'd printed off an updated summary for his own file. This one *wasn't* sanitised. It contained all his suspicions and all his frustrations.

The wrong report had ended up in the wrong file . . . The Bristows got to read all about Peyton Williams . . .

Only later, after Williams had been snatched and tortured by Muriel Bristow's father, and long after he'd given up Muriel's location and she'd been safely returned to her family, did anyone stop to think how Bristow even knew about Peyton Williams at all.

The mistake had been quickly uncovered, and despite Poe having been right all along, and despite an innocent girl being returned to her family, he'd been suspended with immediate effect. A few weeks later, Peyton Williams died of his wounds.

Until Flynn had showed up at Herdwick Croft, Poe hadn't seen anyone from the NCA since.

'You disappeared without saying goodbye to anyone,' said Flynn.

He felt a tinge of guilt. When he'd been suspended, Poe had ignored all the texts and voicemails offering support. A man had been tortured and he'd been responsible. He'd had to learn to live with that. He'd returned home to Cumbria. Got away from his well-meaning colleagues. Hid away from the world. Alone with only dark thoughts for company.

Flynn continued, 'Between you and me, van Zyl told me he thinks the IPCC aren't far off a finding of "No Case to Answer". They can't prove it was definitely you who put the wrong report in the family's file.'

The thought offered Poe no comfort. Perhaps he was getting used to his monastic existence? He opened the case file and began reading everything SCAS had on the Immolation Man.

CHAPTER SIX

Although it was a triple murder and the documentation was copious, Poe had seen enough files to locate the important stuff. He went straight to the senior investigating officer's early description of the first crime scene.

These were often the most useful as they contained first impressions. Later reports were more measured and considered.

The SIO was a detective chief superintendent called Ian Gamble. Normally the Force Major Incident Team would lead on something that big, but they were in the middle of another investigation, so Gamble – who was also head of CID – appointed himself, and, given the media attention Cumbria was getting, it seemed a sensible move.

Gamble had been a detective inspector when Poe knew him. A solid copper who ran tight, if unimaginative, investigations. He was the one who'd noticed a chemical smell above the obvious one of petrol at the first scene. His suspicions had been well founded. The Immolation Man had used a home-made accelerant. No wonder the bodies had been turned to charcoal.

'Scary, isn't it?' said Flynn. 'Apparently all you need to do is add bits of chopped Styrofoam to petrol until it won't dissolve any more. The boffins at tech support say the result is a white jelly-like substance that will burn so hot it'll render down fat. When that happens, the body acts as its own fuel and burns until there's no flesh and bone left.'

'Dear God,' Poe whispered. Prior to joining the police he'd

served for three years with the Scottish infantry regiment, the Black Watch, and had trained with white phosphorous grenades. He imagined the results would have been similar; once it was on you, it wasn't coming off. The best you could hope for was that your flesh fell off; if it didn't, it kept burning.

The first victim had been killed four months ago. Graham Russell had started his newspaper career in a local Cumbrian rag forty years earlier but had soon moved to Fleet Street. There he rose to be the editor of a national tabloid heavily criticised during the Leveson Inquiry. He hadn't personally been implicated in anything, but he'd taken a massive pension and retired to Cumbria anyway. The Immolation Man had abducted him from his small country estate. There had been no sign of a struggle, and some time later he'd been found in the middle of Castlerigg stone circle near Keswick. As well as being burnt to a crisp, he'd been tortured.

Poe frowned as he followed the team's early lines of enquiry. 'Tunnel vision?' he asked Flynn. Inexperienced SIOs sometimes saw things that weren't there, and although Gamble was hardly a junior officer, he hadn't run a murder investigation for some time.

'We think so, though they're denying it, obviously,' she replied. 'But DCS Gamble seemed pretty keen on the first murder being a Leveson revenge crime.'

It wasn't until a month later, when the body of Joe Lowell was discovered, that the TIE enquiries – Trace, Interview, Eliminate – stopped focusing on phone-hacking victims. Lowell had never been involved in the newspaper trade; he was from a family of landowners who'd farmed south Cumbria for seven generations. The Lowells were – and always had been – solid and popular members of the community. He'd been taken from Lowell Hall, the family home. Despite his son living with him, no one reported him missing. His body was found in the middle of Swinside stone circle, near Broughton-in-Furness in south Cumbria.

Consequently, the investigation got even more serious. All

thoughts of Leveson were forgotten – to the point the murder file was amended – and the focus turned to where it had always been heading: a serial murderer investigation.

Poe searched the file for the section on stone circles. With the killer seeming to have a connection to them, Gamble would have collated as much information as he could.

Cumbria had the highest concentration of stone circles, standing stones, henge monuments, monoliths and barrows in the UK. They were all unique and from a range of time periods – from early Neolithic to Bronze Age. Some were oval and some were round, some of the stones were pink granite and others were slate. A small number had an inner circle of smaller stones. Most of them didn't. Gamble had brought in academics to brief the team on their probable purpose but this was less than useful. Theories ranged from death ceremonies and trade routes to an intimate association with the lunar cycle and astronomical alignments.

The only thing academia seemed to agree on was that, in the entire history of stone circles, they had never been used for ritual sacrifice.

Of course, Poe thought, tomorrow's history is written today . . .

CHAPTER SEVEN

Poe was reading about the third murder – Michael James, the South Lakes councillor who'd died two weeks ago with Poe's name carved into his chest – when he came across a document that made him laugh out loud. It had been written by one of the detective sergeants on the case and he was the only man who could get away with describing the smell at the crime scene as having a 'miasmatic quality' to it.

He was one of life's clowns but he was also one of the most intelligent men Poe had ever met. The type of man who could win a game of *Connect Four* in three moves. His name was Kylian Reid and he was also the only real friend Poe had in Cumbria. They'd met in their early teens and had been close ever since. He felt a pang of guilt he hadn't looked him up since he got back; he'd been so wrapped up in his own problems it hadn't occurred to him. Saying that, he and Reid had known each other a long time and had far too much history for them to ever really fall out. Poe borrowed Flynn's phone and opened the dictionary app. He typed in miasmatic. It meant noxious vapours from decomposing organic matter. He wondered how many people before him had been forced to do the same. It was Reid all over. Getting one over on senior managers by making them feel stupid. No wonder he was still a sergeant.

Things were looking better if they were going to be working together again. Poe picked up the rest of the file and read on.

After the second victim had been found and SCAS were called

in, Flynn's name began to appear in reports. The second victim also started a media race to name the killer. In the end – as they always did in matters like this – the red tops won with 'Immolation Man'.

He finished his first readthrough and put down the file on the rear seats. He closed his eyes and rolled his neck. He'd read the file again soon, every document. Get it imprinted on his memory. The first time was simply to get a flavour of what he was dealing with. SCAS were rarely called in immediately, so reviewing files like they were cold cases was an important skill. They weren't just looking at the evidence; they were looking for mistakes the investigating teams had made.

Flynn noticed he'd finished reading and said, 'Thoughts?'

Poe knew he was being tested. He'd been away for a year – she and van Zyl needed to know he was still up to the job.

'The circles and the immolations are probably a dead end. They'll mean something to the killer but we won't find out what until after he's caught. He has an idea of what he wants but he's happy to change if the reality doesn't live up to the fantasy.'

'How so?'

'The first victim was tortured, the others weren't. For some reason, that didn't do for him what he thought it would. So he stopped doing it.'

'Michael James had your name carved onto his chest. Seems like torture to me.'

'No, he put that on for a reason we don't know yet. The pain he caused was incidental. Graham Russell's pain was intentional.'

Flynn nodded for him to continue.

'All the men are in the same age group and they're all wealthy. You've found nothing to suggest they knew each other.'

'You think he's choosing them at random?'

Poe didn't, but he wasn't ready to say why yet. He needed more information. 'He wants us to think he is.'

She nodded but said nothing.

'And none of them were reported missing?' Poe asked.

'Nope. They all seemed to have genuine reasons to be away from home. It wasn't until after they were killed that we discovered the lengths the Immolation Man went to make sure they wouldn't be reported missing.'

'How?' Poe knew it was in the file but sometimes it was better to get an interpretation of the facts.

'Graham Russell's car and passport were logged getting onto a ferry, and his family got emails saying he was holidaying in France. Joe Lowell sent his family texts from Norfolk saying he was staying with friends and he'd be shooting red-legged partridges until the season ended. Michael James lived on his own so wouldn't have been immediately missed, but his computer history still showed he'd been planning a bespoke whisky tour of the Scottish Isles.'

'So you can't be sure when any of them were taken?'

'Not really, no.'

He thought about what that meant and decided all it did was confirm what he already knew. The Immolation Man was well organised. He told Flynn.

'How so? He leaves a chaotic crime scene.'

Poe shook his head. She was still testing him. 'He's in control at the crime scene. No improvisation. Everything he needs, he brings with him. No physical evidence at the abduction sites or the murder sites, and given that evidence transfer is inevitable and retrieval techniques have never been better, that's remarkable. By the third victim there was a fair bit of surveillance on the stone circles, I gather?'

'Most of them. The one at Long Meg had only just been lifted.'

'So, he's also surveillance aware,' Poe said.

'Anything else?'

'Have I passed?'

Flynn smiled. 'Anything else?'

28

'Yes. There's something missing from the files. A control filter, something the SIO is holding back from the media. What is it?'

'How did you know?'

'The Immolation Man might not be a sadist but he's acting sadistically. There's no way he leaves the bodies unmolested.'

Flynn pointed at her briefcase on the back seat. 'There's another file in there.'

He leaned across and retrieved it. It was stamped 'Secret' and someone had written 'Not to be shared without written permission from DCS Gamble'. Poe didn't open it.

'Have you heard of the cutting season, Poe?'

He shook his head. He hadn't.

'It was originally coined by the NHS. It refers to the time of year – the summer holidays usually – when young girls, some as young as two months old, are taken out of the UK, ostensibly to visit relatives abroad. What they're going for is to undergo female genital mutilation. They go in the long summer break so their wounds have a chance of healing before they return.'

Poe knew a little bit about FGM, the abhorrent practice of removing parts of a young girl's genitals to ensure she can't experience sexual pleasure. It was believed to keep them faithful and chaste. The reality was that the victims had a lifetime of pain and medical problems. In some cultures, the wounds were still stitched together with thorns.

It dawned on Poe why Flynn was telling him this. 'He's castrating them?'

'Technically no. He cuts off the veg *and* the meat. Neatly and without anaesthetic.'

'He's keeping trophies,' Poe said. A high percentage of serial murderers kept parts of their victims.

'Actually, he isn't. Open the file.'

Poe did and nearly lost his lunch. The first photograph explained why the victim's screams hadn't been heard.

He'd been gagged.

The photograph was a close-up picture of Graham Russell's mouth: it was stuffed with his own genitals. The next few photos showed the penis, testicles and scrotum – which were still attached to each other – after they'd been removed from the mouth. Blackened at the end exposed to the fire, surprisingly pink and undamaged at the other. Poe flipped through the rest of the photographs and found them to be much the same.

And he was supposed to be the fifth victim? As if the stakes hadn't been high enough already. He crossed his legs.

'We'll get him before he gets anywhere near you, Poe.'

CHAPTER EIGHT

Deep in the heart of Hampshire, in the grounds of the old Bramshill Police College, lies Foxley Hall. The college might have seen its last course, but Foxley Hall was still the home of the Serious Crime Analysis Section.

For a unit that tended to avoid attention and work in the shadows, the building itself was surprisingly quirky. It was wider than it was tall, had sloping roofs that almost touched the ground, so it looked like SCAS worked in an abandoned Pizza Hut.

Flynn had spent the night at home. Poe had checked into a hotel.

He'd had a fitful night. His nightmares had returned. When he'd been working, the dead had always stayed with Poe. They messed with his dreams and they interrupted his peace. Being back in Hampshire had reopened old wounds. Despite what he'd done, Peyton Williams hadn't deserved to die. During the early hearings, Poe had been shown photographs of the injuries Mr Bristow had inflicted upon Williams. Teeth removed with pliers, spiral fractures to all his fingers, the punctured spleen that would eventually kill him. It had been six months before Poe managed to get a full night's sleep.

And now the nightmares were back. Perhaps they'd never gone away . . .

It was eight o'clock in the morning and Poe had to be escorted into Foxley Hall as if he were an official visitor. The receptionist's bored look changed to one of sycophancy when she saw her boss. She handed Flynn some mail and looked at Poe rudely.

'And you are?' Poe asked, glaring back. He might be wearing jeans and look more mountain man than cop, but she was about to learn that SCAS had a sergeant again.

The receptionist looked like she had no intention of answering unless she was told she had to. That was the problem in areas with high employment: no one took their jobs seriously any more. It was little more than pin money.

'I'd answer him if I were you, Diane,' Flynn said as she rifled through the letters she'd just been handed. 'This is DS Poe, and you'd better believe he's not going to take your shit.'

Instead Diane smirked and said, 'Deputy Director Hanson is waiting for you in your office.'

'Is he now?' she sighed. 'You'd better stay out of his way, Poe. He still blames you for not getting the director's job.'

Hanson had never taken responsibility for his own failings. Not being promoted had to be either someone's fault or part of a wider conspiracy against him. That he'd backed Talbot in the Peyton Williams case was neither here nor there. 'Glad to,' Poe replied.

Flynn turned to Diane. 'Go and get DS Poe a cup of coffee. Do that and he'll be your friend for life.'

Poe and Diane looked at each other. Both doubted that, but Poe was in no mood for a fight this early. Flynn went off to see Hanson and Diane led Poe across the open-plan office to the kitchen area. As she poured him some filter coffee, Poe surveyed the office he used to manage.

Things had changed. When he'd been the detective inspector, the tables were arranged depending on wherever people fancied sitting that day, and because of inter-office politics, the office layout was constantly changing. Even though he'd known that had irritated Flynn, he hadn't intervened. If she'd wanted order, she could have put her sergeant's stripes to use.

But now, with her inspector's pip, she'd decided to use her management authority. Analysts, some of whom he recognised, most of whom he didn't, were seated around an ordered central hub. It acted as the centre of a wheel, with offices and specialist pods forming the spokes. It wasn't quite a cubicle farm but it wasn't far off. There was a low hum of noise; muffled phone conversations, the clack of keyboards and the shuffle of paperwork. Despite it being early, no one was eating breakfast at their desks. That had been another thing that had made Flynn's bile bubble: people arriving at work then spending thirty minutes making porridge.

SCAS might have been functioning professionally and efficiently but, to Poe, it had about as much charm as an out-of-office email. If he were forced to spend time there, he knew that within an hour he'd be using the word 'fuck' like a comma.

At least his large map of the United Kingdom was still there. Poe wandered over and scanned it. It dominated the wall. Different colour markers, laid over it like weather patterns, indicated where the various crimes were on their radar. If the colours were the same, it suggested there was enough evidence that the crimes might be linked. Analysts were constantly scanning the media and crime reports from the territorial forces, looking for patterns and anomalies. Part of what SCAS did was crying wolf – seeing patterns and letting police forces know they might have a serial rapist or murderer. Most of the time they were wrong.

Sometimes they were right.

There were three red markers in Cumbria; the Immolation Man was being worked hard.

A hush rippled across the room as people began to realise who had walked in with the boss. Poe heard his name being whispered. He ignored it. He hated being the centre of attention but he knew he was a cause célèbre. Not just because his name had been carved into the chest of a man sleeping in a cold bed at Carlisle's mortuary, but also because of the way he'd run the unit when he was in charge.

And the way he'd left; he shouldn't forget that.

The silence was broken by muffled shouting. It was coming from his old office, technically Flynn's office now. Poe wandered over.

Although most of the shouting was indistinct, Poe heard his name every now and then. He opened the door and eased inside.

Hanson leaned over Flynn's desk. Both his hands were planted knuckles down on the wood.

'I told you, Flynn, I don't care what the director said, you shouldn't have reinstated him.'

Flynn was taking it calmly. 'Technically Director van Zyl reinstated him, not me.'

Hanson stood up. 'I'm disappointed in you, Flynn.'

Poe coughed.

Hanson turned. 'Poe,' he said. 'I didn't realise you'd travelled back with DI Flynn.'

'Good morning, sir,' Poe said.

Hanson ignored his outstretched hand.

Poe knew he should care that the deputy despised him, but he found not giving a shit was far easier. When you didn't care about your job, the people in authority quickly realised just how little power they had.

'Smile all you want, Poe. Van Zyl's made a mistake reappointing you. You'll fuck up again and he'll go the same way as the last director.' He turned to Flynn. 'And when he's gone there are going to be some big changes around here, DI Flynn.'

Without a further word, he left the office. King of the token gesture, he couldn't resist slamming the door.

Flynn had arranged a meeting with Human Resources; the sooner Poe could be formally reinstated, the sooner they could both get back up to Cumbria. A senior HR officer was on his way down to the SCAS building. They took a seat at the small conference table and waited.

Poe took the time to look at what Flynn had done with his old office. Before he'd sneaked in, he'd noticed the highly polished brass plate with Flynn's name. Poe had had a sheet of A4 with his details written in flip-board marker pen. Blue, if he remembered correctly.

The chaos in which he'd worked had been replaced by a sense of calm and order. Blackstone's police manuals were lined up on the shelf. Right at the end was her well-thumbed copy of the *Senior Investigating Officers' Handbook*. Poe had owned a copy of the pocket-sized book – all detectives did – but he'd discarded it after reading it once. It was useful but unremarkable. It led senior detectives through logical and thorough investigations. The problem was that everyone ended up investigating crimes the same way, and while he agreed there had to be standards, the handbook didn't help with catching the *extraordinary* killers.

He scanned the rest of the office. All very corporate. Nothing personal on show.

When he'd worked at SCAS, the clear desk policy was something that happened to other people. Flynn's desk was predictably uncluttered. A computer and a notepad with a clean page on top. A cup with the NCA logo was filled with pens and pencils.

Her phone rang. She pressed the speaker function and answered it. Diane said, 'Ashley Barrett from HR is here.'

'Thank you,' Flynn said. 'Send him in.'

Barrett came in smiling, suited and booted, carrying a brown leather briefcase. He was a tall, thin man. He sat at the conference table.

'Sorry to be curt, Ash,' Flynn said, 'but can we do this quickly? We need to get back up to Cumbria.'

He nodded, glanced at Poe and removed some documents from his briefcase. He placed them on the table in front of him. He coughed gently before launching into a pre-prepared speech. It sounded as though he was talking on autopilot. 'As you know,

DS Poe, suspension is considered a neutral act and it is up to the organisation to decide whether the suspension remains justified. Yesterday, Director of Intelligence Edward van Zyl decided that, despite the IPCC case remaining active, the end of the internal investigation means your suspension should be lifted.' Barrett searched through his paperwork. Handing Poe a one-sheet document, he said, 'This is confirmation in writing. Can you please sign at the bottom?'

Poe did. It had been a long time since he'd had to write his 'work' signature – a careless scrawl he wouldn't have dared use on a cheque. It felt strange but in a comforting way. He slid the document back across the table.

The desk phone rang and Flynn got up to answer it. While she spoke quietly, Barrett busied himself with asking Poe if he wanted employee assistance like counselling, or refresher training on the IT system. Poe answered no to everything, as they both knew he would.

With another box ticked in the big book of HR rules, Barrett got down to the good stuff. From his briefcase he removed a succession of things that Poe considered the tools of his trade. He handed Poe a work mobile; an encrypted BlackBerry. Barrett explained it was pre-programmed with some contact details he might need and his online calendar had been synced to it. It meant anyone with authorised access to his e-diary could enter appointments. Poe made a mental note to disable it as soon as he found out how. The BlackBerry was internet enabled; he'd be able to surf the web, receive his secure emails and text messages. He could even make phone calls with it.

'The BlackBerry has the Protect app installed and it's switched on,' Barrett said.

Poe looked at him blankly.

'It means its location can be logged from a website.'

'You're spying on me?'

'Deputy Director Hanson insisted, I'm afraid.'

Poe slipped the BlackBerry into his pocket. He would disable that later as well.

Barrett gave him a small, black leather wallet that contained Poe's warrant card and NCA ID.

Poe casually opened it, checked it was the right one, then put it in his inside pocket. He felt whole again.

It was time to get back to work.

He glanced over at Flynn. She was frowning as she listened to whoever was on the other end of the phone.

'Since you've been gone, Detective Sergeant Flynn has been promoted into the temporary detective inspector role at SCAS,' Barrett said. 'Director van Zyl has made it clear that this is to remain the case. The conditions of your suspension being lifted are that you will return to work in your substantive post of detective sergeant. In effect, you will report to DI Flynn.'

'Not a problem,' Poe said.

Flynn put down the phone and turned to Poe. Her face was ashen. 'There's been another one.'

CHAPTER NINE

'Where?'

'A hill walker stumbled into him somewhere near a town called Cockermouth. You know it?'

Poe nodded. It was a small market town in west Cumbria. He was surprised the Immolation Man had already changed his MO. 'You sure?'

Flynn said she was, and then asked why.

'There aren't any stone circles in Cockermouth. Not to my knowledge anyway.'

She checked her notepad. 'Cockermouth. That's what the SIO said.'

Poe stood. 'Let's get going then.' It was getting serious; if the fourth victim had just been found, then he was next on the conveyor belt.

Barrett said, 'I'm supposed to give you a reorientation tour before you start . . .' He withered in front of their combined looks. '. . . but I suppose under the circumstances it can wait.'

'Good man,' Poe said. 'I want to take an analyst with us. Someone who can do a bit of everything, I have an idea where to start and there'll be a lot of data mining to do. Who's the best we have?'

Flynn hesitated and her face coloured. 'Jonathan Pierce.'

'And he's the best, is he?'

'Well, officially Tilly Bradshaw is the best. She has a skill set like no other here. She's the one who found your name in all that medical data.'

Poe thought he'd recognised the name. 'What's the problem then?'

'She's one of our special people. She refuses to leave the office.'

Poe smiled. 'What you need, DI Flynn, is a sergeant . . .'

CHAPTER TEN

Poe marched into the open-plan office and shouted for Tilly Bradshaw. A small thin woman stood up. She looked shy and bookish, a typical cube-dweller. She pouted and sat back down when she saw who'd shouted for her.

He turned and spoke to Barrett. 'Can you stay there a moment, Ash? I might need some help.'

Poe had loved being a sergeant. In hindsight he shouldn't have taken the temporary inspector role. It came with more management responsibility than he was comfortable with. He'd been *good* at being a sergeant and by the looks of things SCAS had been without one for too long . . .

'Miss Bradshaw, my office now.'

Bradshaw slouched along to the sergeant's office. As it had recently been Flynn's office, it was scarily tidy. Poe sat behind the desk.

Bradshaw didn't shut the door behind her and that was fine. The unit would do well to pay attention to the new way of working. He gestured to the seat in front of the desk and she perched on the end.

Poe studied her; 90 per cent of being a sergeant was managing people. She wore no makeup and behind her gold-coloured Harry Potter glasses were grey, myopic eyes. She was fish-belly pale. The front of her brightly coloured T-shirt showed the logo of the all-girl *Ghostbusters* remake. Her canvas trousers were khaki with large side pockets. Cargo pants, he thought they were called. Her fingers were long and fine-boned. The nails were chewed to the quick. Despite her earlier show of defiance, she looked apprehensive.

'Do you know who I am?'

She nodded. 'Your name is Washington Poe. You're thirty-eight years old and you were born in Kendal, Cumbria. You transferred from Cumbria Constabulary to SCAS and it is believed that a mistake you made led directly to the torture and death of a suspect. The IPCC are investigating you. You're on suspension.'

Poe stared at her. His piss-taking radar wasn't beeping; she was being serious. This was how she talked. 'Wrong. As of,' he said, checking his watch, 'five minutes ago, I'm *Detective Sergeant* Washington Poe. And from now on, if I ask you to do something, you do it. Are we clear?'

'DI Stephanie Flynn says I'm only to do what she says.'

'Did she now?'

'She did, Detective Sergeant Washington Poe.'

'Poe's fine.'

'She did, Poe.'

'I meant you should call me Sergea . . . actually . . . you can call me what you want,' Poe said, realising he didn't have the energy for a meaningless discussion over forms of address. 'And why did DI Flynn tell you that?'

'Sometimes people like to joke with me. They tell me to do things I'm not supposed to,' she replied, pushing her glasses back up her nose and tucking an errant lock of wispy brown hair behind her ear.

A flickering of understanding crept up on him. 'OK. But I'm your new sergeant so you do have to do what I tell you to do,' he said.

She stared at him.

Eventually Poe said, 'Wait here.'

He walked into Flynn's office. She was talking to Barrett. 'That was quick,' she said.

Poe could have sworn she was suppressing a smile.

'Can you pop into my office and tell Miss Bradshaw that she is also to do what I tell her?'

'Of course.' She followed him into his office.

'Tilly, this is Washington Poe and he's our new sergeant.'

'He wants to be called Poe,' she replied.

Flynn glanced at Poe, who shrugged in a what-you-gonna-do kind of way.

'Well whatever, you're to do what he says as well now. OK?'

Bradshaw nodded.

'But no one else, Tilly,' Flynn added before leaving them alone.

'Now we've got that sorted, Tilly, I'd like you to go home, pack a suitcase and meet me and DI Flynn back here in an hour,' Poe said. 'We're going on a road trip for a few days.'

'I can't,' she said immediately.

Poe sighed. 'Wait here.'

A minute later he was back with a NCA standard contract of employment. He slid it across the desk.

'Show me where it says that, because all I can see is the paragraph that says, "There may be occasions where you are required to work unsocial hours and away from your office base."'

Bradshaw didn't look at it.

Poe continued, 'I certainly can't see anything that says Tilly Bradshaw is exempt.'

Bradshaw closed her eyes and said, 'Section three, paragraph two, subsection seven states that discretionary benefits – in my case not working away from the office – can be considered a binding term of an employment contract if well-established over a period of time. The legal definition is "customs and practices".' She reopened her eyes and looked at him.

Poe was vaguely aware of the HR rule that said if someone had been doing something for a long time it could be considered part of their job, even if it was in direct contradiction to their contract of employment. As stupid as it sounded, people had been awarded money in employment tribunals on that rule.

He stared at her open-mouthed. 'You memorised the employment manual?'

Bradshaw frowned. 'I read it when I signed it.'

'When was that?'

'Eleven months, fourteen days ago.'

Poe stood up again. 'Wait here, please.'

He walked round to Flynn's office.

'Jonathan Pierce will be happy to get out of the office for a few days,' she said.

He wasn't giving up so easily. 'Is she all there?'

'She's fine,' she replied. 'She's had a sheltered upbringing and can sometimes be taken advantage of. She's very literal and tends to believe everything she's told. As much as I can, I keep a close eye on her. When you learn how to handle her she's the most important asset you'll have.'

'But she's not field ready?'

'She has an IQ close to two hundred but probably can't boil an egg—'

'Ash, is there any legal reason why I can't take her?' Poe asked.

'If she claims customs and practices, we'd defend it and she'd lose.'

Poe looked at him. He waited for a yes or no answer.

'No,' he said. 'There's nothing in employment law that offers her any protection.'

'That's settled then,' he said, 'and this time last year, *I* couldn't boil an egg.'

Poe walked back into his office and sat down. He steepled his fingers and leaned forwards to face Bradshaw. He'd try something Flynn had tried on him the day before and hope Bradshaw wasn't in the mood to bluff him. 'You have two choices. One, you go home and pack a bag for a Cumbrian spring, or two, I accept your notice right now.'

Bradshaw looked even more nervous than before.

I'm missing something, Poe thought. 'What is it, Tilly? Why can't you leave the office?'

Eventually she stood, her eyes brimming with tears. She stomped out of his office without a backwards look.

Poe watched as she made her way to her desk. She got to her workstation and slumped in her chair. She put on some headphones and began typing.

He followed her over. Perhaps she hadn't understood the urgency.

'Miss Bradshaw, DI Flynn tells me you're the best we have. I need you up in Cumbria. You're no use to me behind a desk.'

'Duh,' she said, 'what do you think I'm doing?'

An arrogant-looking young man laughed insolently. Poe gave him a look that would've withered a thistle. He read what Bradshaw had typed into Google's search bar: What to pack for a Cumbrian spring?

'You've got to be kidding me?' he said.

She looked up. It was clear she wasn't.

There were no personal items around her workspace. Flynn had tidied up the office since he'd left, but everyone else had managed to personalise their workspaces. Mugs with 'World's Best Dad', cheaply framed photographs of partners and kids, the odd risqué calendar. Bradshaw's was empty.

'Have you just moved to this desk, Tilly?'

She looked confused. 'No. I have been here almost twelve months, Poe.'

'Where are all your things then?'

'What things?'

'You know, your mug, a cuddly toy, a novelty pen,' he replied. 'In other words, where's all your shit?'

44

'Oh,' she said. 'I used to bring things in but people took them for a joke. I never got them back.'

Poe's heart missed a beat. 'Look, just pack as if you're going away for a few days: a change of clothes, some toiletries, that type of thing. I also need you to bring all the gear you need to catch a serial killer,' he said. 'And be quick. There's been a fourth murder.'

'You don't understand how much trouble I'm in,' she muttered.

An hour later, Poe understood.

Bradshaw had left to pack – Flynn had needed to authorise a taxi as Bradshaw didn't have a car and her mother usually dropped her off and collected her – when Diane, the receptionist, walked over. She was smiling and Poe already recognised that as a bad sign.

'Phone call for you,' she said. 'I'll put it through to your office.'

'DS Poe,' he said when he picked up the phone. It felt strange to have a rank in front of his name again. 'How can I help you?'

'Hello, Sergeant Poe, this is Matilda's mother.'

There was a pause and Poe filled it. 'I'm sorry but are you sure you have the right number? I don't know any Matilda.'

'You'll know her as Tilly. Tilly Bradshaw,' she said. 'My daughter's just been on the phone saying she's had to go home to pack a suitcase but she couldn't find the tent. She wants me to leave work to go and buy one. She also said she'd need some canned goods and a tin opener. She wants me to bring it all to the office. You've got her awfully excited, Sergeant Poe.'

'A tent . . . canned goods . . . I'm sorry, Mrs Bradshaw, but I've got no idea what she's talking about. She'll be staying at the same hotel as the rest of the team. I'd assumed that was obvious.'

'Well, that makes a lot more sense, I suppose. But why is she going up to Cumbria at all? It sounds dreadful up there.'

'Hey, I'm from Cumbria!' he protested.

'Oh, I'm sorry. But it does sound awfully bleak.'

Poe was about to reply, 'That's because it fucking is', but thought better of it. He settled for, 'It's Cumbria, not Baghdad, Mrs Bradshaw. She's going to be assisting on a murder investigation.'

'And it won't be dangerous?'

'Not unless the Immolation Man decides to burn the hotel down.'

'And is that likely?'

'No, I was joking,' Poe said. At least he knew where Bradshaw got her social skills from. 'She'll be perfectly safe. She's coming up for analytical support only, I doubt she'll even leave the hotel.'

That seemed to mollify her.

'OK, I'll allow it,' she said, 'on one condition.'

Poe bit back a sarcastic response. He thought about Bradshaw, worrying because she didn't think she'd be allowed to go. She hadn't been deliberately awkward at all. 'Name it.'

'She rings home every night.'

Under the circumstances that didn't seem so unreasonable. 'Deal,' he said.

'Now, there are a few things you need to know about Matilda, Sergeant Poe.'

'I'm listening.'

'Well, first of all, you need to understand that she's a wonderful girl and a marvellous daughter. I really couldn't ask for anyone better.'

'But . . .'

'But she has led an extremely sheltered life. She was at university when she should have been playing outside. She got her first Oxford degree when she was sixteen.'

Poe whistled.

'And she stayed on and got a master's and two PhDs: one in computers and the others in mathematics or something. It's all beyond me. We'd assumed she was going to spend her life at

Oxford, going from research grant to research grant. People were throwing money at her.'

'So how did she—?'

'So how did she end up working for the National Crime Agency? Your guess is as good as mine, Sergeant Poe, but I suspect it's something to do with the wilful streak she got from her father. She just came in from university one night and said she'd applied for a job. Wouldn't tell us what as she knew we'd stop her.'

'Why would you do that?'

'You've met her, DS Poe. Matilda has an extraordinary mind. A once-in-a-generation mind according to one of the professors who came to see us when she was thirteen. The flipside of that is, because she's never really lived in the real world before, she's never developed the life skills you and I take for granted. I suppose it was all about her brain's priorities. She finds social situations extremely difficult and this has caused her problems in the past.'

It was becoming clearer. Perhaps Flynn was right, perhaps Bradshaw wasn't the right person for the job. He was about to tell Mrs Bradshaw not to worry, that her daughter would be home for tea, when Bradshaw walked through the door. She was still looking scared but there was something else. She was exuding a nervous excitement. Now she knew she was going, it looked like she couldn't wait to get started. She walked over to her desk and began packing equipment.

'I'll take care of her, Mrs Bradshaw, you have my word,' Poe said before hanging up.

Poe walked over and was about to help her, when the man who'd laughed earlier decided to entertain the assembled staff. He didn't realise Poe was standing behind him. He stood up and said, 'Look everyone, Little Miss Retard's going on a road trip.'

A couple of people tittered. Most had seen Poe and recognised a shit sandwich when they saw one.

The excitement in Bradshaw's eyes fizzled out. Her cheeks coloured and her eyes dropped to the floor. Poe glanced back at her featureless workspace and everything clicked into place.

She was being bullied.

Before anyone could react, he'd taken three strides and dragged Laughing Man from his chair. Grabbing him by the back of his jacket, Poe ran him across the office and slammed his head into the wall.

'Name!' Poe shouted.

Silence.

'NAME!'

'Jon-Jon-Jonathan,' the man stuttered, his face a mask of terror.

'Ashley Barrett! DI Flynn! Out here, please!'

Flynn rushed out. She was followed by the HR manager.

'Please repeat what you've just said for DI Flynn's benefit.'

Jonathan's eyes were spinning like a slot machine as he searched for a way out. Poe's grip on his throat was vice-like. Without releasing him, Poe turned and addressed the room. 'Most of you haven't met me yet. I'm Detective Sergeant Washington Poe and you all need to know that I absolutely won't tolerate bullies.'

It was true. He wouldn't. Having a strange name, no mother and a total weirdo for a father had been the toxic trio that made him a bully magnet at school. It hadn't taken long to work out that the only way he would survive was if there were consequences for anyone who picked on him. The bullies learned that Poe fought back, that he didn't back down and he wouldn't stop fighting. Start a fight with Poe and you had to be prepared to continue until someone was unconscious. It wasn't long before he was given a wide berth.

'So, take a good look at your friend Jonathan here,' he continued, 'because this is the last time he steps foot in this office.'

The whole office stared, open-mouthed.

'Does anyone think I'm being unfair?'

48

No one seemed to. Or if they did, they were bright enough not to say.

'Did everyone hear what Jonathan called one of his colleagues?'

Everyone had, it seemed.

Poe pointed at one. 'You, what's your name?'

'Jen.'

'What did Jonathan say, Jen?'

'He called Tilly a retard, sir.'

'I work for a living, Jen. Don't call me "sir".' Poe turned to Flynn and Barrett. 'Good enough?'

Flynn turned to Barrett and said, 'It is for me. Ash?'

Barrett paused. 'I could have done without DS Poe assaulting—'

'He was holding a pen,' Poe interrupted. 'I thought he was going to use it as a weapon.'

'Good enough then,' Barrett said. 'Jonathan Pierce, I'm formally suspending you for gross misconduct, bullying and using offensive language. Please let me have your credentials and we'll arrange for a disciplinary hearing, at which point you'll no doubt be formally dismissed from the NCA.'

'But-but-but everyone calls her that,' Jonathan said.

Poe could almost hear the room's sharp intake of breath. Jonathan had just committed the cardinal sin: ratting out colleagues to save his own skin.

Poe said, 'Anyone else here committed gross misconduct?'

No one moved. A couple of people looked guilty, but it didn't look as though anyone was about to fall on their sword.

'Nope? Just you it seems, Jonathan,' Poe said. He leaned in and whispered, 'And if I hear there's been any comeback on my friend Tilly, I'll hunt you down and twist your fucking fingers clean off. Are we clear? Nod if you understand.'

Jonathan nodded.

'Good,' Poe said. 'Now fuck off.' He let Jonathan go and he slumped to the ground.

Turning to Bradshaw, he said, 'You don't need a tent, Tilly. You'll be staying in a hotel with DI Flynn. You got everything else?'

She managed a nod.

'What you waiting for then? Let's go and catch us a serial killer.'

CHAPTER ELEVEN

Poe had assumed the three of them would share the driving. They'd pulled over at some services in Cheshire after Bradshaw had announced, 'I need the toilet', but when Poe threw her the keys and told her she'd be driving the last leg, she'd told him she didn't have a driving licence.

He thought for a moment. 'So why the hell have you been sitting in the passenger seat all this time? Non-drivers sit in the back.'

She folded her arms. 'I always sit in the passenger seat. It's statistically the safest.'

Flynn stopped the argument before it could start by climbing into the rear. 'I prefer the back anyway, Poe,' she explained.

Bradshaw continued lecturing them on car safety as Poe pulled back onto the M6. He stopped listening before he was off the slip road.

He'd never met anyone like her. She didn't seem to understand any of society's basic norms. There was no filter between her brain and her mouth and she blurted out whatever she was thinking. She had little to no understanding of non-verbal communication: she either refused to make eye contact or wouldn't break it. If he ignored her when she said his name, she simply repeated it until he answered.

After a while, they descended into silence.

Poe glanced in the rear-view mirror. Flynn was asleep. 'Can you do me a favour, Tilly?' He reached into his jacket pocket and passed over his BlackBerry. 'There's an e-diary thing and some sort of tracking app on this phone. Can you disable them?'

'Yes, Poe.'

She made no move to take it.

'*Will* you disable them?'

She hesitated. 'Am I supposed to?'

'Yes,' he lied.

She nodded and started fiddling with his phone.

'But if DI Flynn asks, don't tell her,' he added.

'Do you like working for SCAS, Tilly?' he said five minutes after she'd returned his BlackBerry.

'Oh gosh, yes,' she replied, her face lighting up. 'It's marvellous. It's not everywhere you get to adapt theoretical mathematics into real-world applications.'

'Damn straight,' Poe said without cracking a smile. It had been the first time she'd really smiled. When she did, her face was transformed.

After they talked about her SCAS work, they discussed her time at Oxford. It was a one-sided conversation; Poe didn't have a clue what she was talking about. Maths had ended for him as soon as they replaced numbers with letters. It was clear Flynn had been right, though. Bradshaw was an asset. She had an in-depth understanding of all their profiling disciplines but her real strength was being able to devise bespoke solutions as and when they were required. Flynn had told him it was her program that arranged the slash wounds into his name. He thanked her. She'd probably saved his life.

She blushed.

'Why are you called Washington, Poe?' she said minutes later. She smiled shyly when she realised what she'd said. She rephrased it. 'Poe, why is your first name Washington?'

'Don't know. Ask me another,' Poe replied.

'Why does no one like you?' she said.

Poe glanced at her. She wasn't being rude. She didn't seem to understand the concept of small talk; if she asked you something, it was because she wanted to know the answer. 'Boy, you just come right out and say things, don't you?'

'I'm sorry, Poe,' she mumbled. 'DI Stephanie Flynn says I have to work on my people skills.'

'It's fine, Tilly. It's refreshingly honest, actually,' he said, keeping his eyes on the road as he overtook a lorry. 'And I didn't realise I was that unpopular.'

'Oh, yes. I listened to Deputy Director of Intelligence Justin Hanson and Detective Inspector Stephanie Flynn talking about you.'

'Deputy Director Hanson blames me for not getting promoted,' he said.

'Why is that, Poe?'

'A lot of people didn't want me investigating Peyton Williams, Tilly. He was an MP's aide, and Deputy Director Hanson, along with some other senior managers, were terrified of causing a scandal. If they'd listened to me in the first place, Peyton Williams wouldn't be dead.'

'Oh,' she said. 'I don't care for Deputy Director Justin Hanson too much. I think he's mean.'

'You've got that right,' Poe said. 'And anyway, you couldn't have heard them this morning. Even I couldn't hear what they were saying and I was nearer DI Flynn's office than you were.'

'Not this morning,' she said. 'I was in Conference Room B with Deputy Director Justin Hanson, DI Stephanie Flynn and Director Edward van Zyl when I was showing them the MSCT data. After a while, I think they forgot I was there.'

Poe said nothing. He glanced in the rear-view mirror again. Flynn had woken up. Her eyes were red and gritty. Car sleep was never as satisfying as bed sleep.

Bradshaw turned in her seat and said, 'You don't like Poe do you, DI Stephanie Flynn?'

'What are you talking about, Tilly!' she exclaimed. She looked worried, though. 'Of course I like Sergeant Poe.'

'Oh,' she said. 'I thought when Director Edward van Zyl said that the Serious Crime Analysis Section needed Poe because he had an "encyclopaedic understanding of serial killers", and you said, "But a microscopic understanding of not being a dickhead, sir", it was because you didn't like him?'

Poe laughed so hard, hot coffee jetted out of his nostrils.

'Tilly!' Flynn said, mortified.

'What?'

'You should never repeat private discussions.'

'Oh.'

'That wasn't a nice thing to say. About either of us,' Flynn said.

Bradshaw's bottom lip began to quiver and Poe jumped in. 'Don't worry about it, Tilly. Being liked is overrated.'

She smiled. 'That's good, because no one likes me either.'

He turned to see if she was joking. She wasn't.

Bradshaw turned to look out of the window. The conversation was over.

Poe glanced at Flynn in the mirror. Her face was red with embarrassment. He winked to show there were no hard feelings. He was beginning to like Matilda Bradshaw.

The rest of the journey was uneventful and they arrived at the Shap Wells Hotel just after seven in the evening.

Flynn and Bradshaw checked in while Poe collected his mail. Although it wasn't his official address, it wasn't fair to expect a postman to walk over the rough fells to Herdwick Croft, and the hotel allowed him to have his mail delivered to reception.

There was very little. That was one of the perks of living silently; you got very little junk mail.

Flynn met him at reception.

'Sorted?'

'Yeah,' she sighed. 'Tilly wanted a room nearer the fire exit so we had to do some swapping around but she seems happy now. I've told her to get something to eat then have an early night.'

'Let's go and see victim number four then.'

Long Meg and Her Daughters, the scene of the third murder, and Castlerigg, the scene of the first, were two of the most visually impressive prehistoric monuments in the country. They were internationally known stone circles. Cumbria also had countless other Neolithic circles, including some that were so small they could only be identified from the air.

Poe didn't know of any near Cockermouth. He suspected that either the police or the Immolation Man had seen a circle when there wasn't one. Most fells in Cumbria had naturally occurring rocky outcrops and stone formations, and if you were standing in the middle of one, it wouldn't be too much of a stretch to imagine they'd been strategically placed by a Stone-Age civilisation thousands of years ago.

But Poe was wrong.

There was a stone circle near Cockermouth.

Poe navigated the roads as they got smaller and smaller. He turned right at Dubwath, a tiny village on the edge of Bassenthwaite Lake, and five minutes later the flashing glare of blue lights guided them to where they needed to be.

Poe parked at the back of a long row of police vehicles. A uniformed officer was standing at a gate holding a clipboard.

He asked to see their ID and gave Poe a funny look as he recorded his name.

'Is there a stone circle up there?' Poe asked.

The uniformed cop nodded. 'Elva Plain. Supposed to have had

something to do with the trade in Neolithic axes.' When you were on cordon duty in the middle of nowhere there was very little to do but Google things on your phone.

'This is the outer cordon?' Poe checked.

'Yep,' he replied. 'The inner cordon's up there.' He pointed towards a sharply inclined, windswept hill. Poe couldn't see anyone but he could hear voices.

As they climbed, they met another uniformed cop on his way down who told them they were nearly there. They kept walking up until they saw it.

The circle was on a level terrace on the southern slope of Elva Hill. It was bathed in artificial light. Fifteen grey stones formed a circle about forty yards in diameter. The tallest was no more than a yard from the ground; some of the others were barely visible.

It was a hive of activity.

CSI, clad head to toe in white forensic suits, milled about in organised chaos. Some knelt on the ground working, while others focused in and around an evidence tent that had been erected in the middle of the circle.

The inner cordon was set up so the entirety of the circle's circumference was within the blue and white police tape. Poe and Flynn introduced themselves to a cop with another clipboard.

'The boss'll be out soon,' the uniformed constable said. 'Can't let you in without his permission.'

Poe nodded. Good crime-scene discipline usually meant a good SIO. Ian Gamble might not have the flashes of inspiration that cracked the impossible cases, but he played to his strengths. And why not? Ninety-nine per cent of murders were solved by thorough and methodical investigations.

Flynn turned to face him. 'Is there anything to be gained by going in? We'll get the photos when they're ready.'

'I'll have a quick look, if you don't mind. I want to get a feel for him.'

She nodded.

One of the white-suited men looked up and saw them. He left the conversation he was having and walked over to them. He pulled off his face mask as soon as he'd left the cordon. It was Ian Gamble, the SIO. He reached out and shook Poe's hand.

'Good to see you again, Poe,' he said. 'You had any thoughts on why your name was on the last one's chest?'

Poe shook his head. No niceties, no small talk. Strictly business.

'Never mind, we can get into it later,' Gamble said. 'You want a look?'

'Just to see what my first impressions are.'

'Fair enough,' he said, before turning to a man standing near a box of equipment. 'Boyle!' he shouted. 'Bring DS Poe a suit.'

At the sound of Poe's name, another man in a forensic suit pulled off his mask.

It was Kylian Reid.

In a voice loud enough for the whole hill to hear, Reid said, 'Misunderstood by colleagues, ignored by managers, taken for granted by everyone else – ladies and gentlemen, I present the great Washington Poe.'

Poe reddened.

His friend bounded over, leapt the cordon fence, causing Gamble to wince, and wringed Poe's outstretched hand until it hurt.

'I see how it is now,' Reid said, a grin on his face. 'I only get to see you when there's an emergency. That how it is, Poe? Shite show.'

Poe shrugged. 'Kylian.' There'd be time to catch up later.

Reid turned to Flynn and said, 'So, how'd you know this friendless weirdo?'

Poe introduced them. 'DI Flynn, this is my friend Kylian Reid. He *was* a DS in major incidents.'

'*Still* a DS in major incidents,' he said. 'I take it you're all staying at Shap Wells? I'll get a room there one night and we can all have a drink.'

'It'll be the best night ever,' Flynn said woodenly.

Poe decided the reunion could wait. 'So, what's in there?' He directed the question at Gamble. Reid might be the only friend he had on the force, but it was still Gamble's crime scene.

'You know the rule of nines?'

Poe nodded. It was how the extent of burns was medically assessed. The head and arms were all 9 per cent each, while the legs, the front and the back of the torso were all 18 per cent each. That added up to 99 per cent. The remaining 1 per cent was the genitalia.

Gamble said, 'Well, our lad's getting better. Although he was the most heavily tortured, the first victim only had burns covering his legs and back. Not much on his front, and his arms weren't touched. The burns increased on the second, and by the third, the victim was around about the ninety per cent mark.'

'And this one?'

'Come and see for yourself.'

While Poe changed into the suit Boyle had brought over, Gamble replaced the one he was wearing to avoid any cross-contamination issues. Flynn didn't bother – she'd seen victim number three in situ – and stayed with Reid. Poe was signed into the inner cordon and followed Gamble across the footboards CSI had laid down to avoid key evidence being trampled on.

The smell hit him first. Five yards from the forensic tent and the stench became overpowering.

Poe knew there was a myth that burning humans smelled like pork. They really didn't. Human flesh alone might, but people who burn to death haven't been processed the way slaughtered animals have. They haven't been bled and their internal organs haven't been removed. Digestive tracts full of food and faeces remain in the body.

Everything that burns has its own unique foul smell.

Blood is iron-rich and Poe could detect the faint metallic aroma. That was the most pleasant. Muscles burn differently to body fat, internal organs burn differently to blood, and burning guts have a smell unlike any other. The combined odour was thick, sweet and cloying. On top of it all was the unmistakable stench of petrol.

The smell coated the inside of Poe's nose and the back of his throat. He'd be smelling and tasting it for days. He retched and almost vomited but managed to hold it together.

Gamble opened the tent flap for him. He walked inside. The Home Office Pathologist was still working on the body.

It was on its side and twisted into an unnatural position. The eyeballs had burst then dried, and the mouth was open as if the victim had died screaming. Poe knew heat did strange things to corpses, and the mouth could just as easily have opened post-mortem. The hands were burnt to stumps, and although it would no doubt be confirmed later, Poe was sure the victim's '1 per cent' was missing. The corpse was the colour and consistency of rough black leather. It looked as though it had been dipped in lava then dried in a furnace. Apart from the soles of the feet. They were still shockingly pink.

The pathologist looked up and grunted a greeting.

Poe asked, 'You think the same accelerant was used?'

'Definitely,' he said. He was an older man and thin. The forensic suit billowed out like a hot-air balloon. He pointed at the victim's thigh. 'You see that split? The University of West Florida has been researching this for a few years, and they now know that the outer surface of the skin fries and peels first. It takes five minutes for the thicker dermal layer to shrink and split, and as untreated petrol will only burn for a minute or so, additional fuel must have been used.'

Poe didn't want to know why the University of West Florida

had been conducting research like that. He wanted to know *how* they'd been doing it even less. They did execute a lot of death row inmates over there, though . . .

'And if you look here,' the pathologist said, pointing at the thighs, buttocks and waist, 'all the fat has rendered down. Human fat is a good fuel but it needs something to act as a wick. He was naked so we know it wasn't his clothes. I'll know more when I get him back on the table, but I suspect that every time the fire was dying down, the killer added more accelerant.'

'How long?'

'For him to die?'

Poe shook his head. 'To reduce the body to this.'

'Five to seven hours I'd estimate. The muscles have shrunk and contracted, which has caused the peculiar position he's in now, and that takes time.'

'And the soles of the feet?'

'He was standing throughout the whole thing. The ground protected them.' He turned back to the task in hand.

Gamble said, 'You can't see it, but there's a small hole underneath the body. He was staked in the upright position. Staking his victims is one of the adaptations he's made since he started.'

'Must have been a metal one,' Poe said. 'A wooden one would have collapsed after fifteen minutes.'

Gamble said nothing and Poe knew he'd already figured that out.

'I think I know why this one's been burnt more than the others, though,' Poe said. 'I'm assuming you've been up here all day?'

Gamble nodded. 'Since ten o'clock this morning.'

'What you won't know then is that none of this can be seen from the road. You can barely see the crime-scene lights. The circle's hidden from view until you're almost on it, and because this road is mainly used by people going to and from the golf course, most people leaving the club house would be going away from it, back into Cockermouth.'

'So he had more time,' Gamble said.

Poe nodded. 'And if he waited until after last orders at the nineteenth hole, there was virtually no chance of being observed.'

'That's helpful.'

Poe wasn't sure how. They already knew the Immolation Man was careful.

'Any early thoughts?' Gamble asked.

'Just that I'm never accepting a barbecue invite from the University of West Florida.'

Gamble nodded but didn't laugh.

They left the tent and the inner cordon and re-joined Flynn and Reid. Poe was glad to remove the constrictive forensic suit.

'We haven't released anything to the media about DS Poe's connection to the case, DI Flynn,' Gamble said. 'I've agreed with my assistant chief that we can use it as an additional control filter for anyone ringing up claiming responsibility. The information is extremely restricted so don't put it on any documentation.'

'Makes sense,' Flynn said, nodding. 'And I think we should also stay away from the official investigation, sir. Keep Poe out of it completely. We can work from the hotel for now.'

Gamble nodded. Poe got the impression he was relieved Flynn had suggested it first.

'And DS Reid seems to like DS Poe, so he can be your liaison. I'll second him to you for now. He'll make sure you have everything you need,' he said. 'As well as analytical support, can SCAS take the name angle? Try and figure out Poe's involvement. We'll exchange information at the end of every day, even if it's a nil report. How's that sound?'

'Perfect,' she said.

After another round of handshakes, Poe and Flynn made their way back to the car.

As soon as they were out of earshot, Flynn turned to face Poe. 'What was that about?'

'The "liaison" thing?'

'Yes. That.' She sounded angry. 'Do they not trust me?'

Poe shrugged. 'It's not you they don't trust, Steph. It's me.'

CHAPTER TWELVE

Shap Wells was a hotel with a past. Almost as isolated as Herdwick Croft, it could only be accessed via a mile-long drive down the narrowest of roads. During the Second World War, its isolation had been used to the Allies' advantage: it was requisitioned from the Earl of Lonsdale and turned into Prisoner of War Camp Number Fifteen. It had held up to two hundred prisoners, mainly German officers, with the camp leader at one point being a German prince related to Queen Mary.

The main north–south railway line was near and security had been high as trains had facilitated POW escapes from the camp. Two barbed-wire fences had been erected around the hotel, and towers had allowed guards to cover every angle with powerful searchlights. The concrete bases of the guard towers were still visible if you knew where to look. Poe did; he knew the hotel well. His car was permanently parked there, he took advantage of the free wi-fi when he needed to go online, and he ate in the restaurant at least twice a week.

Next morning, before making his way to the hotel, Poe left Edgar with Thomas Hume, the farmer who'd sold him the croft and the surrounding land the year before. They'd become friends and did the occasional favour for each other. Poe allowed Hume to graze his sheep on his land and helped him with the odd bit of dry stone walling – usually when Hume needed muscle rather than technical ability – and Hume looked after Edgar when Poe was away.

Although he usually walked the two miles to the hotel, that morning Poe took his quad bike. He collected his mail from the receptionist, a New Zealand girl who always had a smile for him, and went looking for Flynn and Bradshaw.

They'd just finished breakfast and Poe helped himself to a coffee. Flynn was wearing another power suit, black this time. Bradshaw was wearing the same cargo pants and the same trainers, but a different T-shirt. This one had a faded picture of the Incredible Hulk and the phrase 'Don't make me angry'. He was surprised Flynn had allowed it. Then again, he wasn't – the art of management was all about avoiding pointless battles.

Five minutes later Kylian Reid joined them. Flynn frowned in annoyance but shook his hand. He updated them on the fourth victim. He still hadn't been identified but the body had been recovered and was now being prepped for post-mortem. Gamble wanted to know if SCAS would put it through the MSCT. Flynn confirmed they would.

Flynn had managed to get the use of a small conference room for the duration of their involvement. Poe was pleased they'd be working away from the main investigation. He'd never been the most popular cop in Cumbria: his tendency to speak truth to power meant that he'd been tolerated at best and he knew his suspension from the NCA had been joyfully received in his old force. He didn't care, but he didn't want any ongoing antagonism to get in the way of what they were doing.

They were in the Garden Room on the ground floor. Despite the age and grandeur of the hotel, the room was modern and well equipped. Flynn had chosen a bigger room than they needed. It allowed them to section it off. They spent the first half hour setting up Bradshaw's equipment and arranging the tables so they had a conference area and enough space to move about. They weren't allowed to pin or Blu Tack anything to the walls so Flynn called for additional whiteboards and flipcharts.

Incident rooms were the beating hearts of major investigations and Poe felt the familiar tingle of excitement; there was something exhilarating about setting up a new one. Before long it would be populated with clues and questions, of things they knew and things they wanted to know.

It was going to be different to previous investigations in which Poe had been involved. In the official incident room at Carleton Hall, Gamble would have an army of staff: office managers, action managers, document readers, indexers, exhibits officers, house-to-house coordinators, disclosure officers and file preparation officers.

At Shap Wells there was just the four of them. It was liberating.

When Bradshaw had hooked up the computers, they began.

Flynn kicked it off. 'I'm suggesting we start with why Poe's name was carved into the chest of Michael James. Any one disagree?'

Poe gave everyone the chance to speak up. No one did.

He raised his hand. 'Just a thought.'

They all looked at him.

'I think, for now at least, we should assume it's a red herring. I don't know any of the victims and I know DCS Gamble is going through all my old cases to see if anyone I put away fits the profile of a serial killer. What value can we add?'

Flynn said, 'You have an alternative line of enquiry, I take it?'

Poe nodded. 'There's a far more important question that hasn't been answered yet.'

'Which is?' Reid asked.

'Why the gap between the first and second victim was so long and the gaps between the second, third and fourth were so short?'

Flynn looked slightly annoyed and he knew why. Experience suggested – and it was backed up by statistics – that serial murderers started slowly then speeded up.

Before he could be patronised, he continued. 'I know you're going to give me a lesson in serial killers and how their urge to kill is sated after the first murder, but the amount of time this holds them is ever reducing. Am I right?'

Flynn nodded.

'And none of the victims knew each other, right?'

This time it was Reid who answered. 'The investigation has found no link between them. Of course, I can't speak for the fourth victim; he hasn't been ID'd yet.'

'What's your point, Poe?' Flynn asked.

'My point, Steph, is that you're thinking like someone who doesn't know Cumbria. It might be the third largest county in England but it's sparsely populated.'

'And that means . . . ?'

'That it's statistically unlikely that these men *didn't* know each other.'

Flynn and Reid stared at him. Bradshaw – for whom the word 'statistic' was a starter pistol – began typing.

'I'm from here, and so is Kylian, and we can tell you that everyone seems to know everyone.'

'It's a bit thin,' Flynn said.

'It is,' Poe agreed. 'But if you also consider that all the victims were in the same age and socio-economic group, the odds of them not knowing each other reduces even further. This isn't Knightsbridge. Parts of Cumbria have a lower GDP than the Czech Republic. Just how many millionaires do you think we have?'

The only sound was Bradshaw's keyboard.

'But we're sure they didn't know each other,' Flynn insisted. 'Unless you're saying we've all missed something?'

Poe shrugged. 'Sort of, but it comes back to my first point. Why was there such a big gap between the first and second victims?'

He waited.

'What if these men did know each other but had made

concerted efforts to hide it? And what if these men would know if they were being picked off? A pattern only they could see. Now, when Graham Russell's murdered, so what? He'd overseen the hacking of the phones of murder and paedophile victims all over the country – the list of people who wished him harm must have been huge. And whatever the file might say now, we know that's the line of enquiry Gamble initially took. If I'm right, it's entirely possible the others simply put it down to bad luck on Russell's part. But when victim number two is killed in the same way, even the most optimistic of them would know what was happening. The Immolation Man has no reason to take it slowly any more; in fact, if he's working through a list, he has every reason to speed up.'

Flynn frowned. 'But if they knew they were being targeted, why didn't they go to the police?'

'They couldn't,' Reid said. 'If Poe's right then they might be linked by something they couldn't speak about.'

'And given their individual wealth, it's almost certainly something illegal,' Poe added.

'But we're not sure when the men were abducted,' Flynn said. 'It's possible they were all taken before anyone was killed.'

No theory was perfect, thought Poe.

'Three-point-six per cent,' Bradshaw said, looking up from her computer.

They stared at her.

'Using a program I've just written, I've calculated that the odds of three men from that social group, in a county with a population of seventy-three-point-four people per kilometre squared, not knowing each other are three-point-six per cent. There are some variables that take it as low as two per cent and as high as three-point-nine, but the maths is sound.'

Reid was staring open-mouthed. 'You *wrote* a program?' He looked at his watch. 'In under five minutes?'

Bradshaw nodded. 'It wasn't hard, DS Reid. I simply adapted an existing tool I have.'

Poe stood up. 'That's settled then. We don't argue with Tilly and maths.'

Bradshaw gave Poe a shy, grateful glance.

'Let's get to work then,' Flynn said.

Twelve hours later and they were all in a foul mood.

They hadn't found the slightest hint that the men might have known each other. They hadn't been in the same golf clubs, they hadn't sat on the same charitable boards and, on the few occasions they'd eaten at the same restaurants, it was at different times. Bradshaw had managed to get their supermarket loyalty-card details, and they hadn't shopped in the same stores. Reid rang Gamble who promised to re-interview their neighbours and friends to see if anything was missed, but Poe's theory wasn't looking good.

Adding to their misery was the fact that the room wasn't working. Due to the constant interruptions, they couldn't put anything confidential or graphic on the wall. Tea and coffee being delivered, the events manager checking they didn't need anything, and on three separate occasions residents walking into the room thinking it was the dining room. One numbskull twice.

And at the end of the day they had to take everything down and pack it away as it wasn't a secure room.

Although this was only the first time they'd sat down with everything laid out, the sense of despondency was palpable.

There was a knock on the door and the events manager popped her head in. 'I know you said you didn't want to be disturbed, but can I just check you don't want menus brought in for the evening meal? The dining room's about to shut.'

'Can I make a suggestion?' Poe asked after she'd left. 'Why don't we work from my house tomorrow? Downstairs is open plan and about the same size as this room. I don't have rules about pinning things to my walls, and it's more secure than this place. Plus, most of the time I'll be there anyway.'

'I don't know about that, Poe,' Flynn said. 'You're supposed to be the next victim, remember.'

'All the better that I don't have to travel back and forth to the hotel every day then. If anyone's going to try and grab me, it'll be when I'm out on the moor on my own.'

There was a moment's silence while Flynn considered it. 'Tilly?' she asked. 'Would you get a signal up there?'

'If I don't, I'll tether my phone to anything we need internet access to.'

'How would we get there?' Flynn asked Poe. 'I was happy to tramp across as a one-off but I'm not doing that every day.'

'I'll leave you and Tilly my quad. Any stuff you need to bring can go in the trailer.'

'What about me?' Reid asked.

'You? You can fucking walk,' Poe said.

Reid grinned.

Everyone looked at Flynn, waiting for her decision. 'Well, it's got to be worth a try. Today was a disaster.'

CHAPTER THIRTEEN

Poe collected Edgar then returned the quad to the hotel. The walk across the fells to Herdwick Croft was invigorating. The fading light had turned everything a rich shade of crimson. Edgar ran off to chase a rabbit but soon came bouncing back. Poe doubted he'd know what to do if he ever got near one.

He fixed himself a simple supper: a cheese and pickle sandwich, a bag of crisps and a cup of strong tea. The day might not have been a success but Poe was sure he was right; the Immolation Man was targeting his victims using more than just age and wealth. He reordered the thoughts in his mind. He hoped he was right. If he weren't, then somewhere out there was an organised, forensically aware, technically proficient serial killer who liked to castrate and burn people.

And he was next.

Although Edgar would howl like a wolf if anyone approached the croft at night, for the first time since Poe had lived there he locked the door and shuttered the windows. Surprisingly, he slept well. Not a single nightmare.

As soon as he woke, Poe knew they were in for another glorious spring day. He boiled an egg, walked Edgar, then waited for the team to arrive. Reid had walked over from the side of the road and got there first. Flynn and Bradshaw arrived on the quad moments later.

Bradshaw shouted with delight when she saw Edgar.

'You didn't tell me you had a dog, Poe!' she squealed. For the next ten minutes work was forgotten, as Bradshaw and Edgar became best friends. The spaniel, who'd always been an attention junky, made a beeline for her and lathered her in licks and dog hair. Bradshaw shrieked with laughter and hung her arms around his neck as if afraid he'd run off. Poe passed Tilly some treats to give Edgar and their friendship was cemented.

'Remember, Tilly, if he shows you his lipstick, don't touch it,' Reid said, winking at Poe.

Bradshaw buried her head in the spaniel's neck. 'You don't have any lipstick do you, Edgar? What a silly goose DS Reid is. He must mean your penis.'

After they'd laughed at Reid's open-mouthed look of astonishment, Flynn called them to order. 'You can play with Edgar later, Tilly. We need to crack on.'

Poe had opened all the windows and spring sunlight beamed into the room. The ground floor of Herdwick Croft was rectangular, without fancy nooks and crannies. Two windows at the front, none at the back and one door. Poe explained that, years ago, during bad winters the shepherd lived upstairs while the sheep sheltered in the room they were in now. It offered them protection from the cold and warmed the building. The walls were the same on the inside as they were on the outside: exposed, roughly quarried stone. The ceiling beams were old and sturdy and black after a century of smoke. A wood-burning stove dominated the room. It had wood inside but it hadn't been lit yet. Despite the warm day, Poe would light it later; it was how he heated his water.

Poe put a pot of coffee in the centre of the table and they got to work. As it was his line of enquiry, Flynn let him lead the first session.

'Back to basics everyone. I want us to assume these men did know each other at some point. They may have been hiding that fact, but that's what we detectives do; we detect things.'

71

Bradshaw stuck her hand in the air.

Poe waited but she said nothing. He looked at her, confused, until he remembered that up until a year ago, her entire life had been spent in classrooms and lecture halls. 'Tilly, you don't have to put your hand up. What is it?'

'I'm not a detective, Poe. I'm an employee of the National Crime Agency but I don't have the power of arrest like you, Detective Sergeant Reid and Detective Inspector Stephanie Flynn.'

'Er . . . thanks for clearing that up, Tilly. Good to know.'

Bradshaw nodded.

For the next four hours they delved into the lives – and deaths – of Graham Russell, Joe Lowell and Michael James. At midday, Reid took a phone call.

'We have a name for victim number four. Clement Owens. Sixty-seven years old. Retired solicitor. Worked in the private sector and represented the banking industry. Apart from his wealth, there's no obvious connection to the others. We'll have more info soon.'

Flynn called a break. They were all getting hungry and she'd brought sandwiches with her. Poe suggested they ate outside.

Although Poe enjoyed the harsh beauty of a Cumbrian winter, he'd lived at Shap for over a year now and felt qualified to say that spring was his favourite season. Other than the omnipresent sheep, winter stripped the fells of life. Left acres and acres of bitter, colourless landscape for as far as the eyes could see. Spring seemed like resurrection. The days were longer, dormant plants pushed green shoots through the warming earth and the heather blossomed. Exotic gardens of lichen and moss burst into life. Ferocious, freezing winds became warm, richly scented breezes. Birds nested, animals bred and there was a renewed sense of optimism in the air. It was the time of year that made you appreciate the beauty and slower pace of life in rural Cumbria.

While Flynn was off making a phone call, and Bradshaw chased Edgar all over Shap Fell, Poe turned to Reid and said, 'It's good to see you again, Kylian. How long's it been?'

'Five years,' Reid grunted through a mouthful of ham and egg.

'Five years? It can't be. The last time I saw you was—'

'My mother's funeral,' he said accusingly.

A burst of blood coloured Poe's cheeks. Reid's mother had died of motor neurone disease, after years of illness. He was right, the funeral had been the last time Poe had seen him.

'I'm sorry, mate,' he said, but Reid waved away his apology. 'How's your dad keeping?' asked Poe.

'You know him, Poe. He only retired because mum told him he had to. Still does a bit for a stable in Lancashire. Not even sure they pay him, he does it to fill his time. If he's not doing that, he's napping in front of the fire or reading books on racing.'

Reid's father had been a highly respected vet specialising in racehorses. As a boy, Poe had loved visiting George Reid's veterinary practice. There were always animals to fuss over.

'How's your dad?' Reid asked, smiling. 'Still a beatnik?'

Poe smiled. It wasn't far from the truth. His father lived to travel, and rarely came back to the UK. The only time he'd lived in one place for any length of time was when he was raising Poe. His mother, unable to handle the vanilla life, had abandoned them both when he was a toddler. His father had temporarily sacrificed his nomadic spirit and brought him up alone. As soon as Poe joined the Black Watch, he was off again. They kept in touch via email but they hadn't seen each other for almost three years. As far as Poe knew, his father was in Brazil somewhere. Doing what, he had no idea. He could be deep in the rainforest or running for political office, there really was no way to tell. He loved him dearly but he'd never been what you'd call a 'traditional' parent.

Poe's mother had died a few weeks after he'd been suspended, killed by a hit-and-run driver. He only found out when his father emailed him five weeks after she'd been cremated. He'd been saddened by her death, just as he was saddened by anyone's death, but he hadn't lingered on it. She'd made a choice to put her own needs before his a long time ago.

'You seeing anyone?' Reid asked.

Poe shook his head. He'd always found it hard forming relationships. When he'd been down in Hampshire, there'd been a few women, but nothing that lasted for more than a few weeks. A therapist might have told him it was because he had a deep-seated fear of abandonment, but Poe would have told them they were wrong: he wasn't scared of abandonment: it was all he'd ever known . . .

'You?' he asked.

'Nothing permanent.'

'Well, aren't we a pair of romantic bastards?' Poe smiled.

Flynn returned from her phone call. 'I've just spoken to Director van Zyl,' she said. 'He wants us to stay up here for as long as it takes. I told him about our new line of enquiry and he agrees it's worth pursuing.'

She sat down, poured herself a coffee and grabbed a sandwich. She looked tired and Poe knew the investigation was getting to her. None of it made sense – especially his connection – and SCAS were supposed to answer questions, not pose them.

The sun was bright and the view as stunning as always. Uneven ground, treeless hills and jagged rocks for miles in every direction. Edgar tried to beg Flynn's crusts, but unlike Bradshaw, who'd given him virtually all her lunch, she seemed immune to the sad-eyed, puppy-dog routine. When he realised the treats were over, Edgar wandered off and before long there was a screech. A curlew panicked into the air. Edgar reappeared, looking pleased with himself.

'Leave the birds alone, Edgar!' Poe shouted, before he could find the ground nest. The last thing he needed was the spaniel coming back to Bradshaw with a mouth full of hatchlings. Edgar reluctantly returned to the croft.

Flynn brushed some crumbs from her jacket. She was wearing the suit she'd had on the first day she'd been there, the one with the pinstripes. Bradshaw was wearing her usual cargo pants and T-shirt. Reid was immaculately dressed; he'd always been a clotheshorse and never dressed casually. Even when they'd socialised together, Reid wore a suit and Poe suspected he considered his own lack of effort a burden and disgrace. Poe was still wearing the clothes he had on yesterday, which reminded him – his mail was still unopened in his pocket.

He retrieved the bundle and glanced through it. There was a letter from his gas supplier letting him know that the delivery time for his fresh tank had been changed, and one from the borehole-pump suppliers telling him his warranty had expired. If he wanted to renew it, it would be six quid a month. Poe didn't.

The last envelope was plain brown. His name was typed on the front and the postmark was local. He slid a knife under the flap and slit it open. He shook out the contents.

It was a postcard. A generic picture of a cup coffee. The foam on top had been fashioned into a design by someone with too much time on their hands. Latte art, he thought it was called. Something they did in London, not Cumbria.

He flipped it over. He must have let out a gasp, as Flynn, Reid and Bradshaw all turned to stare.

'What is it, Poe?' Flynn asked.

He turned the card so they could all see what was written on the back.

One symbol, two words.

ʕ

Washington Poe

CHAPTER FOURTEEN

'What the hell?' Flynn muttered. She turned to stare at Poe. 'What is this?'

Poe didn't take his eyes from the postcard. 'I have absolutely no idea,' he managed.

It was clear no one else did either. The only sound that could be heard was Edgar gnawing on a bone he'd found. No one wanted to know where he'd got it from.

'And what the hell's that reverse question-mark thing?' Flynn added. She placed the envelope and postcard into a clear evidence bag while Reid called Gamble to let him know. He promised to get someone across to take it for a forensic test, although none of them was holding out hope. The Immolation Man didn't make mistakes at chaotic crime scenes – he was hardly likely to make one when he wasn't in a hurry.

Bradshaw scanned both sides through the evidence bag so they had an electronic copy. She stared at her tablet for almost ten minutes, occasionally touching the screen and pulling her fingers apart to zoom in on something. She started to frown and mutter to herself.

'What is it, Tilly?' asked Flynn.

'I need to go inside,' she replied. She got up without another word. By the time they'd caught up with her she had her laptop open. She was searching for something. She turned to Poe and said, 'Do you have a white bedsheet you can hang on the wall, Poe?'

He did, and luckily it was clean. Reid helped him put it up while Bradshaw set up the projector she'd brought with her.

When they'd finished, Bradshaw was ready. She aimed the light at the hanging sheet. She moved to Google's home page and typed in 'Percontation Point'. Nothing happened and she apologised for the slow internet connection.

A picture came up. It was the same symbol; the reverse question mark: ⸮

Underneath was the definition:

> The Percontation Point, sometimes called the Snark or
> the Irony Mark, is a little-known notation used to indicate
> that the sentence is to be taken rhetorically, ironically or
> as sarcasm. It can also be used to indicate that there is
> another layer of meaning in a sentence.

'Tilly,' Flynn said, 'where are you going with—'

'Let her speak, boss,' Poe said. 'I think I know.'

Bradshaw looked at him gratefully. 'Thank you, Poe. The point I am trying to make, DI Stephanie Flynn, is, if I do this,' she fiddled with the projector until it was out of focus, 'what does the percontation point look like?'

Poe squinted, although he already knew. He watched Flynn to see if she could see it as well.

'It looks like a number five,' she said.

Bradshaw nodded excitedly. 'We'd assumed the killer had carved a number five into the chest of Michael James, but what if that was simply apophenia, which means—'

'We know what apophenia means, Tilly,' Flynn said.

'—seeing patterns when there aren't any,' Bradshaw finished regardless. 'What if we saw the number five because we're conditioned to look for numbers? And my program works on probability

– it wouldn't have recognised a percontation point so would have simply inserted the nearest thing to it.'

'The number five,' Poe said.

'Yes, Poe,' she replied. 'The number five would be the nearest match to the program's reference points. The letter "S" would have been the closest after that.'

'Is there any way to check the original wounds?' Poe asked.

'Yes, Poe. I still have the data on my laptop.'

She pressed a few buttons on her laptop and the 3D image of his name appeared on the wall. It was the clearest one of his name; the letters were all taken from different slides to ensure each one was the optimum for viewing.

'Can you separate the symbol?' Poe asked. In his mind, he'd already dismissed the number five.

Bradshaw fiddled some more. There were fifty images of the symbol, each one taken at a slightly different depth. She put them on a slideshow, shallowest first. Because of the damage caused by the burnt flesh, the first few did look like the number five. The deeper she went with the image, the clearer the cuts became. The last few weren't clear at all, just some nicks in the breastbone. She came back up a couple of slides.

'There,' Reid said. 'That's the one.'

Bradshaw stopped the slideshow.

They stared at the screen. What they'd earlier assumed had been the bottom part of the number five was in fact a separate, albeit smaller, wound. The Immolation Man had added a single stab wound under the curved part of the percontation point to represent the dot. Probably stabbed then twisted to add depth and definition. When the fire caused the flesh to split, the wound at the bottom had taken the path of least resistance and joined the bottom of the percontation point. While the top MSCT images had looked like a number five, the lower ones most certainly didn't. It wasn't a perfect explanation but Poe suspected that the Immolation Man, when trying to carve an elegant and obscure symbol into the chest of a wriggling, screaming victim, had simply done the best he could.

And because everyone had missed it, he'd followed it up with a postcard.

If they were right – and Poe thought they were – then he wasn't the intended fifth victim. That was good news. The bad news was that the Immolation Man knew where he lived.

He said, 'Well, boss, I don't know about you but if I had to put my money on it, I'd say that wasn't a number five after all, I'd say that was a perforation point.'

'*Percontation* point,' Bradshaw corrected.

'Agreed,' Flynn said. 'It's too much of a coincidence not to be.'

Poe felt a prickle of excitement. Bradshaw had said one of the percontation point's uses was to denote that a sentence or passage had another layer or meaning. He picked up the evidence bag. 'Do we all think this was sent because we didn't get the first message?'

Flynn paused. 'There's nothing else we can think.'

'And there was definitely nothing on the first two victims?' he asked.

'Nope,' Reid replied. 'They've been retrospectively checked.'

'And SCAS were called in after the second victim, but after the post-mortem?'

Flynn nodded.

'So it would be fair to say, if you did have a message for SCAS, the body of the third victim rather than the first would be the one to use.'

'Logically, I can't argue with that,' Flynn said. 'What do we need to do next?'

'I think we should look at Michael James's chest again,' Poe said. 'All the slides, not just the highlights. But this time we put on our lateral-thinking pants.'

Bradshaw's hand shot up.

'Our *figurative* lateral-thinking pants,' Poe said without missing a beat. Her hand went back down.

Bradshaw brought up the 3D image of Poe's name and they all studied it. Reid said, 'That the only one we have, Tilly?'

As before, she took them through a series of slides. The last one was a deeper image and showed fragments of the wounds used to make up the letters in Washington Poe. These were the wounds that had cut so deep they'd caught the ribs. Most of the others hadn't gone as deep. None of the other images seemed to offer up anything new and she returned to the first one.

For five minutes, no one spoke as they absorbed what was projected onto Poe's wall. Tilly opened as many screens as she could fit on the sheet and filled them with different pictures.

'Anyone?' Flynn asked.

Poe was staring so hard his eyes were beginning to blur. Like the percontation point, the top images were the most distorted by the fire. The edges of the wounds weren't as sharp as the ones taken from deeper inside the body.

Bradshaw brought up some more. The new images were different to the ones they'd been viewing previously. The fire hadn't managed to get that deep and the wounds Bradshaw was showing on the sheet were sharper. Thin and precise.

Poe leaned in, squinted at one of the images and said, 'Is it just me or do those letters look different?'

Bradshaw responded first. 'You're right, Poe! The slant of the letters isn't consistent. Neither is the spacing.' She produced a laser pointer from nowhere and aimed it at the sheet. 'I've studied forensic handwriting and I think the second, third and fourth letter in Washington and the first letter in Poe were written left-handed. The difference in the spacing would also suggest they were written before the right-handed letters were put in.'

Poe said, 'Steph? This is your investigation. What do you think?'

She stood and walked to the makeshift screen. She traced the four letters with her hand. She turned and said, 'I think you're both right. I think those four letters are different and I think they do mean something. Unfortunately they're of no help whatsoever.'

CHAPTER FIFTEEN

Poe felt deflated. He waited for Flynn's explanation.

'It's an anagram,' she said.

Poe had never been good at word puzzles; he was a lateral rather than analytical thinker. Reid was even worse than he was, which, for someone with his vocabulary, was surprising. Bradshaw could probably solve anagrams at the same time as she solved advanced equations.

But even he could have a decent stab at a four-letter problem.

Flynn didn't give him time to think. 'It's Shap,' she said. 'That's why the letters were different. It was to make sure we came to *this* Washington Poe.'

Poe immediately reflated; he knew something Flynn didn't. He and Reid exchanged glances. He said, 'You ever googled yourself, Steph?'

She blushed slightly and said she hadn't.

Yeah, you have, he thought. *Everyone has.*

Poe was as 'don't give a shit what people think' as they came, and he'd googled himself. When Peyton Williams had died, and someone – almost certainly Deputy Director Hanson – had leaked his name to the press, he'd stayed off the internet while the press called him a vigilante. In truth, it had been an easy thing to do; by then he'd been suspended and was living at Herdwick Croft where surfing the 'net' to idle away time was no longer possible. But curiosity is a funny thing. One evening he'd been in the bar at Shap Wells, and, taking advantage of the free wi-fi, he'd typed his name into Google. The first time he'd done it.

The results were astonishing. The vitriol aimed his way was bizarre. Peyton Williams had abducted and killed two women, had almost killed a third, and yet, in some people's eyes, Poe was the bad guy. He remembered the good old days when having strong opinions about issues you knew nothing about was considered a negative thing. Facts no longer mattered. Populism and fake news had seemingly turned half the population into mindless trolls.

But . . . the other thing he'd learned from searching Google was that he shared his name with only one other person; an American politician from Georgia who had died in 1876.

He was sure there must be others out there, but he doubted Gamble would have needed his name *and* location to work out to which Washington Poe the Immolation Man was referring. He could imagine the detectives in Cumbria – some of whom he'd worked with for years – saying, 'Oh, *that* Washington Poe. Now he's mentioned Shap, I know exactly who he means.'

He explained that there were no other Washington Poes, but Flynn didn't seem convinced.

'It's too much of a coincidence,' she said. 'And the Immolation Man wouldn't necessarily know there's only one of you on the internet.'

Poe shrugged. 'I think it's worth following up. If he hid Shap in the message just to make sure you came to me, then fair enough, but checking costs us nothing.' He waited for her to make the right decision. She didn't disappoint.

She nodded and turned to Reid. 'I think this might be a job for our liaison officer. Can you get onto Cumbria's intelligence systems? See if anything weird has happened here recently.'

'Like?'

'JDLR,' Poe cut in. 'You'll know it when you see it.'

'Just Doesn't Look Right,' Reid said. 'OK, I'll go to Kendal nick and check SLEUTH.'

SLEUTH was Cumbria police's intelligence system. Any intelligence, whether it was criminal behaviour or not, would be recorded there. Reid said he'd also ring Gamble to brief him on where they were.

After he'd left, Poe said to Bradshaw. 'While he's away, Tilly, can you have a look and see what you can dig up?'

'Can I go back to the hotel, Poe? The wi-fi is stronger there.'

'I'll give you a lift unless . . . unless you want me to show you how to drive the quad?'

Bradshaw looked at Flynn in excitement. 'Can I, DI Stephanie Flynn? Please. *Please.*'

'Can she?' Flynn asked Poe.

'Makes sense,' he replied. 'We don't know how long we're going to be up here and we all need to be mobile.'

'Go for it, Tilly,' Flynn said. She looked at Poe, then added, 'Just don't tell your mother.'

For twenty minutes Poe demonstrated how to drive the quad. Other than computer games, Bradshaw had no driving experience whatsoever, but it was easy and she picked it up quickly. He showed her how to turn it on and off, how to disengage the brake and how to put it into drive. The throttle was on the right-hand grip and the rest, he explained, was a case of not getting stuck. Bradshaw laughed and smiled the whole way through.

After five minutes of supervised riding she was proficient enough to set off on her own.

They watched her leave as if she were their daughter going off to college.

'And mind the road!' Poe shouted. Crossing the A6 was the only time she'd be on a road; technically she needed a licence to cross it. He glanced at Flynn and hoped she hadn't realised.

Bradshaw waved without looking back.

With half the team away on tasks, and with nothing for them to do until they reported back, Flynn and Poe took Edgar for a walk. It was mid-afternoon and it felt like they'd made some progress. The weather was the same as the day before but somehow it seemed brighter. It was funny how mood affected the senses.

Flynn asked him about Herdwick Croft and how he'd ended up living there.

'Bit of luck, really,' he told her. 'I wanted to buy something outright after I sold my flat but I needed something cheap as I assumed I'd be getting sacked. I was queuing at the council offices in Kendal, seeing if I qualified for housing support, and I happened to be standing behind this farmer. He was raging at this poor woman behind the reception desk. I calmed him down and took him for a pint. He told me that he owned large swathes of Shap Fell – the fell we're on now – and some bean counter in the council tax department had decided that, as Herdwick Croft had once been a shepherd's dwelling, albeit over two hundred years ago, it was eligible for council tax. And without any discussion he'd been sent a bill through the post.'

Flynn turned to look at the croft in the distance. 'It's a smallish building, though. Why didn't he just pay it?'

'It might be small but it's near Kendal and that means it's in a high band. He couldn't even knock it down as it's a Grade II listed building.'

'So you offered to buy it?'

'Did the deal that afternoon. Paid him cash for the building and the land. Twenty acres of bleak and desolate moorland. I spent a few grand on a reliable generator, hired a company to dig a borehole and put a pump in. Another lot buried the septic tank; it gets emptied every two years apparently. My only outgoings are generator fuel, gas and my car. Comes to less than two hundred quid a month.'

'And now you're back in the real world.'

'And now I'm back in the real world. The IPCC investigation still stands so it may not be for too long.'

Flynn said nothing. There were no reassurances she could give him and he was grateful she didn't try to sugar coat it.

A week ago, he'd have welcomed his termination. It would have been a full stop to that part of his life, but now, with his warrant card in his pocket, he was no longer sure he was ready to quit being a police officer. It had been depressingly easy to revert to 'cop mode'. He knew one thing for sure though: Herdwick Croft was his home. He'd never move; he loved the land and he loved the solitude too much. Whatever the future brought, the isolated shepherd's dwelling would remain part of it.

Flynn's phone rang. She answered it, then said, 'That was Tilly. She hasn't found anything.'

Damn.

If Bradshaw couldn't find anything, it was unlikely Reid would.

They made their way back to Herdwick Croft. They arrived at the same time as Bradshaw. The quad skidded to a halt and she leapt off with a huge smile. She was breathless with excitement and Poe's first thought was that she'd found something after all until he realised it was simply the exhilaration of driving. She bounded over to Edgar and, with all the guile of a five-year-old, slipped him a piece of meat she must have begged from the hotel kitchen. She looked at Poe with an innocent face.

An hour later, Reid appeared. *I'm going to have to get another quad*, Poe thought. Reid had walked miles that day.

'Anything?' Flynn asked.

'Nothing obvious. No suspicious deaths for years and nothing on the system weird enough to be linked to the Immolation Man.'

Poe could sense a 'but' coming.

'But,' Reid said, 'and I'm loath to even mention this, as I was leaving the office, I gave a last shout out for anything.'

'And?' Poe asked.

'And someone who lives in Shap reminded me that Tollund Man was found up here.'

Poe was nonplussed. His history recollection wasn't perfect, but even he knew the two-and-a-half thousand-year-old mummified body of the Tollund Man had been found in Denmark, not Cumbria. It was one of the weird facts that had stuck from his school days. That, and the Spinning Jenny having had something to do with the Industrial Revolution.

'Not *the* Tollund Man, obviously,' Reid clarified. 'But twelve months ago, a John Doe was found buried in a salt depot up here. Although the salt had dried him out to no more than a husk, he was perfectly preserved. The cops who worked on it gave him the nickname and it stuck. Total fuck-up from start to finish. The guy on the JCB had scooped him up in the bucket, panicked when his workmate saw a hand sticking out. Dumped the full load on his mate, who died of a heart attack.'

Poe hadn't heard of it, but then again, why would he? He'd been little more than a hermit for the last year and a half. 'Who was he?'

'He was never identified. There were no obvious injuries and the pathologist thought the cause of death was probably natural. The prevailing theory is that he collapsed while trying to steal salt for his drive – a lot of that used to go on when the council stored salt and grit outside – and either died immediately or froze to death. The body gets covered with snow and then the digger doesn't notice him when he's loading the lorry.'

'Surely he'd have clogged up the gritter, though?'

'Not necessarily. He was found in the Hardendale Salt Store, that stupid-looking one at junction thirty-nine on the M6.'

Poe knew it well – it was only a few miles from Herdwick Croft. It was dome-shaped and he'd assumed it was some sort of air-defence installation when it first went up. He remembered feeling disappointed when he discovered its more mundane purpose.

Reid continued, 'Anyway, Highways England have a contract with the council to keep it fully stocked. When the council closed some of their smaller depots, most of the salt was transferred to Hardendale. It's likely Tollund Man was stealing salt from one of the smaller, outside deports when he died and was simply transported to Hardendale in the back of a council truck. If it hadn't been for the brutal winter we've just had, it's unlikely the salt would have been depleted low enough for him to be found.'

'And it was definitely natural causes?' Flynn asked.

'That's what the pathologist said.'

'And the man who died at the scene?'

'A walking heart attack apparently. The dickhead driving the JCB resigned before he could be sacked, but there was never any suspicion of foul play.'

'Why was the body never identified? Surely someone must have missed him.'

'He had nothing on him and, because of the salt, the pathologist couldn't be sure how long he'd been dead,' Reid replied. He removed a notebook from his inside pocket. 'The official report is that he'd probably been in his early forties when he died but that could have been years ago.'

'And missing persons was nowhere near as sophisticated back then,' Poe said.

'Exactly.'

Bradshaw had been busy on her computer for a change. Despite Tollund Man being seemingly irrelevant, she'd taken it personally that her beloved internet had let her down.

Poe heard the printer she'd set up whirr into action. She collected the information and passed them a sheet each. It was an article in the *Westmorland Gazette* entitled: Man Dies After Unidentified Body Found in Hardendale Salt Store. It was a summary of what the press knew. It was less than Reid had told them and mostly conjecture.

They read in silence.

Poe got to the pathologist's report. It said that, for the unidentified man to become as desiccated as he had been, he had to have been buried in salt for at least three years, and the clothes he was wearing meant he couldn't have been there for more than thirty. The jacket he'd been wearing had only been available since the mid 1980s.

But Poe wasn't buying such a vague time of death. Not in the context of where they were, and what was happening. Not when you considered one other factor.

'It's him,' he said. 'This is who the Immolation Man is pointing us towards.'

His statement was greeted by silence.

'Go on,' Flynn said.

'The jacket he was wearing,' Poe explained. 'It wasn't an expensive one. Certainly not one you'd wear for years and years.'

Flynn nodded.

'It indicates he'd been dead closer to thirty years rather than the three. Agreed?'

Again, Flynn nodded. 'Maybe. But so what?'

'Yeah, Poe, share what you've got with the rest of the class,' Reid said.

'I'll tell why it's important, boss,' Poe replied. 'If this so-called Tollund Man was alive today, he'd be in the same age group as the rest of the Immolation Man's victims . . .'

CHAPTER SIXTEEN

'Nah. I'm not buying it, Poe,' Reid said. 'It's a coincidence.' He looked round for support. 'How can it not be?'

'I agree with Sergeant Reid,' said Flynn. 'I can't see how this is relevant, Poe. Even if you're right about the date, and that involves a whole lot of guesswork, don't forget, he died of natural causes.'

Poe, who begrudged coincidences at the best of times, wasn't prepared to dismiss it so easily. It was Shap: population twelve hundred. Nothing ever happened in Shap. The percontation point had to be alluding to Tollund Man. At the very least, it merited further investigation. Loose ends and unexplained details bothered him more than they should.

'Fair point,' he conceded. 'But as we've got nothing else to go on, we may as well tug on this thread for a while. See where it takes us. Agreed?'

Flynn nodded but Poe could tell she still wasn't convinced. 'We'll look into it but I don't want us ignoring everything else.'

'What do you need from me?' Reid asked, standing up and stretching. 'I can root out the file; it'll be on the system somewhere.'

'Take the quad to your car, Kylian,' Poe said.

After Reid had left again, Bradshaw opened her laptop but didn't start typing. 'Please may I check the MPB database, Poe?'

'Shit, I'd forgotten about that, Tilly,' he replied. 'You crack on.'

When the National Crime Agency was established in 2013, one of the agencies it subsumed was the UK Missing Persons Bureau; the point of contact for all missing-person and unidentified body investigations. Tollund Man would be registered with them.

'How long, Tilly?' With fifteen unidentified bodies being recorded each month, and over a thousand on the database at any one time, finding him might take time. Each body was assigned an ID number, and basic details to help identification were publicly available.

'Found him, Poe,' she replied. 'Case number 16-004528. I'll print off a hard copy.' The printer spat out a two-page document. Bradshaw handed it to Poe.

There was no photograph; a lot of the cases listed didn't have images. A significant percentage of suicide-by-trains would never be identified; their bodies were unrecognisable, and even more were washed up on beaches having been exposed to the elements for too long. Sometimes an artist was commissioned to sketch an impression of how the corpse might have looked in life, but with Tollund Man having been desiccated, mummified, petrified or whatever the correct term was for someone who'd been stored in salt for years, he doubted there'd have been value in either putting his photo on the site or trying to guess what he'd looked like before every bit of moisture was sucked from his body.

Most of what the document said, Poe already knew from the newspaper article. Usually the site would list details like approximate age, height, build and an estimated date of death. The page he was holding had 'unknown' listed beside every one of those identifiers. Hair colour was listed as brown. What he was wearing was listed but it was unremarkable. Certainly nothing that would make someone jump and shout out: 'That's old Jim that is! He used to wear a top hat and a green cape!'

No possessions were listed.

Bradshaw logged into the database and brought up the non-public information but it didn't add much value. There was a photograph on the NCA-only part of the site, but it looked more like a prop from a horror movie than a human being. Poe wasn't expecting to recognise him.

'At some point we're going to need to see the body,' Poe said.

Flynn looked at him.

Poe shrugged. 'We might not have a choice. If this is linked then it probably wasn't an accident. We'll need to put it through one of those machines of yours. Find out what really happened.'

'The MSCT?'

'That's the one.'

'Do you have any idea how expensive that test is?' Flynn asked.

Poe knew he should. It wasn't that long ago he'd managed the unit that commissioned them. He shook his head.

'We have to book time with the hospital. And, by law they can't bump a living patient for a dead one. The consultant, radiographer and any number of other medical staff are all paid overtime. At night.'

Poe wasn't concerned about the cost. He'd fund it himself if he had to.

'It costs about twenty grand . . .' she said.

Maybe not . . .

'And I'm not blowing our entire diagnostic budget on a whim.'

'It's hardly a whim,' Poe muttered. 'It has to be connected.' To be fair to Flynn, even he thought he sounded desperate.

'Aren't you the one who used to bang on about knowing the difference between facts, opinions and guesses,' she snapped. 'This is a guess, Poe, nothing more. And I can't waste money on guesses.'

He felt like saying, 'Never quote me to me,' but held his tongue. He knew part of the DI's job was curbing the enthusiasm of some staff, but the age Tollund Man would be now was too much for him to dismiss.

'We're supposed to do what's right, not what's easy,' he said.

'What did you just say?' she snarled.

Poe knew there were times when backing down was the right move. He also knew that sometimes shutting up was even better.

They were still glowering at each other when Reid returned. He picked up on the atmosphere immediately. 'What's up?'

'Nothing!' Flynn barked.

'Just a small disagreement,' Poe said.

Reid was shameless in the way he couldn't be embarrassed. He retrieved the file from his rucksack and put it on the table. 'I've not had time to read it.'

Flynn made no move to take it.

Poe picked it up and read the summary. There were photographs of the body in situ; he'd study them later. The last few pages were chronological entries of the actions taken. The superintendent from Kendal had signed off the case. The final entry was dated less than a month ago.

'Bollocks.'

Flynn, despite herself, asked, 'What is it?'

Poe ignored her and directed a question at Reid. 'I thought Cumbria's protocol was for unidentified bodies to be kept for a year before being disposed of?'

'It was. It's just been changed. They're kept for eighteen months if they're to be cremated, nine months if they're going in the ground.'

Poe looked at Flynn.

'No fucking way!' she exploded.

'It's the only way we can be sure,' Poe countered.

'Sure of what, you idiot? Even if I felt like throwing away my career, the coroner declared it death by natural causes and it's their fucking office that authorises exhumations! What? You think we can waltz in there and tell them they were wrong because Tollund Man would have been an old man now? They deal with facts, Poe, not lunatic conspiracy theories.'

'We need one,' Poe persisted.

93

'We don't fucking need one!' she barked. 'And we're not asking for one, so put that idea out of your mind right now. I will not embarrass the agency by applying for an exhumation order we almost certainly won't get and don't need. And that's final.'

Poe expressed his frustration with silence. She was right; unless DCS Gamble was prepared to link the two cases and apply for it himself – and there was nothing in the way he ran investigations that suggested he'd even entertain the idea – they'd never get permission. Forensic exhumation orders were rarely applied for – the police and the pathologist were expected to do their jobs properly the first time around.

Yet he knew there had to be a link. His name hadn't appeared on the chest of Michael James by accident. Someone was dripfeeding him information and he wasn't prepared to give up on the latest offering just yet. He'd concede for now, but when they ran into a dead end he'd have another go. Eventually she'd see reason.

He returned to the file and reread the summary. Some kid, whose dad had wangled a job for him with the council, had panicked when they'd found the body in the machine's bucket, and instead of lowering it to the ground he'd dumped it all over his colleague, a Mr Derek Bailiff. Bailiff had suffered a stress-induced heart attack and died at the scene.

'I want permission to speak to the witness then,' he told Flynn.

'What witness?' she asked.

'Francis Sharples. The one who accidentally killed his mate when they found the body. If I can't examine the corpse, at least let me have a word with someone who saw it. There might be something that seemed irrelevant then but doesn't now.' Poe pressed his advantage, 'Come on, Steph, part of being the boss is knowing when to compromise.'

'Fine,' she said eventually. 'But I'm coming with you.'

CHAPTER SEVENTEEN

Bradshaw was happy to keep working at Herdwick Croft so Poe
didn't have to dump Edgar with his neighbour. She promised she
wouldn't give him too many treats. Poe left out a handful but hid
the rest; Edgar had begging down to an art form and Bradshaw
had already proved to be a pushover.

Reid texted Poe the address for Sharples. Since the incident at
the Hardendale Salt Store, he'd moved out of his parents' house
and into a flat in Carlisle. What he did for a living was anyone's
guess.

Poe knew where he was going and Flynn didn't so they took
his car. They were soon speeding along the A6. A few miles later
they were at the turn-off for the M6, but instead of entering the
northbound traffic, Poe drove over the motorway bridge and
stopped beside a wrought-iron gate. He turned off the engine and
said, 'That's the Hardendale Salt Store. That's where the so called
Tollund Man was found.'

They got out of the car and wandered up to the depot. It was
only a stone's throw from the motorway. From the outside, the
domed building looked like a planetarium or a modern concert
hall. Tens of thousands of motorists passed it every day, wondering what it was. The metal gates were locked; Poe doubted it was
open much during the warmer months, but the small detour had
served a purpose. The journey had taken less than ten minutes and
it emphasised – in his opinion, at least – the possible link between
himself and the body.

'And back there,' he said, pointing the way they'd come, 'is where I live. As the crow flies it's less than eight miles.'

Flynn didn't see it that way. 'It doesn't mean anything, Poe. As DS Reid said, this depot almost certainly wasn't the one he died in.'

Poe said nothing.

Forty minutes later Poe pulled up outside Francis Sharples's flat. It was in a converted townhouse in affluent Stanwix, an area that was all delis and bouncer-less pubs.

'North of the river,' Poe said. 'Very posh.'

'Is it?' Flynn asked.

'For Carlisle, yes. The city doesn't have the wealth of the towns and villages in the Eden Valley or the National Park, but most areas aren't too bad.'

She shielded her eyes and craned her neck to look at the house. 'What do you think Sharples does for a living?'

'God knows. He's a philosophy graduate: I'm assuming he's on the dole.'

She smiled and pressed the button on the intercom with the typed name 'Sharples'. Poe noticed that BPhil had been added in biro.

A tinny voice answered, 'Yah?'

They looked at each other. Flynn rolled her eyes.

She leaned in, and, in a clear voice, said, 'National Crime Agency, Mr Sharples. We'd like a word, please.'

There was a significant pause. There always was after they announced themselves. They might not have the status of the FBI – their American equivalents – but their name was still enough to spook people. Eventually the door clicked open.

Sharples's flat was on the top floor and he was waiting by the door. He was a tall and stringy man. He didn't ask for their ID but they showed him anyway. He turned around without glancing at them. They followed him in.

The townhouse might have been Georgian but the interior was all twenty-first century. The large living room had polished oak floors. Modern pictures hung on the whitewashed walls. A large desk with an Apple laptop dominated the window wall. A bookcase displayed a selection of highbrow books. Tolstoy's *War and Peace*, Dostoyevsky's *Crime and Punishment*, an Old English edition of *Beowulf*: none of the spines were creased and Poe instinctively knew they were for show only.

He offered them his hand. 'My friends call me Frankie.'

This time it was Poe's turn to roll his eyes. He made sure Sharples saw.

After inspecting the rest of the room, Poe said, 'Can I ask what you were doing when we knocked?'

'I was working,' he said.

Poe doubted it. The laptop was in sleep mode and he noticed the Blu-ray player was powered up. The case for a *Transformers* Blu-ray was open and there was a cup of coffee on the table in front of the large TV. Poe didn't wait to be asked; he sat down on the nut-brown leather sofa.

Sharples tried to give him the evil eye. He was a strange-looking man. A pubic beard covered his chin and his moustache could have been made of eyelashes. His Adam's apple was so big it looked like he'd swallowed a triangle. His thinning hair was tied back into a ponytail. He wore shorts, a T-shirt and leather sandals. A black tattoo was just visible on the bone behind his ear.

How had a Grade-A dickhead like this ever worked for the council's road department? Nothing Poe had seen fitted with him ever having had a manual job.

Flynn explained why they were there and Sharples stiffened. The memory appeared fresh. He touched his ear when Flynn asked him if he knew anything that might be of help to them. Poe looked closer and saw he was running his fingers over his tattoo. He continued touching it while he recounted the sequence of events at the Hardendale Salt Store.

He admitted releasing the JCB load instead of lowering the bucket. Derek Bailiff had been his friend and mentor. That he'd caused his death had devastated him. And, no, he couldn't remember anything useful about the body that he hadn't already told the police. He hadn't seen much of it. It was just the hand sticking out initially, and even when he'd mistakenly tipped the load on top of Bailiff, most of the corpse had stayed buried. He hadn't been there when the body had been taken away. He'd resigned before he was fired.

It was clear that he'd told the story many times. He didn't need to pause while he remembered details. It sounded rehearsed and Poe couldn't help feeling that Sharples was leaving something out. He knew witnesses frequently did this; they tried to present themselves in the best possible light, and a peacock like Sharples even more so.

He needed to put him off his stump speech. 'What's with the ink, Mr Sharples?' Poe would rather eat petrol-station sushi than call someone Frankie.

Sharples turned so they could see it. Flynn leaned forward. 'Looks like a circle.'

'It's an ouroboros. A snake eating its own tail. Symbolises the cyclicality of life. It means—'

'I know what it means,' Poe cut in.

'I had it done after the incident. It's a private reminder of the fragile nature of life.'

'I wish I could remember what my personal philosophy was,' Poe muttered. He needed to take him away from the Francis Sharples appreciation society. Needed to needle him, get him talking without thinking. 'And it's a private reminder my arse. You have it behind your ear so people will ask about it. You love talking about what happened. Probably the most exciting thing that's ever happened to you.'

'No!'

Don't let him settle; keep him on his toes.

'What do you do, Mr Sharples?'

'I told you, I was working.'

'No, what do you do for a living? What is your profession?'

'I'm an author. I'm writing about how philosophy's increasing in relevance in a shrinking world.'

'Published?'

'Not yet. But I've had some very promising responses to my proposals.'

'May I see them?'

'See what?'

'Letters from publishers and agents.'

'You clearly don't understand the publishing industry, Sergeant Poe. It's all done verbally these days.'

'Yep. You're talking shit,' Poe said. Before Sharples could protest, or Flynn could intervene, he asked, 'What aren't you telling us?'

Sharples paled and glanced at Flynn. Her eyes bore into him.

'N-n-nothing,' he stuttered.

'How long have you lived here?'

'About three months,' he replied.

'And before then?'

'I lived at home.'

'So, what aren't you telling us?' Poe asked. 'You know we'll find out.'

Sharples stood firm. Poe suspected there was a risk–reward thing going on, and without a stick to beat him, and with no carrot to tempt him, he had no reason to say anything. He was an over-educated dickhead, though; Poe reckoned another half hour would probably crack it. Unfortunately, Sharples thought that too. He stood and said, 'I'm sorry I wasn't able to help, but I really must be getting on.'

Poe remained seated but Flynn thanked him and waited for her colleague.

'I could have had him,' he said as they walked down the stairs.

'Possibly. The reality is he isn't a suspect. Just because pseudo-intellectuals rub you up the wrong way, it doesn't mean they're hiding something from you.'

Poe had no response. She was right; Sharples had pressed all his buttons.

'Come on,' she said. 'Let's call it a day.'

Poe would have offered to take her out for an Indian meal in Carlisle but he just wanted to get home. He had some thinking to do. He knew they were stagnating. The Immolation Man was too clever and too well organised to be caught by a rigid adherence to the murder manual. But the murder manual and predictable investigation strategies were all Gamble and Flynn had.

He had to change that somehow.

CHAPTER EIGHTEEN

Poe arrived at Herdwick Croft to find Bradshaw immersed in her computer. Edgar was curled at her feet, snoring like a fat man. She'd found nothing more on Tollund Man. He was sure that she'd have been quite happy to continue working, but he insisted on driving her to the hotel. He'd have quite liked the company but he needed to think.

When he returned to the croft, he whistled for Edgar and set off on a long walk – the best way he knew of clearing his head.

He walked hard until he'd built up a bit of sweat, then slowed and settled into a pace he could keep for hours. He reckoned he had another two hours of sunlight. He found a flattish stone on a rocky outcrop and sat down. Pulling a pork pie from his pocket, he broke it into two equal pieces. He nibbled at one; the other he passed to Edgar. It was gone in less than a second.

He was in an area he knew well. His thinking zone, he called it. It was a part of the fell where two boundary walls met. Two different craftsmen had worked on them because the difference in style was stark, although both were equally impressive and beautiful.

He stared at the wall he was facing and allowed his mind to focus on it. Dry stone walls – being made without any form of binding agent – were basically large-scale, three-dimensional jigsaw puzzles. Two walls, with smaller stones filling the gap in the middle. Poe reflected on how much they resembled the two facets of solving complex murders.

One side was Gamble and Flynn, methodically building their case, stone by stone. Carefully and thoughtfully. And on the other side were officers like him and Reid. More instinctive, throwing stones into gaps, twisting them until they fitted. Trying different ideas. And although Poe knew that his side of the wall would collapse without the one Flynn and Gamble were building, he also knew that without his side certain cases were never solved.

And there was another similarity before Poe would have to admit he was stretching the analogy too far, and that was the 'through stones'; stones that went through both walls, locking them together. And it was a through stone that Poe was looking for; one bit of evidence that connected both sides of the investigation.

He was convinced the body in the salt store was one of those stones. He either had to find a way to look at it somehow or he had to be allowed a proper go at Sharples.

If he couldn't, the Shap lead was at a dead end. He would be out of options.

Unless . . .

The thought had first occurred to him as he was driving back from Carlisle with Flynn. In the red mist of a lying witness and an awkward boss, it had seemed the logical thing to do. In the cooling evening air, it seemed anything but.

He knew some people thought his reputation for following the evidence wherever it took him was because he felt he held some sort of moral high ground. That he had a calling to a purer version of the truth that was unattainable to other, lesser, cops. The truth was simpler – if he thought he was right, the self-destructive element to his personality took over. It frequently allowed the devil on his shoulder to shout down his better angel. And at the minute, the angel couldn't get a word in edgeways . . .

His face turned to granite. If he didn't do it, who would? Sometimes someone had to step up. Do the unpalatable so others didn't have to.

He reached into his pocket, made sure his mobile had a signal and dialled a number. Reid answered on the third ring.

'Kylian, I need you to do me a favour and you can't mention this to anyone.'

CHAPTER NINETEEN

Poe made his way back to Herdwick Croft. He got another pie, split it with Edgar again, and then sat down to wait. It didn't take long. Half an hour later Reid called him. He had what Poe needed and he told Reid why he wanted it. He made a note, thanked him and hung up.

Leaving the BlackBerry on, he scrolled down until he found van Zyl's number. He tossed up a few scenarios and came down on the side of simply telling the truth.

Van Zyl answered on the first ring and Poe told him what he wanted. The director didn't waste time on amateur dramatics – he was a wily man and still a great cop. He asked Poe some searching questions and he answered them as honestly as he could.

When he was finished, van Zyl went silent. After a few moments, the director spoke. 'Are you sure, Poe?'

'No, sir.'

Van Zyl grunted. 'But you're as sure as you can be?'

How sure was he? Was it an educated guess or was it one last desperate grab by a man out of options? He mentally reviewed what he knew.

'Poe. . .' van Zyl growled.

'Sir,' he said finally. 'I am as sure as I can be.'

'And there's no other way?'

'I don't believe so, sir.'

'Fine,' he sighed. 'Give me what you have.'

'It's a twelve-page form, sir,' Poe said. 'I'll fill it in, then email it to you.'

'You're at home, right?'

'I am, sir.'

'By the time you get to that hotel of yours to use their wi-fi, you'll have wasted half an hour,' van Zyl said. 'I assume you want this to happen sooner rather than later?'

Despite being on the phone, Poe nodded. 'Yes, sir.'

'I'll fill it in then. You need my signature anyway, and if you want this expedited, I'm going to need that extra half hour to get the right people out of bed.'

'What do you need from me, sir?'

'I suggest you get some sleep, Poe. I'll call you if I need additional information. Otherwise you can expect a copy of the fax to go to the hotel.'

It was only after he'd hung up that Poe realised that van Zyl hadn't referred to Flynn once.

Poe was glad. He hadn't had to lie.

And although it would be tricky, if everything went in his favour, he might get away without anyone else finding out.

Two hours later and Poe hadn't heard anything more. He decided to go to the hotel and wait. He had a stomach full of nervous energy and the pages of the novel he was reading weren't registering. Sleep was out of the question.

He wasn't expecting the fax that early but he could check if Bradshaw was still up. If she were, she might be willing to find some dirt on Sharples. He hadn't finished with that prick yet.

He put on his coat and said to Edgar, 'You want to go and see Tilly?'

The spaniel's tail started wagging. Apparently, he did.

* * *

Poe told the receptionist he was waiting for a fax. He asked her to ring Bradshaw's room. She wasn't answering. He checked the clock in the office. It was ten o'clock and he suspected she was asleep with the phone off the hook; just because he was an insomniac it didn't mean everyone else was.

He was about to see if he could beg a coffee when Darren, one of the hotel's barmen, ran up to the desk.

'Where's the duty manager?' he asked.

'Dealing with guests in the Bath House,' the receptionist replied. 'Why?'

The Old Bath House had been exactly what it sounded like: a bathhouse. A detached building at the front of the hotel, it was now used for guests who wanted additional privacy.

Darren looked agitated.

'What's up?' the receptionist asked.

'There's some trouble in the bar.'

Poe didn't work for the local constabulary any more but he was still a cop at heart.

'Show me,' he said. His tone didn't invite discussion. He followed the barman through to the main bar area. It was old-fashioned, a bit worn, resembled a working men's club and attracted a strange mix of clientele. When Poe was having a drink in the hotel he tended to use the smaller bar to the left of reception. He only used the main bar when he needed the free wi-fi.

'I've asked them to leave her alone, sir,' Darren said, 'but they told me to "fuck off".'

Poe looked where he was pointing. His breathing quickened. The animal inside him stirred. *And Bradshaw was just starting to come out of her shell . . .*

She was seated near the window, trying to play a game on her laptop; Poe recognised the headphones she'd slip on when she conversed with other players. Three men surrounded her. They were wearing nametags. He hated conference goers; as soon as they

106

were away from home they seemed to think the rules of society no longer applied, and these clowns had clearly been drinking all day. As Poe watched, one of them lifted the headphones off Bradshaw's head and whispered something into her ear.

'Stop it!' she said, snatching them. Her eyes were wide as she stared at her laptop. The man who'd removed her headphones did so again. Bradshaw again took them back. All three men laughed.

Another man pushed a bottle of lager to her mouth and tried to encourage her to take a drink. She shook her head and it spilt down her T-shirt. The men laughed again.

'Shall I call the police, Mr Poe?'

'I've got this, Darren.'

He walked over. One of the men noticed him. He whispered something to the others and they turned. All three looked like they'd been caught wearing their mother's knickers. Bradshaw looked small and fragile yet . . . there was steel. She wasn't crying and she wasn't screaming for help. She was facing up to them.

'What's up, boys?' Poe asked. His voice was calm but there was no mistaking his intent. When Bradshaw saw him, he knew the look of relief on her face would stay with him forever.

The man who'd been trying to take Bradshaw's headphones said, 'Just having a bit of fun with Mrs Mouse here.' He had a southern accent and was slurring.

Poe ignored him. 'You OK, Tilly?'

She nodded. Her face was paler than usual but she was bearing up. She had guts, he'd give her that. He'd known cops who'd have bottled it by now.

'Tilly? How come this streak of piss knows your name but you won't tell old Karl?' the drunk asked. 'It's almost as if you don't like me. I don't like it when people don't like me.'

Jesus . . .

'Why don't you go and wait by the bar, Tilly? I'll be with you in a second,' Poe said.

Bradshaw tried to stand but the man who called himself Karl put a hand on her shoulder and pushed her down. 'You're going nowhere, darling.'

The animal inside Poe got to its feet. It cracked its knuckles and rolled its shoulders . . . He knew he could stop the situation from escalating by producing his NCA ID card. He also knew he wasn't going to do that; some lessons have to be delivered physically. 'Everything's fine, Tilly,' he said. 'These men are about to leave.'

'Are we now?' Karl said. He stood to emphasise his height and bulk. He grinned when he saw Poe sizing him up.

'Why don't you fucking jog on, mate?' he said. 'I'm not leaving until I've found out whether this frigid bitch spits or swallows.' He lifted an empty bottle by the neck. The threat was clear.

Poe turned to face him but he was speaking to all three. 'Put down your drinks. Leave now. Don't ever come back.' His voice was a growl.

The man who was comparatively sober – Poe could see a nametag with the words 'Team Leader' – said, 'Come on, let's go.' Poe knew he'd recognised trouble even if his drunken colleagues hadn't.

'Sit down!' Karl hissed. 'We're going nowhere. I'm teaching this northern monkey a lesson.'

Poe smiled politely.

'Look, you cunt, you're nausing me right up. Fuck off.'

Poe continued to say nothing. Smiling.

Karl's forehead was now beaded with sweat.

'This is your last chance,' Karl said. 'Just walk away.'

Last chance? Whatever happened to the first chance?

'I'm counting to five,' Poe said. 'That's how long you have.'

'Karl!' said one of his friends. 'Let's go!'

Karl was past the point of no return. 'And what happens at five?'

'One,' Poe said.

'I'm shitting myself,' he sneered.

'I know,' said Poe. 'Two.'

Men like Karl seldom had a Plan B.

Poe said, 'Three . . . four . . .'

Karl's brow furrowed. Poe had backed him into a corner. He was going to fight.

Good.

Poe might have been giving away height and weight but he'd been a Cumbrian cop for almost a decade. Gutter fighting came easily, and he knew what to do when someone was threatening to glass him. With muscles moving ahead of his mind, Poe grabbed Karl's hand. Karl tightened his grip.

Big mistake.

Poe wasn't trying to disarm him. He *wanted* him holding it. He lifted Karl's hand then slammed it onto the table.

The bottle shattered.

Shards of glass flew across the table. Apart from Bradshaw lifting her laptop out of the way, no one moved. The few people left in the bar looked across. They went back to their drinks when Poe glared at them.

Poe continued to grip Karl's hand. He began trembling. His expression changed from lager-fuelled rage to agonising pain. His face whitened. He began to whimper.

Breaking a bottle to use as a weapon isn't like it is in the movies. Banging it against a table to leave a nice smooth neck to grip, and a bunch of deadly shards to stab someone with doesn't work in real life. As Karl had just found out, glass is brittle and unpredictable. When it shatters, you have no control over how *much* of it shatters. Karl had been holding a deadly weapon, *now* he was gripping a handful of razor sharp glass. Blood poured from between his fingers.

Poe squeezed.

Karl screamed.

Poe knew the risk of permanent damage was real but he didn't care; you didn't trade punches with people like Karl. And they needed to understand that retaliation would be met with a disproportionate, life-changing response.

Poe brought his hand down low. Karl dropped to his knees like he'd been shot. He screamed again. With his spare hand Poe retrieved his ID card, and flipped it open.

'Evening, gents,' he said. 'My name is Detective Sergeant Poe and the lady you've just assaulted is my friend. We both work for the National Crime Agency. Now, do we all agree that you three are in deep shit?'

The soberest man nodded.

Poe leaned in to read his nametag. 'MWC Computer Engineering? Never heard of you—'

'We're a company who—'

'I don't need part two, dickhead,' Poe said. 'But if Karl here ever wants to use that hand again, he needs a hospital right now. Not in the morning when you've all sobered up.'

The silence was broken by Karl's sniffling.

'Now, please fuck off out of this hotel.'

Guiding Karl by his ruined hand, he led them back through the bar into the reception area. The sober man turned towards the stairs. 'Where the hell are you going?' Poe asked.

'I'm getting my bag.'

'No, son,' Poe said. 'I told you to fuck off and that means now, not when it suits you.'

'But our stuff. I have computers up . . .' He trailed off under Poe's gaze.

Poe called to the receptionist. 'Zoe, can you order these gentlemen a taxi? Tell the driver he needn't bother driving down to the hotel, these three idiots will meet it on the A6. I think they could use the fresh air.'

He turned to the three men. 'The taxi will take you to hospital.

I'd get a move on if I were you, it's at least a mile to the main road.'

Poe let go of Karl's hand and they staggered into the car park. 'Before you go, how much money do you have?'

'You're robbing us?' the sober one asked.

Poe said, 'Karl's blood is on the carpet in the bar. I don't think the hotel should have to pay for it. Do you?'

Bradshaw was still in the bar. She was trembling but smiled when Poe walked back in. She was stroking Edgar who'd been quiet throughout the whole shebang. He ordered drinks. The barman didn't want his money.

'You OK, Tilly?' he asked. 'Sorry you had to see that.'

'Why do you keep rescuing me, Poe? That's twice now.'

Poe laughed. Bradshaw didn't. She was being serious.

'It was hardly that,' he replied. 'And anyway, I can't stand bullies.'

'Oh,' she said. She looked a little bit deflated.

'And come on, Tilly, we may have had a rough start but you're my friend. You must realise that?'

She didn't reply and for a moment Poe thought he'd said the wrong thing. A single tear was running down her face.

'Tilly—'

'I've never had a friend before,' she said.

He couldn't think of anything to say, so he settled for, 'Well, you do now.'

'Thank you, Poe.'

'Anyway,' he said, 'it's your turn to rescue me next.'

'I will.' She frowned, 'Spit or swallow what, Poe? Whatever did he mean?'

He was saved by the receptionist; she'd entered the bar area with a sheaf of papers. He raised his eyebrows and she nodded.

His fax had arrived. He read the cover sheet.

For some reason it was happening at eighteen minutes past five, but the preparatory work would begin in the next few hours. He wasn't required to be there for that, but he wanted to be.

'I'm going to have to get away, Tilly.' He stood, all thoughts of asking her to delve into Francis Sharples forgotten. 'You going to be OK?'

'Yes, Poe.'

He paused. 'And try not to worry about those idiots, Tilly. If it wasn't you, it would have been someone else. Look at it this way, you're in the NCA. Imagine what it would have been like for some-one who wasn't. Look at it as a glass half-full kind of thing.'

Bradshaw removed her glasses and polished them with a special cloth she kept in her bag. When they were back on, she tucked some hair behind her ear and said, 'The glass isn't half full, Poe. And neither is it half empty.'

'What is it then?'

She grinned. 'It's twice as big as it needs to be.'

She was going to be fine.

CHAPTER TWENTY

Parkside was one of two cemeteries the district council ran in the Kendal area. Poe had been to funerals there so didn't need directions. It was huge, extended to both sides of Parkside Road, and was sectioned according to denomination and religion.

He needed K-section. It was the furthest from the chapel and the car park; and why wouldn't it be? No one would ever visit it.

Finding the grave was more difficult than he imagined it would be. The cloud covering – while keeping the ambient temperature warm – made the blanket of blackness shrouding the cemetery complete. It robbed him of his senses and he cursed himself for not having had the foresight to bring a working torch. He had one in his car but it was little more than a tube for carrying dead batteries. The BlackBerry's torch was barely making a dent in the darkness.

After half an hour of stumbling, tripping over exposed tree roots and walking through cobwebs, he eventually found K-section. Some of the sections were situated in light woodland but K-section was in one of the more open areas.

He began reading headstones. It was an old section of the grounds and most of the graves were simple monuments; weathered stones with fading inscriptions. Names, dates and simple messages of love. The occasional military rank. Some were clean, and others were stained green; half a dozen or so had the full moss overcoat. Some of the older ones leaned together like old friends. He shuddered; how could a place be so full and yet so empty at the same time?

Eventually he found it. It was at the very edge of K-section in a small area he hadn't noticed earlier, hidden from view by a large mausoleum. The reason he'd missed it earlier was because none of the graves had headstones.

The area was slightly covered by a maple tree. He looked down and saw seven wooden plaques in a neat row. Poe knew this was what he'd been looking for.

Logic – and in this part of K-section logic probably did play a part – dictated he should start at the end of the row. He could smell freshly turned earth, and when he shone his light on the plaque to the far right, he found what he'd come for.

The plaque simply said, 'Unknown Male'. The date of interment was there in smaller writing along with an eight-digit reference number that matched the one Reid had told him. The number that was now on the fax van Zyl had sent.

Poe stepped back and viewed the surrounding area. He didn't know what he was looking for and found nothing amiss. It was one of the reasons he'd wanted to get there before the council cavalry arrived; he wanted to look at the area before it was molested and trampled on. See if it had been interfered with. It didn't look as though it had; the grave of Tollund Man was fresh but not *new* fresh.

If he were going to find anything, it was below ground.

He sat down to wait. He checked his watch. It wouldn't be long.

The environmental health officer was called Freya Ackley. She had a shock of ginger hair and spoke with a Newcastle accent. She seemed relieved someone had been there to meet her. 'DS Poe?'

Poe showed her his ID. 'You have things to do before the circus starts?'

She nodded. 'I'm supposed to get five days to do my checks. I was woken by South Lakeland District Council's director of environmental health two hours ago and told the Ministry of Justice had a job that couldn't wait.'

She wasn't moaning; she was nervous. Poe could tell it was the first exhumation she'd officiated. She removed a large file from her rucksack and went to the summary sheet.

'I need to find the grave,' she said.

'Over there,' Poe pointed. 'New one on the end.'

Ackley removed a document from the file's inside pocket. It was the same one Poe had. She walked over to the grave and shone her torch down onto the wooden plaque. She checked it three times then called Poe over.

'I can confirm that this is the grave on the exhumation order.'

'Agreed,' Poe said.

'And can you confirm the reason for the exhumation?'

Poe read it off the fax he was holding. 'To assist in an ongoing serious investigation.'

'And the reason for urgency?'

It was the same reason. Poe repeated it. She stared but Poe didn't elaborate.

Ackley went back to her form. 'As the body's a John Doe there isn't a family to seek permission from and I can confirm that this section of the cemetery is neither consecrated ground nor a registered war grave. I can also confirm that the body can be disinterred without disturbing other remains and that the authority controlling the cemetery has no objection.'

'We ready to go then?'

'We are, DS Poe. My people will be here soon. We'll start at eighteen minutes past five.'

Poe looked at her quizzically, he'd noticed the weird time on the exhumation order earlier.

'It's the official time for sunrise. If we do this during daylight we don't need specialist lighting. And that means I don't need health and safety to certify the generator, the lighting rigs and the cables. Reduces the paperwork and the amount of people who need to be here.'

A council employee who didn't like bureaucracy? Poe liked Freya Ackley.

CHAPTER TWENTY-ONE

At four-thirty, the gravediggers arrived. Three of them. They were prepared for the task in hand. They moved floral tributes from the adjacent graves and erected blue plastic screens to ensure privacy. With the preparation done they disappeared, returning with protective clothing for everyone. There'd be no more people coming; there'd been a thorough forensic post-mortem completed so Poe hadn't needed – and wouldn't have wanted – crime scene investigators. This was all about satisfying his curiosity; if he spotted anything out of the ordinary, he'd stop it all and call Flynn.

As the exhumation order only gave authority for a graveside examination of the remains, two of the gravediggers went for Tollund Man's new coffin, a large casket called a 'shell'. It was made of wood and tarred on the inside. It had a zinc liner and a leak-proof plastic membrane. The remains of Tollund Man, his coffin, and anything else found in the grave would be placed inside the 'shell', sealed, and reburied in the original grave.

Ackley was required to approve the 'shell' – a task that would ordinarily have been completed in her allotted five days. She checked the new nameplate on the lid to ensure it matched the one on the grave and the exhumation order. She asked Poe to double-check. He did. They matched.

They were ready. They only needed to wait until daylight. Ackley took the time to deliver her required briefing. As the environmental health officer, it was her job to ensure that respect for the deceased was maintained. More importantly, it was also her responsibility to ensure that public health was protected during the exhumation. She briefed Poe and the gravediggers on the risk of infection from human remains and the soil surrounding graves. Creutzfeldt-Jakob disease, tetanus, even smallpox were transmittable and were still viable after interment. Ackley was reading from prepared notes and Poe was paying as much attention as he would a pre-flight safety demonstration; Tollund Man had been buried in salt for decades and had been tested and autopsied – there was no risk. He doubted he'd been in the ground long enough to even start decomposing.

Poe glanced at his watch. It was officially morning: five-eighteen had happened. He closed his eyes and tried to calm himself. Tried not to imagine 'Ex-cop Reduced to Grave Robbing' as the lead in tomorrow's newspapers.

It was at that point that someone leaned into him and snarled, 'What the fuck do you think you're doing, Poe?' into his ear.

Poe's eyes snapped open. Flynn was glaring at him. He'd never seen her so angry.

He started to speak but she cut him off.

'How dare you!'

'Steph, listen—'

'Don't, Poe,' she snapped. 'Just fucking don't.'

Poe did. 'I spoke to van Zyl last night. He authorised it and chased everyone to get it done quickly,' he said. 'I'm sorry but here we are.'

'You went above my head?' Her voice was low.

Poe shrugged. 'I'd hardly call it that.'

'What *would* you call it?'

Poe didn't have an answer and he had no intention of hiding behind banal platitudes. He'd have been furious if the roles had been reversed, but the Immolation Man hadn't carved her name into someone's chest. He didn't have the luxury of kowtowing to procedural niceties. 'It's me he's taunting, Steph. Not you, not Gamble. And you know who I am, why van Zyl wanted me in the first place – I go where the evidence takes me. And it's taken me here.'

'Fuck off, Poe,' she growled. 'That's binary thinking and it's unworthy of you. It's not as simple as that. There's a right way and a wrong way to do things and this is absolutely the wrong way. What's DCS Gamble going to say when he finds out the NCA has exhumed a body in his investigation without telling him? He's going to go ballistic.'

'Blame me,' Poe replied.

'Blame . . . who the fuck else would I blame?'

Fair point. This was the Peyton Williams case all over again; even when he was right he was wrong. He handed over the faxed copy of the exhumation order.

'And van Zyl was OK excluding me from my own investigation?' She seemed to have softened slightly. Probably recognised they were going to exhume the body whether she liked it or not. Professional curiosity was blunting the indignation.

'Honestly, Steph, I don't think he realised. I think he assumed I was acting on your instructions.' Poe didn't think that at all. Van Zyl was an intelligent and pragmatic man – if he hadn't mentioned Flynn it was because he hadn't wanted to mention her. He hadn't wanted to hear Poe lie. He'd almost certainly realised he was going rogue and was probably glad Poe hadn't dug up the grave himself. But he wouldn't want to subvert the chain of command too much; there would be repercussions. He'd have to come down on Flynn's side when the body was back in the ground. 'I'm assuming van Zyl called you?'

She nodded. 'First thing. Told me my exhumation order was down in reception. You could imagine my surprise.'

Poe could. He almost smiled but held it in. Now wasn't the time to be conciliatory; Flynn needed to stay mad at him for a bit longer.

She said, 'Look, Poe, when all this is over you could very well be back in charge. And if that happens, it's fine; I'll be glad to be your sergeant again. But until that happens can you please, for the love of God, just give me the respect I gave you?'

Was that what she really thought of him. That he'd circumnavigated her because he didn't respect her? That he was struggling reporting to a former subordinate? He hoped not, because nothing could be further from the truth. Flynn had been an awful sergeant but she was shaping up to be a great DI. She had the potential to be the best boss he'd ever had. It was right that she was angry.

He told her as much and was happy when she reddened. 'This is all on me, Steph. When Gamble finds out I will hold my hands up. Tell him you weren't involved.'

'Fuck you, Poe,' she sighed. 'We're in this shit show together.' She looked at her watch. 'Come on. It's time.'

The earth was soft and damp and the gravediggers made it look effortless. With their over-long spades, they moved the dirt in quick, economical movements. Poe had no idea how deep graves were supposed to be. 'Six feet under' sprang to mind but he didn't know if that was from the top or the bottom of the coffin, or just a phrase with no bearing on modern graveyard regulations. After ten minutes of digging they'd ditched their spades and one of them had got in and was moving the last of the mud with his hands. After a few moments he'd exposed wood. The webbing straps used to lower the coffin were wet and dirty but still in good condition – they hadn't been in the ground for long – and he passed them up to his colleagues. No point fitting new ones when the ones in situ were perfectly serviceable.

'We'll lift it out and place it directly into the shell, Sergeant Poe,' Ackley said. 'You can remove the lid and examine the contents from there. When you're finished we'll widen the grave slightly and reinter.'

120

The man who'd cleared the coffin and located the webbing straps grabbed the hand of his mate and climbed out of the grave. As he did so, part of the webbing caught on his leg. It caused him to slip and he banged against the side of the coffin.

The lid moved.

That was odd. Coffin lids weren't simply popped on like the top on a tube of Pringles, were they? Weren't they supposed to be nailed down?

'The lid. It's loose,' Poe said.

They all peered into the grave.

A sickly sweet stench of putrefaction wafted up.

Flynn's nose wrinkled in disgust. 'What's that?' She removed a handkerchief from her pocket and held it across her mouth and nose.

There was something wrong with the smell.

'I don't know, but it's not coming from someone who's been in salt for about thirty years,' Poe replied. It was too . . . organic.

The man in the grave reached down to remove the coffin lid.

'Stop!' Poe yelled. He reached down and grabbed the man's hand. Hauled him up. He faced the three gravediggers. 'I need you all to put down your spades and remove your protective clothing.' He turned to the environmental health officer. 'You too, Freya. This isn't an exhumation site any more, it's a crime scene.'

CHAPTER TWENTY-TWO

The body in the coffin wasn't the dried-out husk of the uniden-
tified male they'd been expecting – it was another victim of the
Immolation Man. Judging by the smell, it wasn't a new victim.
It was as badly burned as the body Poe had seen in the circle at
Cockermouth, but whereas that body had smelled disgusting but
fresh, this one smelled disgusting and rotten.

'It's the fifth victim,' Poe said, 'or the fifth one we've found
anyway.'

Flynn didn't seem to be able to tear her eyes away from the
blackened corpse in the grave.

'I take it you believe me now when I say the two are linked?'

'What the hell's going on, Poe? And where the hell's Tollund
Man?'

Poe didn't have a clue.

But Flynn had hit the nail on the head; the new victim being
there was incidental and of little interest to them. That was a job
for Gamble and the main investigation. Poe had no doubt that the
Immolation Man's primary objective in replacing the body with
another victim had little to do with mischief; it was to stop Poe
finding out who Tollund Man was.

So why had he led him here at all . . . ?

Unless . . . unless he hadn't been meant to get access to the
coffin so quickly. Going through van Zyl instead of the usual
bureaucratic channels meant he'd got the exhumation order
in hours rather than weeks. His insubordination with Flynn

might have bought them an advantage they weren't supposed to have.

And that meant he had a potential bridge to the truth; all he had to do was find a way of crossing it.

An hour later, the Cumbrian team descended on the cemetery. Gamble and Reid arrived first, all suited and booted. Forensics and CSI were close behind. It wasn't long before the combined ensemble of a murder investigation had ruined K-section's tranquillity.

A forensic tent soon covered the grave. An inner cordon had been set around some gravestones and an outer one around K-section.

When Gamble realised what had happened he turned red-faced with fury. Flynn stood up to him. She showed him the exhumation order. It didn't improve his mood. He snatched it off her and marched up to Poe. 'What the hell is this?'

Poe glanced at the top sheet. It was signed by the Ministry of Justice Coroner and by the head of the Cemeteries Office in South Lakeland District Council. The reason for exhumation was listed as 'Urgent examination of contents of coffin'. More information was given but the gist was that the NCA had reason to believe that evidence vital to the apprehension of a serial murderer was contained within the coffin. It was signed 'Edward van Zyl, Director of Intelligence'.

'It's an exhumation order, sir.'

'I know what it fucking is, Poe!' he snarled. 'Why's DI Flynn's name not on this? Why is your name listed under "applicant"?'

Flynn walked over.

'Perhaps I can explain, sir,' she said. 'As I said earlier, Ian, the postcard Poe received yesterday led us to believe there was evidence in this grave vital to your investigation. I tried to ring but couldn't get a signal. I knew you'd want us to get on it as soon as possible, so I went through my own director to get expedited permission. Thankfully he was able to leap a few hurdles and buy us some extra days.'

Gamble knew she was lying, but he also knew he'd been out-flanked. 'You bloody people . . .' After standing his ground for a moment, he said, 'I want a full report uploaded to HOLMES by midday, Detective Inspector Flynn.' He turned to Poe and said, 'And I want him off my investigation!'

When he was out of earshot, Flynn turned to him. 'I'm sorry, Poe.'

'What?' he exclaimed. 'He doesn't have the authority—'

'Director's orders. I've just spoken to van Zyl. You went behind my back and you went behind Gamble's back. He can't afford a fight with Cumbria and politically he can't insist they host you any more.'

His phone rang. It was Director van Zyl.

If Poe thought he was in for a phoney bollocking over the chain of command he was wrong. 'I spoke to HR yesterday, Sergeant Poe,' van Zyl said without preamble. 'It seems that because you hadn't contacted anyone during your suspension – and more importantly, no one contacted you – you have accrued over twelve months' worth of leave. Now we can pay you for it if you like, but if you were to verbally request some now, I'd look upon it favourably. I'm sure Detective Inspector Flynn would too.'

Poe could only manage, 'Er . . . what?'

'Do you want to take some leave,' van Zyl said, speaking slowly. 'It's either that or you're back in Hampshire today.'

'Er . . . yes then?'

'Good. That's settled then. With immediate effect you're on a month's leave.'

'Why, sir?' Poe asked.

But he was gone.

Poe stared at the phone in his hand. Flynn wandered up. Gamble was in tow.

'Why's he still here?' Gamble barked.

'Sergeant Poe has been reassigned, sir,' Flynn said. 'But I understand he's taking some leave first. Is that right, Poe?'

He nodded. Gamble grunted in satisfaction before stomping off. Flynn and the director had figured a workaround that allowed Gamble to save face but kept Poe in Cumbria. They wanted him working the case, but from now on it would be unofficial.

Just as he preferred.

He knew what he had to do. Scrolling through his phone's contact list, he went to his newest entry and pressed call. Considering it was still very early it was answered immediately. The voice at the other end didn't sound in the least bit sleepy.

'How do you fancy some advanced fieldwork, Tilly?'

CHAPTER TWENTY-THREE

Poe dropped off Edgar, then picked up Bradshaw at the hotel's front door. He didn't bother turning off the car's engine. Bradshaw – a star in the making – had understood he was coming off night work so had somehow rustled up fried-egg rolls and a flask of coffee. Poe ate the rolls before sipping the hot drink until it was cool enough to gulp.

The journey up the M6 took less than half an hour. By eight in the morning they were in Stanwix. Poe parked the car and they headed up the steps of the townhouse. Poe pointed at the BPhil after Francis Sharples's name and asked, 'You know what that means, Tilly?'

'Bachelor of Philosophy, Poe.'

Poe shook his head. 'It means he's a cock.' He pressed the intercom button and didn't let up until a sleep-ridden voice answered.

'Yah?'

'See?' Poe said. After he told Sharples who was at the door, and after ignoring his protests about civil liberties being trampled on, they were let in.

As before, he was waiting for them at the entrance to his flat. He'd either slept in his shorts or had managed to get dressed in the time it took them to walk up the stairs. Instead of the condescending smirk he'd worn last time, he was now struggling to hold a nervous smile.

This time Poe saw no reason to be nice. He wasn't leaving until Sharples told him everything.

'The information you're concealing, it's now part of a murder enquiry.'

'I'm not conceal—'

'Piss off,' Poe snapped. 'I've been doing this job fifteen years and I've never seen a worse liar.'

'How dare you!'

'Whatever.' Poe couldn't tell if Sharples was shocked at the change in tone or the fact someone didn't believe him. 'You can be as pretend outraged as you want, *Frankie*, I'm about to arrest you for assisting an offender and perverting the course of justice.' Before Sharples could object, he added, 'And at this stage, as you're the only person connected with the case who we know to be lying, I am formally telling you that you are now considered a suspect in five murders. At the very least you will be convicted of joint enterprise.'

It was bullshit but Poe was banking on knowing more about the law than Sharples did. 'Get dressed, you're coming with me.'

Sharples was now shaking. Tears were in his eyes. Poe looked round the room. He'd been working on his book the night before. Or at least he wanted to give the impression he'd been working on his book. A neat stack of paper was lined up next to his laptop. It was his manuscript – where anyone who visited would be able to see it, Poe noticed – and there seemed to be about seventy pages. He picked up the title sheet: 'The Increasing Relevance of Philosophy in a Smaller World'.

'Nice computer, Mr Sharples,' Bradshaw said, looking at his Apple laptop. 'This model's top of the range.'

While they talked computers, Poe looked at the expensive décor in the expensive flat in the expensive part of town. He'd wanted to ask Sharples last time how an unpublished philosophy graduate afforded a place like this.

'How did you pay for all this, Mr Sharples?'

His eyes dropped to the floor.

'I can have a forensic accountant here in a matter of hours, Mr Sharples. They'll go through everything, and I mean everything. Better by far if you tell me now.'

Sharples mumbled something but it was too quiet for Poe to hear.

Bradshaw had, though, 'He said he took something from the corpse.'

Poe nodded. 'And what would that have been?'

'A watch,' he croaked.

Poe wasn't a fashion guru but even he knew some watches were incredibly expensive. 'Make and model?'

'A 1962 Breitling 765. The strap must have broken when I accidentally tipped the body on top of Derek. I didn't think, I put it in my pocket. To keep it safe.'

'To keep it safe.'

'Yes.'

'And what, you forgot you had it?'

'I did. When I found it later I was scared the police might think I'd stolen it.'

'Imagine that,' Poe said. 'So where is it?'

He didn't have an answer. Poe suspected he'd sold it. Sharples continued to stare at the floor.

'I said—'

'I don't have it any more!'

'I want the serial number and photographs,' Poe said. He turned to Bradshaw. It was what you did when you wanted something checking on the internet. She was already on her phone.

'Value?' Poe asked her.

'A Breitling 1962 model would cost approximately ten thousand pounds, Poe,' she replied. She seemed to be enjoying her first trip out into the field. At some point Poe would have to explain that it wasn't official. Let her decide whether she wanted to carry on or not. But not just yet.

Poe turned to Sharples and asked, 'Who did you sell it to?'

'I want a deal.'

Poe snorted. Even Bradshaw giggled.

'You watch too much shit television, Mr Sharples,' he said. 'This isn't America. There'll be no deal. What there might be is *mitigation*. That's where the judge looks at something good you might have done, instead of just the bad. And the only way you'll get *mitigation* is if I get hold of that fucking watch. Now, tell me who you sold it to.'

'I can't,' he whispered. 'I sold it on a specialist watch site to an anonymous collector in the States.'

'Tilly?'

'Please can you move out of the way, Mr Sharples,' she said as she pushed past Sharples and powered up his Mac. 'Password, please?'

He told her.

While Bradshaw searched the computer, Poe asked, 'How much did you get for it?'

'Certainly not ten thousand pounds!' he said. He seemed annoyed he'd been fleeced. 'I got five thousand dollars, which came to a touch over three thousand sterling.' He eyed Bradshaw nervously. 'What's she doing?'

Poe said, 'What most people don't realise, Mr Sharples, is that you can delete things from your computer all you want, but everything's recoverable. Tilly here will uncover anything you've written about that Breitling. How long, Tilly?'

'Found it, Poe' she said. 'Do you have a printer, Mr Sharples?'

He opened a cupboard and pressed a button. A green light came on and the printer whirred and clunked its way to being ready. 'It's wireless,' he said.

Bradshaw rolled her eyes and said, 'Duh.'

She printed off some documents. She handed them to Poe without looking at them.

He flicked through them. They were colour and the first few pages were good – certainly enough to secure Sharples's conviction – but it wasn't until the last two that he hit the mother lode.

The buyer had wanted to see what he was buying and Sharples had been happy to oblige. Six full-colour photographs, three to a page. It was the fifth that made Poe smile.

It was of the back of the watch.

And there, as clear as day, was its unique serial number.

CHAPTER TWENTY-FOUR

They left Sharples but told him to stay where he was. Uniformed officers would be coming for him. They would be, but not for a while and not until Poe had finished chasing down the watch's original owner.

Poe told Bradshaw that as he was officially on leave she should head back to Shap, but she was keen to see through the Breitling line of enquiry. Poe relented. They decided to grab breakfast from the Sainsbury's café. Poe chose the full English and Bradshaw got the vegetarian equivalent. They shared a pot of tea.

As the bacon broke over his tongue, the salty flavour like a bomb in his mouth, they discussed the best way to track down the watch's owner. Bradshaw wanted Poe to go straight to Breitling – she assumed there'd be a central database somewhere – but he had reservations. They were a big company, with clients all over the world, and some of them would be extremely wealthy. Breitling weren't going to breach their confidentiality policy just because some dickhead from the NCA asked them. Instead, he planned to hit the county's high-value dealers and frighten them until they gave him what he wanted. There weren't many, and if Tollund Man had been a Cumbrian, it was possible the watch had been bought locally.

As he was mopping up egg yolk with a bit of fried bread, Bradshaw asked him why he was taking leave now of all times.

'Just need a bit of time, Tilly.'

'Are you sure it's not because of me, Poe?'

'What . . . no, of course not. Why would it be about you?'

'People get sick of me.'

'Well, if they do, they're idiots,' he said. 'No, the real reason is because last night DCS Gamble asked me to leave his investigation.'

'Is that why DI Stephanie Flynn rang me to say I was to help if you asked?'

'I didn't know she had.'

'She said I wasn't to tell you.'

'But?'

'Friends should never lie to each other, Poe.'

He nodded thoughtfully. 'Come on, eat your sawdust. The shops will be open soon.'

As they'd been talking Bradshaw had taken advantage of the store's free wi-fi. She'd been trying to shorten the search by finding jewellers with staying power, those who'd been around for a long time. She'd collated a list, then switched to a news channel. It was nine o'clock and the headlines were on. Bradshaw's mouth opened as she stared at the screen. 'No . . . no . . . that's not right at all,' she cried.

'What isn't?' Poe said absentmindedly, as he chased a snide baked bean around the plate with his knife.

'Look at this, Poe!' She turned the tablet round so they could both see it. She turned up the volume and pressed play.

In the middle of a scrum of cameras and oversized microphones, wearing a clean suit as if he hadn't just spent three hours in a Kendal graveyard, was Gamble. The news anchor led into the interview by saying, 'Police have said that the body found in a grave in Kendal early this morning could be another victim of the serial murderer known as the Immolation Man. We'll now go live to Cumbria where Detective Chief Superintendent Ian Gamble will be making a short statement.'

Gamble had been waiting for the go-ahead and he started

speaking as soon as the anchor finished. 'After some exceptional police work by Cumbrian detectives, the investigation team applied for an exhumation order for a grave in the Parkside Cemetery in Kendal. We had reason to believe that a coffin that should have contained the unidentified body found at the Hardendale Salt Store last year had been recently tampered with. As expected, the coffin's original occupant was missing. In its place was the body of an as yet unidentified male who we believe to be a victim of the Immolation Man.'

Gamble's statement was concise, well written, didn't contain a single lie and was total bullshit. The NCA wouldn't dare contradict him; they wouldn't risk exposing their own faultlines. Poe had seen to that.

'Prick,' said Poe. 'Come on, let's get going.'

Although he knew the watch could have been bought anywhere, Poe planned to start looking in Carlisle as they were already there. If he were lucky, it had been bought before online shopping took off, when people tended to buy high-end items in person.

He was happy to discount the cheaper stores and focus his efforts on the smaller upmarket chains and family-owned businesses. There was only a handful of smaller shops that sold watches – although to be thorough they would check the ones that didn't in case they used to sell watches – but even so, they were soon struggling.

Every shop except one was happy to let Bradshaw into their records, and the one that didn't was able to confirm that they'd never sold Breitlings, new or second-hand.

The serial number BR-050608 wasn't on any of the computer databases they checked, and because very few of them had transferred their paper records to electronic, searching old ledgers was slow and laborious.

One jeweller smiled as he dumped ten ledgers on his table, each one thicker than a copy of *Yellow Pages*. Poe groaned, although it didn't seem to faze Bradshaw. She had the kind of analytical mind that relished things like cross-referencing lists.

However, effort didn't guarantee outcome. After she'd finished the seventh and final ledger in a shop that might have sold Breitlings a few years ago, Poe called a halt. It was lunchtime and standing around doing nothing had made him hungry.

They walked to the car and bought another parking ticket before wandering over to a little-known old-school coffee shop he'd recently discovered in Carlisle. Coffee Genius was down Saint Cuthbert's Lane, near the medieval West Walls. It had a high counter, expensive-looking chrome machines and plenty of home-made cakes and scones. They roasted their own beans and it was a coffee snob's paradise. Poe found the smells intoxicating: freshly brewed coffee, the acrid smell of espresso, sweet warm caramel and chocolate, a tingle of cinnamon . . . His mouth watered as soon as he walked in.

It was full of the lunchtime crowd but they found a seat near a window. Poe ordered a slow-brewed Peruvian black and the club sandwich of the day – pulled pork and caramelised onions. Bradshaw ordered a hot chocolate before asking him if she was allowed the meal deal: soup and a sandwich.

'Get what you want, Tilly. My treat.'

She nodded happily and placed her order. Like birds flitting from branch to branch, her eyes were everywhere, taking in all the new experiences. Her mother had told Poe she'd led a sheltered life before joining SCAS, but he had no idea just how sheltered. As they waited for their food and drinks Bradshaw asked what he thought about the morning's search.

'It's a fool's errand,' Poe said. He was beginning to doubt the course of action they were on. It had felt like a wasted morning.

'It's not, Poe,' she said. 'It's just going to take time. If it's out there, I'll find it.' And with that she begged the wi-fi password from the barista and took out her tablet. Within seconds she was immersed in something. Poe knew he wouldn't get another word from her until the food arrived.

The barista came over with the drinks and placed a small triple egg timer on the table. The sand on Poe's right was for a strong brew and he watched as it slowly ran down. It was therapeutic and he could feel his mind unwinding. He'd have to get one. When it ran out, he poured his coffee.

The sandwiches arrived ten minutes later. Bradshaw photographed her food and texted the picture to her mum. 'She likes to know what I'm doing,' she explained.

Poe, who was getting used to her eccentricities, kept his own counsel. She arranged her napkin to her liking then took a bite from her sandwich. 'This is nice isn't it, Poe? I usually eat lunch on my own.'

When they'd finished they ordered more hot drinks.

One of the things he liked about Coffee Genius was that the staff were always happy to stop and chat. While Bradshaw worked, Poe and the barista talked about the benefits of buying your own beans and grinding them at home.

'What do you do?' the barista asked.

Poe told him but left the details a bit fuzzy. 'We're searching for the owner of an old watch today.'

The barista sat down, and without mentioning the murder angle, Poe explained.

'All a bit needle-in-a-haystack, isn't it?' the barista said.

'Tell me about it.'

The barista laughed.

'And that's not even including the shops that don't exist any more. Got no way of searching for them online.'

The barista huddled up to him. 'There's a man and his wife come in here a couple of times a week. He's retired now but I'm sure he used to work in the jewellery business. And the reason I know is that I've just got engaged and he advised me on which jewellers wouldn't rip me off.'

'You got a name?'

'Charles. His wife's called Jackie, I think.' He looked over his shoulder. 'The boss is in, she might know. I'll go and ask her.'

Two minutes later he returned with a bit of paper. 'Charles Nolan. The boss says they come in most Saturdays and Wednesdays. Thinks they do their shopping in Marks and Spencer. If you leave your name and number, I can pass him a message if you want.'

Poe declined. He didn't have the time to wait. He excused himself and walked outside to make a call.

Kylian Reid answered immediately.

'Oi, oi! It's Burke and Hare!' Reid said without preamble.

'Ha-fucking-ha,' Poe replied. 'I kept you out of it, didn't I? And I saw Gamble preening about on TV this morning. He knows I did him a favour.'

'Like that matters. He's still fucking furious.'

'I need another favour,' Poe said.

'OK . . .' Reid said. 'Aren't you supposed to be on leave?' He was wary. If Gamble had found out Reid had passed him the information for the exhumation order, it could have meant his job.

'I am. It's just something I'm following up on. Nothing that'll raise any eyebrows.'

'Going to need more than that, mate.'

Poe was reluctant to tell him. Reid was his friend but he was also a bloody good cop. If he thought the investigation team were better equipped, he'd have no qualms about pulling the plug on him.

'Best you don't know, Kylian.'

'Prick,' he said. 'I meant I'm going to need more than just "I need another favour", I need to know what the fucking favour is.'

CHAPTER TWENTY-FIVE

Within the hour Reid had emailed Poe a list of all C. Nolans, Charlie Nolans and Charles Nolans registered for council tax in Cumbria. There were fourteen. He passed the list to Bradshaw, who asked how she could refine it.

That was easy enough.

Excluding motorway services, there were only four Marks and Spencer stores in Cumbria. He told Bradshaw to remove anyone who lived in West Cumbria or Eden; they'd use the Workington or Penrith stores for their regular shopping. For the same reason, he told her to remove anyone living below junction 39 on the M6 corridor: the Kendal store served the bottom half of the county.

That left the Carlisle area, and reduced the list to four. One lived in the city centre and Poe discounted them – retired jewellers were more likely to live in one of the thousand and one picturesque villages dotted around Cumbria, not in the middle of a grubby city.

One lived in Brampton and the other two lived in villages: one in Warwick Bridge and the other in Cumwhinton. On the basis that it could be any of them, Poe decided to start with the nearest Nolan then work outwards. C. Nolan in Warwick Bridge would be first; it was a nice village just outside Carlisle. They'd then move on to the other C. Nolan in Cumwhinton, and turn back for the Charles Nolan in Brampton.

* * *

They got lucky on the first go – although, as Poe said to Bradshaw, when you've narrowed your search to just four people, how lucky is it?

The man who answered the door was genteel and polite. He was in his early sixties. He wore a frayed cardigan, thick-lensed spectacles and a broad smile. When they'd confirmed that they were the Nolans who frequented Coffee Genius twice a week, his wife put the kettle on and insisted they stay for some cake.

'Washington, eh? There's an ambassadorial name if ever there was one. I can just imagine it being mentioned in high-stakes diplomatic dispatches. The sort of name that stops war being declared. There's a fascinating story behind it, no doubt?'

Everyone's a fucking onomatologist . . .

'You don't know, do you, Poe?' Bradshaw said, unwittingly rescuing him.

Poe smiled at her and shook his head. 'That's right, Tilly. I don't.'

'Ah,' Nolan said. 'Then how can I help you?'

'We're trying to trace a watch,' Poe said.

'Not high-stakes diplomacy then?'

'Definitely not. My boss would be keen to tell you that diplomacy isn't the strongest part of my character,' Poe said, taking a bite of the excellent cake. He told Nolan his problem.

'I assume this watch has been stolen?'

'Of a fashion,' Poe replied.

'And the National Crime Agency gets involved with thefts, do they?' he asked with a twinkle in his eyes.

Poe said nothing.

'Sorry. Of course, I'll help if I can. I used to own three shops and I like to think we had some of the better ones.'

'What happened?'

He flexed his hand. 'Arthritis, I'm afraid. Curse of the jeweller. That and fading eyesight meant I couldn't hold or see anything smaller than a penny. I sold up. The shops are all gone now. One of them is now Coffee Genius, which is why we go there.' He sighed, 'Still, I did well out of it so shouldn't complain. Now, tell me about this watch you need help with.'

Bradshaw handed over the photograph showing the Breitling's serial number.

'This is the one we're trying to trace,' Poe said. 'Do you need the model and year?'

'If you have it,' Nolan said, 'although Breitling's serial numbers are unique across the whole range. In other words, there won't be two different models with the same number. But the model might jog someone's memory.'

Poe breathed out. It was nice finally to talk to someone who knew what he was on about.

Nolan said, 'I'll make some calls and see what I can find out. I still keep in touch with a few folk in the trade so I might be able to point you towards someone who could help.'

'Appreciate it,' Poe said. He wrote his name and number on the same piece of paper the serial number was on and stood to shake Nolan's hand.

'I'll be in touch, Sergeant Poe,' Nolan said.

His wife showed them to the door. 'That'll keep him busy for the afternoon anyway. He's been a bit lost since he retired.'

'Now what?' Bradshaw asked when they were back in his car.

'We wait,' Poe replied.

They didn't have to wait long. Nolan rang back within two hours.

'I think I have something for you, Sergeant Poe,' he said.

Nolan had begun by ringing people who'd had similar shops to him: jewellery businesses and small chains. Most of them didn't sell high-end watches; it was a lot of money to tie up in stock that might not sell, and the kind of thing they did sell was mostly bespoke anyway. They made their jewellery from scratch and had little interest in anything else.

'Even that's a dying art, though,' he moaned. 'These days it's all designed on a computer and then cut with a pre-programmed laser. Flawless results and I suppose it is progress. Makes the end product a bit soulless if you ask me, though.'

Poe wanted to speed him up but knew better than to say anything.

'Anyway, a friend of mine remembered a dealer in new and antique watches who would visit the various shops and leave leaflets and information for customers. He worked for all the major watch manufacturers. The shop would facilitate the purchase and take a cut. That way they could call themselves official suppliers without having to buy any.'

Made sense, Poe thought. It also avoided the smash-and-grab raids thirty grand watches attracted.

'The dealer's called Alastair Ferguson and he's retired.'

'And?'

'And I've just finished speaking to him. He's on his way over here now. He's coming from Edinburgh, though, so it'll be another couple of hours. If you and Miss Bradshaw can come back we can have a cup of tea while we wait.'

'And he knows something, does he?'

'Well, he didn't have records for the serial number to hand but he thinks he knows the watch in question.'

'And why's that?'

'Because as soon as I mentioned the Breitling, he said he'd been waiting for this call for twenty-six years . . .'

CHAPTER TWENTY-SIX

Alastair Ferguson spoke with a strong Scottish accent. He was small and immaculately attired in a three-piece suit, obviously from the generation who still believed in dressing up for appointments. He took a dram of whisky from Nolan, then settled in to tell them what he knew.

A shop that no longer traded had sold the watch he suspected they were following. They had two premises, both in Keswick. One sold costume jewellery to tourists and the other was a more traditional shop.

The owner had been asked to source a Breitling for a customer and he'd had a healthy budget. Alastair Ferguson had driven down from Edinburgh to meet him with a strongbox full of watches and hopefully to secure a nice fat commission.

'Do you remember who the customer was?' Poe asked.

Ferguson nodded. 'The Bishop of Carlisle.'

For several moments no one said anything. *This is going to get 'political'*, Poe thought.

Ferguson added, 'It wasn't for him, though, and it was all above board. He paid with a church cheque and made sure he had a signed receipt.'

'Do you know who it was for?' Poe asked.

Ferguson removed a newspaper cutting from his pocket. It was yellowing with age but otherwise in good condition. He passed it to Poe. The clipping had been taken from the *News & Star*. It was a filler article. A single column on page eight. Probably only interesting to those involved. The date was at the top and it was from twenty-six years ago.

Poe read it, then snapped a photograph with his mobile. He passed it over to Bradshaw. She did something with her tablet and scanned it. Poe glanced at the image she'd made on the screen. It was crystal clear.

```
In a ceremony at Rose Castle, the Bishop
of Carlisle presents a watch to the
Reverend Quentin Carmichael, the Dean
of Derwentshire, in recognition of his
outstanding services to charity.
```

Quentin Carmichael – who was known for holding charity cruises on Derwentwater, the lake near Keswick – was forty-five and had a glittering career with the Church ahead of him.

Poe glanced at Bradshaw and wondered if she'd spotted the importance of his age. She was waiting for him to catch her eye; it was clear that she had. Twenty-six years ago, Quentin Carmichael had been forty-five. That put him right in the target age for the Immolation man.

Poe's suspicions had been confirmed.

If Carmichael were involved, then it meant Poe was right; the Immolation Man wasn't choosing his victims at random. He was targeting them. Find out why and he'd be a step closer to finding out who.

Poe turned to Ferguson and said, 'When I spoke to Charles earlier, he said you'd been expecting a call like this?'

Ferguson nodded. He removed another newspaper clipping from his pocket. Poe read it.

It was another article on Carmichael. This one wasn't so flattering.

* * *

Disgraced church official, Quentin
Carmichael, flees country. Embezzlement
suspected.

The article was full of the usual journalistic bullshit phrases of 'allegedly' and 'according to senior sources' but the gist of the accusations was clear: Carmichael had fled the country because he was about to be exposed for embezzlement. Although it was thin, there'd been corroboratory evidence of his escape from justice: a missing passport and chequebook. There was nothing else of significance in the article and Poe made a mental note to try and get hold of the police file.

'So, you'd been expecting a visit from the police because Mr Carmichael had been suspected of embezzlement?' Poe asked.

'Not exactly.'

Poe waited.

'I kept these clippings because I thought there was something a bit off with him. He asked to see me not long after he'd been gifted the watch, and when this happens it's usually because the person wants to thank me or, even better, they've got the collector's bug and are looking to expand their collection.'

'But Carmichael wasn't either of those?'

'He was not, sir. All Quentin Carmichael was interested in was how much it had cost. He got quite angry when I said I couldn't tell him. He even offered to sell it back to me for two-thirds of what the bishop had paid. As I don't own the watches, I refused. I said I'd be happy to act as his broker but he stormed out.'

'So, the embezzlement thing made sense to you?'

'Oh, aye. He was all about the green, that man.'

A financially motivated thread was appearing. Now all he had to do was gently tug it. 'Could you all excuse me a moment?' He stood and walked to a quiet corner of the large living room. Mrs Nolan came in with a pot of tea and another cake. He was going to put on three stone during this investigation if he wasn't careful.

He called Reid.

'Burke, what you after this time?'

Poe told him what they'd found and he asked how he could help.

'I need to know all about the Carmichael embezzlement investigation. It was twenty-five, twenty-six years ago,' Poe whispered into his phone. He didn't want Nolan and Ferguson knowing he didn't have the authority to request the information through official channels.

'The Church? Aren't you in enough trouble?'

'Please, Kylian.'

'It's going to be difficult to do it without alerting anyone, Poe. All our systems leave footprints, you know that.'

'Tell Gamble then. I was just about to tell DI Flynn anyway.'

'You were?'

'Absolutely,' Poe lied.

'I'll get back to you then,' Reid said before hanging up.

Poe returned to his seat and finished his cup of tea. He asked Ferguson some more questions but it was clear he had everything the ex-watch salesman knew. After thanking Mrs Nolan for her hospitality, they made their excuses and left.

He rang Flynn on the short walk back to his car and was relieved when he got her voicemail. He left her a quick update, and then turned off his phone. He was going to have to do it the hard way and he didn't want any interruptions.

They hadn't even got out of Warwick Bridge when Bradshaw's phone rang. She answered it quietly, then frowned. 'It's for you, Poe,' she said.

Poe pulled over at a bus stop and took the phone from her.

'Poe,' he said.

'Poe, this is DCS Gamble. What the hell do you think you're doing? You're supposed to be on leave.'

Sometimes the best thing to do is to deny everything. This was one of those times. 'Don't know what you're talking about, sir.'

Gamble grunted. 'DS Reid tells me you think you've discovered Tollund Man's identity?'

'Quentin Carmichael, sir. Disappeared about twenty-five years ago.'

'And you think it's linked to the Immolation Man?'

'I do, sir.'

'How?'

Poe didn't have a clue and said as much. Gamble seemed annoyed that he didn't have more. He said, 'And how did you get his name?'

'I've emailed Flynn a full report, sir. I think it would be best coming from her.'

Gamble either didn't realise or didn't care he'd been brushed off. He said, 'I want to make it absolutely clear – you are not to go near any Church officials. Do you understand, Poe? My team will go through the proper channels and set up appropriate interviews if they're needed.'

Poe said nothing.

'Do you hear me, Poe? You don't go near the Church!'

'Sorry, sir, you're breaking up.' He pressed the end-call button and handed the phone back to Bradshaw. She started fiddling with it.

'There's nothing wrong with it, Tilly. I just needed to end the call. It's easier to say things like that sometimes.'

'Oh,' she said. 'What did he say, Poe?'

'Nothing.'

'So, what are we going to do now?'

Poe frowned. He'd always thought that if someone would rather you stopped doing what you were doing, you were probably on the right path, but . . . he didn't want to drag Bradshaw down at the same time. As adorably awkward as she was, she had an important career ahead of her. He told her he would do the next bit on his own.

She refused.

He stared at her, trying to fathom if she really wanted to help, or whether she was blindly following him because of some new-found, misguided sense of loyalty. The only thing he could see was determination. He sighed then thought, *Why not?* He was on leave, what was wrong with taking his new friend round the sights of the Lake District? And if they happened to end up in Keswick, near the Bishop of Carlisle's residence, then so be it . . .

CHAPTER TWENTY-SEVEN

Between 1230 and 2009, the Bishop of Carlisle's official residence had been Rose Castle, near the village of Dalston. A huge and sprawling, culturally significant part of the country's heritage, it had long been considered one of the jewels in the Church's property portfolio. The last bishop, however, had elected to move out, believing it to be inappropriate to live in such opulence when others, including his own parish priests, were living in poverty.

It had made the headlines so Poe knew this without having to look it up. Bradshaw's quick internet search found the bishop's new address. He'd moved into 'Bishop's House' in Keswick. Poe didn't know it, but he recognised the street.

Although he hadn't slept since the day before, he was gaining momentum and no decent detective slept when a case was hot. Twenty minutes into the journey Bradshaw's phone rang. This time it was Flynn warning them away from the Church.

'Tell her I'm driving and don't have hands-free,' he said when Flynn wanted to talk to him. 'I'll call her when I get a signal but we're heading into the National Park for some ice cream and the mountains make coverage a bit thin.'

Poe could hear Flynn swearing through the small speaker. Oh well, couldn't be helped. Anyway, she shouldn't be calling him; he was on leave. It left him with a problem, though: Bradshaw's continued involvement. It was all right him being reckless – he didn't care about the inevitable fallout – but when the big dogs fight, it's the little dogs that get hurt. However, there was no public transport he could put her on and he didn't fancy the two-hour detour back to Shap. He settled for a compromise: he'd take her to Keswick but would drop her off in one of the nicer pubs until he was finished ruining what was left of his career.

He told her.

She said no, folded her arms and refused to acknowledge him until he relented. He tried explaining the potential consequences but she stood firm.

Fair enough, then.

Bradshaw wasn't the most streetwise person in the world, but she was an adult and was allowed to make disastrous decisions along with everyone else. And, as strange as it sounded, they worked well together. Misfits often do, he thought.

Her phone rang.

'It's DI Stephanie Flynn again,' she said, looking at the caller ID.

'Answer it. You don't want to get into trouble.'

She flicked the switch to silent, and put it back in her pocket. 'I don't have a signal.'

Poe flinched. *What had he created . . . ?*

The bishop might have downgraded when he left Rose Castle, but he was hardly slumming it. The unimaginatively named Bishop's House was on Ambleside Road in Keswick town centre. It was an elevated and imposing triple-fronted, slate-faced Lake District building. It sat behind an acre of large garden, which still needed a few years to bed in. Poe could see no drive or obvious place to park so he entered the Keswick on-street parking lottery.

Eventually he found a recently vacated spot on nearby Blencathra Street. He set his parking disc on the dashboard next to a scrap of paper with 'police business' scribbled on it. If the traffic warden was new he might get away with it.

He and Bradshaw made their way back to Ambleside Road, and

walked up the large gravel path to Bishop's House. There was a doorbell and a large black knocker. Poe pressed the bell.

Poe hadn't called ahead, so had no idea if anyone would be in. He didn't know much about the hierarchy of the Church, but he knew being a bishop was a big deal. He imagined they spent a lot of time away on business.

If someone knocked on Poe's door and he didn't answer in ten seconds, he was either out or he was dead, but in this house he was prepared to wait three minutes before giving up. After a minute, he decided he might have more luck with the oversized knocker. He raised it and sent it crashing back against the striking plate.

Poe and Bradshaw looked at each in shock; the noise would have woken the dead. A few seconds later, the large door opened.

A rotund man peered out at them, blinking in the low afternoon sun. He was in his sixties and was wearing a scruffy cardigan. Reading glasses hung from a leather strap around his neck. He smiled at them curiously. Bradshaw had found a recent photograph of the bishop on the way over and Poe knew he was looking at the Right Reverend Nicholas Oldwater.

'You must be Sergeant Poe,' he said. 'I was warned you might visit.' He frowned. 'Although I was told you'd be on your own.'

Before Poe could stop her, Bradshaw stepped forward and curtsied. 'Matilda Bradshaw, your holiness.'

Poe winced but Oldwater laughed and said, 'Nicholas will be fine, Matilda. You'd better come in. Whatever it is, it sounds intriguing, I've never had so much contact with the police. The chief constable's been on the phone twice and someone called Stephanie Finn from the NCA called not fifteen minutes ago.'

'DI Stephanie *Flynn*, Nicholas. She's our line manager at SCAS. That's the Serious Crime Analysis Section,' Bradshaw said. 'We're part of the National Crime Agency, aren't we, Poe?'

Poe nodded. 'We are indeed, Tilly.'

'Well, they all seem very keen on us not talking,' Oldwater said. 'Whatever can it be about?'

He walked them through two rooms and one long hall before they reached his study. He'd been working before they'd interrupted him. A desk lamp was on and several books were open.

He sat back behind his desk and gestured towards the chairs dotted around the room. 'Mrs Oldwater's in London and the housekeeper has gone for the day. I can probably rustle up some coffee if you're thirsty?'

Ordinarily Poe would have declined but he wanted to keep it informal. 'I'll have a coffee please, if that's OK? Tilly?'

'Do you have any fruit tea, Nicholas?'

'I believe Mrs Oldwater enjoys a cup of liquorice tea every now and then. Will that do?'

Bradshaw shook her head, 'No thank you, Nicholas, liquorice gives me diarrhoea.'

Holy hell . . .

The bishop smiled. 'Quite right, young lady. Of course, at my age, I don't really have that sort of problem.'

'That's right, Nicholas. Constipation is a common problem among the elderly,'

Poe stared at her aghast.

'What?' she said, when she saw his expression. 'It is. Thirty per cent of senior citizens have fewer than three bowel movements a week.'

Poe put his head in his hands. He turned to the bishop and said, 'It's sometimes hard to get Tilly to say what she's thinking, Nicholas.'

Luckily Oldwater found it hilarious and he roared with laughter. He said, 'Excellent. Can I get you a hot water instead?'

Tilly said, 'Yes please, Nicholas.'

He left to get their drinks. Poe could hear him laughing to

himself down the corridor. He turned to Bradshaw and gave her a thumbs-up and a way-to-go nod. 'Nice,' he said.

'What is, Poe?'

'Doesn't matter.'

The bishop returned five minutes later. He had a full tray: coffee, hot water and a plate of biscuits. Poe reached for one. Ah . . . rich tea, for when you fancy a biscuit but can't decide between sweet or savoury. He put it on the side of his saucer and concentrated on the excellent coffee.

Poe looked around. There were rare-looking books and manuscripts everywhere. Spilling a cup of coffee in this room could cause irreparable damage; a horrifying thought to Poe, who was in fact holding a cup of coffee. Oldwater saw where he was looking.

'I'm speaking at the House of Lords shortly on what role the Church should play in the refugee crisis. Been boning up on some precedents. See if I can shame the government into doing what's unpopular but right, instead of what's popular but wrong.'

'I'll keep it as short as I can then, Nicholas,' Poe said. 'We're here about Quentin Carmichael.'

'What have you found?'

He didn't say it defensively and Poe knew that putting him on the back foot wouldn't be the best tactic. If he handled it right, the bishop could be an ally. Poe had intended to restrict the outflow of information, but sometimes it was best to go with gut feelings . . .

'I'm going to tell you a story about a missing watch, Nicholas. If possible, I'd like you to hear me out until the end.'

Oldwater smiled. 'Sounds like my evening's not going to be as stuffy as I thought.'

When Poe had finished – with Bradshaw chipping in when there was something technical – Oldwater leaned forwards and steepled his fingers. He asked a few insightful questions and Poe got the impression he'd fully understood everything, and some of what he'd been told had cleared up some long unanswered questions.

'You know it was my predecessor's predecessor who gave Carmichael that watch? A few of the charities he'd worked with had chipped in together for it. The Church wouldn't spend money like that on a trinket.'

Poe nodded.

'And you know both the police and Church investigations found no evidence that he'd embezzled money.'

Poe's working theory was that the Church had covered it up so well that the police hadn't been able to find anything. If the Catholics could cover up child abuse, the Church of England could certainly cover up a bit of theft.

'Ah,' Oldwater said. 'You think we were protecting our reputation?'

'The thought had crossed my mind.'

Oldwater retrieved a slim file from a filing cabinet. He opened it and showed Poe. 'The Church's assets, Detective Sergeant Poe.'

It was a glossy financial spreadsheet. The number at the bottom was staggering. It was in the billions, not millions. He had no idea the Church was that wealthy.

'You're wondering why I showed you that?'

Poe was about to say that it was to demonstrate how powerful his organisation was, but the reply died on his lips. Oldwater didn't seem angry. Perhaps it wasn't that.

'It's not to show you how powerful we are, if that's what you're thinking.'

What was he, a bloody mind reader . . . ?

'Never occurred to me.'

'No, it's to show you how good we are. We have some of the finest accountants in the country. We don't pay our clergy much and occasionally one or two are tempted from the path. My point is, we always find out. And when I tell you that the investigation *was* an investigation and not a cover-up, you can take that as fact. The Church protects its investments jealously.'

Poe looked at the spreadsheet again. It was true, he thought. The very rich seemed to know where every penny was, far more so than people like him. 'OK then, tell me what you know. Tell me why the press thought he'd been embezzling Church money.'

Oldwater seemed to be trying to work things out in his mind. 'Are you really a policeman, Detective Sergeant Poe?'

'I am. Why?'

'Because it appears you haven't read your own files.'

'We're the National Crime Agency, Nicholas. We don't always play well with others. We're having some . . . communication problems at the minute.'

Oldwater nodded. Poe suspected the wily bishop knew there was far more going on than he'd been told, but he seemed keen to help anyway.

'Detective Sergeant Poe, when Mr Carmichael disappeared, he had half a million pounds in his bank account, and it wasn't money he embezzled from us. To this day, no one knows where it came from.'

Poe leaned forward. 'Tell me everything,' he urged.

CHAPTER TWENTY-EIGHT

'Quentin Carmichael was an upstanding member of the Church,' Oldwater said. 'He was ambitious but that's not always a bad thing.' He had retrieved a large manila file from another room, probably a staff file. He read it to refresh his memory then launched into a summary.

'He was a dean?' Poe asked.

Oldwater nodded. 'He had the Derwentshire Deanery. Covers most of Allerdale. A very wealthy part of the county.'

'And the charity work he was given the watch for?'

'Above board and verified. The investigation found that at no point did any of the funds he'd raised pass through any bank account he had access to. He would take on a particular cause and act as a figurehead but leave the details to others.'

Poe paused. 'Any chance he took backhanders from the charities? A sort of "give me some money and I'll raise you ten times the amount" kind of thing?'

'The police investigation considered that. They were all reputable and all had flawless accounts. It wasn't them.'

'Accounts can be faked,' Poe said.

'They can, yes. But there were some serious boys in blue going through them. Are you telling me that over twenty charities all did enough to fool a team of forensic accountants?'

'It doesn't seem plausible, no.'

'But as he was high profile, and the money had been discovered shortly after he'd disappeared, the media put two and two together and came up with a cliché.'

'What happened to the money?' Poe asked. If money were the motive, then following it might lead him to either the killer, or at least Carmichael's connection to the other victims.

'You heard what I said his children claimed?' Oldwater asked.

'That he'd found a calling to do missionary work in Africa?'

'That's it.'

'Did you buy it?' Poe asked.

'I didn't then and I don't now,' Oldwater replied.

'Didn't they say he died of malaria or something?'

'Dengue fever. And there was never any proof.'

'But his assets were released by the courts.'

'They were.' Oldwater sighed. 'Look, you have to see it from the children's point of view. Their father had disappeared and there was a lot of money in the bank. A police investigation couldn't prove it was ill-gotten and, by rights, the law of intestacy applied. His wife had already died so the money would pass to them as soon as he was declared dead.'

'So they faked it?'

'Hard to say. Records indicate that the children got it rough at school when the press went after him. Perhaps it wasn't surprising they came up with a story that explained his disappearance. I don't know if they were thinking as far ahead as getting access to his money.'

'You think they hid his passport and chequebook?'

'They might have. And once they'd lied, they had no choice but to stick with it.'

It would be unusual for three children to keep a lie going when being questioned by the police. More likely one of them had, and then lied to the other two.

'I've read all the statements they made,' Oldwater continued, 'and they were very careful to avoid saying he had left the country. Rather they said they *thought* he'd left the country.'

'And telling the police what you think isn't a crime,' Poe

finished. 'What about the dengue fever, though? Surely that could be checked?'

'A lot of Christian missionaries go to Africa and a lot of them don't come back. War, crime and disease are the big three,' Oldwater explained. 'But if the children were making it up, they were clever.'

'How so?'

'Do you know what dengue fever is, Detective Sergeant Poe?'

He shook his head.

'Well, you only need to know two things. It's an awful way to die and it's highly contagious. In Africa, in those days, anyone who succumbed to a disease like that was immediately cremated.'

'So—'

'So all they needed was a record of an unidentified white male of the right age dying, and they could begin campaigning to have him declared dead. Records out in Africa, particularly in war zones, are virtually non-existent.'

Poe said nothing.

'And don't forget, by that time he'd been missing for years. They applied to the courts, showed some circumstantial evidence, and in 2007 they got a death certificate. The estate was then theirs to do with as they wanted.'

'So what, they just squandered it?'

'Oh, no, nothing like that.'

'What then?'

Oldwater seemed to be coming to some sort of decision. 'You don't strike me as the kind of man who lets things go easily, Sergeant Poe.'

'It's not one of my strong points, Nicholas,' Poe admitted.

'Good,' Oldwater said.

'How so?'

'It's your lucky week,' he grinned. 'Can you get your hands on a suit?'

CHAPTER TWENTY-NINE

By the time Poe had left Bradshaw at Shap Wells, Cumbria was beginning to show its true colours. The weather had changed and an easterly wind was threatening to turn into a gale. Edgar growled at the dark skies but a long walk soon had his tail wagging.

When the wind began rushing through Poe's thin coat he decided he'd better turn back; there was no such thing as bad weather, only bad choices of clothing. As he did so, his phone alerted him to an incoming text. It was from Flynn: I'm on my way to yours, Poe. We need to talk.

There were no prizes for guessing what Flynn wanted, and Poe idly wondered if he had enough time to build a moat round Herdwick Croft to keep her out. The light was already on as he approached. Despite it being his home, he knocked before entering.

Flynn was furious. 'Where the hell have you been?'

Poe walked past her and opened the valve on a gas bottle. After lighting his stove and getting some water on the boil, he turned to her and said, 'What was that? I'm sure you weren't just telling me what I can and can't do when I'm on leave.'

She wasn't fazed, as he knew she wouldn't be. 'Don't give me that shit, Poe. With no authority at all, you went to see a witness.'

'Which one?' Poe asked before he could stop himself.

Luckily Flynn seemed to think he was just trying to wind her up.

'You know fine well who I mean. Francis Sharples rang Carlisle police station asking when they were coming to arrest him.'

Shit . . . he'd forgotten about Sharples. He suppressed a grin.

'It's not funny, Poe! They looked a right set of tits.'

'They are a right set of tits.'

'No, Poe, they aren't. They have an impossible job, and the world's media are second-guessing everything they do. Gamble can't have someone talking to witnesses willy-nilly.'

'But van Zyl—'

'Van Zyl wanted you up here so you could help *strategise*, Poe. So you could think of the things no one else can,' she replied. 'He doesn't want you going rogue. He was on the phone for an hour to Cumbria's chief constable.'

'I'm sorry,' he said. 'You're right; there's no excuse. I should have told someone.'

That seemed to mollify. 'Tell me what you found out. Your voicemail about the watch was a bit vague.'

Poe told her all about his day, although he forgot to mention the subsequent trip to see the bishop; no way could she ignore him disobeying a direct order. Not after he'd gone over her head for the exhumation order. Bradshaw might tell her later – he hadn't told her to keep it a secret – although he hoped she wouldn't. And anyway, he was on leave and Bishop's House was on the tourist trail. Despite her simmering anger, Flynn seemed impressed.

The kettle whistled and they took a break. While his coffee cooled, he took the time to secure all the shutters and make sure everything outside was tied down. He wasn't concerned about Herdwick Croft; it had stood for centuries – builders in the past seemed to understand how to make things properly – and all his modifications were either inside or buried in the ground. He looked up and saw one of the inevitable Herdwick sheep. It was chewing the tough fell grass stoically and seemed untroubled by the gale. And why would it be? The breed was as tough as nails. They'd been known to survive in snowdrifts for weeks by eating their own wool; a little bit of wind wouldn't bother them.

Edgar came out to see what he was doing but soon dived back inside when his ears nearly flapped off. Poe tied the last thing down, a spare gas bottle, and finally he was finished. He went back inside and shut the door.

Flynn was sipping her drink and looking at the board on the wall. Nothing had been added since she'd been there last.

'It's a bit breezy out there,' he said as he took off his coat.

She drained her coffee and put the mug in the small sink. 'So, what's your next play?'

'You sure you want to know?'

'No. But tell me anyway.'

'Tilly and I are going to a charity event with the Bishop of Carlisle.'

Flynn put her head in her hands and groaned.

CHAPTER THIRTY

After he'd driven Flynn back to Shap Wells, Poe tried on his old
work suit. It was frayed, shiny with grease and far too big. He
didn't know how much weight he'd lost since he'd come back to
Cumbria, but the suit that had once been so tight it left him with
flesh wounds was now hanging from him like he was a coat hanger.
He looked like a before-and-after advert for a miracle diet pill, no
doubt due to the hard physical work he'd been doing over the last
year keeping Herdwick Croft viable.

He clearly needed a new suit. Luckily the charity event wasn't
until the following evening. He had a whole day to buy something.
He called Bradshaw to make sure she had a dress.

She told him she hadn't.

'Kendal will have something,' Poe said. 'Pick you up at ten?'

'Yes please, Poe. Can we have lunch out again?'

'Er . . . of course.'

'Good.'

'You talked to DI Flynn?' Poe asked.

'Not yet. We're having tea later.'

'Well, remember if she asks you anything, don't lie.'

'I won't,' she promised.

Despite the weather, which at some point in the night Poe upgraded
from 'breezy' to 'bracing', he slept all the way through. When he
woke, it was as if the storm had been a figment of his imagination.

He opened the window shutters and let in some air. The sun

was out and the sky was a flinty blue. The air was as warm as fresh bread.

He threw on some old clothes and checked outside for damage. He nodded in satisfaction. The croft had survived without a scratch. The sheep from the previous night was still there. It barely bothered to look up from its foraging.

He picked up the file he was compiling and reread the notes he'd made the night before to see if anything popped out with fresh eyes. Nothing did, and he settled on making sure he had a good breakfast. Ordinarily, he and Edgar would have walked across to Shap Wells and eaten there, but he didn't want to bump into Flynn. They'd left on good terms the night before, and he didn't want that to change.

He settled on some good butcher's black pudding, two fresh duck eggs and some buttered toast.

An hour later, he was outside Shap Wells waiting for Bradshaw.

They split up to shop and agreed to meet for lunch. Poe bought a suit in the first shop he entered. He'd considered getting something specifically for the gala, but his new obsession with living frugally persuaded him to get a sensible, machine-washable suit.

With an hour to kill before he was due to meet Bradshaw, Poe popped in to Kendal police station to see Reid.

He wasn't in, and the desk sergeant made it clear he wasn't welcome to come in and chew the fat with his old colleagues. 'Fuck off, Poe' left little room for misinterpretation. Instead, he had a walk around the town; it was a nice day and he was on holiday after all.

Over lunch Bradshaw showed him what she'd bought. The dress was all reds, golds and greens. When he peered closer he saw it was a mosaic of comic-book covers. It would suit her.

'Very nice, Tilly. Very colourful,' he said. He reached into his own bag and threw her a T-shirt. 'Here, I bought you something.'

She opened it up and giggled delightedly when she saw the 'Nerd Power' design. Before long the giggles disappeared and Poe thought he'd fucked up.

'Sorry,' he said softly. 'I thought you'd like it.'

'I love it, Poe!' she said fiercely. She folded it and made sure it was safely at the bottom of her bag. Her superhero dress was on top. Poe could see Spider-Man looking at him.

Tonight was going to be fun . . .

CHAPTER THIRTY-ONE

Poe had never been to the Theatre by the Lake. It was a contemporary building, and although it looked a bit like a local authority office, by using Lake District stone, the theatre had managed to retain a certain amount of charm. The setting made up for the uninspiring building. It was on the edge of Keswick, near the shores of Derwentwater, and sat under the Western Fells. Poe had always thought the fells around Keswick, Grasmere and Ambleside were just a bit too perfect, almost as if someone had photoshopped them into the background. He preferred the wilder fells further west and further south. The tourists he saw on the fells around Shap were either seriously lost or seriously keen.

It was a very pretty setting, though.

The good and the great of Cumbria – or at least those who thought they were – had descended on the theatre in droves. Half of the men were in black tie and the other half were in a dazzling display of modern suits. Blues, greens, even purple. One man was wearing a fez.

The arty-farty set, Poe thought, *always trying to be different, always looking the same.*

Despite the crowd's eclectic dress sense, he and Bradshaw stood out like they were backlit. Poe knew he was underdressed. His suit looked cheap because it was cheap. Even the man checking people's invites was wearing something more elegant.

Bollocks to them. He was hunting a serial killer, not trying to make friends.

Bradshaw was faring a bit better. Her comic-book dress had the advantage of making her look a bit quirky. And because she'd made an effort with her hair – it was now lying gently on her shoulders rather than being pulled back into a severe ponytail – and had discarded her ever-present Harry Potter glasses in favour of contact lenses, she was drawing admiring glances from some of the men. She was oblivious to it.

Poe's eyes focused on a figure in the distance. 'Heads up,' he said to Bradshaw, 'the bishop's here.'

When Nicholas Oldwater had said it was Poe's lucky week, he'd been referring to a gala dinner to raise money for disadvantaged children in the old county of Westmorland. The evening was being hosted by the children of Quentin Carmichael.

It was how he'd answered Poe's question about what they'd done with the money: they had created the Carmichael Foundation.

'In 2007 the children each took one hundred thousand pounds and the rest was put into the not-for-profit foundation,' he'd said.

'Generous of them,' Poe had acknowledged.

'Not really. In 2007 anything over three hundred thousand pounds was subject to forty per cent inheritance tax. By taking a hundred thousand each and putting the rest into their foundation, they avoided paying any tax at all.'

'And I'm assuming they're all on the board. Directors as well probably.'

'With nice yearly salaries to boot,' Oldwater finished. 'You can't blame them, I suppose. Their father had dealt them a pretty rotten hand. They were only protecting what was theirs as best they could. And the foundation does do some good.'

The Right Reverend Bishop of Carlisle was having a night off, as he wasn't in Church attire. He was wearing an old-style suit but still looked twenty times smarter than Poe.

Oldwater winked when he saw them, and if he were disappointed by what they were wearing, he didn't show it. He approached them and said, 'Typical ex-Black Watch, always punctual.'

Interesting. He'd been checking up on him. And he'd still turned up. Poe wondered if he had an ally.

Removing a gilt-edged invitation card from his inside pocket, Oldwater said, 'Shall we?'

The event was a celebration of the first ten years of the foundation. Poe didn't know how the disadvantaged children of Westmorland would have felt if they could have seen the spread of canapés and champagne laid on for everyone, but it certainly made him feel uncomfortable.

'Obscene, isn't it?' Oldwater said.

Poe nodded.

'It's not as bad as it seems. These people,' he waved his arms, 'won't part with their money if they haven't been pampered. It's an old charity trick. Make them think the organisation has so much money, only large donations will be noticed. The more they spend on vol-au-vents and caviar, the bigger their return.'

If that was how it worked, then that was how it worked. Charity had never been a big part of Poe's life. He had a standing order to the Royal British Legion and always gave away his clothes to the local Oxfam shop, but he'd never attended anything like this.

Oldwater said, 'I have a few hands to shake and then I'm giving a speech. Why don't we meet at the bar and have a whisky afterwards? I can introduce you to anyone you want to meet then. In the meantime, I suggest you take advantage of the Carmichaels' hospitality for an hour or so.'

CHAPTER THIRTY-TWO

Poe's experience at the buffet was dismal. The Carmichaels had laid on food that he neither understood nor liked; as far as he was concerned, eating oysters was one step away from eating salty phlegm, and lobsters were nothing more than massive prawns. With the vegetarian options being equally pretentious, he and Bradshaw decided to take advantage of the free bar instead. Poe had a pint of Cumberland Ale and Bradshaw had a glass of sparkling water.

Drinks in hand, they wandered through the theatre. Most areas appeared to be open. There was a podium set up on the stage in the auditorium. To the left and right, along the walls, were linen-covered tables. People taking donations staffed the tables on the left, and they were doing a steady trade. The tables on the right had display cabinets extolling the virtues of Quentin Carmichael and of the foundation established in his honour.

Poe walked over to the left and picked up a donation envelope. There was a section for him to write his postcode; they would get tax relief on anything inside if he did. Something called the Gift Aid programme. He didn't write anything. He didn't have a postcode and he didn't want one. He slipped a twenty-pound note inside and sealed it. He left the name blank. A man in a tuxedo saw his donation and looked him up and down.

'Problem?' Poe said. He stared at him until the man reddened and backed down.

Prick.

He sensed someone else looking at him from across the room.

He was about to give them the same treatment, when he recognised who it was.

'Shit,' he muttered.

'What is it, Poe?' asked Bradshaw.

'It's Cumbria's chief constable.'

'Oh,' she said, 'So what?'

'He hates me.'

'Wow, what are the odds?'

Whoa . . . who was this sassy girl? Bradshaw had just taken the piss; the first time she had. He grinned to show he didn't mind. 'He's a spite-filled fool. Wanted me to stay in Cumbria and tried to block me joining the NCA.' He paused. 'Bollocks, he's coming over.'

The chief constable walked like a man badly in need of a stool softener. He was in full uniform – including medals Poe was sure he hadn't earned – and carried his hat under his arm. His hair was thinning and subject to a criminal comb-over. He had a drinker's nose and his upturned chin resembled a jester's boot. His name was Leonard Tapping and he had all the charm of an East German border guard.

'Poe,' he said.

'Leonard,' Poe replied.

His nostrils flared. 'That's *Chief Constable* to you.'

Poe could have said he wasn't his chief any more, but decided not to have a fight. He put his new-found maturity down to Bradshaw's influence.

'What the hell are you doing at an event like this?' Tapping asked. Before Poe had a chance to respond, he added, 'I thought the Carmichaels had standards.'

'Obviously not,' Poe replied. He took a sip of his pint and said, 'Tilly and I are here as guests.'

Bradshaw offered her hand but Tapping ignored it.

'Which moron invited you, Poe? I've a good mind to have a word with them.'

'Feel free, sir,' Poe said. He turned to Bradshaw. 'Tilly, could you see if the Bishop of Carlisle's free?'

The colour drained from Tapping's face.

She nodded, 'May I tell him what it's about, Poe?'

'Certainly. You can say that the Chief Constable of Cumbria wants to have a word with him.'

Tapping paled even further. He glanced at Bradshaw then turned back to Poe. 'You wouldn't dare!' he hissed. 'And you were told not to approach the bishop!'

'Oh, was that what DCS Gamble's message was? It was a bad signal, sir.'

Bradshaw began walking towards the bishop.

'The Bishop of Carlisle has the ear of the archbishop doesn't he, sir? I wonder how he'll feel about you calling him a moron?'

Tapping's jaw tightened.

'And doesn't the archbishop sit on the advisory board for the Met's vacant deputy commissioner position?'

Tapping's ambitions were well known. They didn't include staying in Cumbria.

'Stop!' he cried. People looked at them.

Bradshaw looked at Poe for guidance. He said nothing.

'Please,' Tapping whined.

'Tilly,' Poe said.

'Yes, Poe?'

'After you've asked him to come over, can you get me another pint of Cumberland while you're near the bar?'

'Of course, Poe.' She turned and made a beeline for the bishop who was momentarily standing on his own.

In silence they watched her approach Nicholas Oldwater. She gently tapped him on his arm and he turned. He bent down to hear what she had to say and they both looked at Poe and Tapping. Poe waved. Tapping didn't. Bradshaw and Oldwater began walking over. It wasn't a quick process. Everyone wanted to talk to the bishop.

'Fuck you, Poe,' Tapping muttered under his breath. 'Fuck you very much.'

'I reckon you have about thirty seconds,' Poe said.

'Thirty seconds for what?' He wasn't trying to hide his panic.

'To convince me,' Poe replied.

'Convince you of what, man?' Tapping couldn't tear his eyes away from the approaching bishop.

'Not to tell the bishop you insulted his guests and called him a moron.'

'How?' he snapped.

'I want back on the Immolation Man case.'

Two more seconds. The bishop got closer.

'OK!'

'Tonight,' Poe said. 'I want a phone call from my DI telling me that Cumbria has had a rethink. Same access as before.'

Tapping gritted his teeth. 'Fine.'

'I'd smile if I was you, Leonard. The bishop's very influential, you know . . .'

'Well, that was fun,' Poe said to Bradshaw. The bishop had just left to go over his speech, and Tapping was making his phone call.

'Come on,' Poe said, 'let's go and see if we can learn something about the Carmichaels. By the end of the night I want to have spoken to all three of them.'

That was easier said than done. Notwithstanding the Bishop of Carlisle, the Carmichaels were the stars of the show. As soon as one sycophant finished talking to them, another two took their place. While they waited for an opportunity to present itself, they idly walked along the right-hand side of the auditorium. The side with the display cabinets.

Starting at the end furthest from the stage, they worked their way along. Whoever had arranged the display had done it chron-ologically and Poe realised he'd started at the wrong end. The first item he read was the invitation card for that evening. The next few cabinets seemed to be the Carmichaels posing with various dignitaries and C-list celebrities, holding oversized cheques or champagne flutes.

Poe had almost finished the most recent decade when he felt a polite tug at his elbow. It was the bishop.

'Sergeant Poe, can I introduce you to Jane Carmichael?'

She was a tall woman in her forties. Her blonde hair was piled high on her head, beehive style, and her understated gown probably cost more than Herdwick Croft.

Carmichael smiled politely and offered her hand, not in the standard vertical position, but palm down as if she were royalty. Poe resisted the urge to bow. He lightly shook her fingers. She ignored Bradshaw, who wandered off, oblivious to the snub.

'Charmed,' Carmichael said. 'What brings you to my event, Sergeant Poe?'

Poe didn't answer. He was watching Bradshaw.

Carmichael coughed. She clearly didn't like being ignored, but that was a burden with which she'd have to learn to live. Bradshaw was staring at something in the display cabinet and her face had turned ashen. She turned and looked at him.

She'd seen something.

'What is it, Washington?' Oldwater asked.

'Excuse me,' Poe said and walked off to join Bradshaw. The bishop followed him.

'What's up, Tilly?' Poe asked as soon as he reached her. His phone rang. He looked at the caller ID. It was Flynn. The chief constable had kept his side of the bargain. He switched the BlackBerry to silent.

Bradshaw couldn't tear her eyes away from a photograph in the cabinet. It was of a boat, one of the steamers that ran up and down the more touristy lakes by the looks of it. Poe leaned in and studied it. He frowned. He couldn't see what had got Bradshaw so rattled.

The bishop leaned in to look as well.

'What's in the photograph, Tilly?' Poe asked. 'Tell me what you see.'

'Look, Poe.' She pointed, but it wasn't the photograph she wanted him to look at. It was the invitation card underneath. It was for another charity event, a boat ride round Ullswater. It pre-dated the foundation, and was probably one of the last Quentin Carmichael had arranged.

Poe leaned in again and read it. It was what today's invitation would have looked like if it had been printed – Poe looked at the date – twenty-six years ago. It was for a charity auction. The beneficiary was a local children's home and the name of the event was called, 'Are You Feeling Lucky?' It was the kind of charitable event held up and down the country. A self-catered bash where businesses donate things and rich people bid on them. There was the usual mix of dinner for two at posh restaurants, weekends away, that kind of thing. Nothing that got Poe's heart racing.

The card said, 'By Invitation Only'.

'What is it, dear girl?' Oldwater asked.

And then, as if the clouds had just parted and the sun had shone through, realisation dawned on Poe. He knew what Bradshaw was looking at.

It was the title, 'Are You Feeling Lucky?' He'd read it the first time without *seeing* it.

'Holy hell,' Poe whispered. He'd expected stilted conversation and snobbery at the gala; instead he'd found something else entirely.

'What is it, Washington? What have you seen?' Nicholas Oldwater asked.

'Everything, Nicholas,' Poe replied quietly. 'I've seen everything.'

Because 'Are You Feeling Lucky?' didn't end with a question mark.

It ended with a percontation point.

CHAPTER THIRTY-THREE

Poe had assumed his discovery of the victim inside Quentin Carmichael's coffin would be his bridge to the truth. He was wrong. Regardless of the obstacles he'd faced, in Poe's opinion, the Immolation Man had pointed him towards the Kendal graveyard. He probably hadn't expected Poe to get there so quickly, but he had expected him to get there.

Up until that evening, Poe was convinced everything they'd discovered had been orchestrated, but he didn't care how clever the Immolation Man was; Bradshaw's discovery of the percontation point on the twenty-six-year-old invitation wasn't part of his plan. And if it weren't, then for the first time in the investigation, the Immolation Man wasn't in full control. Poe wasn't yet sure if the Immolation Man had made a mistake, but if he hadn't, he'd come close.

Every document in every display case was now evidence and he asked the chief constable to use his authority and declare it a crime scene. While Tapping flapped about achieving nothing, Jane Carmichael called her brother Duncan over and shouted that Poe was trying to ruin their evening.

He was a fleshy man with a pouchy face.

'Do you know who I am?' he said.

Poe bristled. He knew he shouldn't, but he turned to Bradshaw. 'Tilly, can you call the mental health team? We have someone here who doesn't know who they are.'

'I will, Poe.' Out of the corner of his eye he saw her remove her tablet and turn it on.

'Tilly.'

'Yes, Poe?'

'Put your tablet away.'

'OK, Poe.'

The three Carmichael children – by then Patricia had joined them – protested Poe's intrusion on their big day. He wouldn't budge.

'Damn it, sir! You are a rank bad hat!' said Duncan Carmichael.

Poe doubted it would be the worst thing he'd be called that night. He tried to call Flynn. He pointed at his phone and said, 'Shh.'

'Oh, I'm sick of this obnoxious little man!' Patricia Carmichael complained. 'I'm asking Nicholas to put an end to this nonsense.'

'I'm here at his invitation,' Poe replied. He still hadn't managed to get through to Flynn.

That didn't stop them marching on the bishop. Oldwater did his best to placate them but it was clear he was on Poe's side.

It seemed he trusted his judgement.

In the end the chief constable did too. He might have been an isolated careerist, but he wasn't stupid. When Poe told him that the Immolation Man's identity might be hidden among the display cases, and that being seen in the company of the Carmichaels might not be politically advantageous for too much longer, he did his job and rang for uniformed backup. When the Carmichaels continued to make a fuss, he threatened to arrest them.

He sidled up to Poe and whispered, 'You'd better be fucking right, Poe.'

Through the glass cases Bradshaw began photographing the items. It meant they had their own records and weren't relying on Gamble to share everything. It didn't matter; Poe knew it was all going to come down to that one obscure punctuation mark.

؟

It was innocuous, and in the context of a charitable auction, completely appropriate. But . . . the last percontation point they'd found had led them to dark places. Poe knew this one would too.

He didn't know how easy it'd be to uncover information on a twenty-six-year-old charitable event, but, if it were online, Bradshaw would find it. He doubted the Carmichaels were going to be much help; potentially they had much to lose. In any case, they'd been children at the time.

A gruff voice made him turn. DCS Gamble was now on the scene. Reid was with him. Flynn would be there soon. Gamble ignored Poe as he strode over to his chief constable. Poe couldn't hear what was being said, but judging by his flamboyant gesticulation, Gamble didn't get whatever it was he was after. He stormed across to Poe.

'I don't know how you've managed it, Poe, but the chief says that you should be given full access again.' His lips were pressed together.

For a few seconds the two men glared at each other. Poe knew Gamble's heart wasn't in it, though. He was angry but a large part of that was misdirected; his own officers shouldn't have been so far behind this. Poe didn't want to fall out with the man so a peace offering was the right move.

'Sir, as far as I'm concerned this is your investigation,' he said. 'I'm happy to help in any way I can, but I would urge you to consider using SCAS as it was designed; to offer analytical support and advice.'

'Fine,' Gamble replied. He gestured for Reid to approach. 'Sergeant Reid, you're back on SCAS liaison, but this time do it properly.'

'Sir,' Reid acknowledged with a deadpan face. That Poe had exhumed a corpse and gate-crashed a gala had hardly been his fault, but he was wise enough not to protest.

Bradshaw interrupted. 'Everything's scanned, Poe.'

He nodded. 'Let's get out of here then.'

'Where to?' Reid asked.

'The pub,' Poe replied. 'I need a drink.'

The Oddfellows Arms in Keswick was still serving food – real food this time – and they grabbed a quiet table in the paved beer garden that overlooked one of the town's car parks. Poe ordered giant Yorkshire puddings filled with lamb stew for himself and Reid, and a vegetable lasagne for Bradshaw.

'What do we need to know next?' Poe asked.

Reid said, 'I don't know what we know now, mate.'

'Fair point,' Poe said. For the next half an hour he and Bradshaw ran through the sequence of recent events. By the time they'd finished, the food had arrived, and rather than spit gravy at each other, Poe called a halt until they'd eaten.

After they'd refreshed their glasses, Bradshaw, who'd been on her tablet since they'd sat down, said, 'There were two companies running cruises on Ullswater twenty-six years ago. One of them ceased trading a few years ago. The father died – of natural causes before you ask – and the children didn't want to keep it going so it folded. The other's still going strong and has been for the last one hundred and fifty years.'

Poe said, 'OK. If we assume that the cruise is important, then both companies need to be checked out.'

'I'll do that,' Reid said. 'I can access Eden District Council's licence department and look into it. If anything needs chasing up I'll put a couple of detectives on it.'

Poe nodded. He'd hoped Reid would take on that task. It would be easier for a Cumbrian to do it.

'You think something happened on that cruise? An accident maybe?' Reid said. 'Rich men are never that bright when they've done something stupid. Their first thoughts invariably turn to covering it up.'

175

Poe shook his head. 'No, if something happened, then the per-contation point on the invitation means it was planned. At least one person knew about it in advance.'

'Quentin Carmichael?' Reid asked.

'Probably. Not definitely.'

'Best guess?' Reid asked.

'Most murders have their roots in money or sex, and at the minute, I see no reason to look any further. Quentin Carmichael died with almost half a million pounds in his bank account. Money that was never accounted for.'

'So . . .?'

'So, I think we need to go and speak to someone at this children's home. See if they actually received anything from this auction or not.'

CHAPTER THIRTY-FOUR

It was the morning after the night before. Bradshaw, Reid and Flynn met Poe at Herdwick Croft at eight. Flynn was leaving for Hampshire later that morning; there was a political storm brewing over Quentin Carmichael. Unsurprisingly, his children were kicking up a stink and trying to stop the investigation going anywhere near their father. They had connections in Westminster – some of whom were equally as keen to preserve the good Carmichael name lest they were tarred with the same brush – and some junior minister had summoned the NCA director. He wanted Flynn at his side.

She wanted to take Bradshaw back down to SCAS but she'd refused. 'We can't justify the expense of a hotel room, Tilly,' Flynn had argued. 'You can do just as much good back at SCAS.'

'I can stay with Poe and Edgar, can't I, Poe?' she'd countered.

Poe was spared having to explain to Bradshaw why perhaps it wasn't such a good idea for a naive young woman to stay with a cantankerous middle-aged man, when Flynn rolled her eyes and caved. 'OK. A few more nights.' In the meantime, she asked them to carry on, and to try not to upset everyone they met.

Poe grinned wryly and said he couldn't promise.

Bradshaw had been up half the night on the internet and she'd found somewhere to start. The children's home named as the beneficiary on the invitation card had been called Seven Pines and it no longer existed. Although it had been owned by a Cumbrian faith charity, like all children's homes, the local authority had over-seen it.

The fact that it no longer existed had raised Poe's suspicions, but when he spoke to the duty social worker at Children's Services in Carlisle, she'd said, 'Cumbria hardly has any homes now, Sergeant Poe. Most of our children are placed with foster families. Better value and a far better environment for them. If a Cumbrian child can't be placed and does need a home, they'll usually go out of county. Costs a fortune, though.'

'OK,' Poe said. He was learning something. 'And if I wanted to speak to someone about Seven Pines and a charity event that was held to raise funds for it, who would be the best person to speak to?'

'Before my time,' she said. But she wasn't a negative-ninny and promised to speak to someone who'd been there longer. She took his number and said she'd get back to him.

While they waited, Poe put a jug of strong coffee on the table and they all took a cup, even Bradshaw. Reid had brought dough-nuts, and a bag of freshly ground coffee to replace what they'd used in the last few days. Poe smelled them and sighed. They were nice beans. Guatemalan and hand-roasted by the shop Poe used. He thanked him although it hadn't been necessary; never in his life had he run out of coffee. His reserves had reserves. Still, it was a nice gesture. He put it to the front of his stash. He'd open it next.

Along with the coffee and doughnuts, Reid had also brought a copy of the Quentin Carmichael file and they spent half an hour familiarising themselves with its contents. Nothing stood out and Poe was happy the original investigation hadn't missed anything obvious. The money was unaccounted for but there was no evidence of illegality. Bradshaw scanned everything into her tablet so they didn't need to carry the paper file with them.

Reid's phone rang. He looked at the screen and held his finger to his lips and whispered, 'It's Gamble,' before answering, 'DS Reid.'

Poe was trying to eavesdrop when his own phone rang. The

number began with 01228: Carlisle's area code. He pressed the green telephone icon to receive the call.

'DS Poe?'

'Speaking.'

'My name's Audrey Jackson and I am the assistant director for Looked After Children. I gather you spoke to one of my duty social workers a while ago. You were asking about the Seven Pines Children's Home?'

Poe confirmed he was.

'Would you mind telling me what this is about?'

'It's come up in a murder investigation.'

'I see,' she said. It was obvious she hadn't been expecting that. 'I gather you're not with Cumbria police.'

After explaining that he was with the National Crime Agency but attached to a Cumbrian murder investigation, she said, 'Are you mobile? Because if you can get to the Civic Centre in Carlisle at midday I can meet with you. I'll have retrieved the home's records from archives by then.'

'Will that include the financial records?' he asked. If it did, there could be a paper trail to follow.

'I've not seen them. But I'll get onto finance when I put the phone down and make sure we get records going back . . .?'

'Twenty-six years,' he answered.

By the time he'd finished with Audrey Jackson, Reid's call was over. 'That was the boss,' he said. 'The body found in Carmichael's coffin has been identified as Sebastian Doyle, sixty-eight years old. Everyone thought he'd moved abroad to be with his family in Oz, which was why he hadn't been reported missing.'

'He fit the same profile?' Poe asked.

'That's all I have. Gamble said he'd keep me updated through-out the day.'

Poe didn't respond. Another victim, another older man and, at the minute, all roads were leading to Quentin Carmichael's charity cruise. He stood up. 'Come on, we'll need to get a shift on if we want to make that midday meeting.'

CHAPTER THIRTY-FIVE

It didn't matter how many charity abseils it hosted, Carlisle's Civic Centre remained the most soulless building in Cumbria. Poe believed that uninspiring surroundings led to uninspired thinking, and it didn't get any more uninspiring than the twelve-storey tower block in which Cumbria's leaders worked. In the county that inspired William Wordsworth and Beatrix Potter, Poe found it shocking that planning permission had been granted to the monstrous eyesore that overlooked the city's historic quarter. The imminent plans to knock it down and start somewhere else couldn't come fast enough.

They were shown into Committee Room C, a characterless room that contained nothing that could cause offence: just an oblong table, plastic chairs and some Perspex-covered posters promoting the council's mission statement. The ceiling light was dim and flickering. Tea and coffee had been arranged for them, along with some biscuits. Reid opened a three-pack of chocolate bourbons and they had one each.

Audrey Jackson arrived promptly at midday. A bespectacled man was with her. Poe introduced himself and everyone else did the same. When Jackson sat, he noticed she did so on the other side of the table. The man took a seat beside her.

The other thing he noticed was that neither had any records with them.

The man with Jackson began. 'My name is Neil Evans, and I'm with the council's legal services, Sergeant Poe. I must insist that you tell me what Seven Pines Children's Home has to do with a murder investigation.'

'I told Mrs Jackson over the phone,' Poe replied.

'And now you're going to have to tell me, I'm afraid,' he said. 'Even though it wasn't one of our homes, Cumbria County Council has a duty of care for every child housed in Seven Pines, and although they're now all over twenty-one, they remain entitled to certain services; one of which is confidentiality.'

'This is a murder investigation,' Poe said.

'That may be so,' Jackson cut in. 'But there's still a stigma attached to care leavers, Sergeant Poe. We've had it before. Rather than look for real evidence, the police simply round up all the kids in our care and see which one most fits the suspect profile.'

Poe didn't respond. It was probably true.

'So, if you're on nothing more than a fishing expedition, Mr Evans will ensure we aren't bullied into giving out the names of our children.'

Poe summarised what they knew and how they'd ended up at the Civic Centre with the assistant director of Looked After Children. He ended with, 'And I have no interest in the children who stayed at Seven Pines, Mrs Jackson. At the moment, I am only interested in that cruise, and the only person we know who was definitely on it is dead. Quentin Carmichael, have you heard of him?'

From the looks that flashed between them, Poe knew they had. Neither tried to deny it.

Evans said, 'I'm sorry, Sergeant Poe, but you haven't passed the reasonableness threshold. I cannot expose the council to the risk of you seeing our records. I appreciate your candour, and I will note that at no point have you asked to see anything to do with the home's former occupants, but if you want to see these records, you'll need a warrant.'

Ordinarily, Poe would have been punching the wall, but Evans had a point. He said, 'If I were to get a warrant, would it be worth my while?'

Evans stared at him. Almost imperceptibly, he nodded.

Poe turned to Reid. 'How long will it take your lot to get one?'

'You've seen them in action. Gamble's a good SIO but he's thorough. He won't rush a decision.'

It was what Poe had expected. He had neither the time nor the inclination to wait for Gamble to keep catching up. He left the room and dialled Flynn.

She answered immediately. It sounded as though she was driving.

Poe updated her on the legal roadblock they'd just hit and how he thought there might be something in the records worth seeing.

'Steph, I need a search warrant and I can't wait for Gamble. Can you get van Zyl to authorise one? If it's faxed to the Civic Centre in Carlisle, I'll get DS Reid to march it straight over to the magistrates' court. They're on the other side of the road so it'll be a two-minute job to get it signed.'

'And they definitely won't release them without a warrant?'

'Nope. They're scared of the legal repercussions.'

'What repercussions?'

'That's what I'm wondering,' Poe said.

'Leave it to me,' she said.

Poe returned to the small conference room and explained what was happening. Evans agreed to wait.

'The magistrates will be more open to a Cumbrian cop, Kylian. You OK going downstairs and waiting for it to come in?'

'You want me to tell Gamble?'

Poe shook his head. He wanted first crack at whatever was in those files. 'We'll tell him if we find something.'

'He's going to be furious,' Reid said, '. . . again.'

'Yep,' Poe nodded. He didn't care.

Neither did Reid, apparently. He left to wait by the fax machine in reception. Poe knew that within five minutes he'd have the receptionists eating out of his hand. They'd be falling over themselves to bring him drinks and cake. By the time the fax arrived he'd know all about them: their husband's foibles, their children's dreams and where they'd be having a cheeky wine after work if he fancied joining them . . .

Poe asked some general questions about the home.

'If it was a charity that ran it, why do you have the records?'

'It's the law,' Evans replied, feeling he was on safer ground. 'Officially we don't buy bed spaces from privately run homes; we go into partnership with them. That means all funding has to be signed off at director level.'

'It's a way of ensuring the council remains accountable for their waifs and strays,' Jackson added. 'We can't just buy services and forget about them. We remain heavily involved.'

It made sense.

'Who was in charge twenty-six years ago?' Poe asked.

Jackson looked at Evans. He nodded.

'We seconded a woman called Hilary Swift. In those days the manager of a children's home had to have a social work qualification.'

'She still with you?'

'Retired.'

Poe had expected more: either an endorsement of her attributes or a damnation of her failings. It was rare to mention an ex-colleague and then leave it hanging. There was something he wasn't being told.

Jackson hadn't got to senior management by gossiping, though. She folded her arms and refused to elaborate.

Evans helped her. 'Employees and ex-employees are entitled to the same level of protection, Sergeant Poe.'

The door opened and Reid walked in. He passed a document to Poe, who examined it. It was a warrant to recover and seize all records pertaining to the Seven Pines Children's Home going back thirty years. He handed it to Evans, who removed his spectacles and replaced them with some readers. He studied it, then said, 'All in order. Now, I have everything in my office because I assumed we'd get to this point. I'll need a hand carrying it over if I can borrow someone . . .'

'Kylian?' Poe asked.

'On it.' Reid stood, 'Lead the way, Mr Evans.'

Before leaving the room, Evans turned and spoke to Jackson. 'Audrey, I am fine if you want to talk to Sergeant Poe now.'

Poe looked at Jackson. She unfolded her arms.

'Have I got a tale to tell you, Sergeant Poe,' she said.

CHAPTER THIRTY-SIX

'Hilary Swift resigned,' Audrey Jackson said. 'And it wasn't a resignation "after years of dedicated service". It was more like a "If you don't resign, you will be sacked" kind of thing. And it all began with that charity event.'

Poe's heart started beating that little bit faster. He leaned forward. 'The one on Ullswater?'

Bradshaw flicked through the images on her tablet until she found the clearest one of the invitation they'd found at the gala. She passed it over.

Jackson barely glanced. 'That's it.'

'You sure?'

'I am. And the reason I know is because I was one of the investigating social workers after the incident.'

Poe looked at her in confusion. 'Why would a social worker be doing the investigating? If misappropriation of funds was suspected, surely the council's financial or legal team would be better placed?'

Her brow furrowed. 'I know nothing about the finances, Sergeant Poe,' she replied. 'Although I haven't seen the file, Mr Evans tells me that there was never a suspicion of any wrongdoing. My understanding is that Seven Pines did all right out of it.'

Poe frowned. His theory had just taken a dent.

But when one door closes . . .

'No, I was involved in investigating what happened *after* the event.'

'Explain,' Poe said.

Jackson said, 'What you won't know, because it doesn't say so on the invitation, is that not only was the event for Seven Pines, it was hosted by Seven Pines.'

Bradshaw began flicking through her exhibit photographs. She looked at Poe and shook her head.

Jackson continued, 'And what I mean is that Hilary Swift was heavily involved in setting it up. Because it was a self-catered event – they basically hired the boat for the evening and did everything else themselves – four of the boys from the home were there working as waiters to cut down on costs. Fetching fresh drinks and plates of canapés for their guests, that type of thing.'

'Sounds like child abuse,' Poe said.

'Not really. The home did this type of thing a few times a year and it was a bit of a racket for the kids really.'

'Why is that, Audrey?' Bradshaw asked.

'Because they knew the more cute and helpless they looked, the more tips they'd get. Those kids were streetwise, and they knew how to tug on heartstrings. When I spoke to Hilary Swift afterwards, she said she reckoned the boys had each cleared more than five hundred pounds.'

'In tips?' Poe exclaimed. Twenty-six years ago, that was a staggering amount for a child.

'In tips,' Jackson confirmed. 'And I suppose when you think about it, it's not an absurd concept. The guests were all there to support the home; why not give to the boys directly?'

'I can think of a few reasons,' Poe said. 'How old were they?'

'Ten and eleven,' she replied.

'There you go then.' He turned to Bradshaw. 'How much was five hundred quid worth twenty-six years ago, Tilly?'

She searched and said, 'According to the Bank of England's inflation calculator, almost two thousand pounds, Poe.'

Poe turned to Jackson, 'How many kids, especially those from deprived backgrounds, can handle suddenly being given the best part of two grand?'

'It's kind of hard when you make my argument for me.'

'What happened?'

'What do you think?'

Drugs, booze. Nothing good. Poe thought things through. He may have started with money as the motive but he wasn't blinkered to everything else; lines of enquiry rarely followed a straight line. If the investigation took him away from where he was expecting it to go, so be it.

'I'm going to need to speak to them, Mrs Jackson,' he said. 'See if they can shed any light on what happened that night. I'm assuming their names will be in the file?'

'That's going to be a bit harder than you think, Sergeant.'

'How so?'

'Because, Sergeant Poe, the very next day they all bought train tickets to London and, apart from some postcards to Hilary early on, no one has heard from them since.'

CHAPTER THIRTY-SEVEN

Poe was gathering his thoughts, when Reid and Evans returned. They were carrying a stack of files.

Reid saw Poe's expression and said, 'What's up?'

Poe remained tight-lipped. He wasn't prepared to venture new theories in front of strangers. Ignoring Reid's question, he addressed Jackson and said, 'What happened? I'm assuming that's why there was an investigation?'

'Partly. Some of the men on the boat said that the boys had been drinking. That they were taking sips of everything they were bringing from the bar. It was a game, I think. See who could get the most drunk.'

Poe hadn't been a shrinking violet in his youth; he knew keeping children away from free booze was a fight no one could win. 'And that was a no-no, I take it?'

'An absolute no-no,' Jackson said. 'It's the main difference between being looked after by the state and being looked after by a family. The state has no discretion whatsoever. If the legal age of drinking is eighteen, then no one has the authority to allow, facilitate or even turn a blind eye to it.'

It was a fair point. The state couldn't have rogue foster carers doing whatever they wanted. Turn a blind eye to alcohol and you might turn a blind eye to cannabis or the age of consent. 'And Hilary Swift didn't stop them?'

'She wasn't there. She should have been; our regulations are clear, no unsupervised activities.'

'So . . .'

'So why wasn't she? I can assure you that it formed part of our investigation, Sergeant Poe. She said her daughter came down with a sudden fever, and as half the boys were on the cruise that night, there were fewer staff at the house to call up for cover. She said in one of the numerous interviews we had with her that the men on the boat were the pillars of the community and the boys had never been in any danger.'

Reid said, 'Sounds like bollocks.'

'It did to us, Sergeant Reid,' Jackson said. 'That and the drinking forced Hilary Swift's hand in the end. Children *do* run away from homes and institutions, and occasionally they manage to evade the authorities until they're of age, but we have processes to minimise the risk of that happening as much as we can.'

'You called it in?' Poe asked.

'Well, not me obviously, but yes, it was called in,' she replied. 'There was a police investigation, but for us, in those days, it wasn't exactly Missing White Girl Syndrome. Mr and Mrs Middle Class's child goes walkabout and everyone panics, but when it was one of ours we got little more than a "Well, what do you expect? That's what they do."'

Poe knew she was right. Although the police had tightened up on children missing from care, he shuddered to think how many had slipped through the net. He shuddered even more when he thought about all the predators out there waiting for children like the boys from Seven Pines. For their sake, he hoped they were alive, well and thriving. He'd recently read that a child forced into prostitution at the age of sixteen would have made a pimp over two hundred thousand pounds before they were too old to attract punters. And with blowjobs costing as little as twenty quid in London, that was an awful lot of perverts to service before their youth had depreciated enough for them to be cast aside.

Reid said, 'I remember reading about those boys, actually.

The investigating officers took it seriously. Their train tickets had been bought for the first train out of Carlisle the day after the cruise. Cumbria contacted the Met and asked them to look out for them.'

'And we contacted all thirty-four councils in London,' Jackson added. 'Told them we were missing four boys, and if they showed up asking for assistance we were to be contacted immediately. A few months after they'd run off, Hilary got postcards from them. Said they were loving London. It didn't mean the search was called off but it did ease the urgency somewhat.'

'That's it?' Bradshaw asked. 'That can't be it, Poe. Can it?'

'Children in care don't always make good decisions, Tilly,' Poe explained. 'Sometimes they put themselves at risk. There's only so much people like Ms Jackson here can do.'

Jackson nodded. 'We assumed they'd pop up again at some point but they never did. They either made a success of things or . . .'

'Or they didn't,' Poe finished for her.

Bradshaw was staring at him. Her eyes were wet. She was upset and Poe couldn't give her the reassurances she wanted. Instinctively society felt an alarm should sound every time a child went missing, but the problem was there *was* no alarm, and even if there had been, some of these kids were fleeing far worse situations. Dragging them back wouldn't always be the right thing to do. Not for the first time in his life, Poe wondered how social workers held on to their sanity. It had to be one of the most thankless jobs there was, even worse than being a cop. There were no good days; everything was on a sliding scale of bad to awful. Vilified for taking children away from families, crucified when they didn't.

Fuck that . . .

Jackson didn't feel like answering Bradshaw either. She said, 'Our investigation found Hilary Swift had breached several of the protocols put in place to prevent children like that running away. She allowed them to drink – and there was no way when they got on that train to London they weren't still drunk – and she gave them access to large amounts of money.'

'And?' Poe asked.

'And finally, she wasn't the best person to be running a home like that anyway. She was far too interested in the social side of it all. And yes, of course the manager had to be visible, the home relied on donations just as much as council funding, but the investigation found that she was obsessed by it. And if some rich and influential men thought it was funny to get children drunk, then even if she'd been there, the feeling was that she wouldn't have stopped them.'

Poe needed to move on. The children running off to London might or might not be important, but getting a look at the file sitting on the table was. He turned to Evans. 'I take it you know what's in these files?'

'I vet everything that goes out. Warrant or not.'

'Direct me to where you think I might need to look then, please,' Poe said.

Evans had a thin file on top. He slid it across to Poe. 'I've copied some of the documents you might want to review first.' He looked at his watch. 'The court is still open. When you've seen the top sheet, you might want to go and get another warrant.'

Poe opened it and removed a sheet of A4. It was a twenty-six-year-old bank statement for Seven Pines. There were the usual mundane items found in everyone's list of monthly outgoings. Food, TV licence, utilities. The amounts were all on the right side of the page. To the left of them was another set of figures. Fewer in number but greater in value. It was where the incoming money was listed. There were three different sources for that month. A grant, which looked as though it was a standing order from the charity that owned Seven Pines, and a local authority payment, which probably differed each month depending on how many bed spaces they were using.

Poe stared at the third. It was a payment by cheque.

He checked the page from the corresponding accounts ledger Evans had also supplied. The cheque was from Quentin Carmichael. It stated it was a donation resulting from the 'Are You Feeling Lucky?' event. It was for nine thousand pounds.

Carmichael's account number was also listed.

What the hell . . . ?

His breath quickened.

'What is it, Poe?' Bradshaw asked. She was getting better at reading his facial expressions.

He slid the page across the table. She stared, not immediately seeing it.

'You've still got photographs of the investigation into the money found in Carmichael's bank accounts, haven't you, Tilly?'

She nodded.

'Cross-reference them with the account the cheque came from.' He didn't need her to. He'd always had the ability to imprint salient details into his memory.

Bradshaw turned on her tablet and began searching. She wasn't as quick as usual. Eventually she looked up with a confused expression. 'I can't find it,' she said.

'Exactly,' Poe said. 'Quentin Carmichael made that payment from a bank account no one knew about.'

CHAPTER THIRTY-EIGHT

A Relationship Manager wasn't a banking position with which Poe was familiar, but as soon as the branch manager had received head office's verification of the validity of the additional warrant, he handed the three of them over to a Miss Jefferson. Poe suspected it was less to do with him not being interested – he clearly was – and more to do with him not knowing his way around his own system.

Miss Jefferson, who wanted to be called Rhona, found the unknown account on her computer. She frowned, 'This is odd.'

She printed off some sheets, stapled them together and handed them a copy. 'As you can see, Mr Carmichael opened the bank account in the May of that year and closed it one month later.' She turned her own copy to show them where she was looking.

Poe studied it. As far as he could tell there'd been a flurry of activity before the cruise with six separate deposits of twenty-five thousand pounds, followed by another three deposits the day after the cruise: one of one hundred thousand pounds, one of two hundred and fifty thousand pounds and one of three hundred thousand pounds. Together, they totalled eight hundred thousand exactly.

'Is there a withdrawals sheet?' Poe asked.

'Page two,' Rhona replied.

He turned the page and read on. There'd been two withdrawals: a cheque for nine thousand pounds made payable to the Seven Pines Children's Home, and a cash withdrawal of seven hundred and ninety-one thousand pounds made by Quentin Carmichael. With the balance at zero, the account had been closed.

What the hell had he been up to?

'I see that the deposits into this account were all by cheque or bank transfer, Rhona,' Poe said. 'Any chance you can get me a list?'

She looked uncertain. 'I'll need to check your warrant covers that.'

'You do that,' Poe said.

Being the good employee that she was, she locked her computer before she left the room. Poe smiled. It was as if she'd known he'd have spun the monitor round the second she was gone.

It didn't matter, though. The bank manager had checked with head office, and if someone had made a deposit into the account on the warrant, their name could be shared with the police. If Poe subsequently needed to dig into the accounts of someone on that list, they would need another warrant.

Rhona printed off another document.

This one had names on.

The sudden chill in the room was palpable. Poe stared at the first five names. In his head, he added a location after each one:

Graham Russell – Castlerigg stone circle, Keswick.
Joe Lowell – Swinside stone circle, Broughton-in-Furness.
Michael James – Long Meg and Her Daughters, Penrith.
Clement Owens – Elva Plain, Cockermouth.
Sebastian Doyle – the body in Quentin Carmichael's
        coffin.

Five men.
  Five victims.
  Poe had his connection.

They'd all deposited twenty-five thousand pounds into Carmichael's account before the cruise, and three of them had subsequently made additional, more sizeable donations after the event. Sebastian Doyle, the man Poe had found in Quentin Carmichael's coffin, had made the largest deposit – three hundred thousand pounds – and Michael James had made the smallest at a measly one hundred thousand. Clement Owens was in the middle with two hundred and fifty thousand.

The sixth man on the list was called Montague Price. Like Joe Lowell and Graham Russell, he'd made a twenty-five thousand pounds deposit before the cruise but nothing afterwards.

He'd have to get Flynn to check the HOLMES 2 database that Cumbria were managing, but Poe was sure Price hadn't come up in the investigation so far. To be fair, until they'd burnt to death, none of the others had either.

Poe and Bradshaw looked at each other in bewildered silence. Reid was still studying the list. From the outset Poe had struggled to accept the men were being randomly selected, but never in his wildest dreams had he thought he'd find proof so absolute.

What he had in his hands was a death list.

Reid was staring at the document. His face was grim. 'Unbelievable,' he said. 'You've found it.'

Bradshaw was looking excited and scared. Sometimes when the big cases broke, the feeling was overwhelming.

'What do you think this means, Poe?' she asked.

He read the list again. Six men got on the boat that night. Five of them were now dead.

'It can only be one of two things, Tilly,' he replied. 'Montague Price is either the next victim or . . .'

'Or?'

'Or he's the Immolation Man.'

CHAPTER THIRTY-NINE

Poe was happy to let Gamble take over. Searching for a killer once he'd been identified was a job for the sledgehammer, not the scalpel; it needed a manhunt, not a man hunting. He'd called Gamble immediately and told him that they'd found the link between the victims. To his credit, he didn't shout too much.

Flynn was back in Cumbria and insisted on being briefed. They met in the bar at Shap Wells and she seemed happy with what they'd achieved in her absence. SCAS had come out of it OK in the end. She said she'd let him know later how the meeting with the director and the minister had gone.

Bradshaw broke down the financial information in greater detail while Flynn took notes. She'd be the one writing up the official SCAS report. It would form part of any subsequent prosecution so it had to be meticulous. Reid sauntered into the bar halfway through but waited until the information exchange had finished.

'What have you got, Sergeant?' Flynn asked, making it clear she was back and in charge. It was how it should be. The DI organised the show; the DS ran it.

'He's gone,' Reid said.

'Montague Price?' Poe asked.

'Yep. I was on the raid. His house was empty but it looks like he left in a hurry.'

'And?' There was always an 'and' with Reid. He was a natural showman.

His face cracked into a smile. 'And . . . it's him. CSI found traces of blood on some of his clothes – the DNA is being fast-tracked. There was an empty bottle that we think contained some of the accelerant he used, and there was also a vial of an unknown liquid. Looks medical. It's been sent to the lab.'

He reached out and shook Flynn's hand. 'I'm to officially thank you, ma'am. DCS Gamble's busy obviously, but he didn't want it left unsaid. He knows it wouldn't have happened without SCAS.'

He turned to Poe. 'Even you, Poe. He asked me to tell you that he still thinks you're a bit of an idiot but—'

'An idiot. That's what he called me, an idiot?'

'I'm paraphrasing. His actual words were "massive bellend" but there are ladies present.'

Bradshaw giggled. Even Flynn smiled.

He'd been there before; the silly season right after a case finished. It was a natural high. Everything was funny. Price hadn't been found yet but he would be. Gamble would use everything at his disposal. He'd be on the news later that day and he'd have already circulated Montague Price's picture to the press. It's what Poe would have done. Close the net. Leave Price thinking there were eyes and ears everywhere. That he had nowhere left to hide. He might be intelligent as far as psychotic lunatics went, but Montague Price had no idea he was about to become the most famous man in the country.

Poe walked to the bar. They all deserved a drink. While he waited for the barman to take his order, he turned to look at his friends. They were laughing and joking. Enjoying a job well done.

So why didn't he feel the same?

He knew what it was. Like a pea under his mattress, Carmichael's money was bothering him.

The amount withdrawn from his secret bank account when he closed it, and the amount found in his official bank account didn't add up. The six men on the cruise had given Carmichael eight hundred thousand pounds. Only five hundred thousand had been found. Not counting the nine thousand pounds donated to Seven Pines, almost three hundred thousand pounds was still unaccounted for.

And there was still no reason why his name had been carved onto a victim's chest.

Poe didn't like loose ends. They were untidy. Sometimes they unravelled.

While everyone else celebrated, Poe brooded and pondered.

CHAPTER FORTY

Poe and Reid stayed up late. Flynn left early to begin writing SCAS's report. Bradshaw stayed until one a.m. but eventually cried off, saying she had stuff to be getting on with.

Reid raised his eyebrows after she'd gone. 'What stuff does she have to do at this time of night?'

'Computer games, I expect,' Poe replied.

Reid decided to stay the night. He booked a room and they drank whisky and smoked cigars until the early hours. They discussed how Gamble would handle the search for Montague Price. Earlier, they'd all watched the ten o'clock news where Gamble had made the first of what Poe was sure would be many public appeals. Although he'd privately thanked SCAS, it must have slipped his mind to do it publicly. If you believed what he said, it was only because of his determined and unwavering leadership, along with the extraordinary skills of his detectives, that the breakthrough had been made.

Oh well, Poe had never been in it for the glory.

A late night and a bellyful of whisky did not make for a pleasant morning. Edgar woke him at eight. His look said, 'A piss, breakfast and a walk, please.'

He groaned out of bed and threw open the front door. The harsh stab of sunlight he'd expected didn't happen. Instead, thick tendrils of fog crept into the croft. Putting on some old trainers, he dawdled outside to see how bad it was. The fog at Shap was legendary and could trap the fells in a thick blanket at any time of the year. Today's was a beauty; like looking out of a 747's window as it flew through cloud. Edgar ran off and disappeared in the vast whiteness. Visibility was down to a handful of yards; like a giant eraser, the fog had eradicated everything from view. He couldn't see Shap Wells. He could barely see his own hand.

Poe wasn't leaving the house until it cleared; it was too dangerous. He got a few slices of bacon frying and toasted some bread. Edgar would find his way back by smell.

His phone rang. It was Flynn.

'Morning, boss.'

'They've got him.'

Poe's stomach flipped, and it was nothing to do with his hangover. 'Price?'

'Yep.'

'Where?'

'They didn't catch him. He walked into Carlisle police station with his solicitor three-quarters of an hour ago.'

Thrown by the unlikely scenario of the Immolation Man handing himself in, Poe could manage no more than, 'Bloody hell.'

'Indeed,' said Flynn.

'What's he saying?'

'Nothing yet. He's still locked in a room with his solicitor. Gamble wants to know if you want to be there when he starts talking?'

Poe didn't, and luckily he had the perfect excuse; every Cumbrian knew of the Shap fog. Gamble would understand.

'It is a bit thick this morning,' Flynn agreed after he'd politely declined. 'I'll go and represent our interests. I think I can just about make out the road from here.'

'OK, boss. Keep me updated?'

'Will do.'

* * *

After his breakfast, he sat outside with a coffee while Edgar exercised. Around 10 a.m. the sun began burning through the fog and Poe reckoned it would be safe to have a wander over to the hotel to see if Reid had surfaced.

He was halfway there when his phone rang. It was an 020 London number. He answered and the director of intelligence, Edward van Zyl, bade him a good morning.

'Who are you speaking to, Poe?' van Zyl asked.

Poe stopped, looked at his handset in confusion before replying. 'Er . . . you, sir. Director of Intelligence van Zyl.'

Van Zyl replied, 'You must be mistaken, Poe. The last time we spoke was just before you went on leave.'

'OK . . .'

'You've heard Price is in custody?'

'I have, sir.'

'What's your take?'

Poe composed himself before answering. 'The discrepancy in the money worries me, sir. Best part of three hundred grand just disappeared.'

There was a pause before van Zyl spoke again. 'Do you think Price is the killer, Poe?'

Poe took a moment. 'It's possible, sir.'

'Only possible?'

'There might be physical evidence, sir, but I haven't found a motive. It might have been over money but, if it were, why wait until now? I think we all need to wait until he's been interviewed, sir.'

'Hmm . . . That's certainly an option, Poe. Have you spoken to DI Flynn about our trip to the minister's office?'

'Not yet, sir.'

'Well, don't. That list you got from the bank has set the cat among the proverbial pigeons, I can tell you. There are people of influence down here who are getting anxious about what else you might uncover. They want this finished quickly and quietly, Poe.'

Poe couldn't work out if he was being threatened or encouraged.

Van Zyl continued. 'Quentin Carmichael threw more than one party and some of the men who attended them now hold positions in government. They don't want to be dragged into anything. Some very senior civil servants have reviewed the case file and have decided that now Montague Price is in custody, everyone should focus on ensuring he is convicted. They're putting pressure on the CPS to do exactly that, and anyone who tries to stand in their way will be crushed. The official line will be that Quentin Carmichael was an early victim of Price.'

'That's what they say, is it, sir?'

'It is, Poe. Despite the concerns we share, Montague Price is the man they want. A convenient full stop.'

The director didn't add anything for a few moments. Eventually he said, 'But that's not the way we do things is it, Poe?'

'No, sir, it is not.'

'And now that the case is finished and SCAS are no longer involved, I'm sure you'll be keen to resume your leave.'

'Yes, sir, and thank you.'

'Why are you thanking me, Poe? We haven't spoken for ages, remember . . .'

Bradshaw was up, headphones on, eyes glued to her tablet. She waved when she saw him. There was no sign of Reid. Poe got his room number from a porter and gave him a knock.

'Piss off.'

Poe knocked again.

The door opened and Reid peered through the crack with bloodshot eyes. Poe hoped he felt better than he looked.

'Come on,' Poe said, 'I'll buy you something to eat.'

'I'm not getting up.' His breath stank of stale whisky.

'Montague Price is in custody. Handed himself in this morning.'

Reid's red eyes snapped open. 'Give me ten minutes.'

'Take fifteen,' Poe replied, 'and brush your teeth.'

Twenty minutes later, a freshly showered Reid met them in the restaurant. Bradshaw was still on her tablet. Poe didn't know if she was fighting crime or goblins; her concentration level seemed to be the same for both. Poe poured hot drinks for everyone and threw Reid a box of paracetamol.

Reid dry-crunched a couple of tablets while he waited for his coffee to cool. For several moments he stared into space. He was quiet. Far too quiet for a detective just after their only suspect had been apprehended. He turned to Poe and said, 'Does any of this feel right to you?'

Reid was a great cop with even better instincts. With them both feeling nervous about Price, someone should be thinking about what to do if things didn't go the way Gamble wanted. Van Zyl had told him to stay on leave. He wondered if that were premature. Gamble might authorise some ancillary investigating. It would need to be done anyway and Poe wanted to keep moving.

'There are two possibilities as far as I can see,' Reid said. 'Either Price is being set up by the real killer or—'

'Or he is the real killer and he thinks he can beat it,' Poe finished for him. 'And if he thinks he can beat it, then we need to assume that he can beat it. Either way, I don't think we're finished.'

'What are we going to do then?'

'Something we should have done yesterday,' Poe replied. 'We're going to pay Hilary Swift a visit.'

Reid looked worried. 'I don't know about that, Poe. We can't question someone who may end up being a key prosecution witness. We should at least wait until Price has been interviewed.'

Poe stared at him.

Reid sighed. 'I'll call Gamble. It's his investigation at the end of the day.'

He was right, of course. It was the SIO's call, not his. 'I'll call him,' Poe compromised.

'Go ahead. He'll tell you to piss off, though.'

Poe moved to the window to get a better signal and called Gamble. He must have been holding his mobile, as he answered immediately. 'Sir, I know SCAS are no longer actively involved but DS Reid and I thought we'd go and speak to Hilary Swift.'

'Why, for God's sake?'

'Background information. Tidy a couple of loose ends, that sort of thing. She might not have been there on the night but she probably knew Price was going to be there.'

'Wait until we've spoken to Price, Poe. He's in with his solicitor now trying to construct a deal.'

'A deal?'

'Yeah, can you believe it?' he replied. 'But he's entitled to try, I suppose. We'll listen to what he has to say, then the CPS will put him away for the rest of his life.'

'Hopefully, sir,' Poe said.

'You're not convinced, are you?'

'Like you say, sir, we need to listen to what he says.'

'Despite our differences, Poe, I know we wouldn't have him without you,' Gamble said.

Poe didn't need his arse wiped; he needed permission to continue investigating. But he had to play the game.

'Kind of you to say, sir, but all I did was come in with a fresh pair of eyes. You'd have got there in the end.'

'Go and see her, then. But take Reid and you're not to do it under caution. Background questions only. If there's anything we can use against Price, I want to know immediately.'

Poe thanked him and returned to Reid and Bradshaw. 'We're on,' he said.

Reid looked at him. 'He said yes? You won't be offended if I check?'

'I will be offended if you check, but do it anyway.'

Reid waved him off. 'I trust you, Poe.' He looked at his watch. 'We'd better have another brew before we set off. Neither of us will be fit to drive yet.'

CHAPTER FORTY-ONE

Reid drove. He said he didn't want to be in the passenger seat feeling as rough as he did. Poe didn't argue.

Despite the children's home being sold years ago, a quick check of the electoral roll told them that Hilary Swift still lived in Seven Pines. Poe was surprised they found it. The satnav said they'd arrived when they were still three miles away – one of the joys of living in Cumbria – but Reid called Ambleside police station and got directions.

Seven Pines was located between Ambleside and Grasmere and was a magnificent building. Detached, full of character and the size of a small hotel. The external wood was painted yellow – for some reason traditional Lake District houses all seemed to have brightly painted wooden beams. It was tucked up a small lane, and had views of Rydal Water.

Poe's antennae started twitching. He looked across at Reid and saw the same sense of unease. They were both aware of how much property cost in the area. It was on a par with London.

Before they got out of the car, Poe sent Bradshaw a text. They waited until she replied and when she did Poe grunted in satisfaction.

He knew how to start the interview.

They'd called ahead so Hilary Swift was expecting them, although they hadn't told her what it was about. Poe and Reid walked up the immaculately raked shale path and knocked on the door. It opened immediately. They presented their identification and she studied each one carefully.

Hilary Swift had the type of accent that grated. An affected upper-class drawl that she'd perfected over the years. Poe suspected he knew more about her than she wanted him to know. She'd been born and brought up in Maryport, although if anyone ever asked, she'd rewritten her history and claimed a more upmarket Cockermouth heritage. Poe was all for people bettering themselves – it was how the human race advanced – but snobbery wasn't the way to do it.

She was wearing a knee-length skirt and matching jacket, and her hair was a perfect Margaret Thatcher rip-off. Poe knew she was in her sixties but in questionable lighting she could have passed for fifty.

Inviting them inside with a smile that didn't reach her eyes, she guided them towards the lounge. It was clearly her showstopper room. The view out of the bay windows was stunning. Through a tunnel of trees, the eyes were guided to distant views of the lake. The interior wasn't in tune with the exterior, though. Where the outside was governed by National Park regulations, the inside was proof that good taste couldn't be bought. It looked like a bottle of Pepto-Bismol had been mixed with glitter then sprayed every-where. And the hideous colour theme aside, Swift didn't believe in clean lines or the minimalist approach to interior design either; Poe had never seen a room with so much furniture. Innumerable tables were heaped with lamps and bowls and clocks. The walls were jammed with bookcases and shelving units. They were adorned with expensive-looking tat. Her philosophy seemed to be, if it shone, she should own it.

Poe was scared to sit down in case he knocked something over.

A social worker's salary didn't come close to paying for all this.

'I can't give you long, I'm afraid,' she said. 'My grandchildren came back from Australia with me, and my daughter follows in a fortnight. We're having a family holiday. They're upstairs, playing nicely for now, but I don't know how long that will last. I'll get us some tea.'

'I'll give you a hand, Mrs Swift,' Reid said.

He knew Reid had gone with her so that Poe could have a nosey. He approached the window and counted the pines. There were five. He was still looking for the other two when Reid and Swift returned with a fully laden tray. She saw where he was looking.

'Storm Henry, I'm afraid,' she said. 'We lost two of them in February 2016.'

He'd long been of the view that if you wanted people to take storms seriously, they needed names like Roof Wrecker or Bastard rather than Henry or Desmond. No wonder the public were constantly surprised by them.

'Can you tell me how you came to live here, Mrs Swift?' Poe asked.

'Can I rephrase that question for you, Sergeant Poe?' she smiled. 'Because what I think you meant to ask was, "How can I afford to live here?" Am I correct?'

'You are.'

'When the charity closed the home, I was given first refusal on the sale of the property.'

'I was more interested in—'

'In how I paid for it?'

'Yes,' Poe said. The text from Bradshaw had confirmed there was no outstanding mortgage. Swift owned Seven Pines outright.

A flash of temper lit her eyes. 'My late husband. He knew when and where to invest our money, Sergeant Poe.'

Although he'd read about her husband – he'd worked for some accountancy firm in Penrith – it was a vague answer. Accountants were well paid but they weren't massively well paid. He decided to leave it for now. A noise from upstairs was followed by the sound of a child crying. Swift left her seat and walked to the door. She raised her voice. 'Annabel! Jeremy! Grandma's downstairs talking. Can you keep it down, please?'

'Sorry, Grandma,' a child replied.

Poe noticed that when Swift raised her voice, her cultured accent slipped and the Maryport girl shone through. 'Do you know why we're here, Mrs Swift?' he asked when she'd retaken her seat.

'If I were pressed, I'd say one of the home's ex-residents has been naughty and you want some background information on them? That's what it normally is. I retired a long time ago but I still keep in touch with some of the children I looked after.'

'Do you remember a man called Quentin Carmichael?' Poe asked.

Her eyes narrowed. 'So, that's why you're here. Because of what happened on Ullswater. But why now? It was over twenty-five years ago.'

'Something's come up,' he replied.

'About the boys who ran away or about the cruise itself?'

Poe didn't answer. Sometimes it was best to let witnesses take you where they thought you wanted to go.

Swift's face hardened as she stared into the distance. 'Those damn boys!'

Poe waited to see if she would expand.

'Over my years here, Sergeant Poe, I looked after more than one hundred children, and I'm not blowing my own trumpet when I say I had more than a small impact on their lives. The children appreciated the home I kept for them, they appreciated the boundaries I set and they appreciated the jump-start their lives needed.'

'Sounds like you were a pillar of the community,' he said.

'But those four boys . . . well, some children just don't want to be helped. I got them a marvellous opportunity with some marvellous people. If they'd done what I'd asked, they'd all have got decent apprenticeships out of it when it was time for them to leave school. Those men had excellent connections and were keen to help in any way they could. All I asked was for them to behave themselves. But did they? No, as soon as they realised they weren't going to be supervised, they all got drunk. Like common yobbos. They thought nothing of the home and nothing of my reputation.'

'Seems they were a bit ungrateful,' Poe said.

'Doesn't it? Well, I don't mind telling you, I tore an almighty strip off them when they came back. Damn near woke the whole house up.'

'Really?' Poe had been in enough interviews to know when someone was lying. Swift's anger sounded forced.

'Yes, really,' she said.

'So they ran off?'

'They did. Took their stuff – and the money they'd made in tips – and hitched a ride to Carlisle station.'

'Why Carlisle?' Poe asked. 'Penrith's nearer.'

Swift said she didn't know. It was just what the police had told her.

He glanced at Reid to see if he had any questions. Other than helping with the tea, he hadn't asked her anything. Unbelievably he was starting to nod off. *How much had he drunk last night?*

However, Poe was starting to flag as well. The room was warm and it had been a late night. Still . . . to fall asleep in front of a witness was something new. His phone was on silent but it vibrated in his pocket. He asked Swift for permission to answer but pressed receive before she had a chance to reply. It was Flynn.

'What's up?' he said.

'Where are you?'

Poe glanced at Swift, who was smiling. His eyelids were starting to feel heavy. If he weren't careful, he'd be joining Reid soon.

'I'm at Mrs Swift's home. DS Reid and I arrived about forty minutes ago, why?'

'Poe, listen to me carefully. I'm going to tell you something but you can't react. Do you understand?'

Poe said he did. He noticed his voice was slurred and his tongue seemed to be thicker than usual. He looked across at Reid who was now flat out. He was drooling.

What the hell . . . ?

'Montague Price has just given a full statement. He's denying he's the Immolation Man,' Flynn said.

'Yes, he is,' Poe said, his thoughts becoming jumbled.

'You're slurring, Poe. Are you drunk?' Flynn shouted.

Poe didn't answer. He *had* been drunk. He didn't think he was now.

Flynn didn't wait for him to gather his thoughts. 'Whatever, I don't have time for this now. Just pay attention, Price has admitted to being on the boat but it wasn't weekend breaks being auctioned.'

'What was it?' Poe could barely understand what she was saying.

'It was the children, Poe,' she replied. 'It was the children being sold!'

That got through. *Oh shit . . .*

He looked across at Swift who was looking at him strangely.

'And Poe, Hilary Swift *was* on the boat.'

Shit. Shit. Shit.

'She and Carmichael organised the whole thing.'

Poe tried to focus on the woman opposite. His vision was blurring and he realised it was nothing to do with a hangover or late-night fatigue.

This was something different.

'We don't have anyone near. You and DS Reid are going to have to detain her. Can you do that, Poe?'

Poe recognised the early stages of sedation. He tried to fight it but had no chance; he was about to succumb to whatever he'd been given. 'Steph,' he slurred, 'she's fucking drugged us.'

He tried to stand but fell back onto the sofa. He dropped the phone. He was vaguely aware of Flynn shouting through the BlackBerry's microphone.

'Poe! Poe! Are you all right?'

Eventually the voice faded and his eyes rolled back. Ten seconds later everything disappeared.

CHAPTER FORTY-TWO

Poe came round in instalments. He tried consciousness a few times before it fully took. He had no idea how long he'd been out; it could have been days, it could have been minutes. He opened his eyes and tried to focus on the people milling around him.

'Jesus, what happened?' he heard Reid say. 'I've a mouth like a camel's scrotum.'

Poe's throat was parched as well. His head was thumping.

He tried putting the pieces together. After a while, fragments of memory began to take shape and his brain could form thoughts. Hilary Swift had drugged them both, and judging by the hideous pink colour scheme, they were still in her house. If that were the case, then they couldn't have been out for long. There were over twenty people in her front room, and some were wearing the green of paramedics. He looked down when he felt something tightening on his arm. His blood pressure was being taken. Some idiot tried to stick something in his ear and he jerked away.

'Poe, stop being a dick and let her take your temperature.'

It was Flynn.

'Steph?' His voice was little more than a croak.

'You and DS Reid have been drugged.'

Poe scowled. 'That much I've worked out.' Another thought formed. 'Where's Swift?'

'She's gone, Poe. DCS Gamble's team are searching the house now but it looks like she left in a hurry. Must have been picked up as her car's still outside.'

'What about the grandchildren?'

'What grandchildren?'

'There were kids in the house.'

'Are you sure?' she asked urgently.

'I heard them.'

Flynn called across to Reid. 'DS Reid, DS Poe says there were children here.'

'Two, I think,' Reid confirmed.

She shouted for Gamble and he hurried over, an annoyed look on his face. 'DS Reid and DS Poe both say there were children here when they arrived, sir. I think she's running with them.'

'That's all I fucking need,' Gamble growled. He turned to one of the detectives with him. 'Get onto the border agency now. Tell them she could be travelling with children.' He turned to Reid. 'Age? Sex? Description? Anything that can help?'

'Didn't see them, boss,' Reid said. 'They were upstairs. I think she said they were called Annabel and Geoffrey.'

'Jeremy,' Poe corrected.

'Annabel and Jeremy,' Reid confirmed. 'The one who called Swift "Grandma" sounded young.'

'Bollocks!' Gamble shouted.

Poe understood his anger. If the UKBA had been told to look out for a woman on her own, they wouldn't have been paying as much attention to anyone with children. And if Swift made it through a border, Poe doubted they'd ever see her again.

'I'll get on to Swift's daughter and get some photos emailed over, boss,' Reid said.

It looked as though Gamble was about to argue. To tell Reid he wasn't doing anything. Instead he said, 'At least you can explain your own fuck-up. Tell her how her children were abducted from underneath your nose.'

Reid reddened and nodded.

It was unfair and Poe wasn't sure of the significance of Swift's rapid disappearance, but the fact she had drugs to hand surely meant she was involved. He'd already heard one of Gamble's detectives voice the opinion that they were now looking for the Immolation *Woman*. A consensus was forming.

It fitted the facts, as they knew them. It answered all Gamble's questions.

That was all well and good, he thought, but it didn't answer all *his* questions. The big one was still unanswered.

Why?

He didn't care what the others were thinking. He had the same problem with Swift being the killer as he did with Price. Why wait all these years? Of course, with all the evidence pointing her way, it was probable Swift was their killer, and that she had a lucid explanation why she'd waited all this time to kill her partners in crime. But Poe didn't want to die wondering; he wouldn't be able to sleep until he'd understood her motive. Or how he was involved.

To coin one of Bradshaw's favourite phrases, he needed more data.

And there was only one place to start.

Montague Price's confession.

He tried to stand up but his legs were rubbery. They collapsed under him.

'Whoa,' said the paramedic. 'You're going nowhere until a doctor has checked you out. We need to put some saline into you.'

'And you can consider that an order, DS Poe,' Flynn said from across the room.

For once he had no intention of disobeying.

CHAPTER FORTY-THREE

The incident room was jammed. Every moulded plastic seat had a hairy-arsed cop wedged into it. The high ceiling had flickering lights and off-white drop-in panels. Some were newer than the rest and were an annoyingly different colour. Like every police incident room, it smelled of fried food, coffee and frustration. Poe found it comforting.

He stood at the back and listened to Gamble update the massed ranks of the team searching for Hilary Swift. It was two days after she'd drugged Poe and Reid and made her escape. It was Poe's first day back on the job. So far there hadn't been a hint of a sighting. She'd either successfully fled the country, or hadn't yet tried.

As well as the search for Swift, Gamble was trying to locate the boys that Price claimed had been sold on the night of the auction. His theory being that if the train tickets had been a ruse to make the police think they'd fled to London, then they had to be somewhere else. Gamble was convinced that if they found just one of them, the rest of the puzzle would slot neatly into place. He had teams of detectives assigned to it.

Poe wished them luck but he wasn't convinced. One of the unintended consequences of Operation Yewtree – the high-profile national investigation into historic sexual offences against children – was that the reporting of abuse was now at a record level. More and more victims were coming out of the shadows. Their allegations were being taken seriously.

But for twenty-six years these boys had said nothing? Even

217

with all the press the Immolation Man's victims had been getting recently? One of them would have come forward. Even if it were just to ask how much compensation they might be entitled to.

In Poe's opinion, the explanation for the boys' continued silence was simpler. And far darker.

They were dead.

It was a thought he kept to himself.

During Poe's overnight stay in hospital, Bradshaw had kept him up to date with what had happened in his absence. Swift had used a drug called propofol to put him and Reid to sleep. The tests on the evidence found at Montague Price's home had been completed. Propofol was the unknown liquid in the vial.

It was one of the most commonly used anaesthetics. It was fast acting, could be taken orally, and didn't stay in the body long. It was a heavily controlled substance, and Gamble had assigned four detectives to try and locate her source.

They might not yet know where she got the propofol from, but its use did provide an answer to one of the unanswered questions: how had five men been abducted without any sign of a struggle? They'd almost certainly been drugged and taken when they were semiconscious. Gamble's working theory now was that they were either in on it together, or Swift had been trying to set up Price. With the 'how' answered, the 'why' could wait, apparently.

All the victims had empty stomachs, which gave additional credence to the theory that propofol had been used to facilitate their abduction. To keep her method unknown, Gamble believed Swift had kept her victims captive until the propofol was out of their systems – at least two days, according to the medical advice they'd been given. The search was on for her makeshift containment facility.

As Gamble prattled on, Poe caught Bradshaw's eye and gestured for her to join him at the back of the room. 'What do you reckon the two of us get out of here?' he said. 'Go back to Shap Wells and do some police work?'

'Thought you'd never ask, Poe.'

Poe knew Flynn had been in on Montague Price's interview, and that she'd already emailed Bradshaw a copy of the video.

'Do you think Hilary Swift is the Immolation Woman, Poe? I'd be ever so surprised if she was.'

'Why'd you say that, Tilly?'

'Statistics. Eight-five per cent of serial killers are male.'

'Still leaves fifteen per cent,' Poe replied.

'And less than two per cent of females have used fire to kill.'

'Go on then.'

'Go on then what?'

'I know you've done the maths. What are the chances of a female serial killer who also uses fire?'

'Statistically improbable, Poe.'

He sighed. An absence of motive and now he had Bradshaw's maths. He didn't care what Gamble thought, Poe's gut was telling him that, although Swift *was* involved, she wasn't their killer.

'Come on, let's go and see Price's confession.'

The video was as clear as a 4K television. The interview room Gamble had used was small and square. Every line was straight and every corner sharp. The walls were cream and bare. The only things in the room were chairs, a table and some recording equipment. It was a serious room with a serious purpose.

Montague Price was a thin man in his seventies. Poe could see liver spots on his hands. He was resplendent in a tweed suit, complete with waistcoat and tiepin; every inch the country gent everyone believed him to be.

He'd been a big man in the hunting and shooting fraternity. He'd represented Great Britain in clay-pigeon shooting. That made him virtual royalty in Cumbria.

He was visibly shaking. Poe suspected the underlying reason was medical, rather than a fear of what was coming. Bartholomew Ward, his solicitor, had travelled up from London and was rumoured to be costing Price three thousand pounds a day.

Gamble, as chief superintendent, was too high in rank to sit in on interviews, but Price and his solicitor had agreed beforehand to waiver this in the spirit of cooperation. Flynn was in the room representing the NCA, and a detective Poe didn't know was also present.

When the introductions had been made, and the recording equipment had been double-checked, Bartholomew Ward kicked it off.

'Gentlemen,' he said, with no deference to the fact Flynn was in the room, 'I am about to give you a prepared statement by my client. I would like it formally acknowledged that my client has surrendered himself to your custody voluntarily.'

Gamble snorted. 'His face was all over the news.'

'Nevertheless.'

'Noted,' said Gamble.

'And agreed?' asked Ward.

Gamble paused. 'Agreed. Your client attended Durranhill voluntarily.'

Without taking her eyes off the screen, Bradshaw asked Poe, 'Durranhill?'

'Carlisle's newest police station. They moved there a few years after the 2005 floods wrecked the old one. Cost eight million quid and it looks like the back of a football stand.'

They turned to the interview.

'And I'd also like it acknowledged that my client has not been charged with anything.'

'Agreed, your client has not been charged with anything . . . yet.'

With those two small victories in the bag, Ward said, 'My client is deeply ashamed of his small part in the terrible events of that night twenty-six years ago. He acknowledges he should have approached the authorities sooner than he did, but you'll note that at no point was he involved in the planning or the execution of what happened.' With his mitigation out of the way, Ward handed Gamble a document.

For the next five minutes no one spoke. Every now and then Gamble would look up in disbelief. Price and Ward remained expressionless.

Gamble put down the document and said, 'I think it would be helpful if I summarised for the benefit of the video and my two colleagues.'

Ward nodded.

'Your client was one of six men invited to a charity auction on Ullswater. He knew something illegal was going to happen as the invitation was coded.' Gamble looked up, and although he already knew, he asked, 'Coded how?'

Price spoke for the first time and his voice was as croaky as Poe's had been two days earlier. 'The invitation had an archaic punctuation mark in the title. It's called a percontation point and it means—'

'I know what it means, it means there's an underlying message in the preceding sentence.'

Price and Ward looked at each other. Ward said, 'May I ask how you have knowledge of this? It is unused today.'

'No, you may not,' Gamble said. He continued. 'Your client believed that the cruise was a cover for an adult party. High-class call girls and unlimited cocaine. Have I understood that correctly?'

'You have,' Ward replied.

'And for this he was willing to pay, upfront I may add, twenty-five thousand pounds?'

'He was and he did.'

'Twenty-five grand for some hookers and coke? Bit steep, wasn't it?'

'My client was not familiar with the going rate for such things. Naivety is not a crime.'

Gamble did an admirable job of keeping calm. Just watching the interview through the medium of a small laptop screen was making Poe's teeth itch. The whole point of Price's statement was to limit his exposure to the bad stuff. He would admit what could be proved and deny what couldn't.

'And once he got on board, he realised it wasn't cocaine and prostitutes, but children that were for sale?'

'That is correct.'

'The four boys Hilary Swift had brought with her to act as waiters?'

Price tried to suppress a smile. Poe could tell that even after all this time he was still getting off on it. 'There were six of us but only three boys were available. Carmichael kept one for himself. He wanted us bidding against each other to drive up the price,' he explained.

Ward put his hand on his shoulder: 'I do the talking. The boys – just like my client – were unaware they were the star attractions, and by the time Mr Price realised what was happening, the boat had long left the shore. He had no choice but to go along with it.'

'Why?'

'He feared for his life,' Ward said. 'A fear you'll agree was rational given the circumstances we now find ourselves in.'

Gamble didn't take the bait. He kept going, summarising the statement.

'The boys were plied with alcohol before the auction began and one by one Hilary Swift paraded them for everyone. When they'd all been up and down a few times, and the men had had a chance to inspect the goods, the bidding be—'

'Hang on,' Flynn interjected. 'Are you saying Hilary Swift was *on* the boat?'

'Most certainly she was. She and Carmichael organised it all,' said Ward. 'Is that a problem?'

Gamble and Flynn leaned in and whispered together. Flynn left the room. Presumably that had been when she'd called Poe and asked him to arrest Hilary Swift.

Flynn being out of the interview room didn't stop Ward. 'Obviously my client was appalled by what was happening and took no further part in the proceedings.'

'Obviously,' Gamble deadpanned. 'And after the bidding the boat came back to shore and the men disappeared with what they'd bought?'

Ward shook his head. 'No, first Quentin Carmichael produced a video he'd taken of the whole thing and explained it was every-one's insurance.'

'And then . . .?'

'And then nothing. My client never saw any of the men again. He cut off all contact with them.'

'And his understanding about the fate of the boys?'

'He doesn't know. He would like it placed on record that he hopes no harm came to them.'

The DC in the room, quiet up until then, burst out of his chair and shouted, 'Lying fucking bastard!' He tried to punch Price but Gamble bearhugged him and shouted for assistance. A pair of uni-formed officers rushed in and dragged the struggling detective out.

Ward spread his arms as if a point had been made. 'This is why he hasn't come forward until now.'

'Wait until he gets to prison,' Gamble murmured. 'They're going to fucking love him there.'

'Ah,' said Ward, 'I think we might have a problem then. Because if you want my client to testify against the real culprits, Hilary Swift and Quentin Carmichael, then he's going to need assurances that he will not be charged with anything more than assisting an offender.'

223

'Fuck you,' said Gamble. 'No way is he walking away from this. I already knew most of what's in this statement. Oh, and by the way, Quentin Carmichael has been dead for about a quarter of a century so half your bargaining chips are already gone.'

This was news to them. They began whispering urgently. Price started gesticulating at Ward. For the first time he looked worried.

At that point the door opened and Flynn rushed in. She bent down and spoke into Gamble's ear.

'Interview suspended,' Gamble said.

Ward and Price both looked at him.

'You're shit out of luck; Hilary Swift's disappeared. Looks like the music's stopped and you don't have a chair, Mr Price.'

CHAPTER FORTY-FOUR

Flynn found them in the Garden Room at Shap Wells. Reid was more useful to Gamble now and had been reassigned to the main investigation.

'Gruesome, isn't it?' Flynn asked.

'To put it mildly,' Poe replied. 'Where is Price now?'

'Still in a cell in Carlisle nick. Gamble's meeting the CPS soon to see what they can charge him with.'

'A holding charge?'

'Enough to get him remanded certainly. The full charges will follow when the investigation ends.'

'The evidence found in his home?'

'Looks like Swift was setting him up. The evidence might be real but he has a cast-iron alibi for the last two murders. He can prove he was hiding out in London. Gamble thinks – and I agree – that Swift was trying to buy some time. Probably wasn't banking on Price handing himself in so soon.'

Poe ignored the assumption of Swift's guilt. She *was* involved; but that didn't mean she was the all and everything. 'If Price was in hiding, by leaving evidence at his home the real Immolation Man could have been trying to flush him out.'

Flynn frowned. 'You think he's a potential victim?'

'Why not?' he replied. 'Everyone else on that boat seems to have been. What makes him so different? And if whoever is doing this had managed to abduct him and quietly make him disappear, would any of us have looked any further than him?'

'Probably not,' she admitted. 'And you said "Immolation Man" instead of Swift. I take it you're not yet convinced of her guilt?'

'She's definitely working with the Immolation Man; her use of propofol can't be ignored. It might even have been her who left all the evidence at Price's. Whether or not she's been burning people is a different matter entirely. Tilly has some sums you probably need to see.'

'I'll have a look later. What else do you have?'

'Well . . . up until now the only motive we'd been able to come up with had been financial,' Poe said. 'And that never made sense. Not really. Castrations and burnings? Over money? I don't think so.'

'Then what?'

'I don't know yet,' he said. He did, but he didn't want to voice it out loud. Not in front of Bradshaw . . .

Flynn steepled her fingers and closed her eyes. She opened them after a minute and leaned forwards. 'OK then, let's do what we're paid to do then. Gamble can chase Swift; we're the Serious Crime Analysis Section, and that means we do the things others can't.'

Bradshaw nodded. Eventually Poe did too.

Poe said, 'We start with the transport. We have five abductions and five murders, and because there was no trace of propofol in any of the victims, we now know for sure the victims had to have been kept somewhere before they were killed. That's additional journeys we didn't know about.'

'So the killer had to drive to the abduction site, from the abduction site to the containment site, then from the containment site to the murder site,' Bradshaw summarised. 'That's a lot of data, Poe.'

'I thought you liked data.'

She smiled and said, 'I love data!' She punched some keys and before long the printer was whirring. 'The more I have, the more I can do. I'll open up our link to the Automatic Number Plate Recognition database and get cracking.'

Poe led Flynn away from Bradshaw, and, making sure she was out of earshot, told her what he hadn't wanted to say earlier. 'I think we need to assume those boys are dead.'

Flynn nodded. Her face was grim. 'That much I'd worked out. You have a theory?'

'I do. I think twenty-five grand bought you the right to abuse them.'

'And the three who paid the six-figure amounts?'

'For that amount of money, I think you got to kill them.'

'That's what I think too,' Flynn said after a long moment.

Neither of them had noticed the printer had stopped. Bradshaw had heard them. 'Oh no!' she gasped. Tears flooded her eyes and before long she was crying. Flynn sat next to her and put her arms around her shoulders.

For over a year, Bradshaw had worked on some of the worst cases in the country, but up until then it had always been long-arm. Even when she'd studied the carving of his name in Michael James's chest, it had been computer images rather than an actual body she'd been looking at. Here, out in the field, she had as much invested as he did. More perhaps – she was nice, Poe wasn't.

It was more than an hour before Bradshaw was composed enough to resume work. Poe felt guilty. If he hadn't insisted she accompanied them up to Cumbria – and he knew he'd only been making a point at the time – she could have been spared all this.

Flynn said quietly, 'You and Tilly seem to be getting on OK. Despite what's just happened, getting her out of the office has done her the world of good.'

Poe looked at his new friend. She'd pushed her glasses up and her tongue was sticking out in determination. Tear tracks were still on her face. A wisp of hair flapped about in the air-conditioning. She stuck out her bottom lip and blew it away from her eyes. A feeling of protective warmth spread over Poe. There were only a few years between them, but in terms of life experiences there were decades. Her naivety and innocence contrasted sharply with his own dark nature, but in many ways they were alike; they were both obsessives, and they both rubbed people up the wrong way.

Thinking about Bradshaw reminded him about something. She'd been the one who'd interpreted the data from the MSCT that uncovered his name in Michael James's chest. And his own connection to the case was still unclear. Hilary Swift was involved somehow but Poe was certain she hadn't recognised him or his name. If she were the Immolation Man's accomplice, then she hadn't been read into the wider plan. Gamble still had a detective going through Poe's background in the slim hope of a name cropping up. So far there'd been nothing.

And Poe doubted the answer was in his past. Up until the Peyton Williams case, he'd been fairly uncontroversial. He'd put some nasty men behind bars, but none of them had been released in the last twelve months. But . . . Poe's name *had* been carved into the chest of the third victim. That was an indisputable fact.

Which meant they were still missing something.

Poe looked across at Bradshaw. The printer was spitting out documents but she'd begun to pin some of the early ones to the wall. Automatic Number Plate Recognition, or ANPR, was the largest database of its type in the world. There would be a lot of data to get through.

'How long do you think you'll be before you're finished sorting through all this chaos, Tilly?' Poe asked, sweeping his arms around to indicate the various piles of documents.

Bradshaw stopped what she was doing. Poe could almost hear the mental calculations in her head; she didn't do guesstimates.

'Four hours, thirty minutes, Poe,' she said. 'I think I can have something for us to review by then.'

Poe turned to Flynn, 'I think we need to consider a different motive, boss.'

'I'm listening,' she said.

'We suspect that the men who deposited the six-figure amounts were paying to kill their victims, yes?'

Flynn nodded.

'And if that's the case, then before they died, the boys suffered appallingly.'

She nodded again.

'Well . . . what if someone found out?' Poe asked.

'And they're seeking some sort of natural justice?'

'It would fit the ferocity of the killings.'

'Could one of the boys have survived?' Flynn asked.

Poe shook his head. 'If one of them had, the six men would have been far warier than they had been. No, whoever's doing this was unknown to them. Plus, why wait twenty-six years?'

'Who then? We've identified everyone now.'

'Have we?' Poe replied. 'I know they were in care but those boys had to have had families at some point. What if someone's latent parental responsibility has woken?'

She didn't look convinced.

'Look, we have five hours to kill. We might as well do something.'

'What do you have in mind?'

'I think we need to go back to the beginning.'

'How Carmichael ended up in a salt store? Surely that's irrelevant now?'

'No, earlier than that,' he said. 'The Seven Pines warrant was made out to us, not Cumbria police, and it's still valid. I say we go back to Children's Services and look at the lives of those boys. I want to know why they were at Seven Pines in the first place.'

CHAPTER FORTY-FIVE

'What do you need?' Audrey Jackson asked. Flynn and Poe were back at Carlisle Civic Centre. After he'd convinced Flynn that they should take advantage of their warrant, she'd been decisive. It seemed she'd grown tired of being Gamble's assistant.

'Background on the boys,' Flynn replied.

'And their families,' Poe added. 'Plus the staff and the rest of the kids who were in Seven Pines at the same time as they were.'

'That's going to be a big list. Part of the home's role was short-term assessments. Some beds had a pretty high turnover.'

Neither of them responded. Flynn folded her arms.

'I'll see what I can dig up,' Jackson said.

She returned with files on the boys. Poe suspected she'd recently been looking at them. She placed them on the table. They were pitifully thin.

There were four of them. One for each boy. Four kids who'd been dealt a shit hand. Looked after by the state because their parents couldn't, wouldn't, or shouldn't. Seven Pines should have been their sanctuary. A place for them to mend, to learn how to love and to be loved. A place for them to trust adults again.

Instead, they were sold for the sport of rich, bored men.

Poe's resolve hardened. He didn't care if he had to look at paperwork for the next ten years, if the answer was in these files, he'd find it.

He opened them all and laid out the basic information side by side.

Michael Hilton.

Mathew Malone.

Andrew Smith.

Scott Johnston.

Four lives snuffed out. He took a sip from the coffee Jackson had brought for them and began reading. Flynn started on the other children.

An hour later and his despair had deepened. Each file was horribly different and depressingly similar.

Michael Hilton: neglected so much that, at the age of nine, he weighed less than the average five-year-old. When the social workers finally managed to remove him from the family home, he'd been eating flies to stay alive. The parents each got a year in custody. Poe hoped they'd been force-fed insects in prison. Michael had been passed around the system, but behavioural problems rooted in the appalling start he had to life meant he couldn't settle. Seven Pines was his last chance and he appeared to have grabbed it with both hands.

Andrew Smith: a star pupil at school until his grades began slipping. When he was asked to stay behind one night to discuss why, he'd freaked out. He told his teacher he had to go to work. Mystified, they'd called the police who found heroin in his satchel. His father had been using him as a drug mule. Both his parents fled to Spain, where they still lived, apparently. They sent Children's Services a birthday card for him every year, along with some money. With no forwarding address for Andrew, the last few were still in the file.

Scott Johnston probably had the most common reason for being removed from the family home. His mother was a domestic abuse victim who refused to leave her partner. Poe wasn't surprised. It happened more than people realised. Regardless of the consequences, some women found it impossible to leave their abusers. When Children's Services said that the home wasn't safe for young Scott, and that she had to make a choice – her partner or her child – she chose her partner. The social worker had tried to locate his natural father, without success. Scott entered the system and never left it. Poe made a note about his father. He'd get Reid to chase it up later. So far, he was the only person who'd had even the hint of motive.

And finally, Mathew Malone. Perhaps the saddest case of all because he'd come from a happy, well-adjusted family in Brighton. His mother had died when he was young and, proving just how fragile family units could be, his father had hooked up with a heroin addict from Zaire. Within a month they'd fled her drug debts in Brighton and moved up to Cumbria. A month after that, the woman was accusing Mathew of being a sorcerer. His father – who by then had an eighty-pound a day habit of his own – had either been oblivious to it or happy to let it happen. The woman was obsessed with the idea of ridding the boy of his demons, and believed the best way to do that was by driving them out with pain. Mathew was tied to a hard-backed chair while she stubbed out cigarettes on his arms and torso. Mathew, to his credit, wasn't having any of that. As soon as he could get away, he fled to Workington police station. His father was imprisoned for four years for allowing it to happen. He served two, and, according to the file, overdosed on the day of release – an all too familiar tale of addicts underestimating the strength of 'street' heroin compared to 'prison' heroin. The woman got nine years for grievous bodily harm with intent but died during her first year in prison – the result of the same type of shit. This time, though, instead of an eight-year-old boy, it was her cellmate, a fifteen-stone Glaswegian head case, whom she'd accused of being a witch. The Scot, a lifer who'd murdered her husband, smashed her accuser's head onto the rim of the cell toilet until her skull had the consistency of an over-ripe banana.

Poe grunted in satisfaction.

He reviewed the notes various social workers, family judges and guardians *ad litem* had made throughout the years. The boys had never stood a chance.

Apart from Scott Johnston's father, there was little evidence that any of the boys' families would be out there somewhere, seeking their revenge. They were either dead, in prison, or didn't give a shit.

There was one photograph of the four boys together. It looked as though it had been taken with an instant camera. It had that thick white band at the bottom, the part you held as you waved it in the air waiting for it to dry. The photograph was poor quality, and had presumably been taken during a Seven Pines outing to a beach somewhere. The boys were smiling in the sunshine. It was tops-off weather. Smith was holding a football. They looked happy. Despite the quality of the old photograph, Poe could see the cigarette scars on Malone's arms and chest. He put it down carefully. His eyes were moist and he wiped them before tears could form.

'Why weren't any of them fostered out?' he asked. 'I know Hilton had behavioural problems, but the other three seemed to be thriving at Seven Pines. Was it because they didn't want to be separated?'

Jackson shook her head. 'Apart from Michael – who as you said had some deep-rooted psychological issues he still hadn't worked through – they all came to us later in life, and at that time it was virtually impossible to get young boys placed. They ended up friends *because* they weren't being fostered,' she explained. 'It became a badge of honour with them, a "nobody likes us and we don't care" kind of thing.'

It was a depressing answer and Poe went back to the files.

When he'd finished skimming them, he put them down. He needed some fresh air before he tackled a deeper study. Flynn, who was reading similar horror stories with different children, followed him. Jackson joined them a few moments later. She sparked up a cigarette and drew the poison deep into her lungs.

'How do you put up with this shit, day in day out?' Poe asked.

She shrugged. 'If I don't, who will?'

It was an answer of sorts. It didn't invite further conversation. Jackson lit another cigarette from the one she'd been smoking. After five minutes, they went back inside. Poe reopened the files, determined to find something.

Flynn's phone rang. She showed Poe the caller ID. It was Gamble.

'Sir?'

Her expression darkened as she listened. 'Shit,' she muttered finally. 'And there's no doubt?'

She frowned some more before hanging up.

Poe raised his eyebrows.

'Hilary Swift's daughter has just landed. She's confirmed that her mother was in Australia when Clement Owens was killed at Cockermouth.'

Poe felt his pulse quicken. 'So, we are looking for someone else . . .'

CHAPTER FORTY-SIX

Gamble called an emergency meeting for later that day, and as the files on the children from Seven Pines hadn't revealed anything actionable, they'd returned to Shap Wells. Jackson had copied everything for them and Poe vowed to take them home and read it all again later. Sometimes his brain needed a calmer environment.

Bradshaw hadn't been slacking while they'd been away. She was surrounded by reams of paper. She'd needed the hotel's strong wi-fi, so the Garden Room, despite its drawbacks, had become their makeshift incident room again. It was as cluttered as the inside of Poe's mind. Bradshaw looked up anxiously. 'DI Stephanie Flynn, I think I've spent all our money on colour printing.'

'Don't worry about it, Tilly, I'm the budget holder . . .' She stared at the masses of paperwork. 'Er . . . exactly how many sheets have you printed?'

'Eight hundred and four,' she replied.

Flynn looked worried.

Bradshaw dug her grave a little deeper. 'The hotel had to send out for more ink twice.'

'It's cheap if we find something, boss,' Poe said. 'Now we know there's another player, ANPR might just be our best shot.'

Unlike Cumbria Constabulary, the National Crime Agency had live access to the Automatic Number Plate Recognition database. ANPR is the law enforcement system that reads, checks and records every vehicle that passes one of the eight thousand fixed and mobile cameras in the UK. With over forty-five million cars in the country, ANPR cameras take close to twenty-six million photographs a day, and because the National ANPR Data Centre, or NADC, holds every image for two years, at any one time there are over seventeen billion photographs in its archives. Poe knew that Gamble had requested mobile ANPR cameras on the likely routes to some of the more prominent stone circles, but had bust out.

'What have you got for us, Tilly?' Poe asked.

Bradshaw, still not sure if she was in trouble or not, coughed nervously and said, 'After I'd downloaded the data from the ANPR cameras I wanted, I ran it through a program I've been working on for a couple of months in my spare time. The way I see it, this is a chaotic system problem so I adapted the Kuramoto model to assess the synchronisation order.'

She looked at them as if she'd just said something they had any chance of understanding.

'Dumb it down a bit, Tilly,' Poe said, not unkindly.

'Oh right, basically, Poe, under the right conditions, chaos spontaneously evolves into a lockstep system.'

Flynn and Poe continued to stare at her blankly.

'I've redefined the parameters,' she sighed.

Neither of them responded.

'You *have* to be kidding me?' Bradshaw said, shaking her head. 'Jeez, do you two still point at planes?'

'Eh?' Poe said.

'I ran a program and I've got you a list of car registration numbers.'

'Ah, a list. Why didn't you say so?'

Bradshaw stuck her tongue out at him before pulling a pile towards her. 'I focused on the journeys the Immolation Man would have had to make. Abduction to containment site, containment site to crime scene.'

Poe nodded. This he could follow.

'We know when and where four of the victims were killed and I correlated that with the cameras nearest their homes.'

It made sense. She was trying to find vehicles that had passed the cameras nearest to the killing sites and had also passed cameras near the likely abduction sites.

'We have five victims,' Flynn reminded her.

'We do, DI Stephanie Flynn, but for analytical purposes the man in Quentin Carmichael's coffin is an outlier. We don't know when he was put in the coffin and we don't know where or when he was killed.'

She paused to let them catch up. Poe noticed that when she was talking about data, she lost her awkwardness.

'Of course, we're not in London so ANPR cameras only cover the M6, the A-roads and some of the bigger B-roads, but I calculated that in all the abductions, some of these cameras would have to be crossed at least once: the ones on the M6 and the ones that cover the roads that cross the M6.'

Poe agreed. A bit like a major river, the M6 corridor bisected the county through the middle. It was inconceivable that the Immolation Man hadn't had to cross the motorway at least once. In all probability he'd passed over it, under it and driven along it several times.

Bradshaw continued. 'But the ANPR list was far too big. It was six figures high.'

'People use their cars more in rural counties,' Poe explained. 'ANPR covers all the commuter routes so I'm surprised the number wasn't bigger.'

'After I'd run the numbers through my program, it became a bit more manageable. I split the list into three. The first list is the vehicles with the highest probability. Eight hundred and four in total,' she said. 'That's the list I coloured in.'

As well as logging all necessary details like a vehicle's registration, where and when it was snapped, that type of thing, ANPR cameras also take two photographs: one of the registration plate and one of the whole vehicle. When Bradshaw said she'd had some of the ANPR data 'coloured in', she meant she'd downloaded those photographs. And probably to appease her analogue colleagues, she'd then printed them off.

The cost didn't matter, though; Bradshaw had two PhDs, she was a member of the Mathematics Institute at Oxford University, and she had an IQ higher than anyone Poe had ever heard of. If she said the killer was in that pile of paper somewhere, then he believed her.

He settled down to read. Flynn did the same.

Bradshaw smiled.

ANPR was a fantastic investigative tool when you knew what you were looking for, but its big weakness was that when you were casting a net, it was virtually worthless. It caught everyone, and Poe knew this was why Gamble hadn't really bothered before. He was sure that at some point he'd have tasked detectives with reviewing ANPR, but it would have been to tick boxes rather than a genuine investigative strategy. He'd have no way of reducing that list from the same six figures Bradshaw found. But Gamble's detectives weren't mathematical geniuses; Bradshaw was.

It was still an immense amount of data to review but Poe didn't lose focus. His faith in Bradshaw was absolute; the answer was there somewhere. After he'd read a page, Bradshaw would take it from him and pin it to the wall in a pattern known only to her. It was a good idea. Looking at the montage gave a different perspective to looking at them individually. Of course, at some point they'd have to deal with the hotel manager's wrath when he saw what they'd done to his freshly decorated wall, but that was a problem for another day. Or for Flynn. During a break to stretch his legs, Poe walked across to the flipboard the hotel had supplied and they had never used – Bradshaw frowned upon such technologically backwards tools – and picked up a marker pen from the tray underneath. He walked to the wall and started putting red crosses through vehicles he felt confident in ruling out.

Out of the 804 vehicles, over 30 were buses full of passengers. He put a red cross through them, doubting the Immolation Man had brought a coachload of supporters to his bonfires. He ruled out all the motorcycles; they might be able to go anywhere, but they couldn't be used to transport victims, containers of accelerant and stakes. There were four minibuses, and although the pictures were small, Poe could see they were charities transporting adults with learning difficulties. He red-crossed them.

There were others he was happy to cross out as well. Police vehicles were an obvious one. It was possible the Immolation Man was a cop, but police vehicles weren't used by one person; they did eight or ten hours with one shift, then would immediately be on the road with the next one. He crossed off ambulances for the same reason.

Next up were the prisoner-escort vans. The county's tagline for years had been: 'Cumbria: A Safe Place to Live, Work and Visit', and, the Immolation Man aside, it usually was. But there was still a hard-core element of crooks and ne'er-do-wells, and although the number of courts had reduced, the number of idiots hadn't. The GU Security vans were a regular sight on the Cumbrian roads as they serviced the county's courts and its sole prison. But they were also shift vehicles. Poe put a red cross through them all.

He also red-crossed the bigger lorries. Although they'd have been ideal for transporting bodies and equipment, the winding routes to some of the killing sites ruled them out.

The number of pictures without red crosses was still unmanageable, though. Poe stood up and down on his tiptoes to stretch his calf muscles while he thought how he could reduce the number further.

He walked back to the wall and, in a fit of pique, red-crossed every car he thought was too small to comfortably transport a driver, a body and a can of petrol. When he'd finished he threw down the pen in frustration.

'Sorry,' he apologised. More for Bradshaw's sake than Flynn's.

'You OK?' Flynn asked.

He nodded.

'Well, keep going. I think you're onto something.'

He walked back to the flip chart and picked up a green pen. He ticked vehicles he wanted to prioritise. Any van with panelled sides got a green tick. Any estate car, four-by-four or MPV got a tick. There was even a hearse. That got a double tick.

Eventually every vehicle either had a red cross or a green tick. Some, after discussion, changed colour, but after an hour they had some sort of consensus.

Poe rocked backwards and forwards on his heels as he scrutinised the wall.

He was sure the answer was there. He just needed a spark of inspiration to find it.

CHAPTER FORTY-SEVEN

They stared at the wall well into the evening. As they didn't want to take down the pinned ANPR pictures, and because none of them fancied eating in shifts, Poe drove into Kendal to get food from the British Raj Indian and Tandoori takeaway. He'd just ordered butter chicken for Flynn, vegetable balti for Bradshaw and lamb madras for himself, when his phone alerted him to an incoming text. It was from Reid saying he'd been to Herdwick Croft. He wanted to know where he was. Poe typed a reply, telling him they were at the hotel and that he should walk across to meet them. He ordered him a lamb madras.

The hotel was kind enough to provide plates and cutlery and they had begun eating when Reid arrived. He said he was famished and wolfed his down, refusing to speak until he'd finished.

Reid wandered over to the wall. Despite the late hour and the heat of the day, he was as immaculately dressed as always. Poe, who'd removed his jacket and rolled up his sleeves hours ago, managed a sly sniff of his own armpits. He'd need a shower soon.

'You heard Hilary Swift's in the clear?'

'She's involved, though,' said Poe.

'No doubt,' Reid said. 'You think she was working for someone? Or someone was working for her?'

Poe shrugged. 'She didn't recognise me. If she is working with the Immolation Man, then she's his apprentice.'

Reid didn't have an answer. There was no answer. Swift was

involved; they just didn't know how. Until she was caught, it would stay that way.

'What did you get from the social worker?' Reid asked, ready to move on. 'I assume you think the boys are dead?'

'That what you think?' Poe replied.

'Hard to see it any other way. I take it by visiting Children's Services again, you're looking at the families?'

'We are, but so far there's no one jumping up and down shouting "pick me". You've never read about a bigger bunch of wankers in your life. They didn't give a shit about the boys when they were alive, I don't see them developing consciences now.'

'So, we're back to an unknown. Someone who hasn't revealed their hand yet?' He sat down. 'Speaking of Hilary Swift, Gamble's asked me to tell you all that there's no evidence she's managed to leave the country. No one using her name or fitting her description has passed through a UKBA controlled point. Gamble's convinced – and I agree – that she's holed up somewhere.'

Poe grunted.

Reid stood up. 'Well, it looks like you're all on a mission so I'm going to love you and leave you. I'll call tomorrow if there's an update.'

'Call regardless, Kylian,' Poe said. 'We can tell you what we've found.'

He nodded and left.

Bradshaw walked to the board. Poe joined her. She said, 'How about we use a third colour, Poe? Vehicles we've ruled out that we want to reconsider?'

Poe picked up a blue pen and said, 'Let's get started then.'

They worked through the night, taking turns to nap on a sofa the porter had brought in.

By nine in the morning they'd used four more colours and had stared at the photographs until it felt like their eyes were bleeding.

'This isn't working,' Poe snapped. He turned to Bradshaw. 'Tilly, can you please put that big brain of yours to use? Find me something I can recognise because at the minute I can't see shit.'

Bradshaw flinched. He apologised. It certainly wasn't her fault.

'That's OK, Poe,' Bradshaw said. 'You and DI Stephanie Flynn go to breakfast. I'll try an old university trick: if you can't see the pattern, change your perspective.'

She didn't explain what she meant or wait for permission, just walked up to the wall and started unpinning pictures. Poe had seen her like this before and knew there was no point talking to her; she wouldn't be listening.

'Come on, boss. I'll buy you a bacon sandwich.'

When they returned, the pictures were back up but in four different blocks. There was a mixture of red crosses and green ticks. Poe looked at Bradshaw quizzically. The printer was clinking as it cooled. Bradshaw had printed off more photographs.

'We added more vehicles, Tilly?' Poe asked. It would be a backwards step if they had.

'I haven't, Poe. I've rearranged the photographs so they're now displayed on the day the victims were murdered. Each block is a separate day. I only had one photograph per vehicle so if they appeared on more than one day I had to print another copy.'

She'd obviously hammered more of SCAS's printing budget because some of the vehicles were on all four days. Bradshaw had put the date and the victim's name beside each block. Poe ran his eyes over how the information was now being presented to them.

Bradshaw said, 'While you look, Poe, I'll go and get a boiled egg.' She glanced at her watch. 'Rats. Breakfast finished at ten. I've just missed it.'

'Only on Wednesdays and Sundays, Tilly. They need to set up for the carvery lunch on those days. It's open until eleven today, you go and get your boiled . . .' The rest of the sentence died on his lips.

'What is it, Poe?' Bradshaw asked.

He ignored her and marched up to the block of the second victim. Joe Lowell had been immolated in the middle of the Swinside stone circle near Broughton-in-Furness. Telling Bradshaw about the hotel's breakfast had jolted something in the recesses of his mind. He could almost reach it. Almost but not quite. Poe stared at the vehicles until they were burned into his retina. For twenty minutes he looked without seeing anything.

Five times he studied the block of vehicles. And on the sixth he saw the photograph that changed everything.

There it was. Bold as brass. The anomaly. The vehicle that had no right to be there. Poe felt the hairs on his neck stand up.

Surely it couldn't be so simple?

'Poe?' Flynn asked.

For several moments he didn't dare open his mouth, and when he did he ignored her question. Instead, he said to Bradshaw, 'Tilly, can you get on to the HMCTS website and see which Cumbrian courts sat on the day Joe Lowell was murdered? Check Preston Crown Court as well.'

She glanced between Poe and Flynn, unsure what to do.

Flynn said, 'Do as he asks, Tilly.'

They waited while Bradshaw logged into Her Majesty's Courts and Tribunal Service website. The information Poe wanted was publicly available and he could have found it himself, but Bradshaw was quicker. Flynn had known him long enough to know she wouldn't get anything out of him until he was ready so she didn't bother trying.

Five minutes later Tilly said, 'No courts sat on the day Joe Lowell was murdered, Poe. It was a Sunday.'

Poe nodded. He was right. He jabbed his finger against a vehicle in the Joe Lowell block, before turning to face Bradshaw and Flynn.

'So what the fuck is that GU prisoner-escort van doing there?'

CHAPTER FORTY-EIGHT

Like most cops, Poe held strong views on the prisoner-escort service and the shameful low it took in 2004 when it was taken out of the hands of the prison service and sold to huge multinational companies. For some time, those companies had been looking upon the annual one-and-a-half million prisoner transportations with their insatiable lust for profit. The fact that it was a Labour government that did this was no surprise to him; they were as susceptible as anyone else to those false promises of the private sector: efficiencies and innovations.

Innovations that included cramming prisoners into cells measuring no more than two feet squared, and efficiencies that included refusing to stop for toilet breaks, with the result that prisoners – some of whom were on remand and hadn't been convicted of any offence – had to piss and shit in their cells. Legally, animals being taken to slaughter were entitled to better conditions. By the time the Home Office realised what was happening, it was too late – palms had been greased, directorships had been promised and contracts had been signed – so they did what every government does; they lied and manipulated statistics. Poe knew there were no votes in telling the truth.

As an extra kick in the public's teeth, and as an example of the law of unintended consequences, no one in the Home Office had considered what would happen when the first tranche of contracts ended and new providers took over. In a remarkable lack of foresight, no one had thought to regulate what happened to the vehicles owned by the original contractor when they were no longer needed.

Entire fleets were offered for sale on the open market, and although a *Daily Mail* article highlighted the potential for abuse, the government was powerless to stop it. While the minister in charge blamed his civil servants and the civil servants blamed their minister, the result was that, for a few thousand pounds, anyone could legally purchase a vehicle that was, in all but name, a mobile prison.

The prisoner-escort van that Bradshaw had placed on the Sunday block of vehicles was one of the smaller models. It contained four cells. Poe knew that some of the larger ones could transport three times that number. The smaller size meant it was nippy enough to get to all the locations to which the Immolation Man had been.

None of the photographs had the driver in shot. The windscreen seemed to have been treated with some sort of tinting agent. Poe was unsurprised.

There was some immediate work to do. Flynn called Gamble to tell him what they'd uncovered, and Bradshaw checked PNC. She found the registration number was still with GU Security. A call to their operation's centre was met with an unsurprising eagerness to cooperate; image is everything with the private companies who compete for public sector contracts.

Yes, that was one of their four-cell vans.

No, it had never been in Cumbria, and no it had never been involved in any part of the north-west's prisoner escort contract. Vehicle Number 236, as they called it, was used for a UK Border Agency contract in the south-east.

And, yes, they could prove it. All their vehicles were fitted with satellite tracking equipment so the control room knew where they were at all times.

After GU promised to email the information, Poe ended the call. Bradshaw said, 'What does that all mean, Poe?'

'It means the registration number was cloned to make sure it wouldn't be flagged as false or on the wrong type of vehicle.'

'Gosh. How clever.'

It was. 'And because GU have the north-west prisoner contract, they're on our roads all day and well into the evenings. You get so used to seeing them, they blend into the background.'

The Immolation Man had been hiding in plain sight.

Flynn had left for her emergency meeting with Gamble. Hopefully a coherent strategy on how to trace the GU van would emerge.

But just in case it didn't . . .

Poe glanced across at Bradshaw. She had begun to pack. She looked despondent. The excitement of the discovery had fizzled out once the information was passed to Gamble. The change in her was remarkable. A week ago, data was simply a puzzle to solve, and once she had, it had been passed to Flynn and forgotten about. Other than in the abstract, Poe knew she'd never had to think about the human cost behind the data she deciphered. And now she had, he knew she'd be a better analyst for it. Sometimes cold reason wasn't enough; sometimes you needed skin in the game. Being personally involved forced you to go the extra mile.

'You don't think we're done here, Tilly?' Poe asked, smiling. 'Get yourself comfortable, we have work to do.'

Bradshaw clapped. She opened her laptop, pushed up her glasses, and waited for instructions.

Poe sat beside her and said, 'DCS Gamble's going to start checking the sales of those vehicles, Tilly. He'll need a warrant.'

She waited for him to make his point.

'But if the Immolation Man is as intelligent as we think he is, the van purchases are going to be hidden. He won't have paid for them with a credit card. And GU wouldn't have sold them directly to the public themselves anyway: they'll have sent them to one of those companies that buy cars in bulk. The van we want could have

247

been bought through an auction, or through a subsidiary company of a subsidiary company of a . . . well, you get the point.'

'I'm not sure I do, Poe.'

'I'm saying we need to find a quicker way, Tilly. Let Gamble track the van through the paperwork. He'll get there in the end, but while he's doing that, I want you to think of another way to catch this prick . . .'

CHAPTER FORTY-NINE

Bradshaw smiled shyly. 'Poe, what did I tell you a couple of days ago?'

It could have been anything. The topics of their recent conversations had been wide-ranging and varied; from the bowel habits of the elderly, to why he was called Washington.

'I don't know,' he said, before taking a guess. 'Something about the gaming industry now being bigger than the music industry?'

'About data points,' she prompted.

He remembered something about data points. It had been one of those discussions where Bradshaw missed all his non-verbal clues and had enthused at length about some technical point in chaos theory. He found it easier to let her finish than try to stop her. It hadn't been long before his mind went into screensaver mode. 'It's possible I might have forgotten the salient details,' he admitted.

'I said that, with enough data points, I can find the pattern in anything.'

'So?'

He got the impression his stupidity with statistics remained a source of intense frustration to her. Although part of him missed her unintentional rudeness, the fact she was now keeping her comments to herself was testament to how much she'd changed.

'So,' she said, pointing at the photograph-covered wall, 'when I downloaded all those photographs, all I was working on was the days of the murders.'

Realisation dawned on Poe.

Of course!

Now they knew the vehicle, they could get every ANPR record for it. Every time the Immolation Man's mobile prison passed a camera, they'd know about it. ANPR records were kept for two years, and although they would end up with two records – there was still a GU van with legitimate plates working in the south-west – it should be easy enough to separate the two.

Bradshaw was already inside the ANPR database. Within minutes the printer was churning out sheet after sheet of information. She said, 'This is a good example of Edward Lorenz's butterfly effect, isn't it, Poe?'

'Hmm,' Poe muttered, his mind full of auction houses and other ways vehicle fleets could be sold.

'The butterfly effect.'

'I'm not following you, Tilly.'

'I said, this is a good example of it. How one small, seemingly insignificant event can snowball into what we have here.'

'Explain.'

'Well, all of this,' she waved her arms at everything on the desks, computers and walls, 'and everything you and I discovered, all came from that one small thing.' She shook her head as if she were amazed. 'The one thing that anchored everything else.'

It was often how the harder cases broke. Small pieces of evidence led to larger pieces and so on. 'Yeah, we got lucky with that body in the salt store,' he admitted.

'Really? I think it goes back further than that. I think this whole thing goes back to a chance remark.'

The printer's out-tray was overflowing. Poe walked over and emptied it. As he picked up the sheets that had fallen on the floor, he asked, 'What chance remark was that, Tilly?'

'When someone in Kendal police station reminded Kylian Reid about the body in the salt store. He'd forgotten about Tollund Man and

250

you didn't know about it. It wasn't recorded as a crime so I wouldn't have found it. Just think, *everything* started with that chance remark.'

She was right. Sort of. Poe was inclined to think it started when a psychopath carved his name into someone's chest, but essentially she was correct. Without Reid coming back from Kendal with Tollund Man, they wouldn't be where they were now.

Bradshaw mistook his silence for disagreement and began pushing her point. Poe was no longer listening. He'd picked up the top sheet off the printer and was staring at it. Bradshaw had searched in reverse chronological order, so the most recent records were first.

He hadn't been expecting to see anything he would recognise – this was Bradshaw's area, not his – but two results halfway down the page caused him to stop. A feeling of dread came over him. Acid churned in his stomach. His mouth went dry.

The results he was looking at were from one of the cameras covering the A591. They were there to help track the gangs that supplied drugs to the heart of the Lake District. Unless they had extraordinary local knowledge, anyone travelling to Ambleside or Windermere – whether it was from the Keswick end or the Kendal end – would pass one of the A591 ANPR cameras.

And Ambleside and Windermere weren't the only places accessed via the A591.

There were several other small villages.

Once of which was Grasmere.

Where Seven Pines was located.

The dates matched.

The times matched.

If Poe's notes were accurate – and he knew they were – the prisoner-escort van had driven past the ANPR camera about ten minutes before he and Reid had. Hilary Swift wasn't the Immolation Man's accomplice at all. She was his next victim.

He'd abducted her.

And taken her grandchildren with him.

CHAPTER FIFTY

'The Immolation Man has the kids as well!' Poe shouted into the phone. Flynn was on her hands free and the reception was scratchy. As she was on her way to see Gamble, giving her the information directly was the quickest way of getting it to the right people.

Flynn got the message, and even through the poor reception, Poe could hear the car's revs increase as she put her foot down.

On the thousand-to-one chance that Flynn had an accident, Poe decided to cover all bases. He rang Reid but it went to voice-mail. He left a message and hung up. As far as he was concerned, the information had been passed on. He emailed Flynn the document showing that the Immolation Man's vehicle had been in the Grasmere area on the day Swift and her grandchildren had disappeared.

He tried to calm his racing thoughts. Things were making a bit more sense. Swift being abducted was a better fit than her being involved in the murders. And in the scheme of things – including Poe's new-found theory that the case was motivated by revenge rather than money – it all clicked. Whoever the Immolation Man was, he was systematically working his way through everyone on the charity cruise that night. Only Montague Price had avoided his fate, and that was because he'd had the foresight to flee as soon as he recognised the pattern.

The mechanics of snatching Swift from under the noses of two experienced cops were troubling him. How had the Immolation Man administered the drugs? Had he been in the house at the same time as they were? Had he sneaked in while they were talking to Swift and put propofol in the milk? A plan that relied on knowing when police officers were going to be drinking tea seemed too random for the Immolation Man; he'd never left anything to chance so far. It was typical of the case: each time they made a breakthrough more questions were posed.

Bradshaw was still working on the ANPR data for the prisoner-escort van, trying to find a pattern that might help them. In contrast to Poe's hunt-and-stab method of typing, her fingers moved so quickly across the keyboard they were a blur. The printer had been a constant whir of noise, and for the next half hour Poe was little more than an office junior. He loaded the printer with paper and replaced empty ink cartridges. The staff must have been getting sick of Bradshaw's printer – she'd exhausted the hotel's conference stock again, but Poe convinced the staff to steal ink from other machines in the building.

Eventually Bradshaw stopped. 'I'm going to need an hour to look at this. Can you go and get a map of Cumbria, Poe? The larger the better.'

Poe was about to say he'd send someone out for it, but realised she probably wanted him out of the way while she worked. He'd been like a caged beast while he waited.

'Will do,' he replied.

An hour later he was back. Getting a map of the area hadn't been an issue; the shops were full of them. The issue was that the maps the shops sold were for tourists. They were geared for fell walking, not for driving.

He'd been about to give up. He knew Kendal police station had a map that covered the entire wall; he and Bradshaw could take their data there and start plotting it. He was pondering this – the drawbacks as well as the advantages – when he glanced in the shop window he was standing beside. It was an Age Concern charity shop and he saw a basket of maps in the window. He found what he needed: an Ordnance Survey Tour Map. He opened it up and saw the scale was just right for their needs. He gave the woman twenty pounds and told her to keep the change.

The map was pinned to the wall and Bradshaw had fully plotted it. If there was a pattern there, Poe couldn't see it. Red and blue pins had been placed in clumps. He recognised some of the larger, more intense groups as the county's main thoroughfares: the M6, the A66 and the A595. Some of the smaller groups were around known victim-abduction sites. Long Meg and Her Daughters aside, the other stone circles the Immolation Man had used as murder sites weren't heavily covered by ANPR – they were too rural.

Bradshaw was frowning at the map as if something wasn't working.

'What's up, Tilly?'

Eventually she said, 'This doesn't make sense, Poe.'

'How?'

'It doesn't conform to my model.'

'Explain, and use the crayon method please.'

Bradshaw usually smiled. This time she didn't.

'Well, you know that this type of profiling is to assist with understanding the offender's spatial behaviour?'

Poe didn't have a clue what she was talking about. He wasn't even sure he knew what 'spatial' meant. 'Dumb it down a bit more can you, Tilly?'

'An offender will have a natural aversion to committing crimes close to home,' she said. 'It's called their buffer zone.'

Not shitting on your own doorstep, he'd have called it, but he knew what she meant. Even low-life heroin addicts tended to move into the next street before they started shaking hands with door handles.

254

'Well, conversely they'll also have a comfort zone in which they feel safe. It's usually somewhere they know well. It's called the distance decay theory; the farther someone is away from their regular activity space, the less likely they are to offend.'

That made sense too. Poe was convinced that the Immolation Man knew the areas he was working in; it was the only explanation for him having avoided so many of the fixed-point cameras on the roads. 'But we now know he wasn't picking his victims at random. He had a list he was working through. He had no control over where they lived,' he said.

'I've built that into my model.'

Of course she had.

'So what is it?'

'It's the murder sites. That's the thing that doesn't make sense. There are three variables involved in each killing: where he abducts the victim, where he keeps the victim and where he kills the victim.'

Poe thought he knew where she was headed but he let her finish.

'As you say, the abduction points are out of his control, and if we assume that the site he keeps them at is a fixed point, then the only random part is the selection of the murder site.'

'And there's no pattern?'

She shook her head. 'There should have been, even if it was just the way he travelled to them, but I can't see it, and that means there isn't one.' She wasn't boasting, simply stating a fact.

'Perhaps the pattern is there *is* no pattern.'

Bradshaw stiffened and stood up. 'I'm such a silly goose, Poe! You said Cumbria had sixty-three stone circles. He's used four – where are the other fifty-nine?'

'All over the place,' he replied. 'Off the top of my head I don't . . .'

Her fingers moved over the keyboard as if they were possessed.

Twenty seconds later a document listing the county's stone circles shunted its way out of the printer. For the next thirty minutes they plotted their locations on the map with yellow pins. He stood back.

Bradshaw joined him. 'I told you, Poe. Data *never* lies – there's always a pattern.'

Without looking at each other, they silently fist-bumped.

He didn't need her to explain. The Immolation Man's pattern could only be seen when it was placed within the context of the circles he hadn't used.

He'd killed his victims at the so-called 'big three': Long Meg, Swinside and Castlerigg. They were sites of historical importance and known to an international audience. Huge and impressive. Leaving a burning body in the middle was impact heavy. But . . . he'd also picked Elva Plain in Cockermouth. Why? There were more impressive circles he still hadn't used. Elva Plain didn't even look like a stone circle. Most people were unaware of its existence.

Why hadn't he chosen a circle from the biggest mass of yellow on the map? Why hadn't he chosen one from the area known as the Shap Stone Avenue? There were countless circles to choose from – some of them close to where they were now. Some of them were isolated but well known. They even had easy access to the M6. Pretty much everything the Immolation Man needed.

He thought about Bradshaw's buffer zone. Was it possible the Immolation Man hadn't committed any crimes in the Shap area because he lived nearby? Had they been looking out when they should have been looking in?

The back of his neck started to bead with sweat. The room was getting warm again. He removed his jacket, put it on the back of his chair and rolled up his sleeves. He could sense he was close. The answers were all there; he needed to look at everything through a different lens. He rocked his chair backwards and forwards, trying to think of something new. The rocking caused his jacket to fall on the floor. He bent down to pick it up.

And paused.

He caught his breath. His intuition had been telling him that the answers would be found in the past. That Price, and then Swift, becoming suspects, were nothing more than a distraction. He'd never believed either of them had been capable of being the Immolation Man.

His eyes moved from his jacket on the floor to one of the photographs on the wall. The four boys – topless and happy in the sun, puffing out chests they didn't yet have. He stood up and draped his jacket over the chair again. He looked at it, damp with sweat and hanging limply like a sock on a shower rail.

His mind brought up a succession of images. Through memory after memory, he searched for the one that would disprove his growing suspicion. He couldn't find it. He blinked and the images disappeared.

His jacket.

The photograph.

There was a connection.

His thoughts drifted back to something Bradshaw had said earlier. He hadn't paid too much attention, but it had been marinating because it was now jumping up and down in the front of his mind.

The butterfly effect, she'd called it. She'd said that someone reminding Reid about Tollund Man being found not five miles from where they were now was the catalyst, the butterfly flapping its wings in Brazil that causes a hurricane in Texas. Without Tollund Man they wouldn't have found the disturbed coffin, probably wouldn't have discovered the stolen Breitling. Quentin Carmichael would still be listed as dying in Africa and the insidious purpose of the charity cruise would have remained hidden.

But what if . . . ?

Sometimes Poe's mind lay coiled and quiet, processing data at its own speed, but at other times he was capable of making huge intuitive leaps. A horrific, half-formed suspicion grew in the pit of his stomach and began to gnaw and gnaw . . .

Neurons were firing. Faster and faster as he made link after link. All the disparate parts of the puzzle came together and clicked into place. Confusion was replaced by understanding.

Poe knew most of it – maybe all of it.

No one had been able to answer how the Immolation Man had managed to stay a ghost for so long. Fair enough, anyone could learn police procedures these days; the Freedom of Information Act meant that most police manuals were publicly available. It was feasible that an intelligent, careful man could teach himself to be forensically aware. But how had he evaded the surveillance Gamble had laid down? The mobile ANPR cameras, the human surveillance on the stone circles, all the patrols. There was only one possibility. The Immolation Man had to be getting current intel.

As Poe inched towards confirming his own theory, he thought of everything they'd uncovered over the last two weeks. He looked at his jacket and corrected himself. He went back further. To the night of the charity cruise and a plan that had taken almost twenty-six years to come to fruition.

Logically, there was only one person it could be. The thought chilled him to his very core.

'Do you have the information sheet on propofol, Tilly?'

She found it and handed it over. Poe turned over the top sheet and looked for the sections on other uses. He ran his finger down the list and stopped when he found what he was looking for.

Shit . . .

He glanced up. Bradshaw was watching him. 'I need you to check something for me, Tilly.'

'What is it, Poe?'

After he'd told her, she frowned. 'Are you sure?' she said softly.

He found he couldn't speak. He nodded.

As Bradshaw ran the information he'd given her, Poe paced up and down the room. It was the worst thing he'd ever had to wait for. He prayed he was wrong, but knew he wasn't.

The result came on to Bradshaw's screen and she turned and nodded. She had tears in her eyes.

She wasn't the only one.

Poe knew who the Immolation Man was.

CHAPTER FIFTY-ONE

Poe stared at the number on his mobile. There would be no going back if he made the call. No bell could be unrung. His finger hovered over the dial icon. Eventually he touched it. He closed his eyes as he waited for the call to be answered. She might not. She'd be involved in the search for the abducted children and trying to identify the owner of the prisoner-escort van. He had to tell her before anyone else. He needed to convince her.

After eight rings – and Poe counted them with a heart that grew heavier with each one – Flynn answered her phone.

'Poe,' she whispered, 'I can't talk. DCS Gamble's just delivering his briefing.'

'You need to go and get him, Steph.'

'It'll have to wait. I've got—'

Poe spoke firmly. 'You need to go and get DCS Gamble and you need to do it right now.'

'I'm going to need more,' she replied after a small pause.

Poe told her.

There was a delay of three or four minutes as Flynn manoeuvred her way through the briefing room. Despite the fact it sounded as though she was holding her phone at her side, Poe could still hear her as she 'excused me'd' her way to the front of the room.

It was tinny, but when she arrived, Poe could hear both sides of the conversation.

'It's DS Poe, sir. He says he needs to speak to us.'

'Does he now?' Gamble replied. 'Well, he's going to have to get in the queue. When I've finished here, the chief constable wants me to accompany him to the PCC's office. We're both in for a bollocking.'

'You need to take this, sir. Trust me.'

Poe heard Gamble sigh. 'Look, I know he's been a small help on this investigation but we have missing children now. I really don't have time to waste on another of his theories.'

Flynn didn't respond.

'Fine,' he said. 'We'll go into my office.'

A minute later Flynn put the mobile on speakerphone.

'Out with it, Poe,' Gamble snapped.

'I know who the Immolation Man is, sir, and we need to act now.'

'You do, do you?' Gamble said sceptically.

Poe ignored the rudeness. Gamble was under enormous pressure. 'It all comes down to a suit jacket at the end of the day, sir,' Poe replied. 'A suit jacket and the flap of a butterfly's wings.'

'What are you talking about, man?' Gamble snapped.

'It's Kylian Reid, sir. The Immolation Man is Kylian Reid.'

CHAPTER FIFTY-TWO

It was Bradshaw who'd pointed him down the road he'd just travelled. Rattling on about that stupid butterfly and how it kept causing hurricanes. She'd said the body in the salt store wasn't the anchor for this case. The anchor – the first flap of the butterfly's wings – was that someone had thought to mention Tollund Man at all. Without that chance comment in Kendal police station, they'd have been nowhere.

But what if it wasn't luck? What if it had been intentional? Other than fluking their way into the charity gala, the Immolation Man had been in control. To date, he'd been the puppet master.

But why let them make any progress at all?

It could only be because he wanted Poe involved and he didn't want him too far behind. And as soon as he thought about it that way, like a beacon through fog, his connection to the case shone through.

The Immolation Man wasn't trying to evade justice – he was delivering it.

He wanted his story told, but only after the players had been punished. And with the investigation initially stalling and following clichéd theories, the Immolation Man had engineered the involvement of the one man who might see through the smog of confusion. Poe, with his stupid 'follow the evidence anywhere' mantra, became part of his narrative.

From the beginning, Poe had worried about motive, and with a case like this, when you had the motive, you had everything: the identity of the killer, what really happened on that charity cruise, how the victims were selected, everything. Poe could even take a stab at why the Immolation Man had killed the way he had.

It all made a twisted sense. From the Immolation Man's perspective, it really did.

It was a child snuff ring that went to the top of Cumbria's social elite. A landowner, a solicitor, a media baron, a council member and a member of the clergy. The Immolation Man was killing the people involved, but that was only half the story: he also wanted them exposed.

But he didn't trust his own police force to do what was right. He knew his chief constable had ambitions higher than Cumbria. For advancement, he'd cover the reasons behind the castrations and burnings. He'd focus on the killings and nothing more. His story might never be told.

That was where Poe came in. The Immolation Man needed his dogged determination to see behind the headlines and get to the real story.

Reid had integrated himself into their investigation from the beginning, monitoring his progress, nudging them in the right direction if they needed help. It was Reid who'd sent him that postcard. It was Reid who'd told them about the salt-store connection; Poe doubted anyone had reminded him; he probably hadn't even been to Kendal police station. Just came back to Herdwick Croft with an answer he knew Poe would obsess over.

And because he lived in Kendal, he fitted Bradshaw's buffer-zone and distance decay models.

Poe even knew how he'd managed to abduct Hilary Swift.

All that was suspicious, but ultimately circumstantial.

Where was the motive? Why was he doing these monstrous things? Why would Reid, a decorated police officer with over fifteen years' exemplary service, suddenly decide to become a serial killer?

The answer was he hadn't. He'd decided a long time ago.

It was the jacket that provided Poe with the missing motivation.

It didn't matter what the weather was doing, Reid never removed his jacket. For years, he'd taken the piss out of Poe's lack of sartorial elegance. Whether they were at work, or on a night out, Reid always dressed well. In all the time he'd known him, Poe had never seen him without a shirt, jacket or jumper on. He'd certainly never seen him in a T-shirt, even when they were teenagers.

In the photograph of the boys, one of their nightmare starts to life had visible reminders. Mathew Malone had cigarette burns all over his torso and arms. Terrible scars that would never heal.

Kylian Reid's arms were always covered.

Kylian Reid was Mathew Malone.

And Mathew Malone was killing the men who'd murdered his friends.

CHAPTER FIFTY-THREE

'You're out of your fucking mind, Poe!' Gamble said. 'Out of your fucking mind!'

Poe had finished explaining. Gamble wasn't buying it. Even Flynn was reticent.

'It is a bit of a stretch, Poe,' she said.

He needed them to believe him, and their reaction – although not unexpected – wasn't helping. 'Tilly,' he said calmly. 'Can you tell DI Flynn and DCS Gamble what you found, please?'

'I can, Poe,' she said. Leaning into the phone, Bradshaw said, 'DS Poe asked me to check all vehicles registered to the Scafell Veterinary Group.'

'What the heck is that?' Poe noticed Gamble didn't swear at Bradshaw. Drunks in Shap Wells aside, everyone seemed to regulate their language when talking to her.

'They're a veterinary practice and they used to have a lot of vehicles. Mainly four-wheel drives and Land Rovers. Since the company went dormant, they haven't bought anything.'

'Tilly, can you get to the—' Flynn said.

Showing a resilience she hadn't had a week ago, Bradshaw clipped her boss's sentence. 'Until ten months ago when two vehicles were bought from a car auction in Derbyshire.'

There was silence. Everyone on the call knew that GU Security had their UK headquarters in Derbyshire.

'Are you saying what I think you're saying?' Flynn asked. Gamble seemed to have lost his voice.

'It was easy enough to check,' Poe said. 'Because of money-laundering laws, all car auction companies are registered with HMRC as high-value dealers. That means they can't accept cash transactions of over ten thousand pounds so—'

'So those vans would have had to be paid for via a bank transfer,' Gamble cut in. 'I know how the fucking money-laundering law works, Poe! I am still failing to see how this leads back to one of my finest officers.'

'GU were very helpful, sir,' Poe said, as if Gamble hadn't spoken. 'Among the vehicles sold to the auction company were four-cell vans and some of the larger ten-cell trucks. The auction company confirmed that the Scafell Veterinary Group bought one of each. I've sent you their email.'

'But—'

'Sir, the Scafell Veterinary Group is owned by Kylian Reid's father.'

It took a further ten minutes for Gamble to get to grips with the fact that one of his detectives might be a serial killer. He clung to the one thing he thought Poe couldn't explain. 'It doesn't make sense, Poe. Reid was drugged at the same time as you.'

'He was, sir,' Poe agreed.

'Well then?'

'What do you know about propofol, sir?'

'It's an anaesthetic,' Gamble replied.

'It is, sir. But thanks to Tilly I know a lot more about it now. It has a multitude of other uses. It's been used as part of the lethal injection cocktails on American death-row inmates, and it's used recreationally by some of the more discerning drug users. It's even—'

'Get to the fucking point, Poe!'

'Veterinary medicine, sir!' Bradshaw blurted out. 'Vets also use it as an anaesthetic.'

266

'Are you saying . . .'

'The Scafell Veterinary Group purchased some last year, sir,' Poe finished for him. 'Propofol is heavily regulated and the drugs company keep an excellent record. I've sent you that email as well.'

There was a pause, 'It still doesn't explain how he managed to drug himself *and* abduct Hilary Swift at the same time, Poe.'

'That's because he didn't, sir,' Poe said.

'I don't unders—'

'The Immolation Man isn't one person, sir, it's two,' Poe cut in. 'Reid drugged himself to avoid suspicion, then his father abducted Hilary Swift and her grandchildren.'

Flynn took control. 'OK, Poe. Sir, I think we've heard enough. We need to at least detain DS Reid until we've cleared this up,' she said.

'And can I suggest that someone makes sure Montague Price is where he's supposed to be?' Poe said.

That got Gamble's attention. It was one thing to not see the enemy within, another thing entirely for a prisoner in his custody to be abducted.

'It's ridiculous, DI Flynn,' Gamble said, no doubt thinking ahead. The world was about to crash down on his head.

'Steph,' Poe said, 'if DCS Gamble can't, can you? Price is now the only one left from that boat. Kylian will want him.'

'Leave it with me.'

Ten minutes later Poe received a text from Flynn: Reid not at Cumbria headquarters. No one has seen him. Gamble's in meltdown. Any ideas?

Poe sent one back saying he didn't have any, but he'd get Bradshaw working on it. He doubted Reid would have left a paper trail leading to his location but he had to do something. After he'd made sure Bradshaw knew what she was searching for, he'd head into Kendal and have a look through Reid's flat before it was declared a crime scene and off-limits. It wouldn't be Reid's containment site, but it might offer something.

As soon he'd sent the text, his phone rang. It was Flynn. 'What you got, Steph?'

It sounded as if she was running. 'Poe, Reid signed Montague Price out of Carlisle police station two hours ago!'

Shit!

'Escorted him personally to a—'

'Four-cell GU Security prisoner-escort van,' Poe finished for her.

'Exactly. Gamble's staying at HQ to coordinate the search for him but he's totally lost it now. I'm coming back down. It seems it's only you and Tilly who have a grip on what's going on.'

'We'll keep trying to find the address they've been using then. They won't be at Reid's or his father's. Far too busy. Reid's flat is in the middle of Kendal, and although his father has a small farmhouse, he converted and sold the two barns so he now has neighbours.'

'You think the Scafell Group owns a property we don't know about?' she asked.

Despite having this discussion over the phone, Poe shook his head. 'Tilly's checking but the company has literally nothing left. George Reid seems to have liquidated his assets. The only things he owns now are the vans.'

'Best guess?'

'No idea, Steph,' Poe replied. 'But they've obviously been planning this for years; no way do we find them because of a utility bill.'

'Nope, I think . . .' He didn't get to find out what she thought, as at that moment her other phone rang. 'Hang on, Poe,' she said. 'My personal mobile's ringing.'

Poe could only hear one side of the conversation. It didn't sound good.

'Shit! Shit! Shit!' Flynn shouted. 'Right, I'll tell him to go there now.'

Flynn tried to sound calm. 'Poe, we need you to go and check something out for us. Apparently, a train passenger has reported seeing someone on fire in a field.'

'Where?' He thought he might know.

'A short distance from where you are now. I've sent Tilly the coordinates. Go and check it out and let's hope it's just kids starting Guy Fawkes early.'

He stared at the map Bradshaw had just put on her screen. It was as he feared. 'Shit,' he said.

'What is it, Poe?' Flynn asked.

'Those coordinates are where the West Coast Mainline bisects the Kemp Howe stone circle. The train tracks run through the fucking middle of it. If someone did see something burning in the stone circle, they wouldn't have been more than ten yards from it. Hard to mistake a burning body for a wheelie bin at that distance.'

'Oh, shit,' she whispered.

CHAPTER FIFTY-FOUR

When he'd been in uniform, Poe was frequently the first officer on scene. Beat cops were usually the first to see unexplained deaths, natural deaths and suicides. When panicked relatives discovered a body, or neighbours smelled something suspicious and organic, their first thoughts were invariably to dial 999. Poe knew how to secure a crime scene.

Later in his career, when he'd moved into CID and had been on-call, he'd possessed a grab bag: a small rucksack containing things like crime-scene tape, a torch and batteries, a mobile-phone charger, forensic suits and warm clothing. His car was always fully fuelled and there'd be pre-packed food in the fridge.

This time the only thing he had was a greenhorn analyst on her first field trip.

Bradshaw had refused to stay at the hotel. 'I'm coming with you,' she said, and time was too important to spend on an argument he'd surely lose.

On the way, he rang Flynn to determine it was the northbound Carlisle train the passenger had been on. Poe grunted in satisfaction. That meant they were on the right side of the railway track and there was no need for a long detour.

Ten minutes later they were at the side of the narrow field that hosted what remained of the Kemp Howe stone circle. Poe stopped the car but kept it in gear while he searched for signs of Reid or his father. He hadn't expected any; the abduction of Price was a bonus, an unexpected opportunity to get the full list of victims while Gamble's briefing had everyone's eyes elsewhere. Price's murder would have had to be rushed; there wouldn't have been the time for any elaborate staging or ritual. And it didn't matter if Reid were observed or not. Everyone knew who he was now.

Price's murder wasn't the endgame and Reid wouldn't have hung around waiting. Poe checked anyway. There was a part of Reid that Poe hadn't known about and there was no point taking unnecessary risks. He got out of the car, climbed onto the bonnet and recced the immediate area. It appeared clear.

He cast his eyes towards the Kemp Howe stone circle. It was perhaps the strangest in Cumbria. Against a backdrop of ancient moorland, it formed part of the Shap Stone Row, a collection of rocks that ran for a mile and a half alongside the A6 and the West Coast Mainline. It would have been about twenty-five yards wide if the Victorians hadn't bisected it when the railway was laid. More than half the circle was under the embankment. The remaining six pink granite stones were large and visible from both the road and the railway.

In among them, something was smouldering.

Poe jumped down, got in the car and moved it into the middle of the road to ensure no one could get past. He put on his hazard lights.

Turning to Bradshaw, he said, 'Until I tell you otherwise, you're the outer cordon officer. That means no one gets into this field without my permission. Understand?'

She nodded. 'You can rely on me, Poe.'

'I know I can, Tilly. There'll be some help here soon. Get the first police vehicle to park twenty yards up that way,' he pointed up the road, 'so we'll block off the road completely. If anyone gives you any shit, shout for me.'

Bradshaw stepped away from the car and stood in the open entrance facing out. She looked resolute. Pity the idiot who tried to argue with her.

Poe took a moment to make sure he'd done everything he needed to do. Conduct a quick risk assessment: check. Secure the crime scene: check. Allocate resources appropriately: check.

Time to go and see if it was a burning sheep – kids did that sometimes in Cumbria – or a burning paedophile. If anyone had asked Poe for his preference, he'd have had to flip a coin.

For Reid, haste would have become more important than subtlety. Poe suspected that he'd have driven into the field and directly up to the circle. Poe walked along the wall. He had no way of recording the route he'd taken, and this was as good a way as any of ensuring vital evidence wasn't trampled on later. From this point on, everyone approaching the crime scene would use the same route.

He was still fifty yards away when the possibility of it being a six-months-too-early bonfire-night prank disappeared.

It was a body.

Poe approached it cautiously. It was clear that the victim's injuries were incompatible with life. His charred remains were blackened and smoking. The heat was beginning to crack the skin. Parts of his flesh glowed red. The smell was acrid. Poe bit down on his tongue to stop himself retching. He needed to pull himself together. People were relying on him.

The body's arm moved and, for one heart-stopping moment, Poe thought it was still alive. He was about to rush in and start . . . well, he didn't know what, until he realised that it was the heat causing the muscles to contract. By the time it cooled, the body would be as twisted as a corkscrew.

Although he'd have to be formally identified through DNA and dental records, Poe was certain it was Price. He wasn't as badly burnt as the body at Elva Plain and he could see features he recognised from the video interview. It looked like Reid had been in too much of a hurry to stake him properly. He'd probably only had enough time to cover him with accelerant and set him on fire.

As Poe neared the body, he reconsidered – Reid had also made his signature statement. Price's trousers were round his ankles. Reid had castrated him. And judging by the amount of blood on the grass, Price had been alive and unrestrained when his genitals had been removed. Poe scanned the area, but couldn't see the amputated flesh. He suspected it was where everyone else's had been: in his mouth.

He looked back towards Bradshaw – he didn't want her seeing this – and was relieved to see she was still facing the road. His phone rang and he answered it, unable to tear his eyes away from the horror unfolding in front of him.

'Poe,' he said.

'It's Ian Gamble. Are you there yet?'

'I am, sir.'

'And?'

'Bad news, sir. I think it's Montague Price. He's dead, I'm afraid.'

'Mother of mercy,' Gamble whispered. 'What have I done . . .?'

Poe understood. Gamble had Price in custody and now he was dead. Killed by someone under his command. There'd be investigations after this and Gamble would probably lose his job. He'd certainly never be an SIO again. Poe had a measure of sympathy for the man. No one could have been properly prepared to manage a case like this. A serial killer who was part of the investigating team? Poe had never even heard of anything like that before. Reid knew all the lines of enquiry. He'd helped shaped strategy. He'd led on certain things. He knew where Gamble had deployed his mobile ANPR cameras. He knew which circles were being staked out. He knew what the police were doing and he knew what the NCA were doing. He knew everything.

How could that possibly be countered?

Yet Gamble had made mistakes. He should have doubled down on Montague Price's security as soon as the Immolation Man's method of abduction had been identified; the Prison Officers Association had long ago identified the possibility of ex-prisoner transport vans being used to facilitate escapes. As unlikely as it was, Gamble should have at least considered it.

And yes, he should have listened to Poe more often, instead of trying to block him at every turn. Hindsight was a wonderful thing.

'What do you want me to do, sir?' Poe asked. 'At the minute I'm protecting the scene and Tilly is acting as outer cordon. We could do with some professional support.'

'Uniform will be there soon, Poe. Can you make sure they secure the scene? I've also rerouted a DS from the public protection unit. As soon as she gets there, hand the scene over to her. She'll manage it until everyone arrives.'

'Will do, sir.'

'And, Poe?'

'Sir?'

'I'm sorry.'

'About what, sir?'

'About everything.'

Poe didn't answer immediately. 'Try not to worry, sir. This is unprecedented, just remember that. No SIO has ever had to deal with the killer sitting in their own briefing room.'

'Thanks, Poe.' The line went dead.

He glanced across at Bradshaw. She was waving to get his attention. He could see blue flashing lights.

The cavalry had arrived.

CHAPTER FIFTY-FIVE

Before long, Poe and Bradshaw were superfluous. The well-oiled machine that is a murder investigation had taken over, and they were rightly characterised by the first detective on scene as being unauthorised personnel: people with no need to be on the inside of the cordon. Poe didn't take it personally; if the chief constable had turned up, he'd have been told to get lost as well.

More and more police and support staff arrived. They all changed into white forensic suits and the field looked as though it had a moving mushroom infestation.

Poe and Bradshaw offered to help, but, in their civilian clothes and with no one to vouch for them, they were told everything was in hand. A gnarly old detective inspector who Poe had had a fight with over something trivial a few years ago arrived. He firmly told him he was relieved. They retreated to Poe's car to avoid getting under everyone's feet.

Although they would be far more use back at Shap Wells trying to figure out where Reid was holed up, Poe knew he'd better wait for Flynn. At some point detectives would need to interview him. With Reid identified as the Immolation Man, Poe's name being carved into Michael James's chest and his subsequent connection to the case became clearer. They would want to know everything he knew. He had information that would be needed when the scapegoating began. Someone was going to get the blame for all this.

Putting the political ramifications aside, Poe reviewed what had happened. He didn't think Reid would kill Hilary Swift's grandchildren; he was acting psychotically but up until now it had been cold and calculating. Everything had been done for a reason. Poe believed taking the children was tactical: leverage in case he was located before the job was finished.

He also believed that Reid was somewhere near. He'd driven Price from Carlisle police station to Shap, ignoring all the circles in between. Poe suspected that Reid had set Montague Price on fire then driven straight to where he was holed up. It would be close by.

Unfortunately, being in the right postcode didn't help much. The Shap Fells were huge and remote. They could be anywhere.

'Poe?'

Bradshaw was staring at him. She was biting her bottom lip, a sign he'd come to recognise that she was worried about something. 'What's up, Tilly?'

'If Reid is Mathew Malone, how are he and George Reid related?'

How indeed?

Where did George Reid fit into all this? How did Mathew Malone become Kylian Reid? They weren't the only unanswered questions. How had Reid survived Quentin Carmichael and his cronies? When did he and George Reid decide to do something about it? Was it after Reid had joined the police or was it earlier? Had Reid joined the police so he *could* do something about it?

There was so much missing information.

What wasn't missing, though, was the pain Reid must have been feeling for all the years he'd known him. That he'd managed to keep it hidden was almost beyond Poe's comprehension. Would he ever see his friend again? Had he ever really been his friend?

Had Poe been part of his grand plan from the beginning?

A text alert wrenched him from his deliberations. He looked down at the display, expecting to see Flynn's name. It was an unknown number; different to the one Gamble had used. Poe clicked on the message. His mouth opened in astonishment.

Come alone and the two children live. Come with Gamble
and they burn. When your satnav says you're there,
you're not. Keep driving for .6 of a mile then take the next
left. After one hundred yards you will see a sign for Black
Hollow Farm. It is literally the end of the road. Park your
car and walk towards the house. Kylian

It finished with a postcode. Blood began pounding in his temple.
This was it: the beginning of the end. Reid had asked for him and
Poe knew he would answer.

In his heart, he'd always known he'd end up facing the
Immolation Man alone. He typed a single word reply – OK – and
pressed send. He put the phone in his pocket and thought about
what to do next. He didn't have long; Flynn would arrive soon
and no way would he get to sneak off then. If he was going, then
he had to go immediately. Bradshaw was looking at him strangely.
She inclined her head in a silent question.

'Just need to run a quick errand, Tilly. You stay here and make
sure DI Flynn has everything she needs.'

'Where are you going, Poe? Who was that text from?'

'Do you trust me, Tilly?'

She stared at him, her myopic eyes burning fiercely under her
spectacles. She nodded. 'I do, Poe.'

'I have to do something and I can't tell you what.'

'You're my friend. Let me help.' She said it so earnestly he
nearly caved.

'Not this time, Tilly. This is something I have to do on my
own.'

CHAPTER FIFTY-SIX

The address Reid had given him was on the other side of the M6 but the satnav directed him to a nearby underpass. Poe wasn't familiar with much of the area after Shap village; if he needed to go north, he took the M6 not the A6, but he was soon heading up into the fells.

Cumbria was one of those counties where you could be on a single-lane track only a few hundred yards from a major motorway and the road quickly turned rural. Poe doubted he'd see any other vehicles. The people who used this road lived on the fell. It wasn't a route to anywhere and he suspected it would simply stop at some point. Sheep grazed freely, unencumbered by fences. Poe had driven over three cattle grids near the M6 but none recently. Before long he was high enough up to see the motorway below him. He was on Langdale Fell. The air was beginning to thicken with another ominous fog. It wouldn't be long before visibility was reduced to zero. The satnav said he had another five miles to go. He crested Langdale and began navigating down a smaller road on the other side of the fell. Even though the satnav was working, he stopped to check his AA roadmap. He wanted to get his bearings. He was now on Ravenstonedale Common, the Cumbrian Deliveranceville. He'd never been there before in his life.

The road and fog didn't allow a speed much above thirty miles an hour. He followed the satnav's instructions, and by the time it told him he was at his destination he couldn't see a single sign he was on an inhabited planet. He couldn't even see sheep any more.

Poe stopped to check Reid's instructions.

In the distance, jagged peaks rose above the fog like head-stones. Their definition was fading, though; the fog would reach him soon and then he would be cut off. Ravenstonedale Common was made up of crags, scree slopes and unyielding granite out-crops. It explained the lack of sheep; there was nothing for them to eat. The wind whistled down the slope and Poe could hear water trickling.

And nothing else.

It was eerie. The moors and fells that usually gave him a clarity of mind impossible in Hampshire, now seemed close and oppres-sive. The fog was low enough for it to have a dreamlike quality. He really was isolated.

He put the car into gear and followed Reid's instructions. He took the next left and after a few hundred yards he saw the Black Hollow Farm sign, exactly where Reid had promised it would be. Large rocks on the drive and deep ditches either side blocked vehicular access to the farm. The earth was fresh and wet where the rocks had been dragged – the makeshift roadblock had been recently constructed. He wondered why Reid had bothered. It wasn't as if Poe had planned to drive up to the front door. From now on, Mr Caution was his friend.

Black Hollow Farm was the end of the road. The track stopped where Poe was parked. He turned off the engine and surveyed his surroundings.

The farmhouse was bleak and imposing. Poe had thought he lived an isolated existence, but he realised, compared to the men and women who worked these fells, he was almost a city boy. This was extreme farming.

Black Hollow Farm was well named. A dark atmosphere hung over it like a veil: fear, despair, anger. It was in a deep basin – Poe suspected it had once been a quarry – and was cast in perpetual shadow. It was the type of Lake District farmhouse that would never make money from the lucrative bed-and-breakfast trade. It was a low and stocky building, built to withstand ferocious winters with little regard to aesthetics. It stuck to the ground like a limpet on a rock and looked to be two hundred years old.

A sheepfold – a stone pen that afforded sheep shelter in the very worst weather – was attached to the side of the main building. Poe had one on his own land. They were usually circular or oval, the walls about three feet tall, and there was a single narrow entrance. The one at Black Hollow Farm was slightly different. The entrance had been widened and a huge military camouflage net covered it.

Inside was the ten-cell prisoner-transport lorry no one had been able to locate.

Three other vehicles were parked by the side of the building: the four-cell van Poe had spent hours studying, Reid's old Volvo and a beat-up Mercedes that was presumably George Reid's personal vehicle.

Poe took this all in without leaving his car. He removed his phone. Unbelievably, he still had a signal. Now that he'd arrived, the foolhardiness of what he was doing came home to him. No one knew where he was and, even if they did, he was a good forty minutes from assistance.

So why *had* he come? The smart play would be to call Gamble and leave it to a hostage negotiator or an armed response unit. Anything else was foolhardy. But . . . Reid was his friend. A friend with secrets but a friend all the same.

He didn't know what to do.

His text alert went off again. It was the same number as before. It was a five-word message: You're in no danger, Poe.

Still he didn't move. Getting out of the car and walking the shale track to the farmhouse was the end of his career. Whatever happened, people would say he should have waited.

He thought back to the boy in the photograph. A boy covered in scars. A boy who'd survived against overwhelming odds.

His friend. And Reid – despite what he'd become – had been his friend. Nobody could fake a friendship for that long. And Poe owed him the chance to tell his story.

Another text: It's OK, Washington.

His jaw hardened.

Washington Poe swallowed his rising bile, got out of his car and walked towards hell.

CHAPTER FIFTY-SEVEN

What was left of the fog-trapped sun was behind the farmhouse. The front was cast in long shadows. It was as silent as the sheeted dead. Although the air was cooling, Poe was sweating; it ran down his spine and pooled in the small of his back.

When he was seventy yards away he stopped. In front of him, and less than forty yards away, were rectangular shapes. The shadows made it difficult to see what they were. They must have been placed in his path deliberately, like stage props. He approached them.

Coffins.

Three of them.

Oh no . . . Surely not?

His forehead knotted with tension. They were laid out on clean blankets. Poe ran his fingers along the warm pine of the first one. The polished brass fittings gleamed.

He found his phone's torch function and shone the light on the brass plates. His heart felt as though it would burst.

Three names that would forever remain etched into his soul.

Michael Hilton.

Andrew Smith.

Scott Johnston.

The three boys were missing no more.

Poe snapped some photographs, then looked at the bleak and silent farmhouse.

Where the fourth boy waited for him.

*　*　*

Poe walked towards Black Hollow Farm. The front door was made of oak, and was dense and heavy. It was mounted on huge forged hinges, built in an age when things were only made once. The windows were shuttered with the same heavy wood. The natural courtyard was well-trodden shale.

It looked more like a fortified keep than a domestic home.

As he got closer, a familiar chemical stench assaulted his nostrils.

Petrol . . .

Poe's stomach lurched. The back of his throat began burning. Judging by the pervasiveness of the smell, the farmhouse was primed like an incendiary bomb. It was time to run like hell, but not before he found the two children. He looked towards the ten-cell prisoner-escort lorry. The wheels had been removed. If the farmhouse burned, the lorry went up too.

Were the children in there? He headed towards it.

One of the farm's wooden shutters opened.

Reid appeared at the first-floor window.

'This our *High Noon*, Kylian?' Poe said. 'Or should I call you Mathew?' He kept on walking towards the truck. He had to find Swift's grandchildren before anything else could happen.

Reid said, 'I don't suppose I can ask you to stop?'

Poe entered the sheepfold and walked up the metal steps to the mobile prison. He tried the door but it was locked. A keypad, black, with silver numbers, kept whoever was inside from getting out.

Reid called out. 'The number's one-two-three-four. I'll be here when you've finished. Don't be long.'

Poe punched in the code and heard an electronic click. He opened the door.

He was hit by a putridness the likes of which he'd never smelled before. It coated the inside of his nostrils and overpowered even the smell of petrol. Faeces, urine and vomit competed with sour sweat and rancid bodies. It was the stench of misery and death. The floor of the central corridor was wet with a brown liquid.

The smell worsened as he entered the cell corridor. There were five cells on either side and Poe looked through the thick glass observation windows without seeing anything except the remnants of long and unpleasant stays.

They were all empty.

CHAPTER FIFTY-EIGHT

Poe climbed back out of the lorry and took a deep breath. He marched round to the front of the building and tried the front door. It was locked. He attempted to force it but only succeeded in hurting his shoulder.

'The children. Where are they?' shouted Poe.

'You know they're descended from evil?'

Oh God . . . What have you done? 'Where are they, Kylian?'

'They're fine, Poe. They're staying at the Whinfell Forest Center Parcs with a friend of mine. I checked in this morning and they're having a whale of a time. They think their mother arranged it all.'

Whinfell Forest was about three miles from Carleton Hall, Cumbria police's headquarters building. Unless Reid was lying, they'd been under everyone's noses all that time. While they'd been checking the airports and ferry terminals, they should have been checking the swimming pool.

'I'm texting Flynn.'

Reid nodded.

As he typed, a thought occurred to him. 'Their photographs were circulated. What if they'd been recognised?'

'Do you know what they look like?'

'Of course.'

'How?'

'I've seen the photos . . .' Poe trailed off. 'You swapped them. You told Gamble you'd get the photographs from their mother and you swapped them when they came in.'

'At the minute my colleagues are looking for two American kids I pulled off Facebook.'

'So—'

'So why bother taking them at all? Why not leave them both at Seven Pines?'

Poe nodded.

'I needed to get you up here. I thought you'd probably come on your own regardless if I asked you to, but the children guaranteed it.'

Poe had been played again.

'You'll have questions,' Reid said.

'Why am I here, Kylian?'

'How much do you know now?' Reid asked.

'I know that four boys were supposed to die after that charity auction but only three did. I know the fourth boy somehow escaped and has been taking his revenge.' Poe continued. 'So, do I keep calling you Kylian or would you like to be called Mathew again?'

Reid nodded. Tears had begun running down his face. 'Mathew Malone died that night. I'm Kylian Reid now.'

'OK, Kylian,' Poe said. 'Where's Hilary Swift?'

Reid disappeared inside. Poe could hear something being dragged to the window. Swift appeared. Her head was bloodied and bruised but she was alive. She was gagged with masking tape and looked terrified. Reid ripped it off and said, 'Say hello to Poe again, Hilary.'

'Help me! You must help me!' she screeched.

'Help you?' Reid said before punching her in the face. 'Poe isn't here to help you, Hilary.'

Poe knew that Hilary Swift was going to die. There wasn't a thing he could do to save her. She'd made a deal with the devil twenty-six years ago and this was the price she had to pay. A thought occurred to him. 'Where's Quentin Carmichael's body?' he asked.

Reid flicked his head to what Poe had earlier assumed was a discarded hessian sack. He walked over and lifted the opening with his shit-covered shoes.

Inside was the wizened body of a man who'd been lying in salt for almost three decades. His exposure to some moisture over the last year or so meant he'd finally started to decompose. It would be a long and drawn-out process. Reid had discarded him like a piss-stained mattress. His fingers and toes were missing. It looked as if foxes and rats had already been having a go at him.

Poe stepped towards Reid's window. Swift was no longer visible.

'Are you sure you're ready to hear this, Poe?'

Poe wasn't but he nodded nevertheless.

'You don't have to,' Reid said. 'Every bit of evidence I've collected over the years, the confessions I've recorded, it's all in a secure box in the four-cell van over there.'

Poe said, 'Tell me what happened, Kylian.'

CHAPTER FIFTY-NINE

'I've read your notes on Seven Pines, Poe,' Reid said. 'I know that Audrey Jackson told you and DI Flynn that the four of us had been as tight as any group of children in care she'd ever seen.'

Poe gestured for him to continue.

'We loved Hilary Swift. Everyone did. She seemed kind and dedicated. If my friends were my brothers, she was certainly my mother. When she asked if we wanted to make a bit of money, we jumped at it. Why wouldn't we? She told us if we behaved she would take us to London to spend it. Even had us fill out some postcards to save time when we got there.'

So that was how the postcards had been sent. That was why the search for the boys had been down south and not up north where it should have been. They'd been drip-fed into the postal system, probably every time one of the men had been down there on business. The handwriting and fingerprints had matched. How could anyone have predicted it was anything other than what it seemed to be?

Reid began talking again. 'You've got to the truth of that night, Poe – a bit earlier than planned, I may add – and Montague Price filled in the rest. It *was* us being bid on. Carmichael had arranged it with our surrogate mother. So, while we were showing off and generally acting the way boys do when they're excited, the men were bidding for the right to own us.'

The sun was almost gone now and the shadows had all but disappeared. The full moon gave off a pale, ethereal light. It was enough for Poe to see how much Reid was suffering as he relived his nightmares.

'Carmichael told the men that he would be keeping one of the "prizes" for himself. He was clever. Three boys, six paedophiles. Supply and demand. I'm sure Swift could have got him more children, but if there was one for everybody, the price would stay low.'

Montague Price had already hinted at this.

'Did you realise what was happening?' Poe asked.

'We were getting wind of it. The men were getting giggly and grabby. But no, I thought this was what rich men did when they were on the piss. It wasn't until we went back to a house somewhere for a "party" that the truth became apparent. You can imagine what happened there.'

'Jesus,' he muttered. 'And Price? Was he as blameless as he claimed?'

'No, he was not,' Reid snarled. 'Which was why he burned along with the others.'

It was what he'd feared, but to hear Reid tell it was heartbreaking. 'And the men with the winning bids took their boys away with them?'

'Yes. I went off with Carmichael. Drugged and drunk. Spent the next few weeks in a room somewhere. He would bring men to "play" with me every now and then, but most of the time it was just him. I assume my friends went through similar arrangements.'

'So, the party after the boat was the last time you saw them?'

'I wish,' he spat. He looked down and stamped on something on the floor. Swift groaned but it faded into a gurgle. 'No, these men were sadists, Poe. Not satisfied with abusing us for weeks, when it came to finally disposing of the evidence, they gathered together one last time. A way to bind everyone together in murder. Can you guess where my friends were killed, Poe?'

Poe didn't need to guess. 'A stone circle, they were killed in a stone circle.'

CHAPTER SIXTY

'A stone circle,' Reid agreed. 'They drove us to a remote one not far from here. I was forced to watch as, one by one, my friends were set on fire. I don't think the men were all comfortable with it but by then there was an escalation of commitment thing going on. Carmichael had videoed them on the boat so no one could back out, and I think, from his perspective, the worse the murders were, the safer they'd all be. Nothing binds people together like a shared atrocity.'

Poe had started this case with the assumption that he was hunting a monster killing innocent men. He might not be able to condone what Reid had done, but he understood it: those men had created the monster they deserved.

'How did you survive, Kylian?' For their security, all the boys had to die. Leaving one alive was worse than leaving them all alive.

'Carmichael,' he said. 'The other men begged him to kill me as well but he refused. "It belongs to me" he said. He referred to me as an "it", Poe.'

'So . . .?'

'So eventually he either tired of me or – and this is what I think – he'd started to listen to the men on the boat. Why keep me alive? The risk was too great. He woke me early one morning – it was pitch black and snowing – and drove me to Keswick. Told me we were going to take a walk up to the Castlerigg stone circle. I think he wanted the thrill of doing it outside like the others had.'

'And you escaped?'

'No. We were walking through one of the council yards – I later discovered it was a short cut to the circle. It meant he wouldn't have to park his car too close. We were climbing over one of the salt piles when he suddenly keeled over. Dead before he hit the ground. I think it might have been the excitement of what he'd been about to do.'

Common sense suggested Reid would have gone straight to the authorities yet . . . that didn't happen.

'You're wondering why I didn't run to the police?'

Poe didn't say anything. It *was* what he'd been wondering but it couldn't be as simple as that. Not when he was carrying that amount of baggage.

'I think there were two reasons,' Reid said. 'One of the men who raped me at Carmichael's invitation said he was a cop. I had no idea where he worked. In my mind, I was only eleven at the time, all cops were bad. I was scared of them.'

'And the second reason?'

'Carmichael had told me that I was complicit in what had been going on. That I was alive and my friends weren't. He convinced me that if anyone found out, I'd go to prison along with everyone else.'

At that age, and after that much abuse, you'd believe anything. Carmichael had got off easy with a heart attack. Evil bastard.

'So, I did the only thing I could think of – I took Carmichael's wallet and money and ran.'

'And Carmichael?'

'Left him where he fell. The snow must have covered him.'

It fitted with what he knew. The fact it was snowing meant that the gritters would have been working. He doubted the road crews bothered to clear snow off the salt before they loaded their wagons. Carmichael must have been scooped up with the mound he was on and taken to the Hardendale Salt Store as part of the M6 reserves. He'd stayed there for quarter of a century.

'And then I did what I was supposed to have done all those weeks ago,' Reid continued. 'I got on a train to London. Got another one to Brighton and went and found my aunt.'

'No,' Poe said. 'I've been through your file. You didn't have an aunt in Brighton. You had no relatives you'd have been happy staying with.'

'Poe, don't be stupid. We're northerners. You don't have to be related to someone to call them auntie. It was my mum's best friend I went to see – Victoria Reid. She'd always been nice to me and I trusted her. I thought she'd know what to do.'

'And she did?' Poe accepted his explanation. He'd called Reid's mother Auntie Victoria and his father Uncle George. It's just what you did when you were a kid.

'Not really. How could she? She didn't even know I'd been in care; my father hadn't stayed in touch with anyone when we moved up here. I told them what had happened. Everything. George was all for going to the police but she was thinking of me, not the men who killed my friends. She was a cognitive behavioural therapist specialising in PTSD. It had only just been identified back then and she didn't think I would get the help I needed. She thought the criminal justice system would eat me up and shit me out an even bigger mess than I was.'

'So?'

'She convinced George to keep quiet until she could work out what was the best thing to do. The best thing for me. First time in a long time someone had put my needs before theirs. I liked it.'

'And she helped you?'

'She did, Poe. It wasn't easy but she knew what she was doing and she had the patience of a saint. It didn't take her long to realise that I was trapped in a cycle of reliving my ordeal. It's the big issue with PTSD and she needed to break it. I needed to be able to remember what happened without *reliving* what happened.'

'So, you moved up here?'

'You know we did, Poe. We were at school together. They both loved the Lake District and she wanted me to visit the places involved: Ullswater, the stone circle where my friends were killed, Carmichael's house. Show me that it was over. She got a CBT job in Westmorland General Hospital and George opened his practice up here.'

Victoria Reid had uprooted her life for a boy who wasn't hers. Her husband had done the same. Poe didn't come across good people very often – he felt a hypocrite when he did – and now he wished he'd spent more time with them.

'And gradually you got better?'

'It took a while but, yes, gradually I got better. I stopped wetting the bed. I stopped cringing every time someone came near, or touched me. I stopped reliving it.'

'And you became Kylian Reid,' Poe stated.

'In those days everyone assumed you were who you said you were. I was registered at school as their son. I met you. No one questioned my past. And as Victoria worked for the NHS it was a simple job for her to slip some new birth records in.'

For someone to have gone through so much in such a short time beggared belief. For that person then to finally get the chance to have a life was heart-lifting. A testament to human endurance.

So what had happened? He asked the question.

'Why didn't I enjoy the rest of my life with parents who loved me?'

Poe's eyes were moist. He didn't trust himself to speak.

'You know, I think I might have. I really do. The plan had always been that, when I was ready, I would go to the police. Report it and take my chances in the criminal justice system. But . . . when I was ready, I found that I didn't want to. The thought of a peaceful life with two good people appealed to me more than revenge.'

'So what happened?'

'Fate happened, Poe. I went to a vets' function with my dad.

One of those networking events. A meal and a few drinks afterwards. It was at the Masonic Hall in Ulverston and, lo and behold, guess who was there?'

Poe didn't answer.

'Graham fucking Russell, that's who. Larger than life, laughing and joking, brandy stains all over his shirt.'

Shit . . .

'Victoria had helped me stop reliving everything I associated with my past, but when I saw that fat, flabby piece of shit something inside me snapped. I was no longer in the Masonic Hall, I was back in Carmichael's basement – Russell sweating and heaving on top of me.'

'And that was when you decided to kill them?'

Reid shook his head. 'No. Even then, Victoria's therapy held.'

'What then?'

'The evil bastard came over and introduced himself to my dad. They chatted while I was struck dumb with fear. I listened as he bragged about this and that. About how influential he was. About how, even though he was retired, the rich and powerful still feared him. He knew where the bodies were buried, he said. George assumed he was talking about his time on the newspaper. All the scandals and secrets they'd uncovered when they were tapping the rich and powerful. I knew he was talking about my friends.'

That would do it . . .

'The feeling of hate overwhelmed me, Poe. It was all I could do not to slit his throat there and then. For more than a minute, I stared at my steak knife as I considered it. Prison would have been a small price to pay to avenge my friends.'

'But . . .?'

'But something inside stopped me. A cold logic stayed my hand. Killing one of them made no sense.'

Reid stared at Poe.

'Not when I could kill them all.'

CHAPTER SIXTY-ONE

Victoria Reid had been diagnosed with motor neurone disease later that year, and Reid vowed nothing would happen while she was alive; he loved her too much.

That didn't stop him preparing. He decided that to give himself the best chance of succeeding, he would join Cumbria police. George had been wary – he'd wanted Reid to join him at his practice – but Victoria encouraged it; she thought that by helping others it could form another stage of the healing process. He planned to dedicate himself to passing the detective's exam, then get attached to major crimes. And once there, he'd make sure he *stayed*. Poe often wondered why Reid had refused to go on the inspector's course or to consider more interesting roles, but this explained it: he'd planned to be in the middle of his own investigation, subtly steering it in the direction he wanted, staying ahead of the hunting pack.

Gamble hadn't stood a chance.

Poe had attended Victoria Reid's funeral, and although hindsight gives you twenty-twenty vision, he remembered Reid showing steely determination rather than the grief he'd expected. Instead of something more sinister, he'd put it down to watching someone you love waste away in front of your eyes, and having mentally prepared for their death many months ago.

'Did you know the men involved?' Poe asked.

'Only Russell. I wanted to take him and force the rest of the names out of him but I opted for caution. I wasn't ready. Ideally I'd have liked another year.'

'But then Carmichael's body was discovered . . .'

'That was my starting pistol. If I'd left something on the body that could identify him – although by then his children had done a bang-up job of convincing everyone he'd died abroad – the other men involved might have taken precautions. I needn't have worried. Carmichael's identity was never discovered. Not until you turned up.'

'So you started earlier than you wanted to?'

'There were some things I did immediately. Buying the vehicles and some other equipment. I needed somewhere to work. My dad had told me about this place. Said it hadn't been farmed for years. I'd stolen some paperwork when I investigated a burglary a few months before I started, and I'd applied for a passport in case I needed formal ID for anything. I used it to lease this place, and paid cash for a year.'

So that's why Bradshaw couldn't find it. The farm wasn't in his name.

'When I was as ready as I could be, I went live.'

'You abducted Graham Russell?'

'And with a little persuasion he gave up everyone except Montague Price, who'd never used his own name. Only Carmichael knew his real identity and he'd been dead for over twenty-five years. I didn't find out Price's name until you uncovered that bank statement. By then he'd worked out what was happening and was in hiding.'

It explained why it was only Russell's body that had the additional signs of torture.

'And then I went to work on finding them.'

'How long did it—?'

'Not long. I killed Graham Russell to ensure a major investigation was launched. It gave me every excuse I needed to look in databases that would have earlier raised suspicions. I found them quickly and compiled dossiers on them all. One by one, I abducted them.'

296

'How?'

'Come on, Poe, you know how easily a police badge opens a door. A cup of tea while we discussed their security, a good dose of propofol and into the van they went. It was easy.'

Murder *was* easy if you were organised and knew what you were doing. It was the unorganised killers who got caught. 'What about George, though? He's no psychopath; he wouldn't have had truck with this. Not unless you forced him.'

'George? You think George had something to do with all this?'

'You didn't do this on your own, Kylian. You had an accomplice.' He said it as a fact. He pointed at the van and the lorry. 'And it was the Scafell Veterinary Group that bought these vehicles.'

'My father died over a year ago, Poe. Opened a book one night and never got to the end. I guess he just wasn't as interested in living after Victoria died. He had nothing to do with any of this.'

Poe said nothing.

'It's possible I forgot to report his death,' Reid added.

'I'm sorry.' And he was; George had been a good man.

Reid cleared his throat and Poe knew he was struggling to hold it together. 'I buried him on these moors, Poe. It's not far from here. I've marked the grave with a simple cairn. The PM will show when and how he died. Other than me using his company as infrastructure, George wasn't involved in any way.'

'You didn't do this on your own, though,' Poe said. He had been saddened when he thought George had been assisting a serial killer. He was relieved. But everything did point to an accomplice. If it not George, then who?

'No, I didn't. I did have help. But the "who" isn't important and I won't discuss it now. Just so you have peace of mind, though, I've included the information with the evidence in the four-cell van.'

'You're shopping your accomplice?'

Reid shrugged. It didn't seem important to him.

'As soon as I drugged them, my accomplice would drive them

away in the four-cell van. I also disguised their abduction dates. I'd already made it look like Graham Russell was in France. I sent Joe Lowell to Norfolk and Michael James on a whisky tour in Scotland. I followed it up with emails and texts, enough to stop their families worrying. I had them at the farm for longer than anyone realised, even you, Poe. Lowell, James, Owens and Doyle were all here at the same time.'

The planning and preparation were extraordinary. Poe rubbed his neck. It was beginning to ache – he'd been looking up at Reid for nearly twenty minutes.

'Anyway,' Reid continued, 'I had the four of them all nice and secure in the ten-cell. But killing them wasn't the only goal. I wanted confessions, I wanted information gaps filled, but, more importantly, I wanted the locations of my friends' bodies.'

'And they told you? Just like that?'

'Not at first, they were still thinking of their reputations. It wasn't until I hit upon the idea of making an example of one of them that they came round.'

'Sebastian Doyle,' Poe murmured. It had always bothered him why Doyle had been stuffed into Carmichael's coffin rather than displayed publicly.'

'Sebastian Doyle,' Reid agreed. 'I showed the others what happened when they didn't talk. Until they watched Doyle burn, I think they still thought they could buy their way out of it. I put him in Carmichael's coffin to keep you interested. Make sure you kept going.'

Poe had plenty of questions about why he'd been involved. For now, though, it seemed best to get a linear version of events. 'They told you everything?'

Reid nodded. 'And, unbelievably, none of the sick bastards had wanted to get rid of their prizes completely. They'd all been buried somewhere close to where they lived. James admitted to visiting his site at least once a month.'

'You recovered them?'

'One at a time. Carefully. These were my friends.'

'And Swift?'

Reid scowled. 'I'd always intended to kill her last – hers was the greatest betrayal of all – she didn't have the sick urges of the others; for her it was purely financial. You want to know where Carmichael's missing three hundred grand went? It was her fee.'

Poe had suspected as much. The depth of her involvement meant it was the only reasonable explanation. 'But why didn't you take her when you took the others? Surely she'd have spotted the pattern?'

'She was the only one of them whose abduction I couldn't disguise. By the time I was ready, she'd booked her holiday to Australia. If she didn't turn up there'd have been a missing person's investigation, and as it wouldn't have been conducted by major crimes, I would have been in no position to steer it.'

'How could you be sure she wouldn't run? She must have realised what was happening.'

'She'd always denied ever being on the boat, remember? As far as she was concerned, the only people who could contradict her were dead. Running would only establish her guilt to whoever was doing this.'

Poe understood the perverted logic behind it all. 'You should have told me, Kylian,' he said softly. 'Just think how formidable we'd have been together. We'd have got justice for your friends. They wouldn't have stood a chance.'

'This wasn't about justice, Poe. It was never about justice. This was about *vengeance*.'

Vengeance . . . Poe was reminded of the Chinese proverb: 'He who seeks vengeance must dig two graves: one for his enemy and one for himself.' Poe could pretty much work out the rest of his narrative – Reid didn't intend to leave Black Hollow Farm. The building *was* the second grave.

He looked up and held Reid in his gaze. Asked the question that had plagued him since day one. The only question that mattered. 'If you weren't seeking justice, Kylian, then why involve me at all?'

Reid looked down and smiled. 'Three reasons. First, you're the best detective I've ever met. You're intuitive and relentless, and you aren't scared of doing what's needed. You don't care who you piss off and you don't accept the first explanation that presents itself. Although I'd misdirected the early stages of the investigation with the Leveson-revenge angle, I needed it to start catching up. Even when they had a second victim, Cumbria police couldn't see past a random serial killer. They weren't looking for a motive beyond the usual psychobabble bullshit.'

'But you knew I would?'

'I wrongly assumed that with the crimes being committed where you grew up, worked and now lived, SCAS would have lifted your suspension immediately.' He stopped to smile. 'But it seems you've managed to make as many enemies down there as you did up here, Poe. When they didn't recall you, I took matters into my own hands. I sent them a message.'

'You carved my name into someone's chest.'

'No more than he deserved. And because I needed to make sure you didn't become a suspect yourself, I killed Clement Owens when you were down in Hampshire.'

'Thanks,' Poe grimaced. 'I assume it was you that sent me the postcard?'

'Yep. I hadn't realised just how deep the burns on Michael James had gone. The percontation point was virtually destroyed. I needed to give you a nudge when I found out that the MSCT report said the symbol next to your name was the number five. I needed you to re-examine it to get the Shap link. And also, I didn't want you thinking you were my intended fifth victim.'

'Kind of you,' Poe said.

'The second reason for your involvement was that I didn't have a clue who the last man was. He'd not given his name to anyone other than Carmichael. I knew my best chance of identifying him would be to set you loose.'

Jesus . . .

He hadn't thought about it like that. His discovery of the bank statement had given Reid Montague Price's identity. Poe might as well have killed him himself. Although it was hard to feel sympathy for someone who'd been complicit in the rape and murder of children, Poe knew he'd made a mistake. He'd been Reid's puppet.

'By then, Price had already gone to ground. During the raid I planted evidence at his home to ensure Gamble made him suspect number one and started a national search. I was confident that when he was caught, he'd have solid alibis and make bail. And as soon as he did that, he'd be mine. All I had to do was wait.'

'But he didn't get caught. He handed himself in and tried to make a deal.'

'And that meant Hilary Swift's charade of not being on the boat would come to an end and she'd be arrested as well. With them both in custody, neither of them would get bail because the full story would start to come out. Using the van, I had a contingency plan to abduct one person from custody, but it was a trick that wouldn't work twice.'

'You needed to get to Swift before Price talked.'

'Before we left Shap Wells for Seven Pines, I called my . . . accomplice and told him to get on the road. He knew the address. By that time, I had the dosages bang on. I made the drinks and I gave Swift a smaller dose. I wanted her drowsy but awake. My accomplice came in, took Swift, then went back for the kids.'

'And half an hour later we woke up. She was gone, and you were a victim just as much as I was,' Poe finished for him. It was genius, really.

'Which gave me a little bit of breathing space. I knew you were close, though, and the way Tilly had the board laid out in Shap Wells was exactly how you'd figure it out. That fucking money-laundering law – I knew that if the van was ever identified as the abduction vehicle its paper trail would be my undoing, but the rewards of having it outweighed the risks. I'm assuming that's how you put everything together?'

'The Sunday abduction. There wasn't a special court on and prison transfers are strictly Monday to Friday.'

'Jesus, you're a clever bastard, Poe, you really are. And with the van, you got me? That was quick work. I thought it would have taken you longer to track down who'd bought them. GU had put nearly two hundred vehicles on the market over the last couple of years and you didn't have the van's original registration number.'

'It wasn't just the van,' Poe said.

'Oh?' Reid said.

'You never take your jacket off.'

'I never take my . . . ?' he said, before it dawned on him what Poe meant. For several moments he said nothing. The tears that had dried began running again. 'My scars.'

'In all the time I've known you, I've never seen your arms. Not once,' Poe said. He had almost everything now. But . . . there was still something he wasn't being told. Everything Reid had said could have been said by phone or sent via email. For some reason he wanted Poe here.

'You said you had three reasons for involving me, Kylian,' Poe said. 'So far you've only mentioned two. What's the third?'

CHAPTER SIXTY-TWO

Reid stared at Poe with a ferocious intensity. 'I need to ask you something first, Poe. And I need you to be honest.'

'I've nothing to hide,' Poe replied.

'You sure?'

Poe hesitated. 'I'm sure.'

'What happened with the Peyton Williams case?'

'You know what happened!' he snapped.

'That DI of yours asked me, you know? Wanted to know why you hadn't stayed to fight the charges. Why you were just lying down and letting everyone fuck you over.'

'And what did you tell her?' Poe said, his voice less sure.

'I told her that you were struggling to come to terms with having made a mistake that cost a man his life.'

Poe nodded.

'I was lying, of course,' Reid continued.

Poe held Reid's gaze.

'What really happened, Poe?'

'I made a mistake.'

'You don't make mistakes.' Reid paused. 'There's a darkness in you, Poe. A desire for justice that goes beyond what's normal. I have it and you have it. It's why we've been friends all these years.'

Poe didn't respond. He couldn't hold Reid's gaze.

'Tilly told me about how you beat up that man who'd been bullying her in the office in Hampshire—'

'I hardly—'

'And how you seriously hurt one of those drunks in the bar at Shap Wells.'

Poe said nothing. He knew both incidents could have been handled differently. Jonathan had called Bradshaw a retard in a room full of witnesses – he was getting the sack regardless – and those idiots in the bar would have stopped the moment he showed them his NCA badge.

Instead, he'd chosen violence.

Reid was right. And his perennial state of anger predated anything that happened with Peyton Williams. The Black Watch had given him a temporary outlet, but the Army hadn't challenged him intellectually. He'd soon grown bored. He'd never dared look too deeply into the root cause of it all. Instead, he'd used it. It gave him an edge. The ability to see into the shadows. It allowed him to do things others wouldn't. It saved lives.

But at what cost?

'Until you face the demons you're harbouring in there,' Reid said, pointing down at Poe's head, 'they'll keep pushing you into more extreme things. And at some point, your anger will turn into something more sinister. Trust me, I have experience in these things . . .'

'But—' Poe protested.

'Go and see your dad, Poe.'

'My dad? Why would I do that? What's he got to do with anything?'

'Swallow that pride of yours and ask him why you're called Washington. It'll help you to understand.'

Poe was about to tell him to piss off. That Reid knew nothing of his life. But it wasn't true. Reid had stayed with Poe and his dad for days on end sometimes. With Poe living in Kendal, and Reid a few miles out of town, the two boys would often stay with each other's families. Reid knew everything about his life.

'You couldn't see the darkness in me; your own blinded you

to it. But your dad recognised it. He tried to draw it out, and to do that he would occasionally tell me things. Things he probably should have told you first,' Reid said.

'What did he tell you, Kylian?' Poe wasn't sure he wanted to hear what Reid knew.

'He told me about your mother.'

'You leave my fucking mother out of this!' Some things were off-limits, even in a situation like this. He didn't want to think about her, never mind discuss her. As far as he was concerned, he'd never had a mother.

Reid ignored him. 'Just go and see your father. Ask him. Nothing was what it seemed, Poe.'

Poe didn't respond.

'Please don't make me say it,' Reid said. 'It needs to come from your dad. I will tell you this, though: your mother didn't hate you, Poe.'

'She abandoned me. She was a selfish bitch who resented me.'

'Not true, Poe,' Reid said. 'Your mother loved you. Very much indeed.'

'Bullshit.'

'And it was because she loved you she had to leave.'

What did Reid know that he didn't?

'You'll tell me or I walk away now, Kylian. I'll ring it in and you can take your chances with whoever drives up that road next.'

'I can't tell you, Poe. Your father has to.'

Poe hesitated. If his father knew something about his mother he hadn't told him, then they needed to have a conversation. But . . . why had he told Reid? It didn't make sense. Unless . . .

'My dad's not a brave man, Kylian,' he said. 'You know that. If he had something bad to tell me that he could put off, you know as well as I do that he'd put it off. Indefinitely, if he could. Did it ever occur to you that he told you because he expected you to tell me? That he wanted you to tell me because he knew he couldn't.'

305

This time it was Reid who hesitated.

'OK, Poe, if you're sure?'

Poe nodded.

'Did you know that your mother and father went through a period where they saw other people?'

Poe shook his head. It didn't surprise him. His parents were hedonists. Monogamy had never fitted the profile he had for either of them. He'd always assumed they'd been liberal with their marriage vows.

Reid continued. 'Your dad told me that they had almost eighteen months apart. He went to the subcontinent to study some sort of mysticism. She went to the States with a group of CND protestors.'

Poe was vaguely aware his father had studied under a guru in India – they didn't teach the ridiculous yoga positions he used to practise in England. He didn't know his mother had been to America. He knew very little about her at all.

'Your father told me that your mother wrote him a letter saying she was in trouble and that he had to go back to England. They might have been apart but they did love each other. He flew back as soon as he could. When they met up, she was two months pregnant.'

The news hit him like a sledgehammer. *His dad wasn't his dad* . . . All those years raising another man's child. On his own. The man was a saint. But . . . that made no sense. If it were true, there'd be no reason not to tell him. That his mother had been promiscuous was hardly earth-shattering. Even in those days, there was no shame in raising someone else's kid. There was something else. Something worse.

'Go on,' he said to Reid.

'While she was in the States, one of their group had managed to get a brief audience with someone in the British Embassy, and they'd all been invited to a cocktail party afterwards. The way your dad tells it, they were only there to be the butt of everyone's jokes. A "let's all laugh at the hippies" kind of thing.'

'In Washington?'

'What?'

'The British Embassy, it's in Washington, DC.'

'It is.'

'So, what are you saying? That my father was some sort of diplomat?'

Reid held off answering.

'What is it, Kylian?' he said. 'Tell me who my father is.'

Still he said nothing.

'Kylian,' Poe said. 'You can tell me. I won't be angry.'

Reid looked down. There were tears in his eyes. 'Your mother was raped, Poe,' he said gently. 'She went to that party to protest against nuclear weapons and someone raped her.'

Poe's brain registered no thoughts other than he was shocked. He opened his mouth to say something but no words came out. The crushing ache of abandonment lifted, only to be replaced by something far worse: guilt. All those years hating her? *Wasted* years. What must she have thought of him? As if his internal light had gone out, darkness washed over him. He stood trying to comprehend what it meant. *His mother had been raped?* Why had no one told him? He was a policeman. He could have done something about it. The future seemed an unwalkable road now. Where did he go from here? What did he do next?

'I think I'll go now.' He turned to leave – all thoughts of the case forgotten.

'Wait! You haven't heard everything. You haven't heard about the good that came from the bad.'

Fuck that! He hadn't heard why he'd been named after the city his mother was raped in. Bollocks to the good that came out of it, that was the question he wanted answering. He turned back.

'Your mother hated the idea of bringing you to full-term,

307

Poe. She didn't want you – you were right about that – but not for the reasons you thought. She came back to the UK to get an abortion.'

'Fucking great . . .' Poe snarled. There was a red storm rising. Anger was controlling all his thoughts now. Before long it would consume him.

'But when she got to the clinic, she couldn't do it,' Reid said. 'She and your dad – because he *is* your dad, Poe – decided that something good should come of it all. According to your dad, she asked him if he would be prepared to raise you. She intended to give birth and leave the country before you'd drawn breath.'

'And that's what she did?' he asked. 'She gave birth then dumped me? I thought she'd hung on for—'

'But instead of hating you as she'd expected to, she loved you intensely. "A burning love," your dad called it. An immediate bond neither of them had expected.'

'So . . .?'

'According to your dad, she never wanted you to know about your start in life. And she knew if she stayed, there'd come a time when you'd begin to look like the man who'd raped her. She had to leave before that happened. She didn't want you to see her expression when that happened. It would have broken her. She had to leave. But she couldn't. She loved you too much. She needed something to make it easier. She needed something to remind her. She needed to force the issue before it became too late. Otherwise she'd keep putting it off.'

'So, she named me Washington as an ever-present reminder,' Poe finished for him. Every time someone said his name, it would have been a dagger in her heart. A constant reminder of who he was and who he'd eventually become. 'She named me after the city she was raped in so that she'd have the strength to leave.'

'Yes,' said Reid.

'My name was like the health warning on a packet of cigarettes

308

then,' Poe said. 'Don't get too attached to him; he will turn into his father.'

'I wouldn't put it like that.'

'How would you put it?'

'Nicer,' he replied.

Poe's anger fizzled and died. His name had allowed his mother to make a huge sacrifice. And he'd been embarrassed by it. Well, no more – he'd wear it with pride from now on.

He put it to one side. He'd deal with his parentage later. If whoever had raped his mother was still alive then he hoped they'd gone all cold because he was coming for them. It might take him months, it might take him years, but at some point in the future, he and his 'father' were going to meet.

But first he had a job to do.

And before they could move on, Reid had wanted an answer to a question. He *deserved* one. Reid had been raped. Poe's mother had been raped. Little wonder they had a bond. So, if Reid wanted to hear the truth about Peyton Williams, then Poe would tell him.

Poe thought back to the day he visited the family of Muriel Bristow. He only had bad news for them. He had a suspect but he couldn't tell them who. Worse, Peyton Williams knew they were on to him. If she were alive, Muriel would die of dehydration within the week. He had a choice: her life or his career.

And he'd known what would happen. How could he not? Muriel's father was a tough, working-class man. Used to settling things with his fists. And his brother had a garage in the middle of nowhere.

Poe had handed over Peyton Williams's name, knowing he was going to be abducted and tortured until he gave up Muriel's location.

He'd known that and did it anyway.

'It was no mistake,' Poe said. 'I gave them the wrong report on purpose.'

Reid nodded as if he'd known all along. He probably had. He knew Poe better than anyone. 'And why did you do that?'

The answer to that was far from simple. He could spout all the excuses he'd used at the time to convince himself he was on the side of right. That they were exceptional circumstances. That he was out of time and out of options.

Flynn had accused him of binary thinking that night in the graveyard, but the truth was more complex. While he remained resolute in his belief that it had been the right thing to do – if the choice was between the rights of a murderer or the rights of an innocent victim, well . . . that was no choice at all. If he could have gone back in time, he'd have done the same thing. Because making sure the girl had a chance to live; dealing with Tilly's bully in Hampshire and the idiots in the bar; all the ignored instructions – everything that others viewed as self-destructive was part of who he was. Who he'd always been.

The truth was, he did these things because the guilty had to be punished.

Was he sorry Peyton Williams was dead?

Of course he was.

Would he do it again?

In a heartbeat.

'Don't answer, Poe,' Reid said. 'I already know why. You've been wondering lately if you're a sociopath. You're not. Your nightmares prove you have empathy. You tell people you hate bullies but that only scratches the surface. What you hate is *injustice*. It's why it had to be you.'

'I'm not following,' Poe said. His head was spinning. The revelation of his mother, and the need to admit his role in the torture and death of Peyton Williams, had combined to throw him. Reid was now reading him completely. No secrets were hidden to him. He wondered if it had always been the case.

'Why do you think I made you jump through so many hoops, Poe?' he asked. 'The body in the graveyard, the instruction to leave the bishop alone that I knew you'd ignore. Why did I not just leave you a note somewhere? Why didn't I just kill them all, tell you everything I knew, then quietly disappear?'

Reid might be the sanest insane man he'd ever met, but by anyone's definition he was mad.

'I needed to make sure you were still the same person, Poe. That living at your croft hadn't softened you. This is the culmination of my life's work, and if you weren't prepared to challenge the clergy or disturb a grave, you wouldn't be able to do what I need you to do next.'

'You've been testing me? What for?'

'You're going to tell my story, Poe.'

'So all this,' Poe replied, 'is just so I can be your fucking biographer?' He was struggling to keep up. He had sensory overload. He needed to sit in a dark room for a week. He needed to speak to his dad.

Reid remained silent.

'Anyone could have done that for you,' Poe continued. 'People with more credibility and technical expertise than me. Hell, why not just put everything on the internet? Let the conspiracy nuts do the work for you.'

Reid shrugged. 'There are supporting documents I don't have. The bank statement you found. The party invitation. The thing with the Breitling. Things that corroborate their video confessions.'

He was right. They both held two halves of the same puzzle. Without Poe's evidence, the confessions were just frightened men saying whatever their torturer wanted them to say; without the confessions, the evidence was circumstantial at best. He understood now. It had to be him. He wasn't just the only one who could, he was also the only one who would.

'He'd held these parties before you know,' Reid said.

'Carmichael?'

'Yes. I don't know if they had the same level of depravity as ours, but you can be sure nothing good happened at them. I know that some of the people who'd attended his earlier parties are very powerful now. The establishment will try to protect itself. You must realise this.'

Van Zyl had already told him that people in Westminster wanted it finished quietly and sensitively. He could imagine them whispering in the ears of Cumbria's chief constable: Everyone involved is now dead. Let sleeping dogs lie and all that. No need to look beyond the actions of a mad man. And by the way, how's your application for the Met coming along? *You must let me know if I can help. See if I can call in a few favours.* No way would the full truth get out. The men and women who controlled the media, the CPS, the courts and the police would do their masters' bidding. Sure, a few of the more liberal papers might suspect a cover-up, but without Poe's assistance there'd be nothing for them to find.

Reid spoke carefully. 'You've always claimed you'll follow the evidence wherever it takes you, but I'm asking you, if I give you the evidence, will you make sure it gets out? Will you tell the world our story, Poe? My friends deserve nothing less.'

'I'll make sure it gets out, Kylian. All of it.'

'Thank you, Poe.'

He looked up when Reid said, 'I told you not to tell anyone.'

A vehicle was threading its way along the road to the farm. The headlights could be seen through the fog.

'I didn't tell anyone,' Poe replied. He turned to Reid but he'd disappeared. When he returned, he wasn't alone. A semiconscious Hilary Swift was with him. They were now handcuffed together. He was holding a Zippo.

CHAPTER SIXTY-THREE

The light from the approaching vehicle was illuminating Poe's car.

'Who's that?'

'No bloody idea,' Poe replied. 'But I promise you I told no one. If I had, they'd have been here before now.'

He figured that whoever it was, they were still ten minutes away. The distance wasn't far, but because of the sharp incline there were another seven or eight hairpin turns for the vehicle to navigate. As the crow flew, it had two hundred yards to travel, but by road it still had at least a mile. They both knew the vehicle was coming to them. Black Hollow Farm was the end of the road.

Reid said, 'I don't suppose it matters any more. I've finished.'

Reid's part in the story was about to come to an end. He was handing the baton to Poe.

'You don't need to do this,' Poe said.

'Swift needs to feel the same pain my friends did.'

'What about you? Throwing your life away is a poor way to honour their memories.'

Reid stared at him. 'You're right. Please make sure I'm not buried alongside them. And look after my evidence. It's been an honour to have called you my friend, Poe.'

With a flick of his thumb he lit the Zippo and threw it over his shoulder. The sound of it landing was followed by a soft 'whoomph' and a burst of orange light. Shadows began dancing across the cold dark fell.

Reid shut his eyes, and stepped out of sight.

Hilary Swift began to scream.

CHAPTER SIXTY-FOUR

Poe didn't know how Reid had rigged the building but he'd clearly been having arson lessons. Within a minute, thick smoke poured from the open window.

Regardless of what Reid wanted, Poe wasn't ready to let him die. He wasn't ready to arrest him either, but he'd cross that bridge later.

He needed to find a way inside. He eyed the sturdy door.

On television, kicking down doors looks easy. In practice, the police use weighted battering rams and aim for a door's weak points – normally locks and hinges. When you're using your shoulder, you have fewer options.

Poe charged, and bounced off it like a rubber ball.

White heat spread from the top of his shoulder to the tips of his fingers. He tried to move his arm and found he could barely move his fingers. He'd damaged something.

The shuttered windows had metal bars embedded in the thick walls that could only be removed from the inside. They were impregnable.

Swift was still screaming but Poe could tell she was weakening. He searched desperately for options.

He looked at the four-cell van.

He sprinted towards it. The door was open and the key was in the ignition. He turned it and the diesel engine grumbled into life. He glanced at the passenger seat. The secure box containing Reid's evidence was there. He would deal with that later. Poe put the van into reverse and backed up, manoeuvring the van into the right position. He gunned the accelerator and fired the van towards the door of the building.

A number of things happened. The van hit the door and the driver's airbag hit Poe's face. The plastic cover that held it in the steering wheel hit him on the nose and broke it. The sound of the ruined engine was horrendous. Poe staggered out of the van and saw that the front door had been breached.

Poe had never suffered from paralysis by analysis. He climbed over the van's bonnet and walked through the shattered door of the burning farmhouse.

As Poe entered the building, a mass of fresh oxygen via the recently opened door caused the flames to surge like a blast furnace.

The heat was outrageous.

Visibility was zero.

He couldn't breathe and he didn't know where he was going.

Poe steeled himself. His friend was up there.

He remembered something about fire, something from his days as a cub scout: smoke rises: the lower you are, the cleaner and cooler the air. Poe dropped to his knees and began crawling. The smoke was making his eyes stream and he clamped them shut.

He reached out to feel his way around the building, and he hit the stairs straightaway. He scrambled to his feet, figuring it would be better to run up blind rather than crawl partially sighted.

Poe gripped the banister, ignored the bubbling varnish that stuck to his hands, and took the stairs two at a time. They ended before he stopped running and he tumbled forwards on to his hands and knees. He hadn't drawn breath for almost thirty seconds and there was no chance of breathing up there. This was either going to happen quickly or not at all.

Swift was no longer screaming, so he had no direction to follow.

He moved forward, hoping to find a wall and get organised. Try a quick grid search. He estimated that wherever Swift and Reid were lying, together they had to be at least four feet wide. He moved a few feet to his right and his hand touched a cast-iron radiator. It was hotter than a spitting griddle. Poe jerked his hand away. He knew it was badly burnt but he needed to keep moving.

Halfway across the room he found them. Two bodies. He reached out and parts of them were still burning; other parts were crispy. Reid must have drenched them both in accelerant.

They were dead.

Poe felt between them. As he'd feared: they were still hand-cuffed together. Tethered in death as they had been in life. Poe wondered if that had been Reid's plan all along.

He couldn't leave him where he was. He might have said he didn't want to be buried with his friends, but he *would* get a burial. Even if only he and Bradshaw turned up at his funeral.

Poe began dragging them by their feet, but with just the one good arm and only a sliver of breath left, it was slow and hard going. He grunted with the effort.

He reached the stairs.

He'd have to throw them down. Ignoring his bursting lungs, Poe dragged them to the edge of the stairs.

He nearly made it.

He really did.

But old buildings have exposed wooden beams and wood burns quickly.

An ear-splitting crack was followed by so many sparks the room looked like the inside of a firework. He looked up and saw the sky. Part of the roof had collapsed. The oxygen-starved fire flared and burned brighter. The heat intensified against his already scorched skin. Flames shot through the roof, driven skywards.

Another creak, and the roof collapsed.

A shower of burning timber covered Poe. In his fear he sucked in a lungful of the toxic air. He felt himself beginning to lose consciousness and knew he had little time left to save himself. With heavy arms and laboured movements, he freed himself from the burning debris. He started crawling towards the stairs but his arms and legs felt like lead.

The idea of sleep became strangely alluring.

A voice broke through the roar of the fire.

'Poe! Poe! Where are you, Poe?'

Something touched his foot. He looked down and instinctively pulled his foot back. He was hallucinating. He had to be. A mud monster, a golem from his nightmares, had hold of his foot. It was trying to drag him down to hell. He gasped in panic, and the little breath remaining in his lungs left his body.

The room began to spin. The golem was going to get him; he could feel the monster's hands on his legs again.

His eyes bulged as he gasped for air. He found he didn't care any more.

Washington Poe put his head on his burnt hands, closed his eyes and passed out.

CHAPTER SIXTY-FIVE

Poe heard sounds. They'd been there for some time although he hadn't been conscious enough to identify them. He wanted to open his eyes but they seemed gummed together.

He tried to figure out where he was.

Beeps, hums, people talking in hushed tones. He was in a bed. The clean sheets were rough and tucked in too tight at the feet. The air smelled of lemon disinfectant.

Poe knew a hospital when he was in one.

He attempted to open his eyes again but they stayed shut. He tried using his fingers to pry them open but they were heavily clad in soft cloth – bandages presumably. His hands throbbed, almost certainly from the burning banister. Or the cast-iron radiator. Or the burning corpses. Or the roof collapse. Poe gave up using his hands, and, ignoring the excruciating pain, forced his eyes open. With a rip, they opened further. Searing pain caused him to cry out loud. A narrow beam of light pierced his vision. It felt like molten steel being poured into his head.

He tried to sit but was too weak. He looked and saw his hands *were* bandaged. A bile-coloured liquid had leached through them. Probably iodine.

What the fuck had happened?

The heavy feeling of sedation was making it hard to think. Poe leaned back on the pillow and shut his eyes.

When he woke, his headache had improved slightly. He tried his eyes again and this time he could fully open them. He gave himself the once-over. His skin was either bandaged or exposed and raw. His nose was splinted. A cannula with a split feeder was attached to the back of his right hand. Poe looked at the IV stand. A bag of saline was half full. Another smaller bag, which he assumed was an antibiotic, was almost empty.

The ward lights were muted and it was dark outside. He was on his own in a two-bed room on a ward. The bed had high-sided rails to stop him falling out.

He wondered how long he'd been there.

He was desperately thirsty but the water jug was out of reach. Poe grabbed the patient alert box and pressed the button. The door opened and a uniformed nurse walked in. She smiled at him.

'I'm Sister Ledingham. How are you feeling?' She was ruddy-faced, and spoke with a rich Scottish burr.

'What happened?' he croaked. He didn't recognise his own voice. It sounded like he was speaking through gravel.

'You're in the HDU at Westmorland Hospital, Mr Poe. You were burnt in a fire. Lucky to be alive.'

'HDU?'

'High Dependency Unit,' she replied. 'You're not really in any danger but burns are easily infected and this is the best way to keep you sterile until the skin begins to heal.'

'How long have I been here?'

'Almost two days. There's a queue of people waiting outside to see you, if you're up for visitors?'

Poe sat up, fought the urge to vomit and nodded.

Instead of the queue Sister Ledingham had promised, one person walked through the door. It was Stephanie Flynn.

She was back to wearing her official two-piece trouser suit. She looked as tired as he felt.

'How you feeling, Poe?'

'What happened, Steph?' His voice came out little more than

a whisper. He gestured towards the water. Flynn filled the plastic beaker. She inserted a straw then held it close enough so he could get it in his mouth. No drink had ever tasted so good.

'What do you remember?' she said.

He remembered Reid telling him about his mother and he remembered the burning room. He had vague recollections of trying to drag Reid and Swift out of the burning building. He also remembered something about a mud monster but he decided to keep that to himself.

'Not much,' he admitted. He had fragments of memory but they were jumbled and unorganised. 'The children . . .'

'Alive and well and where you said they were. They're with their mother now and are unaware anything untoward happened.'

'And the man who took them?'

'Wore a baseball cap and sunglasses.'

'Shit.'

'Yep. A police artist has sat with them but got nothing usable. The woman who took them to Center Parcs was a registered nanny. Reid had hired her but made it look like the request had come from their mother. The email said it was a treat for them, and a rest for Grandma, before she landed in the UK. They stayed at Reid's flat until he found time to drop them off with her. She took them straight there. She's innocent.'

It made sense. Reid had needed him to think the kids were in danger, but given his own experiences at the hands of monsters, he hadn't wanted to harm them.

'There was a box. A metal box on the front seat of the—'

'Of the van you drove into a burning building?'

'What happened to it?'

'Same as the van. Burnt to cinders,' she replied. 'I don't know what it was but it must have been a big deal because when CSI found it, the chief constable took it away personally.'

'And?'

320

'The official line is that nothing inside survived. All burnt to cinders. We asked to see it but were politely told it was a Cumbrian matter now.'

He put his head in his hands and rocked backwards and forwards. Before long he was sobbing uncontrollably.

Flynn called for the nurse. A doctor came instead. He adjusted one of the drips and soon Poe's crying subsided and he fell asleep.

'He was a killer but he had his reasons, Steph,' Poe said. It was three hours later and he'd woken thirsty and ravenous.

'What was in the box, Poe?' she asked. 'What is it that has everyone so worried?'

For the next thirty minutes Poe replayed the conversation he'd had with Reid at the farm. He omitted the discussion about his mother and the origins of his name.

Flynn asked a few questions and made a quick call when he told her about George Reid's grave – otherwise, she let him tell his story.

'I want to make a statement,' he said when he'd finished. 'I know it'll only end up as hearsay but I owe it to Kylian to air his side of the story.'

'There are a lot of people and organisations who could be embarrassed if that happened, Poe. And with no witnesses, little corroborating evidence and all the key players dead, the CPS have already said there will be no charges. There *is* no one to charge.'

'What about Montague Price's confession?'

'Already suppressed.'

'How?'

'Technically it was only information he was offering towards a deal, and because Reid abducted him before he could be charged, the family solicitor said they'd sue if all records weren't destroyed. Cumbria handed over Price's statement and the video interview this morning. We've been told to destroy our copy of it.'

'And the bodies of his friends?'

'All down to Reid. The working theory – or at least one that fits the bullshit they're spinning – is that he killed them when they were children and he's been reliving the thrill of it all with these new murders.'

'Bastards,' Poe whispered.

'It does have the bouquet of a cover-up,' she admitted. 'I've been digging around and some of the people who took advantage of Carmichael's hospitality are . . . men of influence, shall we say? And if Carmichael had opened a bank account for one specific event, who's to say he hadn't done it before? Nobody wants to look under that stone.'

'Perhaps someone should,' Poe said.

'While you were out, the Secretary of State for Justice made a statement thanking Cumbria Police, and the chief constable in particular, for their hard work and professionalism "during this trying time". Said that the Immolation Man was a police officer with mental health issues and his prayers were with the victim's families. He singled out Quentin Carmichael, said he was a shining example of the type of selflessness that makes this country great and all that bollocks.'

Poe was staring at her aghast. He couldn't believe what he was hearing.

'There's literally nothing we can do. Even if you were prepared to go on record and repeat what Reid told you, nothing would happen. I've been told to tell you that if you say anything other than the official line, you'll be sacked. And as well as losing your job and pension, some of the most powerful and well-connected families in the country will come after you. They'll sue you for everything you own.'

She was right. With no evidence he'd be pissing in the wind. Without the confessions, Poe's evidence was worthless. He had half the story but it was the wrong half.

'We know the truth, Poe,' she added. 'That means something.'

'He deserves better, Steph.'

'He does, but he won't get it.'

Even if Poe were reckless enough to try and get an interview with a tabloid, he knew that the people suppressing the story were the same people who controlled the media. It would never be printed.

He would think about it later but he'd decided he wanted no part of the NCA any more. He would leave and spend some time digging around. See if there was some concrete evidence to be found. He owed his friend that much. He also needed some time away to think about what he should do about his mother. He'd need to speak to his father first, and tracking him down would be a job in itself.

'I need to get off and ring van Zyl, Poe, but before I go is there anything else you want to know?'

'There is, Steph,' he said. 'Something that's been bothering me ever since I woke up.'

She inclined her head.

'How the fuck am I still alive?'

CHAPTER SIXTY-SIX

Flynn had some calls to make first and he needed his dressings changed. They agreed to discuss it again in an hour.

'The heat was cracking stones and boiling glass,' Poe said when she returned. He lifted his bandaged hand. 'Even touching a body was enough to cause third-degree burns.'

'We know,' Flynn said. 'I've seen the preliminary fire report. The house was drenched in that accelerant. It was little more than an empty shell by the time the fire went out.'

'Went out?'

'The fire engines were there within half an hour of getting the call but they couldn't get near enough to the farm because—'

'—of the stones blocking the road.' So that's why they'd been dragged there. 'Who called them? And half an hour seems too long for me to have been lying in a burning building.'

'Who do you think called them?'

Poe thought about it. He doubted Reid had. He'd planned to die in the furnace he'd created. Ashes to ashes and all that. And no one else had known where he'd been going.

Except someone had . . .

He remembered the headlights winding through the fog to the farmhouse. He hadn't seen who was driving; Reid had set fire to the building as soon as he saw them approaching, but someone had been coming.

Other than Bradshaw, everyone else would have assumed he'd

headed back to Shap Wells after leaving the Montague Price crime scene. But she couldn't have worked out where he was.

Could she?

He shrugged.

'The same person who dragged you out of there by the scruff of your neck: Tilly. Our real-life hero of the hour.'

'But . . . how did she know how to find me?'

'Your BlackBerry.'

The little minx! When Ashley Barrett had made him sign for it, he'd explained that the Protect tracker app had been turned on. On the journey up to Cumbria Poe had asked Bradshaw to turn it off. She'd told him she had.

'When you'd asked her to disable it, she didn't know you well enough so she only told you she had. Thank God she hadn't. When she realised you were heading off to do something stupid, she followed you.'

'How did she get to the farmhouse? She can't drive.'

'I think your insubordination must be rubbing off on her. She rang me to say you'd gone off on one. I said I'd be with her soon and that she was to stay put. She said it was urgent. She got a lift with uniform back to the hotel, and then using her own phone to track yours, she followed you up there. She reckons she was about half an hour behind you.'

'Still doesn't answer—'

'Your quad, Poe. She drove your quad all the way up.'

Jesus . . .

Poe was lost for words.

'Is she OK?' It didn't seem to convey the magnitude of what she'd done for him. What she'd risked for him.

'She's fine. Her lungs needed time to get back to normal as she'd inhaled some smoke, and she had some superficial burns on her hands from dragging you out, but she's already been discharged. Her mother came to take her back down south but she refused.'

'No, it doesn't make sense. The roof had collapsed and the fire was raging, Steph. No way could someone make it up the stairs without serious breathing apparatus and protective equipment.'

'She's not stupid, Poe. Unlike you she didn't dive in with no thought of a plan.'

'So how . . .?'

'She googled what to do.'

'You are joking!'

'She was calm enough to spend a moment searching what to do. She found a page that told her to cover herself in something damp. She didn't have the recommended wet blanket so she improvised and ended up using—'

'Mud,' Poe said. She'd smeared herself in wet mud. So, there hadn't been a golem monster; it had been Bradshaw. He could feel his eyes welling but he didn't want to cry in front of Flynn. He thought of Bradshaw, thin and short-sighted, bewildered by the new world she was experiencing. He remembered her sitting in the lounge at Shap Wells when those drunken arseholes had been messing with her. She'd shown courage then. Poe might have seen them off, but they'd been behaving like they had because she'd refused to do what they wanted. It had been the first real indication that underneath her awkwardness was something special.

'How can I ever thank her?'

A noise outside made them both turn to look. Bradshaw stood in the doorway. She was smiling shyly. She gave Poe a little wave. There were bandages on her hands and her eyes were smoke-tinged red. She was wearing the cargo trousers, but this time, instead of her usual film or superhero T-shirt, she was wearing the one he'd bought for her in Kendal. The one that said 'Nerd Power'. When she saw where he was looking she gave him a double thumbs-up.

'Hello, Poe,' she said. 'How are you feeling?'

The tears began rolling down his face and before long he was openly crying. There was a rawness to it. His sobs were for more than Bradshaw and her bravery; they were for Reid, and they were for Poe's own failure to see proper justice done.

Flynn quietly got up and left.

Bradshaw sat down on the chair beside the bed. She waited for him to stop crying.

'Sorry,' he said, wiping his eyes.

'That's OK, Poe,' she said. 'DI Stephanie Flynn has told me what Kylian Reid said to you. It is very sad and I feel sorry for him.'

'I do too, Tilly.'

Something occurred to him. Something he'd said after he'd chased away those thugs in the bar. 'Tilly,' he said, 'tell me you didn't run into that burning building because I told you it was your turn to rescue me?'

She stared at him with that penetrating gaze, the one that ordinarily made him feel so uncomfortable. This time he held it.

'Is that what you think, Poe?'

'Honestly, Tilly? I don't know what I think. My best friend turned out to be a serial killer, I'm not feeling too clever at the moment.'

'But you are clever, Poe! Look at all the things you worked out.'

'*We* worked out, Tilly.'

'We worked out then. And no, Poe, I didn't follow you up there because of what you said at the bar. You were being flippant then because you felt awkward. You do that sometimes.'

'I do?'

'Yes, Poe, you do.'

'Then . . .'

'I told you,' she said. 'You're my friend.'

There wasn't a lot left to say after that.

An hour later Flynn looked in on them. They were both fast asleep.

CHAPTER SIXTY-SEVEN

Poe was forced to spend another day in Westmorland Hospital before he was allowed home. The doctors, initially concerned that his throat had been damaged, were happy to discharge him as soon as it began to heal. They wanted a district nurse visiting his house once a day to change his dressings. He compromised by agreeing to attend outpatients; he didn't think it was fair to ask someone to walk over two miles of moorland with a bag full of medical supplies.

During the next few days he received a plethora of phone calls. Director van Zyl thanked Poe, and, despite everything that had happened, offered him his inspector's job back, this time on a permanent basis. Poe refused.

'Flynn should get it, sir,' he'd said. 'She's a far better DI than I ever was. This case was solved because she had the discipline to make us do our jobs. I only ever see trees, she sees the whole forest.'

Van Zyl agreed. Poe suspected he was only offering him the job because he knew he'd turn it down.

'Is there anything you want to tell me, DS Poe?' he'd asked finally.

Poe knew he was referring to Reid's confession. Van Zyl wanted to see if he intended to do anything about it.

'No, sir,' he'd replied. He wanted to tell the director that the Peyton Williams case had been no mistake. That he'd purposefully put the unabridged document in the family file, knowing what would happen. Accept whatever came his way. He might have saved the life of Muriel Bristow, but a man had died because of his actions. He'd seen what happened when someone tried to keep hold of dark secrets and he didn't want to end up like Reid. But in the end, he said nothing. Admitting it now would be selfish. Old cases would be reopened. Appeals would be filed. His integrity would be called into question. Killers would walk free.

The burden was his alone to carry.

Deputy Director Hanson rang, ostensibly to apologise for the hard time he'd been giving Poe lately. They'd made awkward small talk until Hanson got round to the real reason he'd called. There were a lot of clichés and platitudes: things best left unsaid, no need for careers to be ruined, sleeping dogs being allowed to lie. The upshot was: he also wanted to know Poe's intentions.

Poe pretended he didn't understand and Hanson didn't have the balls to come out and ask him directly. Eventually he blurted out, 'This alleged confession, DS Poe, it was the ranting of a mad man. Nothing more.'

The Bishop of Carlisle called, and Poe had some sympathy for the man who'd helped them so much. Oldwater wanted to know how much damage was going to be inflicted upon his beloved Church. In the end, Oldwater told him to follow his conscience.

For two weeks, Poe rested and took Edgar for long walks in the spring evenings. His scorched lungs healed and his voice returned. His hands recovered. Flynn called occasionally. Pretended she was keeping him up to date with what they were up to. Really she was just making sure he was OK. Poe appreciated it but couldn't find the words to tell her.

Bradshaw emailed him twenty or thirty times a day. Each one made him smile. She told him she was settling back into the day job but couldn't wait to get out into the field with him. She was learning to drive and planned to come up and see him and Edgar as soon as she'd passed her test. Now that Reid was dead,

Bradshaw was probably the closest friend he had. They were polar opposites – her light to his darkness – but sometimes those friendships were the strongest. She asked him when he'd be back at work.

He didn't have an answer for her. He didn't know if he would be. He wanted to see if he could do right by Reid first. Then he needed to speak to his father. He'd emailed and asked him to get in touch next time he was in the UK. So far there'd been no reply but that was OK; Poe had waited a long time, he could wait a bit longer. But there'd be a reckoning. One day, he and the person who raped his mother were going to be alone in a room together. There couldn't have been that many diplomatic parties in Washington with a bunch of hippies in attendance. Someone would remember something. Poe never needed much to kick off investigations and he'd certainly worked rape cases with far less to go on.

The evidence at the farm had been analysed. DNA of all Reid's victims had been found in the cells of the larger truck. Urine, vomit, blood and faeces had been in most of the cells. For some reason one cell had been bleached sterile. Gamble was satisfied that the farm was where the men had been held before making their final journey. George Reid's grave had been found a few hundred yards from Black Hollow Farm, as Reid said it would be. He'd been telling the truth – the PM showed he'd been dead long before the killing spree began. The cause of death was a stroke. Cumbria police were looking for the other person involved in the murders: Reid's elusive, unknown accomplice. Poe doubted they'd find him, though – his identity had disappeared along with the rest of the evidence and they had nothing to go on. They'd keep looking – they didn't have a choice – but Flynn was privately admitting they weren't holding out much hope.

The DNA results confirmed that the bodies found on the top floor of the farm were Swift and Reid.

The fire report stated that the farm had been stripped of anything toxic, which explained why the smoke hadn't been as black as

Poe would have expected. Gamble reckoned that Reid had wanted Swift to burn to death rather than succumb to smoke inhalation.

Poe and Gamble were seeing eye to eye for once. The cantankerous DCS had known Reid well and believed Poe's account of what had happened at the farm. He'd done his best to seek the truth. Against the chief constable's wishes, he'd ordered a post-mortem on the remains of each of the three boys Reid had recovered. Time and fire had beaten him, though. The pathologist was unable to find anything to suggest that they'd had contact with any of Reid's victims. The coroner's inquest recorded an unlawful killing verdict.

They were buried in the same cemetery where Poe had conducted the exhumation. Not in K-section, though, Poe insisted on that. There'd been a high turnout at the funerals. It was covered extensively in the news. Men from London came up, offered mealy-mouthed platitudes to the waiting cameras, then got back in their cars and rushed away as fast as they could.

With the case almost closed, the bodies of Reid's victims – which technically belonged to the coroner – were released to their families. Poe was treated to a succession of grand funerals on the TV. Eventually he stopped watching them. The Home Secretary himself came up for Carmichael's. Apparently, they'd known each other for years. They'd met at a charity event . . .

Reid's funeral was a different matter. He was interred in a smaller, less well-maintained cemetery and, as no undertaker would accept Poe's business, Reid ended up in a local authority coffin. Poe, Flynn and Bradshaw attended. From Cumbria police, there was only Gamble.

Poe was curiously unemotional.

After the funeral Gamble sought out Poe and told him he wouldn't be taking things any further. He was close to retirement, felt he'd been lucky to keep his job, and still had children at university. Poe understood. Those men had ruined enough innocent lives.

The press and the spin-doctors had done what they'd been told, and painted Reid as a worse version of the monster he'd become. They'd twisted the facts, and rewritten their history to ensure the official narrative showed that Reid had been reliving the murders he'd committed as a child. Poe found it worryingly convincing. And then they shut up. The tabloid press might have the attention span of a sugar-filled two-year-old, but a police officer had been castrating and burning powerful men – it should have been more than a three-day story. They'd clearly been told not to linger on it.

The liberal press, despite smelling a turd, had no proof so remained quiet; the families involved were very powerful. The Carmichaels were even threatening to sue Cumbria police and the NCA. Van Zyl had called Poe and said he wasn't to worry. 'They wouldn't fucking dare. They're as terrified of the men in grey suits as we are. Duncan Carmichael is going be given a service-to-charity knighthood to shut him up. It's how silence is bought with these people.'

It sickened Poe and he found he could no longer stomach hearing about it.

After one particularly distressing phone call when Flynn had informed him that Leonard Tapping, the Chief Constable of Cumbria, had been shortlisted for the Met's vacant deputy commissioner's job, Poe decided to stop working the case. It wasn't doing him any good and it was pointless. The evidence had been burned. Or been destroyed later. It didn't matter which; the results were the same.

When he made the decision to remove all the information they'd pinned to the wall at Herdwick Croft, Poe realised it was all over. He'd left it up in case something jogged his memory. Nothing had, even though he'd been staring at it for hours at a time.

He fetched an empty box and started dismantling the last pieces of their work. There were photographs and maps and statements from experts. There were analytical documents from Bradshaw and

Post-it notes from everyone – everything they'd uncovered during the course of the investigation.

The last thing to come down was Bradshaw's laminated copy of the postcard that Reid had sent to Poe at Shap Wells – the one with the percontation point on the back. It was the postcard that had led them to uncovering the same punctuation mark on the chest of Michael James.

The postcard that had kick-started their investigation.

He threw it on the top of the pile.

It flipped in the air and landed picture side up.

Poe stared.

CHAPTER SIXTY-EIGHT

Poe vaguely remembered the picture; the information they'd needed was on the back so they'd not paid much attention to the front. It had been irrelevant. Now he wasn't so sure.

The picture was of a brimming cup of coffee. The foam had been fashioned into a design by a barista with too much time on their hands.

Poe stared at the image.

It was a dove. The international peace symbol. It was in the negative space created by what was presumably chocolate powder.

Without realising, Poe had stopped breathing. Reid had sent him this postcard and he didn't do anything without a reason. He left clues and puzzles. Was this another?

Poe continued to stare at the photo, willing more information from it. There was a dove, and doves were associated with peace. It was a cup of coffee. He ran it through his mind like a mantra.

A dove.

Peace.

Coffee.

A dove.

Peace.

Coff . . . Fuck!

Reid had brought him a bag of coffee!

Poe hurried across his kitchen. He yanked things from the shelf above his kettle. Reid had said it was to replace the stuff they'd been drinking. There it was. A brown bag full of freshly ground beans.

After searching for a sieve he knew he'd never find, Poe settled for a large saucepan. He ripped open the bag and upended the contents into it. A metallic clang told him he'd been right. There was more than coffee in the bag. He searched through until he found the item.

Item*s*. Two to be precise.

One was a USB stick and the other was a metal badge.

Poe walked over to his desk and turned on his laptop. When it had booted up he plugged in the USB. A new window opened. It was full of folders. It looked like there was one for each of his victims. One was unnamed. He opened the named folders in the order they were on the screen.

Each one contained videos, audio files and documents. Everything Reid had on them. Everything he'd forced them to admit. All the evidence he'd collected but had been unable to share.

Poe smiled. Reid hadn't trusted the police. The whole thing had been too well planned to leave to chance.

Of course he'd had a backup.

He picked up the metal badge. It was an enamelled shoulder pin. Poe recognised the insignia from the investigation. It was from the company that had ran the cruises on Ullswater before they'd ceased trading, the company that provided the boat for the 'Are You Feeling Lucky?' event.

There was a word above the company insignia.

Captain.

Poe studied it until the realisation hit him.

The men on the boat that night were all executives or higher. Hilary Swift was a social worker and the rest were children.

So, who'd sailed the boat?

Although it had been a self-catered event, someone would have had to navigate them around the lake. They couldn't have done it themselves. There'd been six men bidding, there'd been Carmichael and Swift, and there'd been the four boys.

And there'd been the captain of the boat.

Who must have seen everything and not said a word. And to Reid, that made him just as culpable as everyone else.

How had they all missed that?

Reid hadn't. He had the man's badge.

But where was he?

Who was he?

He wasn't the owner. Bradshaw confirmed he'd died of natural causes.

Poe went back to the laptop. There was one folder still to open; the unnamed one.

It was another video interview. Two men. One was wearing a balaclava and Poe assumed it was Reid hiding his identity in case things went wrong early on. The other was a man Poe didn't recognise. He hadn't come up in the investigation. He was in his late fifties or sixties and looked like a sailor. He had skin like saddle leather and his face wore a map of the world. He had the healthy complexion of a man who spent his working day outdoors and the physique of the manual worker.

Poe pressed play. The video lasted for almost an hour. It was the man who'd piloted the boat around Ullswater. He told the camera that he'd been unaware of what was going to happen on the 'Are You Feeling Lucky?' cruise but realised something was up during the auction. He'd been paid ten thousand pounds for his silence, and a combination of the money and the risk of upsetting powerful people had ensured he hadn't breathed a word to anyone.

After the man had confessed everything to Reid they'd made a deal. He would stay in the ten-cell truck until it was all over, only leaving to do some small tasks for Reid. Nothing too illegal. Mainly driving jobs. Poe suspected it was the man who'd driven Graham Russell's car to France and left it there. He was also in no doubt that it was this unknown man who'd taken Hilary Swift and her grandchildren. He was getting on a bit, but a lifetime on the lake had given him wiry strength – he would have been more than a match for the partially sedated Swift.

And if he did all that, the video confession – and his role in the boys' murders – would never see the light of day. He could go home. But . . . if he let Reid down, two things would happen: he'd suffer the same fate as everyone else and his family name would be disgraced. The man agreed without hesitation. He seemed eager to please.

Poe had found Reid's accomplice.

Another thought flashed through his mind. One of the cells in the ten-cell truck had been bleached clean. Was that the one in which the man had been kept? Earlier, when Poe had been reviewing the case, there'd been so many unanswered questions it seemed he was reading a book with missing pages. Now, it was making more sense.

Why had one cell been cleaned with bleach?

Why had Reid chosen to burn with Swift?

Why hadn't he wanted to be buried with his friends?

A reluctant accomplice put a different slant on everything.

Had Reid done what he'd promised: let the man go when he'd fulfilled his side of the deal, or . . . had he killed him then kept his body until it was needed?

What did they really know about what happened that night at the farm? The official version was taken from his own eyewitness statement. But that was just his perspective. It didn't mean it was the truth.

What if it had all been an illusion?

When Reid threw the Zippo and stepped back, Poe assumed he'd fallen and waited for his death. But Reid could have had time to switch with someone else. It would have been tight, but not impossible.

And Black Hollow Farm had a window at the back. Poe remembered seeing it when the fire blew the roof off.

Evidence of tricks like that can usually be detected for a long time after the event. *Usually.* But because of the blocked road to the farm, the fire had burned for a long time . . .

All detectives have to submit their DNA so it can be discarded at crime scenes, but with an accomplice to take samples from, who was to say what Reid had submitted. Poe was in no doubt Reid could have doctored a DNA sample. He knew that Gamble and his team had also taken DNA from Reid's flat. Some hair, a discarded cotton bud, a toothbrush. All of it matched the sample he'd submitted at the beginning of the investigation. It was irrefutable evidence that the body at Black Hollow Farm was Sergeant Kylian Reid.

But . . . why had one of the cells in the truck been cleaned with bleach?

Was it possible Reid had fooled them all?

Poe considered the man piloting the boat. Would Reid really have let him go back to his life? He'd known what had been happening and had been paid to say nothing. Poe didn't think Reid would have allowed a man like that to live. Everyone involved had to die. As well as being his early accomplice, was it possible that Reid had finally used him as a body alibi? Was it the accomplice whom Poe had tried to drag out of the burning farm, not Reid? It was a theory but one he'd never be able to prove.

And with that, Poe came full circle. Back to the dove.

Had his friend finally found peace?

Was he out there somewhere? Soaking up the sun, flirting with waitresses. Toasting his friends.

Being happy.

He had to tell Flynn. He reached for his phone. His finger hovered over the call icon. She deserved to know. She'd know what to do.

Or would she? Would anyone?

Poe threw his phone down.

Deputy Director Hanson had given him some advice he was happy to follow for once.

Let sleeping dogs lie.

CHAPTER SIXTY-NINE

Poe sat in a café off the M5. He'd taken public transport to travel south, and then he'd stolen a car from a long-term car park. With luck he'd have it back before the owner knew it was missing. He was nursing a pot of tea. In his hands he had a cheap tablet. He'd bought it second-hand from one of those cash shops that were cropping up everywhere after years of austerity. He didn't know how easily an IP address could be back-traced and he was taking no chances. He could have asked Bradshaw how to cover his tracks but that would have abused their friendship. If there was any fallout from what he was about to do, he didn't want anyone else dragged into it.

He'd been sitting staring at the screen for over three hours.

Poe had compressed all Reid's evidence into a file small enough to be emailed as an attachment. He'd included everything but the accomplice's file.

There were important aspects of the case that weren't in the email attachment: the information from the bank and the video interview of Montague Price trying to cut a deal would have been helpful but they hadn't been available when Reid compiled his evidence. Still . . . what Poe was about to send was the other half of the puzzle that Flynn had talked about, and this time it would be the *right* half.

The email was set to go to every editor, sub-editor, freelance reporter and blogger he could find. Newspapers abroad as well as at home. Almost one hundred names in total.

There'd be no proof it was Poe. In fact, it couldn't be him. He'd been unconscious when he'd left the farm in an ambulance. His clothes had been burnt to a cinder and taken away for forensic examination. Cumbria police knew for certain he hadn't left Black Hollow Farm with anything incriminating. Everyone would assume it was the unknown accomplice. Officially, he was the only actor left on the stage. Cumbria were still looking for him but Poe knew they were chasing their tails. And he couldn't enlighten them without letting Reid down.

If he pressed send, within five minutes nearly one hundred people would see the evidence; by morning that number would be thousands.

There'd be an enquiry. There'd have to be – the public would demand one. He wouldn't need to do anything more: everything they'd uncovered – Carmichael and Swift's cruise, the Breitling, the secret bank accounts, Reid's verbal testimony – Poe would be legally compelled to hand it all over. Someone from Cumbria would leak the Montague Price interview. Too many people had seen it for it to remain secret. Poe would be called as a witness. He'd be ordered to testify under oath.

People would be listening.

He wouldn't let his friend down.

If he pressed send.

His finger hovered. The problem was that he didn't know what would happen next. Bradshaw's butterfly was in his head again. There'd be consequences he couldn't predict. Two cabinet members had been on TV assuring the public that there was no crime beyond Reid's madness. Another cover-up wouldn't be tolerated. There could be civil unrest. Democracy only works when you let it.

Distributing the email was reckless.

But . . . Poe thought about Reid and the trust his friend had placed in him. He thought about Flynn and Bradshaw and the work they'd done to expose what had happened twenty-six years ago. He thought about everyone who'd been involved in suppressing what had really been going on. He thought about the snidey politicians falling over themselves to label his friend a monster. If he didn't press send they'd win again. Edmund Burke had said that 'All that is necessary for the triumph of evil is that good men do nothing'.

And . . . Duncan Carmichael had called him a 'rank bad hat'. Poe wasn't the kind of man to let insults like that go unanswered.

'For you, Kylian,' he whispered.

Poe pressed send, leaned back and waited for the future to arrive.

ACKNOWLEDGEMENTS

Writing a book is easy. Getting one across the finishing line is anything but.

First of all I'd like to thank my wife, Joanne. Without her support none of this would have been possible, and, more importantly, she's the person I have to impress first. She sees the first draft long before anyone else and helps me shape whatever story I'm trying to tell.

Next, a huge thanks has to go to my agent, David Headley, at DHH Literary Agency – you're a true force of nature; thanks for putting up with me. And, while I'm there, a big thanks to Emily Glenister for fielding a lot of my inane questions . . .

Krystyna Green at the Little, Brown imprint Constable gets a big thumbs up for taking a chance on the unpolished script that landed on her desk at the back end of 2016. Your enthusiasm for Poe, Tilly and Steph, and the scrapes they continue to get in to, is remarkable.

Martin Fletcher, Howard Watson, Rebecca Sheppard and Jan McCann – each one of you has made the book incrementally better. And thanks too to Sean Garrehy for such a killer cover – without using images, you were able to convey the dark menace lurking inside the book's pages.

Next I'd like to thank my three beta readers: Angie Morrison, Stephen Williamson and Noelle Holten. If something didn't make sense or wasn't working the way I thought it was, they were honest enough to tell me.

I now need to thank some of the people who helped when I was researching the book.

Thank you to my good friend Stuart Wilson (of the real Herdwick Croft), who patiently explained how Poe would have been able to make his croft on Shap Fell habitable.

Thank you, as well, to an old probation colleague and occasional verbal sparring partner, Pete Marston, for talking me through Cumbria's stone circles (there really are sixty-three . . .). He may not even remember the conversation, or that he loaned me his book on them, but the information stuck in my head somehow, ready to be used five years later . . .

Jude and Greg Kelly get a shout of thanks for helping me with some of the technical aspects of murder investigations and for providing some of the anecdotes I have drawn on to add a bit of depth.

Steve at Shap Wells gets a nod for showing me round the non-public areas. It's a real hotel, grand and isolated, and it really was commandeered as a prisoner-of-war camp.

And finally, a big thanks to the real Serious Crime Analysis Unit. I've taken huge liberties with you, and for that I apologise. Keep on doing what you do, guys – we're all much safer for it.

Inevitably I will have forgotten to thank someone – please know it is a fault with my memory and not with my appreciation.

Thanks, everyone – it's been a blast.

THE evolution SECOND EDITION

COMPANION WEBSITE
www.sinauer.com/evolution

The **evolution** Companion Website is a valuable companion to the textbook that can help you master the material you will be studying in your evolution course. Available to you free of charge, the site is designed to help you learn the concepts and terminology introduced in each chapter, and to use that knowledge to analyze real-world research.

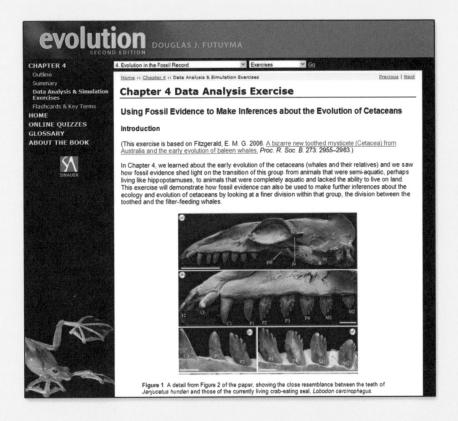

Features of the Companion Website

Data Analysis Exercises: These inquiry-based exercises challenge you to think as a scientist and to analyze and interpret experimental data. Based on real papers and experiments, these exercises involve answering questions by analyzing the data from the experiment.

Simulation Exercises: These exercises include interactive modules that allow you to explore some of the dynamic processes of evolution. Each exercise poses questions answered by running the simulation and observing and analyzing the outcomes.

Online Quizzes: For each chapter of the textbook, the companion website includes a multiple-choice quiz that covers all the main topics presented in the chapter. Your instructor may assign these quizzes, or they may be made available to you as self-study tools. (Instructor registration is required for student access to the quizzes.)

Flashcards & Key Terms: Flashcard activities help you master the many new terms introduced in the evolution course. Each chapter's set of flashcards includes all of the key terms introduced in the chapter.

Chapter Summaries: Concise overviews of the important concepts and topics covered in each chapter.

Chapter Outlines: A convenient outline of each chapter's headings.

Glossary: A complete online version of the glossary, for quick access to definitions of important terms.